Talk To
a Movie Star

LM Foster

This is a work of fiction. Names, characters, places and incidents are products of the author's imagination. Any resemblance to actual events, locales, organizations, or persons, either living or dead, is entirely coincidental.

9th Street Press
www.9thstreetpress.com

For Marie, who quotes movies

It's the movies that have really been running things in America ever since they were invented. They show you what to do, how to do it, when to do it, how to feel about it, and how to look how you feel about it.

– Andy Warhol

ACT I

Now You Too Can Talk To a Movie Star
Variety.com – Biz Section

If you're not a *Talk to a Movie Star* subscriber, you shouldn't call yourself a fan of the movies.

TTAMS, for those of you that live under a rock, is a service that allows fans to have conversations with a vast stable of actors and actresses, living or dead.

Or so it would seem.

Variety caught up with Valerie Whitly, 25, the creator of *Talk to a Movie Star*, and its CEO, Joyce Vinson, 28, to help explain their revolutionary service to any of the remaining fans that haven't yet heard of it.

Variety: Give us a basic overview of TTAMS.

Joyce: For a low monthly price, TTAMS offers the illusion of speaking directly to your favorite actor or actress. We have a few directors, also.

Variety: You say the illusion of speaking to them. So it's not a real conversation?

Joyce: (Laughs.) No. It's a fantasy. You can compare it to a computer game. You're not actually shooting a real enemy in *Halo*, are you? A basic TTAMS subscription allows you to ask basic questions of your favorite stars, and they will answer you. They'll use your name.

The premium subscription allows you to ask anything you want. Ask Brad Pitt how the weather is in Hollywood. Ask Edward Norton what he thinks of the situation in the Middle East. The stars will answer you. They'll have a conversation with you, about any subject you desire.

Variety: But it's not really them.

Joyce: No. The person to whom you are speaking is an operator. Most work from one of our offices, but we also have many that work from their homes. Through the art of performance capture technology, our operators assume the appearance of the famous on your device. A voice synthesizer changes the operator's voice to complete the illusion.

Variety: How real is it?

Joyce: Our voice and performance capture technology is state of the art. The stars appear and sound as real as they did in any movie in which they appeared, as any character.

Variety: So I can talk to Travis Bickle?

Joyce: Yes. And he'll even say, 'You talking to me? Well I'm the only one here,' if you so desire. Or you can talk to Jack Byrnes from *Meet the Parents*. Or you can talk to a young DeNiro, or you can talk to him how he looks today.

Variety: But of course, it's not really him. The first thing that a new subscriber sees upon joining is TTAMS's disclaimer: *At no time will you be interacting with the actual celebrities portrayed on TTAMS. Therefore, all opinions expressed by TTAMS performers do not reflect the views, beliefs, opinions, etc. of the celebrities themselves.*

Joyce: Of course, we strive to be accurate on the details of the celebrities' backgrounds, and our operators make every attempt to stay in character. In other words, in might be difficult for you to engage Travis Bickle in a conversation about puppies and flowers.

Variety: Since it was launched, TTAMS has added thousands of stars, as well as the characters they have portrayed. The service boasts over twelve million subscribers, from every demographic. The only commonality: they are all fans of the movies, and they must be at least 18 to join the premium service.

For the first eight or ten months of its existence, TTAMS was an archive of actors and actresses of the past. The interface was as the basic subscription is today: a list of questions was available to the subscriber, mostly regarding historical information on the actor or character. Ask Rhett Butler about Tara, or ask Hitchcock for a little background information about *The Birds*. TTAMS's info on the stars and movies of yesteryear is encyclopedic; it's like a *Wikipedia* page come to life.

But in its most recent incarnation, TTAMS has branched out into simulacrums of modern, living, still-working celebrities.

Can you explain the technology behind the service?

Valerie: An operator sits in front of a console; he or she wears a facial motion capture device. After the subscriber chooses a character or celebrity, that person's program is loaded. The operator then appears to the subscriber as that celebrity.

The subscriber can choose to show herself to the operator via her webcam; or she can simply type her questions and responses. Either way, it seems as if the celebrity is actually interacting with her.

Variety: Valerie and Joyce met at UCLA; Valerie was a Computer Science major and Joyce was attending UCLA Law. Within eighteen months of graduation, they launched their ground-breaking service.

Blonde, perky and vivacious, with bright blue eyes, dimples and an infectious smile, Valerie dresses casually, as befits a computer genius. Today, she wears jeans and a black t-shirt, bearing a declaration in a tiny white font: *code-monkey.* Joyce has dark brown eyes, and wears her dark hair in a conservative bun. She's dressed in an expensive, pin-striped charcoal suit today. She appears studious, serious, successful. She might be the young lead counsel on a big case, striding purposefully out of the courthouse. Before launching TTAMS with Valerie, Joyce was in fact an up-and-comer at a prestigious LA law firm.

Before TTAMS, Valerie worked at 20th Century-Fox, in the motion capture division. In a Winklevoss-Zuckerberg scenario, the studio is currently suing TTAMS, claiming that many of the performance capture techniques utilized by TTAMS are proprietary; it is the studio's contention that Valerie stole them from Fox for her service.

Joyce: While I can't really comment on ongoing litigation, I can say that Fox's claims are simply not true. We expect this lawsuit to never see the inside of a courtroom. If we stole their technology, why is Fox one of our major sponsors?

Variety: Joyce insists on using that word, *sponsors,* instead of the more accurate *investors.* And while it is true that one arm of Fox is suing TTAMS, another division has invested in the service. Other sponsors include the Academy of Motion Picture Arts and Sciences, as well as every major studio in Hollywood. And while actual numbers are not available, all are no doubt **interested** in a portion of the staggering profits that have been estimated.

Joyce: (Laughs) I wouldn't say staggering. We have to pay our employees – operators, programmers, technicians. We have to pay licensing fees to use the characters, and of course, the studios, actors and actresses get a cut.

Variety: Where did you get the idea for TTAMS?

Valerie: My mother is a huge fan of everything Hollywood, so I couldn't help but be a fan, too. My father was in a band [he is rock legend Dennis Whitly], so I know a little bit about fans. I realized that there was a void where they and performers should be interacting. Sure, there are the movies themselves, as well as magazines and fan clubs on the internet, and the red carpet. There are CDs and concerts for recording artists. But there has never been a way for the average person to interact on any kind of a personal level with their idols. Until TTAMS.

Variety: Except it's not real.

Valerie: No it's not real, any more than are the movies themselves. But Hollywood has never been in the business of reality, now has it? TTAMS offers you the fantasy of what it would be like to have a conversation with your favorite star, in a way that is just not possible in real life. No traveling to premieres, no crowds, no velvet ropes, no hoping that he might just glance your way as he walks up the red carpet. Just intimate, one on one conversations.

Variety: Critics have likened your service to old-fashioned phone sex lines, or more modern webcam-based sites, only with famous people.

Joyce: There is no nudity on TTAMS. What subscribers choose to talk about with the stars is their own business. Surely, there is a romantic element to it, but how many times do you need to tell Brad Pitt you love him and have him say it back? Our subscribers talk to their idols about everything, not just romance. We also have movie buffs who like to talk to the stars of yesteryear about what it was like being in the business back then. We have film students that like to talk to stars and directors as a creative exercise. TTAMS is different, thought-provoking, and, as the saying goes, *all in good fun.*

Joyce closed Variety.com on her tablet and grinned at her business partner. Her best friend. *"My mother is a huge fan of everything Hollywood, so I couldn't help but be a fan, too.* Why didn't you tell the nice man from *Variety* about Eddie, Val?"

"The first rule of Eddie is: you do not talk about Eddie. The second rule of Eddie is: you do not talk about Eddie." Valerie grinned back. *"Prettiest man I ever saw."*

"Just keep talking to him, Val. He's making us millionaires." Joyce nodded at the tablet. "It wasn't a bad interview. I didn't care for that phone sex reference too much, though."

Valerie shrugged. "We're crying all the way to the bank, Jo. Some people can't get enough of hearing Brad Pitt say he loves them." When Joyce still frowned, she added, "There's not going to be any startling exposé claiming that it's just the stars talking dirty. The system keeps out the journalists."

When Joyce still didn't look convinced, Valerie explained again how it worked, for probably the millionth time.

"There are all kinds of factors, Jo. There is the psych profile, based on the questionnaire. *I'll be asking you a few questions, Doug, so we can fine tune the ego program. Answer honestly, and you'll enjoy yourself a whole lot more.* The program begins by prompting the operator based on what the subscriber has said on that.

"The conversations follow a certain pattern, Jo. If someone just signs up and starts talking dirty to Brad, chances are it's a reporter. She's in a hurry, anxious to write that exposé, earn that Pulitzer. She doesn't have time to act like a regular subscriber, get to know Brad a little first." Valerie grinned. "So technical difficulties usually arise, and we shut down the session. Brad has feelings, too, after all. He doesn't want to feel used."

"Someone's going to beat it someday."

"So what if they do? *And everyone can say what they want to say, it never gets better, anyway. So why should I care about a bad reputation . . . anyway?*

"That's really all it is, Jo, if you're honest with yourself, *my brother and only friend.* A lonely hearts' site. We could've called it Rent a Famous Boyfriend. All the film students and movie buffs that you told *Variety* about – that's just window dressing. Most of them really just want to hear Brad Pitt say I love you."

Joyce grinned slyly. "Or Eddie Forbes."

Valerie wouldn't be baited. "Eddie talks to me. Even though he's—"

"Have you ever looked at his stats, though? He's not really one of our largest draws . . ."

"Except for the Canadian demographic."

"But not too many Americans." Joyce consulted her tablet. "Less than two thousand subscribers, in all of these United States, has ever chosen a conversation with Edison Forbes."

Valerie shrugged. "Yet there are a few million Canadians . . ."

"So you have looked at his stats! Have you ever . . . Have you ever talked to him online, Val? Young Eddie, older Eddie. Eddie from that cop flick you liked so much?"

"I wrote the program, Jo. The protocols. It wouldn't seem real to me, now would it?" Valerie paused. "Besides, Eddie talks to *me.*"

"All the time." A statement.

"Yes. And you don't tell anyone about that?"

"You know I don't. But people still know that you're a fan. Anybody that walks by your desk has seen *all* the pictures—"

"But no one knows that he talks to me. Except you."

****

Mitch Barlo wore his sunglasses at night.

He didn't go out very often: TMZ camera crews were always lurking around downtown, and they *still*, even after sixteen months, they still always had to ask him something about Janna's death. Not, *How's the new movie coming along?* Or, *What's it like to work with David Cronenberg?* No. It always had to have something to do with Janna. *Were you aware that she was using again, after she got out of rehab?*

12

Hadn't he gone through the whole thing in his interview with *Rolling Stone?* The entire, doomed, tragic story: famous star meets stunning ingénue on set; they fall in love, get married, begin happily-ever-after. Too late Mitch discovered the starlet's fatal flaw: she had a prescription drug problem. The entire world found out with the ambulance ride and hospital stay that he couldn't keep quiet. They tried to pass it off as an unfortunately serious case of food poisoning, but nobody bought that.

Then there was his press conference in March, last year, after Janna checked in to Betty Ford. He said that his love and prayers were with her, that he whole-heartedly backed her brave choice to get help.

Then the leaked 9-1-1 call in July, wherein he quietly, resignedly asked for his own help: "Could you please send an ambulance? My wife has overdosed."

The lack of panic, the lack of emotion in his words – that was why they were still asking him about it. All of Janna's fans had held that impossible hope that she would get help, that hers would be another druggie-actor-turns-her-life-around story, like Robert Downey, Jr.

But Janna's true Hollywood story was the more common one, the druggie-actor-dies-too-soon tale, like Cory Monteith, or Phillip Seymour Hoffman; like Chris Farley and John Belushi, and a hundred more, stretching back to the dawn of Hollywood. Janna's fans had mourned. She had played plucky, resilient heroines, and they couldn't believe that the girl who had stood against an empire in *The Roman Maiden* could fall to drugs. Only Mitch and her directors and co-stars knew Janna for the fragile train wreck she had actually been.

There had been Mitch's request *to be left alone at this sad time;* there had been a few tributes. Then he had spilled his guts to *Rolling Stone* a year ago, had made the cover. *Life With an Addict.* Her fans had been surprised at her overdose, but Mitch had not been. It had been inevitable.

He'd been thankful for the part in Cronenberg's film because it allowed him to get out of the country. But now that the thriller was in post-production, he was back in town. And still they asked him about Janna.

Mitch thought he saw the flare of lights from a news crew or damnable TMZ down the street, so he ducked into a bar. Maybe he was being paranoid. It wasn't like they were looking for him specifically. No one expected Mitch Barlo, movie-star-still-in-mourning, to be wandering the mean streets of downtown Los Angeles on a Tuesday night.

13

He looked around the bar. No one seemed to have recognized him yet, except for one portly redheaded chap seated at the bar, closest to the door. He smiled shyly, but still, like they were old friends. The stars seemed like old friends to their fans, because movies were like old friends, like stories that they had experienced in their own lives. That was the draw of movies.

Mitch didn't have any trouble with his fans. They paid the bills, and if they really thought he was like one of the characters he played, that was all right, too.

But he didn't want to be mobbed, so he smiled back at the fan, approached, before the guy could say his name and alert the whole bar.

"I know you," the chubby guy said. "In fact, I *am* you."

Mitch stopped, his *Hi there, nice fan, you want an autograph?* smile frozen on his famous face. Was this a nutcase?

The fat guy grinned. "I'm a TTAMS operator, Mr. Barlo." He held out his hand. "I'm Morris Baker. I play you online."

Mitch shook his hand, astounded. "Really?"

"Really, really." Morris grinned at Mitch and sipped his beer.

Mitch knew about TTAMS, as did every actor in Hollywood, maybe every actor in the world. Like the cover of the *Rolling Stone* for a musician, all the Wikipedia and IMDb entries in the world didn't matter – anymore, you hadn't made it in the business until you had a TTAMS presence. You had really arrived when it acquired a following and you started making sick money.

Mitch had such a following. He didn't know exactly how much money he was making – he had an agent to keep track of such things – but he knew it wasn't bad.

The studios insisted on a TTAMS presence, nowadays, even if an actor wasn't totally comfortable with another actor pretending to be him. Mitch had recently done a TTAMS clip, as a matter of fact, the only kind that the real celebrity ever did. The subscriber got a quick blurb from Mitch about the new movie when she logged on: "Hi. Before we chat, I just wanted to remind you about my new film, *The Erskine Dilemma*, in theatres this fall. Do you want to watch the trailer with me?"

A *(y/ n?)* prompt appeared, and if the subscriber pressed *y*, then the trailer would play. If she had any questions, the operator had a list of answers, provided by the studio.

"Are you getting any input about *The Erskine Dilemma?*" Mitch asked his operator.

Morris shook his head. "I play the young you. *Shamus Alive* days."

"Really?" Mitch said again. Morris nodded.

The actor was fascinated. *Shamus Alive* was a critically not-acclaimed Western/comedy; it was his third film. He had played the girl-crazy farmhand to Bruce Willis's more sedate rancher. Bruce was trying to woo the widow, and young Mitch was wooing several of her daughters simultaneously. Hilarity ensued, but not much. The movie was panned: *Tomatometer* rating – 30% – although diehard Mitch Barlo fans loved it. After the fact, of course. After he'd made it big, they'd gone back and discovered the Western, and the period piece wherein he'd died in the second act, and his first movie, a cookie-cutter slasher flick, wherein he'd died *before* the second act.

Shamus Alive had been fifteen years ago; Mitch had been twenty at the time. He'd made a forgettable comedy after the not-funny Western, then landed the starring role in *Two of Swords*. Mitch played a gambler who could predict how Lady Luck would treat him, based on his interpretation of the mystical Tarot. Various sex kittens and criminal kingpins attempt to seduce him or threaten him out of his secret, respectively. It hadn't been Oscar material, but it had been a blockbuster, *better than James Bond,* quoth *Variety.* The movie had rocketed Mitch Barlo to stardom, made his name a household word, blah, blah, blah. It had made him a lot of money.

He'd starred in a lot of movies since then, a few closer to Oscar caliber. One had even been nominated for Best Picture, and he'd been nominated for Best Actor. That was the one on which he'd met Janna. He'd played a brilliant but self-loathing, self-published, indie novelist. Janna's character finds one of his books lying on a subway seat one day – it moves her to tears. She aims to find its author, to show his talent to the world, to make him famous. The ups and downs of their relationship, the agonies and ecstasies, the price of fame and its effects, made for a compelling story. The film hadn't won a single statue, but it was true what all the losers said: a nomination was still great.

Mitch and Janna had fallen in love on the set of *A Random House Is Not a Home.* They had married, and the tabs had dubbed them the next Hollywood power couple, had christened them *Langlo,* a cutesy coupling of their last names. There was talk of babies and happily-ever-afters; they seemed to be one of those rare celebrity couples that were truly in love, one that just might last.

But it was not to be; their life together had only lasted for two short years. Janna was not the plucky heroine of *The Roman Maiden,* not the tireless advocate of her man and his talent that she portrayed in *Random House.* She was a gifted actress; she lost herself utterly in her parts because the thing she despised and feared more than anything else

15

was the day-to-day business of being Janna Langly. When she wasn't acting, Janna wanted to escape from herself. She had finally succeeded.

Mitch's close personal friends at TMZ hadn't put too fine a point on it on their website. But then TMZ never put too fine a point on anything.

> *Janna Langly's Death*
> *Overdosed on Vicodin and Booze*
>
> Janna Langly, star of *The Roman Maiden* and the Oscar-nominated *A Random House Is Not a Home*, OD'd on a lethal mixture of alcohol and drugs, including Vicodin.
>
> TMZ brought you the stunning 9-1-1 call last July, in which Langly's husband, screen great Mitch Barlo, said sadly, "Could you please send an ambulance? My wife has overdosed."
>
> The Los Angeles County Coroner's Office says toxicology results showed a fatal combo of prescription meds – Hydrocodone, Lorazepam, and Paroxetine (Paxil), along with alcohol.
>
> Janna had successfully completed the drug rehab program at the prestigious Betty Ford Center in Rancho Mirage, California, less than thirty days before. The Coroner also said years of chronic prescription drug and alcohol abuse played a factor in her death.

Mitch didn't want to think about Janna and her demons anymore. He had tried; he had vowed that he would stay with her, in the sickness of her self-hatred, in the health of her film success, for the richer that came daily, for the poorer that wasn't likely. He had vowed to stay with her until death did them part, and if the fact was inescapable that Janna had invited that death to come to her, despite her husband's love, then it was something that Mitch would just have to deal with. He was dealing with it the best he could. He had tried.

Mitch pushed the sad memories away, and again smiled at the operator, considered what the man was saying. Mitch couldn't believe that anyone remembered *Shamus Alive*.

"Let me buy you a drink, Morris. Explain to me how this thing works."

"All right, Mr. Barlo." That shy smile again.

"Please, call me Mitch."

"All right," the operator repeated.

Mitch recognized Morris as a fan from the young man's demeanor. There was that shy, amazed, confused friendliness: Morris *knew* Mitch Barlo, but of course he didn't, not really. *He's got to be a fan,* Mitch thought. *He plays me.* But Morris didn't seem to be a *rabid* fan, one of those dudes that wanted *to be* Mitch Barlo, or imagined what kind of perfect buddies they could be, if only Mitch would sit down and have a drink with him sometime . . .

Mitch was doing just that, and Morris didn't seem too overwhelmed by it. That was good. Mitch was grateful for his fans, but there was a line that couldn't be crossed, and he knew it, instinctively, like all actors did. Fans didn't see him as a person, as someone just doing a job, someone just playing a part. There was a little hysteria to fans, some more than others. They were great and all, but Mitch was overly cautious about the prospect of attempting to befriend one of them.

The bartender blinked when he recognized the actor, but that was the only thing he did. He worked in a little dive in downtown LA; maybe actors came in here all the time. Maybe they didn't, but either way, the bartender wasn't going to make a big deal of it. He took Mitch's drink order, and Morris's request for another beer, and went back down the bar.

Morris took out his phone and called up the TTAMS service.

"Okay, the first thing you do is pick who you want to talk to." He grinned faintly at Mitch. "Here's you." He showed Mitch two columns of pictures: on one side was the character he played, and beside it was a picture of how he looked at the time the movie was released.

"There's a landing screen, if you're using a bigger device." The interface was self-explanatory, but Morris explained it anyway. "They can either talk to the character, or they can talk to you from that timeframe. Young you, old you. The trailer for *The Erskine Dilemma* plays when they chose the current you. Don't want to confuse the subscribers."

Mitch must've looked confused himself, because Morris added, "You don't really look like you did in *Shamus Alive,* anymore, now do you?"

"I do not," Mitch admitted. His hair had been black then, while nowadays, the make-up lady had to touch up a sprinkling of salt amidst the pepper. His still played the romantic lead, but at thirty-five, it wasn't the lucky-kid-that-got-more-women-than-he-could-handle kind of part, like it had been when he was twenty. He had been *People Magazine's Sexiest Man Alive* when he was thirty-two, but Mitch didn't think that there would be a repeat of that. There was the whole thing with Janna: heartbreak and drug deaths didn't lend themselves too much to anyone's idea of sexiness, regardless of Mitch's looks. And *People* and Hollywood lionized youth culture. There were plenty of *younger* blue-eyed actors, who still had black hair, not out of a bottle. When those first strands of gray had appeared, Mitch had thought about just letting it show – the aging-gracefully shtick had worked for George Clooney – but neither his agent nor Mitch himself was ready to face Father Time's reality just yet.

"So they run the trailer with the current you," Morris repeated. "If the subscriber chooses a younger you, she obviously wants to talk to a younger you. A trailer for the old you in a new movie would just confuse her."

"What are they like? What do they want to talk about?"

"The subscribers? I signed a confidentiality agreement, Mr. – Mitch. I'm not allowed to tell you what they're like or what they talk about, if I wanna keep my job." Again Morris grinned. "But I may be able to show you."

He swiped the TTAMS site away and said to his phone, "Mitch Barlo wants to know what it is we do with his face."

The phone beeped.

"Yes. The real Mitch Barlo."

There was a pause of several seconds, then Morris's phone beeped again. He showed Mitch the text: *Bring him on in, then.* "As soon as I finish my beer," Morris said to his phone, then put it back in his pocket.

****

Morris remained mysterious about exactly what it was that TTAMS subscribers said to him while he was masquerading as a young Mitch Barlo. Instead, he gave the actor a great deal of insider information about how the game was played, how the computer would prompt him with appropriate answers, whether they were factoids, or just a response that the subscriber might expect Mitch to say.

"It's all psychological," Morris confided, and tapped the side of his head. "Each conversation is recorded – the program remembers what you and she talked about the last time, you see. It remembers *everything* you talked about.

"You know how sometimes, you'll be looking for something online, like, say, you go to Walmart.com and look at TVs, or you go to

18

HomeDepot.com and you look at tools or paint or lumber or something?"

Mitch nodded, although he'd never actually done any of those things. Obviously Morris was not familiar with the concept of *movie stars are not like us*.

"Then, later on," Morris continued, "you're doing something else online, and you notice an ad from Walmart or Home Depot on the side of the screen, and damned if they're not listing just the products that you were searching for earlier. TTAMS programming is just a more complicated version of that. It remembers what the subscriber talked about before, and prompts us to talk about the same things again."

"It sounds sophisticated."

Morris nodded and sipped his beer.

Mitch was utterly intrigued at the idea that thousands of fans were growing simulated relationships with him through TTAMS. Because, if the program remembered what had already been said, then after a while, it would almost seem that they had become *friends* . . .

"Here's the best part. All these conversations are reviewed by another program. That's where the prompts about what to say next come from. All the previous responses have been analyzed; if they asked you how you liked doing *Shamus Alive,* and you said you hated it, their next response was evaluated. If they said *That's a shame,* or, *I'm sorry to hear that* . . . That's a negative response.

"So the program tells us that the statistical probability is that we should reply with, *Oh, that movie was a lot of fun to make,* or something like that. So that's what I say. And the subscriber's response to that it analyzed, and so on."

"So I'm telling them exactly what they want to hear."

Morris shrugged. "That's what they're paying for."

****

Valerie Whitly had a glass-walled office at the TTAMS headquarters in downtown LA. Most of it was glass-walled, anyway, so she could look out at the rows of operators on the floor whenever she had the hankerin'. *To bask in your success,* as Joyce put it. The cubicles below had doors and walls for privacy, but no ceilings. The office was at the top of a set of diamond-stamped steel steps; there was a narrow landing with a railing in front of it, where Valerie could sometimes be seen gazing forth at her employees, if they had the mind to look up.

Joyce had designed the whole thing. *It'll remind them who's boss, when they see you standing there.* The rest of Valerie's office – the bathroom and

19

the tiny bedroom where she spent a lot of nights after working – were not visible to her employees. Joyce's own office was off the lobby, far away from the business-end of her business.

Valerie sat behind her desk and sighed, then opened her laptop. She preferred it to an antiquated desktop or a modern tablet. She had been writing code for practically as long as she could remember, and she liked a full keyboard, damn it. A slick HP rep had been in to see her, had offered her a king's ransom to appear in a commercial and say that she used their premier laptop, but Valerie had had Joyce show him the door. Valerie would not be a shill for HP or anyone else, even if she did use their product, and besides, she already had more money than she could ever spend.

As she always did, Valerie paused to admire the pictures of Edison Forbes that changed, every ten seconds, on the desktop of her computer. She felt the same sentiment every time: *Hot damn, he's cute!* Not a single male *homo sapiens* on the planet came close to Eddie Forbes as far as looks were concerned, to Valerie. There was just something in the amused curve of his smile, the knowing twinkle in his eye. Edison Forbes was the single most attractive man that she'd ever seen.

Anybody that walks by your desk has seen all the pictures, Joyce had said.

And how many times have I had to tell people who he is? Valerie thought. Eddie had made enough movies, had starred in a few television series – he was *kind of a big deal* in his native Canada, and he enjoyed a cult following in Russia. But as for the rest of the world . . .

Less than two thousand subscribers, in all of these United States, has ever chosen a conversation with Edison Forbes.

So what? Valerie thought. *What do Joyce or American women know about foreign talent? Two thousand of them know, just like I do. He's absolutely awesome.*

Valerie's phone buzzed. It was Joyce. It was never anyone but Joyce. All phone calls for Valerie were routed first through Joyce's staff. If a management decision was required, the call was forwarded to Joyce herself. If Joyce deemed the call important enough for Valerie, then she patched it through. Valerie was the brains behind the program at the core of TTAMS. She didn't need to talk to very many people. That's what underlings were for. Joyce had wanted to fire the one that had let the HP rep slip through, but Valerie was kinder. The young man had been transferred to another office instead.

Joyce was the brains behind every other aspect of their venture besides the programming, but she had always seen her primary function as *taking care of Valerie.* They had been friends since college, and Valerie was a genius. Maybe it was true that she wasn't all there sometimes, that she lived in a world a little bit different than the one everyone else inhabited. Such eccentricities were allowed to geniuses. And since Joyce had perhaps been the cause of at least some of Valerie's oddness, she felt it was her duty to look after her friend.

"I've got some bad news and some worse news," Joyce said now. "What do you want to hear first?"

"The bad news."

"I'll give it all to you. Brett's in town. He wants to have lunch with us."

Valerie felt as if she had been punched in the gut. She gasped. She hadn't seen Brett since the day she'd graduated from college.

"That's what I thought," Joyce said.

"Why would I . . ." Valerie fought to catch her breath. "Why would Brett think that I would want to have lunch with him?"

"You're famous, Val," Joyce said. "Creator of the hottest up and coming service in the world. You're bigger than Mark Zuckerberg. Of course Brett wants to see you, to congratulate you. He doesn't know that you—"

"No. I don't want to see Brett. If I'm so famous, I'm too busy to have lunch with—"

"Okay. I just wanted to let you know he was back in town."

"I don't want to see Brett, Jo. You keep him away from me."

"Okay, honey. That's my job."

"Thanks, Jo," Valerie said with infinite gratitude. She told her friend to enjoy her lunch anyway, and hung up.

She looked out of her office at the rows of operators below, all talking to fans, each making her unspeakable profits with every word. But Valerie didn't see them. She glanced at her laptop, and for a moment, she didn't see Eddie's picture, either. Or, more accurately, it *was* Eddie, but in this particular picture, he looked a lot like Brett . . .

But that's just ridiculous. Eddie doesn't look anything like Brett.

Valerie was over Brett, even though she still couldn't bear to see him. Why, if it hadn't been for Brett, and Joyce, and Eddie, she might still be slaving away at Fox, writing code and looking at actors in motion capture monkey suits . . .

Someday I'll thank Brett. Send him a case of Moet & Chandon Ice or something equally as expensive. But not today.

****

21

Valerie was just twenty-one, had just started her junior year at UCLA when she met Joyce. Joyce was twenty-four, in her second year of law school. They had shared a table at a bar called Q's one Friday night, and before last call, they had become inseparable friends.

Valerie learned that Joyce's father had once been District Attorney of Los Angeles. Afterwards, he had gone into private practice and had become wealthy. His daughter aimed to follow in his footsteps.

Valerie's father was also wealthy, but the ostentation and luxury of Beverly Hills or Malibu was no longer his thing. He had been in a famous band when Valerie was a child, but now he lived a life of obscurity with his wife in Riverside. Valerie told Joyce that she was roughing it in a dorm, despite her dad's money.

It was the roommate that had been assigned to share Valerie's quarters with her this term that was the problem. The girl's name was Sharon, and she was a hard-partying tramp from West Covina.

"I helped her take measurements," Valerie told Joyce. "For the revolving door on our room. She's got a different guy with her every night."

Joyce had laughed heartily at the computer tech's wit. She liked Valerie immensely. She was cute and funny, with a wide-eyed, innocent expression always present in her bright blue eyes. She constantly used lines from movies in her conversation. They were often non-sequitur, so Joyce always had to ask, "What's that from?" After a while, she didn't even do that, accepting the quotes as just another aspect of her friend's oddness.

Law school was brutal, cut-throat. Joyce never felt completely at ease with her competitive fellow students. She never felt that she could trust any of them very much. But Valerie was great. All she wanted to do was write code and go out and have an occasional beer. She wasn't interested in the Greek life, could not possibly care less about cars or clothes. She hadn't even bothered to look for a private place to live.

Valerie's only snobbery was that she refused to date anyone other than good-looking men, and Joyce figured it was because she dealt with enough shy, bespectacled types in the IT world. It always fascinated Joyce, the way her friend didn't care what these pretty boys thought or what they said. They were attractive, and that was all Valerie cared to notice. She went out with any of them that asked her, but she never became attached. She slept with some of them; it was all part of the fun of college life to Valerie.

"They're just nice to look at," Valerie explained. "I don't want to take any of them to raise."

Joyce thought she might like to find a life-partner someday, but just didn't have time for emotional entanglements right now; law school was tough. So she and Valerie were perfect friends. Joyce liked to talk to men, to see if any of them encompassed the same drive and ambition that she did. Valerie just liked to look at and occasionally sample the pretty ones.

But Valerie's roommate, Sharon, sampled them all, and the constant stream of suitors was disrupting Valerie's study habits this semester. So Joyce invited Val to come live with her in the guesthouse of her father's Beverly Hills estate. The computer major became Joyce's sidekick, her pet, her best friend. Joyce looked past the quirky movie fan; she grasped Valerie's genius. She knew that Valerie Whitly wouldn't be a nameless techie from Riverside forever.

They laughed and loved their way through college; no two coeds were ever happier or more problem-free. But then, at the beginning of their final year, Joyce met Brett Cooke. And worse than that, she introduced him to Valerie.

Brett was a player. He was intelligent, witty, utterly charming, devastatingly attractive. Joyce quipped that it was a shame that he wasn't a med student. Brett Cooke could've made millions, had he chosen to become a gynecologist, and Joyce told him that. He might be majoring in business, but his minor was obviously women.

Joyce resisted Brett's charms, however. He was just too cute, and she knew that he would be just too good. Her mother had always told Joyce to beware of ladies' men: *They get to be ladies' men by knowing a lot of ladies. You might be the next, but you'll never be the last.*

Brett was just the type that Joyce thought she would fall in love with, against all better judgment. He was smart and ambitious, in addition to being fine *all day long and three times on Sunday.* Joyce had school and an exciting legal career ahead of her. She would not allow herself to become involved with a good-looking, insouciant business major who would in the end bring her nothing but heartache, no matter how many rewarding conversations they had.

Brett was intrigued by Joyce's reticence. He was not accustomed to women telling him no, so he enthusiastically pursued her for several weeks before he finally accepted that she just wasn't going to give in. Brett could tell that Joyce loved him – hell, everybody loved him, especially women – but she loved him like a brother, like a friend. She loved him for his mind. He found that to be refreshing, too. Brett Cooke didn't have many friends of the opposite sex that he hadn't slept with, at least once.

23

Graduation for all three of them was on the horizon before Joyce finally got around to introducing Brett to her best friend. Valerie spent most nights behind her computer, studying or watching movies, and Brett didn't come to the house – he had more accommodating *friends* to entertain. So Joyce's two pals had never run into each other.

But Valerie liked to go out to Q's and look at the pretty boys on the weekend, and kismet delivered the prettiest one of them all to her one Friday night.

The good-looking business major came up to their table and embraced Joyce. He noisily nuzzled her neck, as he always did, as if he would devour her. Joyce allowed it, because Brett smelled good, and it tickled, and it always served to remind her that he greeted all his lady-friends similarly.

Joyce wished that she could be like Valerie, who played with the players. Val didn't care that she was next, but would never be last. Joyce, on the other hand, knew she could fall for Brett. So easily.

"Stop, Lover Boy," she said with a giggle. "You're raising my blood pressure."

"So you are alive! I've had my doubts." He smiled at Joyce's companion.

Valerie blinked expressionlessly, then her dimpled smile slowly blossomed.

"This is Valerie," Joyce said. "She's a computer genius. Valerie, this is my friend, Brett."

"A computer genius? Maybe you can fix my phone. I can't seem to get this app to run right."

Joyce rolled her eyes. Anytime she told *anyone* that Valerie knew something about computers, they invariably had a problem with their cellphone and wanted her to look at it. Valerie had the perfect answer, however, a variation on the one med students had used from time immemorial. *Does it hurt when you do this? Yes? Then don't do that. Your app doesn't work? Maybe it's time for an upgrade.*

"Valerie's not a cellphone repairman, Brett."

But to Joyce's surprise, her friend said, "Let me see it."

Brett smiled again and handed his phone to Valerie. "The Plenty of Fish app. It's really slow."

Joyce rolled her eyes again. "You can't get a date quickly enough?"

"I'm just looking, Jo."

"You can't look quickly enough?"

Brett smiled and glanced around the bar. He asked Joyce a few questions about how school was going, just little meaningless sentences, until Valerie handed his phone back to him.

"You have seventy-five messages. It should work smoother now."

Brett's phone rang in his hand. "I have to take this. Nice meeting you, Valerie. Thanks for fixing my app."

Valerie nodded and Brett wandered off to find a quieter place to take his phone call.

Joyce watched him go. She sighed.

"Where have you been hiding *him?*" Valerie asked. "Your new boyfriend's too cute for Valerie to have a look at?"

"He's not my boyfriend, Val." Joyce noted the enthused sparkle in her friend's eyes and frowned. "And he's definitely too cute for Valerie to have a look at."

His brief phone call ended, Brett was whispering in some girl's ear at the bar. Joyce watched her shake her head and nod at the bouncer. *Be careful, Lover Boy. Some girls do have boyfriends.*

She said to Valerie, "He's too cute to do anything *but* look at him."

"I don't know about that," Valerie commented. "He is *exceptionally* cute. *One Cute to rule them all, One Cute to find them, One Cute to bring them all and in the darkness bind them.*"

Joyce considered her friend with familiar amazement. *Where does she come up with this stuff?* "Brett's not the binding kind, Val."

"But I bet he's a lot of fun in the darkness, nonetheless?"

"I wouldn't know," Joyce replied with a touch of primness.

Val grinned in surprise. "Why the hell not?"

"Ah, Brett's okay for a friend. But I could never trust him."

"I know what you mean, Blair. Trust's a tough thing to come by these days. Tell you what — why don't you just trust in the Lord?"

Joyce ignored this remark. "It would be too easy to fall in love with Brett," she opined, mostly to herself, as she watched him talk up a waitress.

"What is love?" Valerie sang. *"Lady, don't hurt me, don't hurt me, no more . . ."*

Joyce turned her attention back to her friend. She asked seriously, "You've never been hurt, have you, Val?"

The computer genius was philosophical. "Marilyn said, *A wise girl kisses but doesn't love, listens but doesn't believe, and leaves before she is left.*"

"Isn't Marilyn the poster child for heartbreak?" Joyce asked. Valerie didn't have a response for that. "So, no. You've never been hurt."

"As long as you know men are like children, you know everything!" Valerie grinned. "It was something my mother told me. Coco Chanel said it." She looked at Joyce curiously, with a trace of concern. "Were you hurt once, Jo? You never told me–"

Joyce spoke quickly. "Oh, there was this guy. Jeremy. In high school. It all seems so silly in retrospect, now that I'm an adult. But I thought I loved him, because I thought he loved me." Joyce shook her head.

Perhaps this was from where her caution regarding Brett had sprung. *The burnt child fears the fire.* They were the same type, Brett and Jeremy, gorgeous, friendly, without a care in the world. Joyce had given her all to Jeremy, just because he'd casually asked her for it.

Jeremy had been *the one;* Joyce had been entirely sure of it. She'd loved everything about him, his laugh, his smile. She'd loved the way she felt whenever she was around him. She'd imagined a future with him, after high school was over. Maybe she'd find a little paralegal job after graduation – she wouldn't have time for law school now, because she'd be too busy, too happy, loving her beautiful husband, raising his adorable babies. Her ambition took a backseat to her love for Jeremy.

But in the spring before high school ended, when it seemed like one of those babies might actually materialize, Joyce discovered that there would not be a happily-ever-after with Jeremy, nor with anyone like him. When she'd told him that she thought she was pregnant, he'd blanched, and immediately volunteered to go to the ATM and get the money for her so she could get rid of it.

"But . . . I thought we would . . . I thought you'd be happy. I know it's a little too soon, but . . . I thought we were going to be together . . ."

Jeremy had looked at Joyce in confusion then, as if she was speaking in a foreign language. "You're great, Jo," he'd said earnestly. "I like you a lot, but I don't want . . . You and me, we're not going to . . . I'm eighteen years old, for Christ's sake. I'm not looking to settle down yet, not with anyone, and a baby . . . Jesus! I don't want that. I don't think I'll ever want that."

It had all been a fantasy, this idea of a white picket fence and a family with Jeremy; it had all been in Joyce's imagination alone. She'd loved Jeremy, so she'd just naturally assumed that he'd loved her back. It was not the case: it had suddenly become obvious that Jeremy didn't love anyone but himself, at least not yet. Just like Brett, he was not yet capable of it. Like Coco said, he was a boy.

Stoically, she had told the *boy* that she'd considered to be her one true love, "I guess I'll see you around, then." Joyce had the self-respect not to beg him, the pride not to let him see her cry. He said nothing. Not *I'm sorry,* or *It was fun,* or even *Okay.* He said not a word.

Joyce vowed that she would assume the martyr's role, that she would have Jeremy's child, that she would figure out some way to raise it and attend school at the same time. With Jeremy's exit, her ambition returned. Her parents would help – they would get over the shame of her incredible stupidity after their grandchild arrived.

But fate was kind to Joyce. She was only five days late, and before she had to take a deep breath and break the news to Mom and Dad, the curse arrived. She was not pregnant after all.

Joyce was eternally grateful – she'd never refer to it as *the curse* again – and she'd made sure to never make the same mistake again. There would be a time for love someday, perhaps. Time for those babies. Now it was time for study and fun, and she would not again give her heart to another pretty boy, just because he asked for it. The next time, Joyce would make sure that *he* loved *her*, first, before she let her imagination run away with her.

Valerie already seemed to have that concept firmly in mind. *"No time for love, Doctor Jones,"* she would say, if Joyce noticed that she was going out with some guy more than just a couple of times. *"Another prop has occupied my time . . ."*

This one goes out to the one I love. No, Valerie had never been hurt, because she'd never been in love.

But Brett Cooke was the oft-cited horse of a different color, and Valerie was not asking to hear the sad tale of Joyce and Jeremy and what had not been, because she was watching him work the room.

Brett was different. He hadn't started college right after high school; he was two years older than Valerie, a year younger than Joyce, and he was a little better-looking, a lot more confident and sure of himself than most of the college boys that Valerie was used to playing with. Brett was a little more sophisticated.

"Hey, nerd-girl," Joyce said, to get her friend's attention, "We're not in Kansas anymore. You'd better take a moment for sober reflection. Brett Cooke will *turn you out.*"

Valerie's eyes widened in delight. "You think so?"

Joyce nodded seriously. "You're thinking of whacking the wrong hornet's nest this time, Val." She liked her own metaphor. "You're gonna get stung."

"When the legend becomes fact, print the legend." Valerie stood and straightened out her clothes, ran a hand through her hair. Joyce knew that her friend's mind was made up.

But Valerie Whitly was a big girl. Joyce shrugged. "Don't say I didn't warn you."

"We're going to live like we're telling the best story in the whole world. Are you ready?"

"Just make sure *you're* ready, Val."

27

"I was born ready." Valerie glanced again at Brett, then back at her friend. *"I'm gonna make him an offer he can't refuse.* Don't wait up."

****

Valerie caught Brett's eye and he smiled at her as she approached. "Are you stalking me?" he asked. "Because that would be super."

Valerie wondered if Joyce's cute friend knew that he'd just said a line from *Van Wilder*. She thought she'd try an obscure one on him. She asked, *"Is it safe?"*

Brett's grin widened. He understood the reference. He glanced down at his empty glass. *"Why is the rum always gone?"*

"Fat, drunk, and stupid is no way to go through life, son."

"White man's burden, Lloyd, my man. White man's burden." The barkeep appeared, as if on cue, and Brett told him, *"I like ya, Lloyd, I always liked ya. You were always the best of 'em. Best goddamn bartender from Timbuktu to Portland, Maine, or Portland, Oregon for that matter."*

The bartender rolled his eyes at Valerie. He had heard this praise from Brett, from *The Shining*, before, so he supplied the next line. *"Thank you for saying so."* He asked Valerie what he could get for her.

"Do not drink wine nor strong drink, thou nor thy sons with thee, lest ye shall die."

"The Bible?" the bartender asked.

Brett grinned. "Sort of. It's from *The Wild Bunch*."

Valerie said to the bartender, *"I love to drink martinis. Two at the very most. Three, I'm under the table. Four, I'm under my host."*

"Everybody's a comedian," the bartender replied and went to fetch their drinks.

Brett winked at Valerie. *"You know what your problem is, it's that you haven't seen enough movies — all of life's riddles are answered in the movies."*

"Who said that?"

"Steve Martin."

"Tarantino said, *I have loved movies as the number one thing in my life so long that I can't ever remember a time when I didn't.* I've spent most of my life watching movies." But Valerie didn't want to go into all the whys and wherefores of that, so she just added, *"The previous occupant had been a bit of a shut-in."*

"Only child, are ya?"

Valerie nodded, amazed at his perceptiveness.

Brett said, "Yeah, me, too. It was just me and my mom. I kept her company. We watched a lot of movies. She's quite the film buff. She knows all kinds of stories about old Hollywood, too."

28

Valerie was fascinated with how much she had in common, already, with this strikingly attractive guy. Her mother was a film buff, too – that had to be the understatement of the century – and like Brett, Valerie had spent a lot of her childhood and adolescence watching movies with her.

But the only men Valerie had ever met that could quote lines from films were always little wormy fellows, usually with bad skin, who stared at her breasts as if she couldn't tell where they were looking. There was a lot of that type writing code, whether they knew about movies or not.

But Brett was . . . *stunning.* He was tall, broad-shouldered but slender, like a swimmer. He had black, curly, shoulder-length hair, and the most gorgeous blue eyes.

"Your husband told me you were the most beautiful woman he'd ever seen, but he didn't say anything about the most beautiful woman I'd ever seen," Valerie told him, and he smiled. It didn't matter to Brett if the line was non-sequitur, if the gender was wrong. He recognized it as being from a movie, and he understood.

"I get so tired of just being told I'm pretty," he replied and batted his phenomenal eyelashes at her.

Valerie doubted that. *"Vanity is definitely my favorite sin,"* she told him.

"Mrs. Robinson, you're trying to seduce me, aren't you?"

"Would you like me to seduce you? Is that what you're trying to tell me?"

The bartender returned with their drinks, and Brett said, *"Here y'are, baby. Take this, wipe the lipstick off, slide over here next to me and let's get started."*

They smiled at each other over their drinks, and even though it was the corniest line of all, Valerie was thrilled when Brett said, *"Here's looking at you, kid."*

"I may be an outlaw, darlin'," she told him, *"but you're the one stealing my heart."*

Brett slammed his drink, his eyes never leaving hers. He set the glass on the bar. *"I find you attractive. Your aggressive moves toward me indicate that you feel the same way. But still, ritual requires that we continue with a number of platonic activities—"*

"— before we have sex. I am proceeding with these activities, but in point of actual fact, all I really want to do is have intercourse with you as soon as possible."

Brett blinked at her straight-forwardness. Her just plain *forwardness.* But on the other hand, he had started the line from *A Beautiful Mind.* Beautiful Valerie had just finished it for him.

"Alll-righty, then," Brett said, and kissed her lightly on the forehead. He looked down the bar, caught the bartender's attention and said, "Check, please!"

****

Joyce sipped her drink and watched as Brett and Valerie left the bar, hand in hand. She noted the sparkle in her friend's eye, visible even from across the room, as she waved goodbye.

No, Val's never been hurt, because she's never been in love. Until now.

Joyce sighed. She wasn't much of a movie fan, but one picked things up, being around Valerie Whitly. She said aloud, *"Fasten your seatbelts, it's going to be a bumpy night!"*

****

Joyce was correct in her theory about why Valerie Whitly wasted her time only with good-looking men. She had spent her life around ones of her kind: code writers, gamers, all manner of computer geeks. The fact that they were male was mostly an inconvenience to Valerie: they either stared at her dumbly, like they were in love, or they made puerile, sexist comments. Valerie had met her share of geniuses in the coding world, and she had infinite respect and admiration for them. But she purposefully overlooked the fact that they were men. They were all either shy, or they leered. Valerie had no use for their brand of childish masculinity. They were all boys.

The pretty ones, the ones she met when she went out with Joyce, they were boys, too, but they were so much more fun. Like her IT peers, good-looking men pretended to be interested in whatever she had to say – Valerie was convinced that this aspect of their interest was all a sham – but good-looking men had the self-control and confidence to make it seem like it was a normal, casual thing to be talking to an attractive young woman. They didn't stare, didn't practically drool; nor did they nudge their buddies and make crude, off-color remarks.

And the good-looking ones invariably knew what they were doing. Valerie had heard all of Joyce's chuckled admonitions about how ladies' men got to be ladies' men, but she disregarded the advice. She didn't care about who had come before, or who would come next, as long as it was her turn for the weekend. They were all just adorable, talented playthings to Valerie. She didn't care about their politics or their ambitions; she had Joyce with which to discuss the important things in life. She didn't want to talk to them – if they were cute enough, she

30

wanted to touch them and kiss them. Valerie liked them all, but she didn't love any of them. She was just having fun.

"Catch and release," she'd often told Joyce with a giggle.

But Valerie didn't realize that it was she who had been caught this time. She liked Brett immensely, already. He was *stunning*, and he knew the movies. That combination was enough to get Valerie's motor running at a little higher RPM as they drove back to his apartment.

The thought didn't cross her mind that she shouldn't be going home with Brett, scant moments after they'd been introduced. Like any good mother, Sophia Whitly had schooled her daughter in the mores of their culture, warned her that men didn't put a value on things obtained too easily. Valerie had never cared in the past – it had been she who had been doing the obtaining – and their opinion of her willingness had not mattered to her in the least. She wasn't taking them to raise, after all.

And even though Brett seemed different to Valerie, special – she wasn't going to play coy and shy with him, either. He understood. *Ritual requires that we continue with a number of platonic activities . . .* Brett knew what she wanted, and he wasn't going to judge her for it. He'd quoted the line to her. That was explanation enough.

Brett's apartment was small and tidy. "Would you like another drink, Valerie?" he asked, as they entered. *"You know? A drink?"*

"I have always depended on the kindness of strangers."

Brett proceeded into the kitchenette, and Valerie followed him. When he opened a cabinet and extracted a bottle of gin, she decided that she didn't want a drink. The *platonic activities* had gone on long enough. She put her arms around him, hugged his back to her.

Brett turned; she kissed him.

He smiled. *"What'd you do that for?"*

"Been wondering if I'd like it."

"What's the decision?"

"I don't know yet." And she kissed him again. But the decision had been made. Brett was awesome; he knew Bogie and Bacall's classic exchange from *To Have and Have Not*.

It's even better when you help, Valerie thought. When Brett broke the kiss, she said, *"Joey, do you like movies about gladiators?"*

Brett grinned. *"You ever seen a grown man naked?"*

"Well, it's not the men in your life that counts, it's the life in your men."

Brett forgot about drinking, too.

****

31

Valerie was enthralled with Brett Cooke. The way he smelled, the way he tasted, how he moved, the things he whispered. She moaned, she screamed his name.

Brett chuckled. *"Listen to them! The children of the night! What music they make!"*

Valerie panted, smiled. *"And how can this be? For he is the Kwisatz Haderach!"*

Brett smiled back, kissed her tenderly. *"Louis, I think this is the beginning of a beautiful friendship."*

The stuff that dreams are made of, Valerie thought, and kissed him back.

Eventually, she drifted off into a contented sleep beside him. When they awoke in the morning, the first thing she said was, *"Please, sir. I want some more."*

"Go, get the butter," Brett replied playfully.

"Yippee kay-yay, motherfucker."

****

Brett liked Valerie. She was beautiful, and always eager, and didn't make unreasonable demands on his time. She was busy finishing up school, so she was perfectly happy if he only called or texted her during the week, and she always went back home to Joyce's place on Sunday night.

Like everyone who discovered that her father was *the* Denny Whitly, of Sonic Daydream, Brett wanted to know why he had given up music, at the peak of success.

Though still a child when the band quit touring, Brett remembered their catchy, *Billboard*-topping tunes. He had stood in front of the mirror a few times and pretended to be Denny Whitly, even though he didn't play the guitar or sing. When Denny quit, it had been in all the papers.

"Something about an accident?" Brett asked.

Valerie nodded, appropriately somber. She had told the story a million times. Sonic Daydream had been *big*. "An auto accident. My mother was severely injured. She was in a wheelchair for a while. Dad retired so he could take care of us."

And that was all the explanation Valerie was going to give to Brett, or anyone. Joyce, of course, knew the whole story, but Joyce was Valerie's best friend. They were as close as sisters.

ACT II

Valerie sighed inwardly. *Ah, yes, the whole story.* The truth. A programming Prof she'd had her freshman year had been of a philosophical bent; he'd quoted Galileo: *All truths are easy to understand once they are discovered; the point is to discover them.*

Valerie would not learn all the motivations surrounding her father's life-altering decision to quit Sonic Daydream until she was almost seventeen years old.

She had heard all the family histories, of course, the saga of how Mom and Dad met, how they fell in love. Tales of Sonic Daydream's meteoric rise to fame. The accident. But family histories often contain holes, gaps, omissions; details and events that parents might feel are too sad or embarrassing to relate to their child are left unrevealed. Because her father had been a famous rock star, it would take an uncomfortable private discussion of an unfortunately public speculation for Valerie to discover the truth.

Valerie's maternal grandparents were deceased; both had passed a few years before she would even be a twinkle in her not-yet-famous father's eye. Sid Carlin had died from an aggressive pancreatic cancer, and then his wife had followed him to *the undiscover'd country from whose bourn no traveler returns* less than a year later. Mandy Carlin's malady had been more difficult to diagnose. The doctors said it was complications from congestive heart failure; family legend put it down to simply a broken heart.

Mandy had passed in August of 1987, when her daughter Sophia had been seven months away from twenty-one, and her sister Elise still two months shy of turning sixteen. Life insurance had paid off the house in Riverside, but college became unworkable for the eldest Carlin sister. Now she had to be the breadwinner, as well as both mother and father to her orphaned, teenage sister. Sophia got a job as a secretary to support them. As they had no other family, when she turned twenty-one, she legally assumed responsibility for her sister's care.

Sophia was uncomfortable in the role. She and Elise had never been close. Their parents had valued personal privacy and an individual's space, so the sisters had never been forced to share a room. Even so, the years that separated them in age might've been overcome, had it not been for a vast difference in their temperaments. Sophia had always been introspective, if not introverted. She watched other people, gauged their moods and personalities. She would speculate on their motivations, try to ascertain what they wanted from a situation, what they wanted from her. Only then would she act.

Elise, on the other hand, acted based solely on her own motivations. She had always been, in child-rearing parlance, *a spoiled brat*. Where Sophia had always recognized that other people had wants and needs and desires and rights – she would respect theirs, because she expected them to respect hers – Elise had always attempted to manipulate these same things to get what she wanted.

She would play Daddy's little angel, Mommy's little helper, or Teacher's pet, if she believed that these façades would compel Dad to let allow her to go to that concert, even though she was far too young; if it would guilt Mom into giving her a little more allowance, even though she hadn't really earned it; if it would convince the teacher to allow her an extra day to complete her assignment, even though the rest of the class had handed theirs in on time.

Sophia didn't think that her little sister was inherently bad; she was just thoroughly, deviously manipulative. At an early age, Elise had hit upon a schema in life that worked for her, so she had enthusiastically run with it. Telling people exactly what they wanted to hear, doing precisely what they wanted her to do – if the end result benefited Elise, then that was all that mattered. If what she told them was a lie, if she only seemed to do what they had asked of her – that was all part and parcel of getting what she wanted. The ends always justified the means.

At the tender age of sixteen, almost immediately after their mother's death, Elise demonstrated a new wildness. She acquired a shady boyfriend named Sammy, who was twenty-five. He worked as a bouncer at The House of Ale, a bar in downtown Riverside which showcased all the local bands.

Sammy was smart enough to see to it that Elise didn't try to buy a drink when he let her past the sign on the door of a Saturday night, the one that said *You Must Be 21*. But he wasn't smart enough to see that Elise was only using him as a ticket to meet the guys from the bands that played at the bar, musicians who were all so much more desirable to Elise than he was.

Sophia didn't care for Sammy and she didn't like Elise hanging out with him at his place of employment, but Sophia didn't consider her sister to be irredeemable. She imagined that Elise would drink a beer if she was offered one, maybe smoke a little weed if it was available. This only went along with being sixteen, with dating bouncers and sneaking into bars to which she shouldn't be permitted entrance for another five years. And Sophia knew that Sammy was not her little sister's first boyfriend.

But neither had Sophia ever seen Elise drunk or stoned, and if she had been shocked the first time she had discovered that Elise had spent the night with Sammy – she hadn't actually stayed overnight at her girlfriend's house after all – Sophia had never actually caught Elise *in flagrante delicto* with him or any of her other beaux. Nor were there telephone calls at all hours of the night, nor rude honks from the curb.

Sophia was grateful that Elise was neither a drunk nor a druggie, and that she was discreet with her boyfriends. It was just unfortunate that she was in such a big hurry to be grown up, that she was using the big bouncer to gain entry to where the musicians were.

Sophia reckoned that it only followed that her sister would choose the groupie path to the Wild City neighborhood of adulthood. All things considered, it couldn't have gone any other way.

There was a framed photograph in the hall of their house, showing four-year-old Elise wearing pink, footie-pajamas and a giant pair of old-fashioned, leather-cushioned headphones. She was smiling up at the camera, an expression of surprised delight on her face. The picture had been taken in the extra room upstairs, one door down from Elise's bedroom, which the family had always called *Dad's Record Room.*

Sidney Carlin had never been a musician, nor had either of his daughters ever picked up an instrument. He was a civil engineer by trade, had held a high-ranking position with a local land developer, almost until the day he died. He drew plans for the roads, curbs, gutters, and sidewalks of the new neighborhoods built by his company. Sid was good at his job, and it paid well. He was a responsible, hardworking man, who'd made sure that there would be money enough for his wife and daughters to continue life as they had known it, after he was gone.

But Sid's imagination had belonged to music.

There was a little couch in the record room, and an expensive, complicated sound system connected to those headphones. And there were records. Sid was fifty when he too-soon passed; he enjoyed most

35

kinds of music, and had been collecting records since he was fourteen. There were thousands, neatly lined up on the shelves that occupied all available wall space in the room. After a hard day creating the streets for housing developments, culs-de-sac and meandering sidewalks, driveway approaches and cross-gutters, Sid would retire to this little room, don his headphones, and immerse himself in his music.

There was a little jazz, a tiny selection of country and classical artists, but the bulk of his collection was good ol' rock and roll. There were all the famous bands: the Stones and The Doors, The Who, The Beatles, Bowie, Led Zeppelin. But Sid also had the hopeful first offerings of all the flash-in-the-pan, one-hit-wonders, bands who had produced a few clever tunes that had only lasted for a season, sounds that could be tied down to a specific decade, but had faded with the onslaught of the next one.

Sid's beloved wife spent the occasional evening or Saturday afternoon enjoying this cross-section of sound with her husband, as did his daughter Sophia. But they had other interests. It would be Elise who would take up the mantle of music lover from her father. Elise thoughtlessly broke her toys, tore her new clothes, made and discarded friends at her whim. But music would become important to her, vital, as it was to Sid. The only things Elise ever handled with any care or respect were Dad's records.

It was the subtle bass line, the tinkling keyboards and the sounds of rain and thunder on *Riders on the Storm* that had produced the look of wonder and amazement on four-year-old Elise's face in that photograph. Long before she understood the import of *If you give this man a ride, sweet family will die,* Elise was hooked on the sound of Morrison's haunting voice, the rhythm of Krieger's guitar, the relentlessness of Manzarek's incomparable electric piano. Elise would come to love all the old famous bands, the new famous bands, the one-hit-wonders, as much as her father.

Sid shared with his daughter what histories he knew of these musicians that he idolized, but not being one himself, the mechanics of the sounds were not important to him. Neither he nor Elise would ever know that *Riders on the Storm* was composed in a diatonic scale. They had no concept of meter, mixed or otherwise. They felt the beat, the melody, the words, in their hearts and souls. They were moved by rhymes that fired their imaginations. As his never-met granddaughter Valerie would one day sprinkle her conversation with lines from movies, so did Sid Carlin and his youngest daughter often quote song lyrics to each other.

Music fans like Elise and her father were common, a dime a dozen, however. Sophia speculated that perhaps her sister had her heart set on an actual musician lately, not only because she was a rock and roll fan, but because a musician was something that their father had always admired, but had never been. Sophia thought that perhaps Dad would always be alive to Elise if she could surround herself with people who knew how to play, who could accommodate her requests for one of Sid's favorite old tunes whenever the memory struck her.

Sophia decided it was as good a reason as any to explain why her sister had suddenly decided to hang out at bars and try to meet musicians. This wildness had not taken her until after Mandy had also passed, but now it was the thing that Elise did. She had immersed herself in being a fan. She went to concerts, she talked constantly about *amazing* bands, she chased guitar players.

Sophia was pretty sure that Elise had not as yet caught any. Her sister had previously only gone to see famous names that probably didn't wallow around too much with sixteen-year-old girls after the show. But now, big, dumb Sammy had let her in to where the local boys performed on Friday and Saturday nights. Any one of them might show an interest in Elise, might take advantage of her single-minded desire to have a musician for a boyfriend. Sophia worried about that more than the fact that Sammy was too old for her, or that he was letting her into the bar in the first place.

Sophia worried unduly. It was true that Elise was using Sammy's affections to be where the bands were, but she wasn't randomly soliciting just any of the guitarists and singers that performed there. There were cute ones with no talent, and talented ones that were unattractive. Elise watched them all patiently, but spoke to none of them, because there was really only one band in particular that she wanted to see.

Unbeknownst to Sophia, Elsie had snuck into a frat part with a few of her more adventuresome girlfriends some weeks before she had even met Sammy. Anita from her English class had played a demo from Sonic Daydream for her, and when they heard that the band was going to play at the frat house, they just had to go. *Wait to you see this guy!* Anita had enthused. A groupie from way back, Anita had been chasing musicians since she was fourteen.

It was at this college party that Elise had beheld Dennis Whitly for the first time, had heard him sing. Anita was right. Even though she only got the chance to hear them play a few covers, Elise thought the band was great and the singer was incredible. She was entranced.

The happiest people are those that know exactly what they like, Elise thought. *There's some trigger of stimulation for everybody – a whisper, a scent, a fall of hair, the curve of a smile – and if you recognize from the start what that special formula is, then time wasted with football players and bouncers and other boys that would just end up boring you can be saved.*

Elise knew what she liked, knew exactly which type never failed to get her motor running, just by watching them. Elise liked musicians.

To her, there was just something inescapably alluring about singers, about guitar players; and Dennis Whitly had it in spades. There was just something in his voice, in the expressions he made when he sang, when he played his axe; it was like the act simulated. Elise wanted to see Denny make those same faces, but just for her, in private. The very thought of it raised her to the very pinnacle of arousal. She *would* have him.

Neither Anita nor Elise nor their cohort Candace managed to talk to Denny that night, however, because one of the more sober-minded frat boys hustled them out of the party in the middle of Sonic Daydream's set. A few discreet questions put to his brethren was all that was needed to discover that the three cuties at the front of the crowd were all underage. Greek scandals had not touched UCR – never had it appeared in the paper that *a Roman toga party was held, from which we have received two dozen reports of individual acts of perversion so profound and disgusting, that decorum prohibits listing them here* – but he wasn't taking any chances. There were enough drunken college girls on hand, so it wasn't necessary to entertain any jailbait.

But Elise would not give up on meeting the frontman from Sonic Daydream, even after catching just half a set. Anita said that the band frequently played The House of Ale, and after that, it was just a matter of Elise's ingratiating herself – that was a euphemism, if there ever was one – into the affections of Sammy the bouncer.

After a very short period of time, Sammy believed Elise to be his girlfriend. Sure, she was a little young for him – almost ten years – and he should've known better. But she had come on to him, and she was cute, and if she was at the bar with him when he was working, then she wouldn't be out on the boulevard talking up some other bouncer, so why not let her in?

Elise became a regular attendee at all of Sonic Daydream's shows at The House of Ale. They were good, far too good to remain at some little nothing bar in Riverside. Elise knew that they would make it, and she aimed to go with them.

It was not just the band's obvious talents that drew Elise, of course, nor even the promise of the big time that ran through every one of their songs. It was their singer. Elise Carlin had become besotted with Denny Whitly after seeing him only once.

Eventually, she was at last able to worm her way through the crowd of eager fans before Denny left. At last, here was the object of her own sonic daydreams. Elise paused to picture herself at Denny's side, to imagine herself as the one girl that always had a backstage pass. She would be the one cuddled up beside him on the luxurious tour buses that were to come. This talented, gorgeous singer would be her ticket out of Riverside.

"Hello, Denny. My name's Elise."

He looked up at the silky, sibilant *S* on her tongue – *in a dark brown voice she said, 'Lola.'*

"I think you're great."

If her voice got Denny's attention, her looks kept it. Elise wore tight black pants and a t-shirt with his band's name on it. His brother had had a bunch of them printed up and handed them out for free, along with the demos they had recorded, stereotypically, in their drummer's garage.

The girl standing in front of him had curly blonde hair, enormous blue eyes, and a seductive, cruel, red mouth. She struck Denny as wholly sensual, in some undefinable, instinctual, animal kind of way. She wasn't overly made-up, she wasn't showing a lot of skin, and at twenty-one, Dennis Whitly was already used to dealing with pretty girls that came up to him after a show and breathily said, *I think you're great.* In the short time that he'd been fronting for his brother's band, he'd shown more than his share of them whatever aspect of his supposed greatness that they had wanted to see.

But there was something extra about this girl, something more, unmistakable, there in the gleam in her eye. Her smile told Denny that Elise was not just another groupie out to nail any ol' guitar player. She wanted him and him alone, and something about the look on her fabulous face told him that she might be a little bit great herself.

He smiled at her. "Can I buy you a drink, Elise?"

Elise remembered an afternoon spent fishing at Lake Evans with her daddy when she was a little girl. *Wait 'til you feel him bite, honey, then just give a little jerk to set the hook.*

"No, that's okay." Elise giggled and the sound bounced around in Denny's head like a Mexican jumping bean, leaving a small, smudged streak of pleasure behind. "But I'll sit with you while you have one, if you'd like."

Denny had already had a few, and, "I have to help load our equipment."

39

He nodded at his bass player, his older brother Lenny, as he carried his bass in one hand and Calvin's high-hat in the other. It would be a little while yet before a cadre of well-paid roadies would perform these tasks for Sonic Daydream, before these same roadies would count as an extra perk the frequent opportunities they received to console girls just like Elise, who had waited around outside for an appearance by Denny Whitly that never materialized.

"He's already gone, darlin'," they'd tell the disappointed groupies. "On the bus, on the way to the next town. I can show you his guitar, though . . ."

But that was all in the future.

Denny said to Elise, "If you'd like to wait for a few minutes . . ."

Elise nodded and again offered him her toothy, knowing smile. *Damn*, Denny thought, despite the fact that she was just another girl, another sparkly-eyed, head-strong young woman that liked the way he sang. Another one that liked it so much that she was willing to stand around in the chilly wee hours behind a dive bar and wait while he loaded his instruments, just so she could have the chance to find out what she thought she knew for sure: Dennis Whitly just had to be a demon between the sheets. Denny didn't know if it was true or not, but he'd never had any complaints.

He was so mesmerizing on stage, his words and rhythms so full of dark, sweet promise, and Elise felt the same way as a million, billion girls had felt since the dawn of rock and roll: there was nothing sexier than a guitar player that one thought was sexy.

Elise thought Denny was just that, and it looked like she was going to get to fulfill her fantasy. She was surprised at how easy it had been. Now she just had to be a little patient and wait a bit longer while he handled the nuts and bolts and pesky responsibilities of being in a band, and then it was gonna be, *Just me and you, I'll show ya lovin' like you never knew* . . .

Elise was nothing if not patient, so she went outside with him and leaned against the side of the building. She lit a cigarette, one from the pack that Sammy had bought for her. She was still too young to buy them for herself.

A chain link gate blocked the little alcove between the buildings where the truck was parked, effectively keeping out any other girls that wanted to get to know the band. A few of them milled around outside of it anyway, looking in hopefully, calling out to Denny or his brother, or Calvin, the drummer, or Ernie, the other guitar player. They each waved quickly, maybe bestowed a little smile. But they hurried about their task. There would be time for socializing with the fans after their

40

instruments were strapped down and the truck was moved out of the bar's tow-away loading zone.

****

Leonard Whitly was twenty-five, and his day job was as an assistant at a local accountant's office. He and Calvin and Ernie had formed Sonic Daydream in high school, and had been playing parties ever since. He'd started out playing the six-string, but then had found he liked a bass guitar better. He and Ernie had taken turns singing and writing songs, but covers had always been their specialty. Sonic Daydream could switch effortlessly from Pink Floyd to Metallica to the Stones, and damn near anything in between. They played by ear, and their ears were always dead-on. The band had written enough of their own material to make a few demos, however. They had garnered a few fans.

But it was only since his little brother Dennis had joined them that they had started to glimpse success. It was only because of Denny's pretty face, his voice, his words and music, his talent, that they were a party band no longer. No more playing covers for drunken, uninterested people who were present to find a hook up, not there to listen to a band. They had a more or less permanent, *paying* gig at The House of Ale these days, and the girls (and many dudes, too) lined up around the block specifically to see Sonic Daydream, to hear Denny sing the songs he'd written.

Lenny never ceased to be amazed at his brother's skills. He had given the kid a few lessons when he was sixteen, mostly just to keep him off the boulevard, and surely, after he had learned the basic chords, playing the guitar *was what Denny did,* but he did it alone, shut up in his room after school, sometimes late into the night. Lenny never would've guessed that his little brother was any good – what kind of guitar player that's any good never plays for anybody?

Their parents were glad to see that Dennis had adopted the same hobby as his brother, one they saw as innocuous. They were pleased that he didn't spend hours playing video games, that he didn't waste all his free time on mindless sports, so Mr. and Mrs. Whitly had granted Dennis all the free time he wanted. Lenny's little brother had never worked a day in his life. He'd just sat around in his room, playing his guitar, practicing, waiting for the time when he deemed himself skilled enough to reveal what he knew to his brother's scorn.

He'd waited for almost five years. And when Denny at last said, "Hey, let me play you guys a little something I wrote," Lenny didn't have a chance to be scornful, because he was too busy being astonished by little brother Dennis's riffs, his melodies, his lyrics. As was the rest of the band.

That had been at the beginning of 1988, a scant five months ago, a few days after Denny's twenty-first birthday. He'd been Sonic Daydream's frontman ever since. One of the first songs Denny wrote was called *Tomcats*, a paean to the adventures of a Friday night. It would later become a chart topper.

Leonard Whitly had never expected fame, but he could see it coming now. It was just a matter of time. Some guy from a record label had already expressed an interest.

He never would've believed that his little brother would be the one to lead Sonic Daydream to the big time, but apparently, being a musician came naturally to Denny. Lenny wondered if the kid was prepared for all the other things that accompanied an instinctive talent for the guitar. Before The House of Ale, the band had really only played parties, but Lenny was nonetheless familiar with the late nights, the partying, the girls, as if they were a more famous act. How would Denny hold up with all that, as well as the fame that was right around the corner? *Welcome, my son, welcome to the machine* . . .

Since it had been Lenny who had introduced Denny to a musician's lifestyle, had awakened his talent so to speak, the bass player frequently wondered what his brother's future was going to be like. So far, there had been no warning signs. Denny liked to have a few drinks, but he was no alcoholic, and he didn't go in for drugs. He did enjoy his adoring fans, however . . .

Now Lenny looked at the groupie that had picked Denny for the evening. She leaned against the wall, smoking, and keenly studied his brother as he helped the rest of the guys load out. She was young, hot, eager, and Lenny was suddenly put in mind of a trip the family had taken to the zoo, when he'd been eight and Denny still just a four-year-old.

They had been inside the Big Cat House, where plate glass and concrete block walls separated them from those most apex of predators. While Mom and Dad were looking at the lazy, sleeping tigers, Lenny was watching Denny running back in forth in the middle of the room.

He soon discovered that he was not the only one observing his baby brother. A young cheetah paced slowly back and forth in front of the thick glass, never removing her cold auburn eyes from Denny, who was utterly oblivious to the fact that he was being stalked. For Lenny, it was a fascinating glimpse into the single-mindedness of a predator. Had it not been for the plate glass, no force in the universe could've saved his baby brother from becoming the fast cat's lunch.

"Look, Denny." Lenny pointed at the lithe, spotted feline. "Cheetah wants to eat you."

An almost human expression of wonderment crossed the cat's face as Denny ran up to the glass, put his chubby hands upon it – her lunch was delivering itself!

The kid had not a clue as to the danger he was in, if it hadn't been for the glass. The ravenous expression on the cheetah's face totally passed him by. Denny smiled up at the cat, then turned to his brother. "Pretty kitty!"

When all the pretty kitties started waiting for Denny after their shows, almost paternally, Lenny had instructed his brother: "Make them no promises, tell them no lies. Be antiseptically, obsessively, compulsively safe. And don't be surprised when they go home with the drummer from some other band next week."

Lenny hoped that his advice had struck home, because, like the cheetah, tonight's groupie watched his brother with a focused, unblinking, hungry stare. It was clear to Lenny that this girl wanted to *eat* Denny, just like the big cat, and there was no glass barrier to protect him this time.

****

It was Calvin's truck. He kept it parked in his parents' big garage, which was also where Sonic Daydream rehearsed, where they had recorded their demos. No time for groupies tonight; Calvin and Ernie had other places to go and people to see, so they hopped into the truck, bid the brothers Whitly goodnight, and departed.

Denny explained to Elise that he and Lenny lived in a little apartment within walking distance from the bar, and asked her if she would like to see it. His brother rolled his eyes. Denny aimed to take advantage of this biggest perk of rock and roll without further formality. Lenny understood; it was the main reason he worked in an accountant's office during the day and played bass at night. Women loved musicians.

Lenny left Denny to the groupie's reply; he was pretty sure what it would be. He went back into The House of Ale.

The bass player's guess was correct. Elise assented to his brother's invitation without hesitation – it was her adolescent fantasy come true. Going home with Denny Whitly was the culmination, the exact consummation for which she had so devoutly wished from the moment that she had seen him sing at that boring college party.

She had put up with weeks of Sammy's sloppy, clumsy attentions, just so he'd let her into The House of Ale whenever Sonic Daydream played. But it had all been worth it. Sammy was forgotten. Elise was finally going to get to experience gorgeous, sexy Denny Whitly. He would become her boyfriend. She would go on tour with him . . .

Almost before the door to his apartment swung all the way closed, Elise launched herself into Denny's arms. He was surprised. While he was a good-looking, talented musician, not unaware of his own appeal, still, he usually had to at least offer them a drink, make a little small talk, before getting on to the main event.

But this blondie was ferocious in her desire.

Denny let Elise kiss him. She broke the kiss after a few minutes and looked at the two doors in the hallway, then questioningly back at Denny. He nodded at the door on the right and she silently took his hand and led him to his bedroom.

The streetlight outside cut the bed into slanting geometric sections of yellow and black. Elise reclined languidly on the bed. Her red mouth smiled seductively, her blue eyes glittered with desire and anticipation. *Now then, tell me baby, do you need my love? Tell me baby, are you thinkin' of me? Tell me baby, what it is you need? What kind of satisfaction guaranteed?*

Denny took off his shirt, approached the bed, and then there was a hammering on the door.

"Dennis! I need to talk to you."

"Not now, for Christ's sake, Lenny!" He smiled at Elise. "I'm busy." *I'm about to have my hands full . . .*

"She's sixteen, Denny!" came his brother's reply. His voice was muffled by the solid wood of the door, but the words rang like a fire alarm in Denny's head, shrilly, indicating danger.

Watch out for the jailbait, my Jimmy Page wanna-be, Lenny had told him once. *They think they know what they want, and like a little kid screaming for the newest toy, they're gonna go for it. They're too dumb to know any better, so there are laws to protect them from themselves. Make sure you're sure she's of age, little brother, or her daddy and the man with the badge will make sure you don't forget next time. After you get out of the slammer . . .*

But Denny had believed himself to be safe from all that in this case. Sure, she looked a little young, but Elise, with the sexy, slippery *S's* and the promise-filled kisses, had been in The House of Ale, where there was a big, dumb-looking bouncer at the door, checking IDs. So she had to be at least twenty-one, right? The same age as he was?

"Are you only sixteen, Elise?"

Elise had always been calculating, and it had lent her a sophistication beyond her years, but not enough: she glanced down guiltily. Words were not necessary.

All of Denny's lust evaporated. He reached hastily for his shirt. "Get out of my bed, Elise."

She was cute, but she was in no way, shape, or form cute enough to risk going to jail over. She was cute, but Denny was horrified when he realized that she was just a kid. He was five very formative years older; they had nothing in common. But still she'd wanted to –

"It doesn't matter, Denny. I won't tell anyone."

"Go home, little girl." Denny sighed, switched on the lights, opened the door. Lenny, his warning delivered, was sitting in the living room, watching television.

"Please, Denny! I . . ." *I love you!* Elise almost said it, but caught herself.

He turned around, surprised, appalled at the childish, pleading tone to her formerly sexy voice. "You have to go now, Elise."

Denny was pissed off, angry at her for being in a bar where she didn't belong, angry at himself for letting thoughts of her mouth and her body make him forget the most important question, the one that, according to Lenny, should always be foremost in a musician's mind when these situations arose: *How old are you?*

He added, unkindly, "Isn't there a curfew in his town? Goodbye, Elise."

She reluctantly arose from the bed, then held out her arms as if she would embrace him. *I'm gonna make you, make you, make you notice . . .*

Denny said, "You've got to be kidding."

Elise dropped her arms, looked forlornly at the floor. She hitched a long sigh, as if she might burst into tears. "Goodbye, Denny," she said in a small voice. A little girl's voice.

Denny suspected that it might be the real Elise peeking out for a second, around the borrowed sophistication and adult desire to bed a guitar player. *She's just a kid! Christ!*

Elise brushed past him and out of the room. She spared a hateful glare at Lenny – she would ever afterwards despise Denny's brother. The bassist didn't even glance in her direction as she quickly fled the apartment.

Denny looked briefly at the door after Elise slammed it, then asked, "How did you find out she's only sixteen?"

"Her boyfriend told me. The bouncer." Lenny paused for effect. "So, yeah. You would've had to deal with that, too."

"Maybe he's lying. Maybe he's just jealous because she left with me."

Lenny grinned at his younger brother's arrogance. "Oh, he didn't know she was with you. If he did, maybe it would've been him pounding on your door instead of me."

Denny waited for an explanation.

"So, I'm sitting at the bar, and this big dude comes up to me and says, 'Have you seen my lady, man? She went outside with your band.'

"I asked him, 'Which one is she?'" Lenny grinned at his own arrogance now. "He described her, and I said, 'Yeah. I saw her. Congrats, man. She's nice. I wish I could get girls like that.'"

Denny rolled his eyes. Leonard Whitly could have any girl he wanted.

"Big 'un is flattered. He says, 'Yeah, she's somethin'. You'd never know from looking at her that she's only sixteen. Did you see where she went?'

"I shook my head. He wandered off and I paid my tab and high-tailed it over here to save your dumb ass."

"Thanks," Denny said genuinely. He shook his head. "Goddamned *kids.*"

"I believe this is what they call a near-miss, Dennis. Your first."

"Indeed, Leonard. It'll be my last, I promise you."

"Perhaps you should start asking for ID, before you just bring 'em right on home."

"Perhaps I will."

****

The following Friday night, Sonic Daydream had the prime spot: they were the third band out of five scheduled to perform. Lenny had pointed out the guy from Sony Records to his bandmates. Flashy, overdressed for a little Riverside tavern, he was sitting at a corner table with two beautiful, equally out of place women.

The second band had just finished their set and were clearing their instruments off the stage. Denny was at the bar, getting in a quick drink before he had to go help load in, when someone tapped him on the shoulder.

He turned, saw that it was Elise, and almost choked on his drink. He told her to leave him alone.

"Look, Denny, you asshole, I'm here to apologize. I'm sorry I didn't tell you I was sixteen."

46

Only sixteen, Denny thought. *Christ, how I would've hated myself, how I would've hated her . . .*

"You're not supposed to be in here, Elise," he said tersely, under his breath. "You could get this place shut down. Why don't you go where you belong? The jailbait club's three blocks over." When she didn't move, he added, "Don't I hear your mommy calling you?"

"My mommy's dead," she replied flatly, and her lip curled at his mortification. "But I'm here with my sister. She's my legal guardian. I'm allowed to be in here if I'm with her."

Denny suspected that this statement was bullshit. The sign on the door said *You Must Be 21*, not *All Lying Jailbait Must Be Accompanied by Legal Guardian.*

"I told her about you." Denny eyes widened in embarrassment and Elise grinned further. "Not about *us*. I told her about your band, how great you guys are. Real up and comers." Before he could stop her, Elise squeezed Denny's face between her thumb and index finger, then playfully slapped him on the cheek.

She half turned, scanned the crowd. "There she is now. Sophia!" Elise waved.

Sophia. What an old-fashioned name. She's probably Jailbait's much older *sister, probably dried up and —*

But when the rock-star-yet-to-be beheld Sophia Carlin for the first time, his life changed, forever. Irrevocably.

"Uh, check. Paging Dennis Whitly," Ernie said breathily into the mike. There was a titter and a smattering of applause from those gathered to hear Sonic Daydream, but the frontman didn't hear it.

Sophia had made her way through the packed bar. She glanced at her sister, then curiously at the guy standing beside her. Denny noticed that her eyes were big and blue and beautiful, like Elise's, but the teenager's purposeful cunning was refreshingly absent.

"I'm Dennis Whitly," he said, and offered his hand.

Sophia shook it and giggled. "You're being summoned."

Denny glanced at the stage. He had forgotten why he was there in The House of Ale. Now it all came back. His band was about to perform, there was a guy from the record company over in the corner . . . But none of that mattered anymore. Elise's sister was the most beautiful woman Denny had ever seen.

"Will you . . . Will you wait until after we play?" These were words Denny had never spoken so earnestly before, and they sounded odd in his ear. He'd never wanted a girl to wait for him quite this much. Most of the time he couldn't get rid of them. "I'd like to . . . talk to you."

Sophia smiled and Denny felt faint, as if the one quick drink he'd consumed had gone directly to his head. But it wasn't the alcohol, it wasn't even the money in the audience, waiting to hear him perform. It was *her.*

"Sure," she said matter-of-factly, with not a trace of innuendo. Just friendliness. "I'll wait. Elise says your band's great. I'm looking forward to hearing you sing."

Denny almost said, *Who?* Elise was standing right there, looking adoringly at him. But she was forgotten, along with everyone else. Only this blonde vision remained in his mind.

"Okay. I'll see you after the show. You'll wait?"

She nodded, amused at his repeated request. "I'm Sophia, by the way."

"It's so nice to meet you," he said sincerely, then added again, "I'd really like to talk to you."

"I'll be here."

Denny reluctantly left to join his band. When he hopped up onto the stage, there was applause, cheers. He flashed a crooked smile, waved in grateful acknowledgement of their appreciation.

While Sonic Daydream quickly finished setting up, Sophia had time to wonder if Dennis Whitly had been coming on to her. If he was . . . She just couldn't be sure whether he was or not. He had seemed so intense, so serious: *I'd really like to talk to you.* What did he want to talk to her about? Her rude kid sister had not even introduced them properly.

But Sophia knew who he was, because Elise had raved about him. Gorgeous and green-eyed, she had no doubt that he was Sonic Daydream's frontman, even before his bandmate called him to the stage. Denny Whitly, singer, songwriter, irresistible; Elise had made him sound like the best guitarist since Clapton, sexier by far than ten Morrisons.

Sophia had made a deal with Elise. *Pass your math final and I'll go to the bar and see this* phenomenal *band with you. Promise me that you won't go in there again until you're twenty-one, and I'll go with you and listen to Denny Whitly sing.*

Elise had passed her math test, but Sophia had little hope that she'd stay out of The House of Ale. Sophia wanted to believe her sister's promise, but Elise's penchant for lying to get what she wanted had become her dominant personality trait since Mom and Dad had passed.

Their parents had been unaware of their baby's manipulative tendencies – Elise had never gotten into any trouble, she had done well in school, she had always been a good girl. Maybe Mom hadn't really believed that the kitten *had just followed Elise home*, but she'd let her keep it anyway. Maybe Elise hadn't really missed the bus, but she was only twenty minutes late for dinner. These were just harmless fibs, after all, and Mandy Carlin had loved her baby girl. She had been indulgent.

Now that Sophia had had to shoulder the motherly burden of looking after Elise, however, the fibs that she told had taken on a darker, entirely too grown-up aspect. Bouncers and bars and musicians. Elise's behavior worried her sister. She had *run wild*.

So Sophia held little hope that Elise would honor her promise and stay out of The House of Ale. The kid clearly had a thing for this singer, and Elise didn't give her things up very easily.

Hopefully, Sophia wouldn't have to drop a word in the manager's ear about serving minors and revocation of liquor licenses to keep Elise out of the bar, to keep her away from way-too-attractive Denny Whitly. It was tiresome, this role of policeman that Sophia had had to assume for her sister's sake. Sophia didn't care if they let minors into The House of Ale, as long as one of those minors wasn't Elise. She didn't care if Sonic Daydream catered to underage groupies, as long as Elise wasn't one of them.

****

Onstage, Denny Whitly was like a force of nature. He strutted, swaggered, pranced; he transported the crowd beyond the tiny bar. It seemed as though the stage was suddenly vast, like the Hollywood Bowl or Wembly Stadium, just by the way he moved upon it. He smiled, he winked, he reached out and accepted high-fives. He held the crowd in the palm of his hand. He whispered, he screamed; his playing was flawless. He was a rock star.

Sophia liked Sonic Daydream's sound; she thoroughly enjoyed their set. While they played, she glanced around at the women in the crowd, saw the hungry looks in their eyes. Drinks and boyfriends were forgotten while they watched Denny sing. Beside Sophia, Elise watched him with the same astonished focus, her pupils round and black, lips slightly parted, breath coming in small pants. Denny's voice, his movements, his charisma, had mesmerized every woman in The House of Ale, not least of all the teenage girl whom an unkind fate had made Sophia's sole responsibility.

Sophia watched Denny, too, and decided that she would definitely wait for him after the show, that she would definitely like to hear whatever it was that he had so instantaneously decided that he had to say to her. He was undeniably attractive: tall and spare, with long,

49

straight, shaggy brown hair, and that killer smile – Dennis Whitly would've been cute if he was a plumber or a house painter, a cab driver or a student. Sophia, just like every woman in the room, was attracted to Denny, but unlike them, her interest wasn't heightened – and certainly not to near hysteria – by the fact that he was a musician.

Sophia was not much of a reader, but she knew a little Shakespeare. She had a passing knowledge of most of the great characters of literature because Hollywood had put them on the screen for her. She didn't have to read. She was an avid fan of the movies.

Cinema had been a thrilling escape from everyday life when she was a child, and had lately become a respite from the sorrow of her parents' loss, the challenges of workaday life and looking after Elise. All the fascinating characters in the adaptations of classical literature, as well as clever thrillers, witty dramas, happy and sad romances, scary horror – Sophia loved them all.

As a movie fan, she had picked up a little info about actors and actresses, also, but it was only collaterally. To Sophia, all the highly-paid celebrities were just people whose job it was to portray these indelible characters; she wasn't overly interested in their lives and loves. She enjoyed the *people they pretended to be, the stories.* She was a film buff. She was not a fan of movie stars just because they starred in movies.

And this perception colored the way Sophia looked at Dennis Whitly. Surely, he was gorgeous. But so was Tom Cruise, yet he was neither Stef Djordjevic from *All the Right Moves,* nor Jack from *Legend;* nor was he Maverick. Like Denny, Tom was just an attractive man that Sophia didn't know as a human being. What was he *really* like? Was he kind or mean, was he bright or dull? Sophia would never meet the talented movie star, so she really didn't concern herself with these questions. She only paid attention to the characters he portrayed.

And so it was with this singer. He was another type of actor: the part he played was that of the quintessential tomcat, just like he sang about in his clever, catchy little tune. An irresistible lover, a sex-god with a guitar. And all the women in The House of Ale were buying into the character of Denny Whitly, rock star.

Singer, songwriter, guitarist: that was what Denny *did,* but *who was he?* Sophia would never get to meet Stef or Jack or Maverick because they were imaginary people, brought to living, breathing, unforgettable life by the talented Mr. Cruise, whom she would never get to meet either. In the same way she liked Tom's performances, Sophia enjoyed watching Denny's portrayal of a sexy, devil-may-care rock star. She understood the fiction that Elise and all the rest told themselves about him, based solely on how his looks and his music made them feel. But

Sophia knew that the persona Denny displayed onstage wasn't real. She had watched him turn it on with that crooked smile, the moment he hopped up on stage.

What was he really like, once the bar closed and the fans went home? Who was Dennis Whitly, after he flipped off the rock star switch? Sophia thought she had caught a glimpse of just an ordinary guy, even if he was gorgeous; someone who had shown a flattering intensity in his desire to talk to her. That was enough to pique her interest, enough to make her willing to wait to see what he had to say.

The unrealistic fantasy of the awesomely sensual musician was unnecessary for Sophia. If she would come to like Denny, it would be for his personality, not because he could play the guitar.

****

When Sonic Daydream's set ended, the applause, the whoops and cheers and screams, were deafening in the little bar. The A & R man left his out-of-town lovelies at the table, arose and enthusiastically shook Denny's hand. Over the noise of the crowd, the singer heard the phrase *sign you*, so he immediately turned the guy over to his brother. Lenny was the businessman, and besides, Denny had other fish to fry.

He told Ernie and Calvin that he would help them load out in a minute, then he caught Sophia's eye from the stage. He held up his index finger, again asking her to wait just a little bit longer. Sophia smiled and nodded; again Denny felt a tiny bit faint. There was witchcraft in her smile.

Elise waved dotingly at him. Denny ignored her and jumped off the stage. The crowd closed in around him, guys telling him how much they liked his show, girls smiling hopefully at him. Elise attempted to follow him across the packed floor.

Denny shook hands and gratefully accepted his fans' praise, all the while navigating toward the front door. At last he made it.

He had gone out of his way to make the acquaintance of the bouncer during the previous week. The idea that Sammy, someone Lenny's age, would waste his time with a teenage girl fascinated Denny. It also disgusted him a little bit. Sure, she was cute, but so were puppies and bunny rabbits. Soft and innocent and big-eyed. Denny had almost fallen for Elise's put-on sensuality, but once he'd discovered that she was just a kid . . . That kind of thing was wrong to him. She still had a lot of living to do before he would be able to find anything in common with her, even enough to . . . Well, that was never gonna happen now.

51

It was clear that Sammy had no such compunctions. The only thing that he needed to have in common with baby Elise was that she had expressed an interest in getting to know him better. She had wanted to be his girlfriend. To Sammy, if she was old enough to want such a thing, then she was old enough for him to give it to her. The idea that she was playing him, that she was using him as an all-access pass to the adult world – to Denny Whitly – had not crossed his mind.

Denny thought that the big man, a quarter of a century old, perhaps had a little learning yet to do about women. The musician was sure that Elise would teach him, and he was just as sure that Sammy wouldn't enjoy the lesson.

The bouncer was flattered that Sonic Daydream's frontman had befriended him. He thought the band was awesome, and now he'd be able to tell people that he'd known them when. "Yeah, I know Denny Whitly. We used to pal around at The House of Ale, before anybody had ever heard of Sonic Daydream. But I knew they were gonna be big."

Sammy was standing his post at the open door, and Denny smiled, slapped him on the back. He leaned in close to the big man's ear, and said, "I've got a little favor to ask you, my friend."

"What can I do for you, Denny? You guys were great, by the way!"

You wouldn't think I was so great if you knew what your woman tried to pull last week about this time. Woman. That's a laugh. She's just a kid.

Denny said thanks, then, "Here's the deal. I have an urgent desire to speak to your girlfriend's sister, if you know what I mean. Alone." Denny showed Sammy his sly, always-lucky, guitar player's grin.

Sammy grinned back.

"But Elise is like her shadow. I was wondering if you could keep her occupied for a few minutes, so I could . . . well, you know. Have a few words with the sister." Denny winked slowly.

"Sure, Denny. No problem. I understand completely."

"I owe ya, Sammy." Denny shook the bouncer's hand, surreptitiously passing him a $20, thereby settling that debt on the spot.

Sammy was neither surprised nor flattered by the gratuity. It was the way of the world, almost expected: favors cost money. "Good luck, Denny."

The singer nodded and slipped out the door, then loped around the building to the little alcove where the truck was parked. The drummer and the second guitarist for Sonic Daydream – who were not a signed act just yet, who still didn't have any roadies – were loading it.

"Let me in, Calvin!" Denny said at the gate. "I'm with the band."

"It's not locked," Calvin replied. Sonic Daydream wasn't big yet. A closed gate still kept the fans out. Closed was necessary, but not locked. Not guarded. Not yet.

Denny slid it aside, then quickly shut it again.

"Lenny's talking to the guy from . . ." Calvin began, then discovered that he was talking to empty space. Denny had already darted into the bar through the back door.

The crowd had thinned; the band that most of them had come to see had already played. Denny slid up beside Sophia, slipped his hand into hers. "Come on. Let's get out of here."

"Elise is—"

"She'll be okay for a minute. I told the bouncer to look after her."

Sophia narrowed her eyes suspiciously, but couldn't help but smile. So everybody knew who it was that was letting the minors in. "I haven't paid my tab – "

Denny caught the bartender's eye, gestured at Sophia and her glass. "Hey, Karen. This is on me." Karen nodded. "Anything else?" he asked Sophia.

She shook her head. Denny tugged on her hand. "Let's get out of here," he repeated.

Sophia hesitated another second, glanced down at her half-full drink. Denny took it from her and drained it, set the glass on the bar. He inclined his head toward the back exit. Sophia smiled and let him lead her outside.

"Hey, Denny, where ya going?" Calvin asked, as the singer walked past the truck, holding hands with some blonde.

"I'd gladly pay you Tuesday for a hamburger today," Denny replied. He reluctantly released Sophia's hand and pushed the gate open. They stepped through it, and he closed it again. He hooked his fingers in the chain link and said to Calvin, voice full of mock pleading, "If you release me this time, O Great Master, I will help you doubly next time."

Ernie set an amp on the back of the truck and looked appraisingly at Sophia. Calvin waved them away with a flutter of his hand.

"Thanks, Cal," Denny replied. It was with real gratitude, Sophia noted.

"Name it after me!" Ernie called as they rounded the corner of the building.

****

Denny once again took Sophia's hand. He headed down the alley, away from the front of the bar. After the noise and light and heat of The House of Ale, the cooler quiet of the darkness hugged him like an old friend. He was silent at first, then he asked, "Where would you like to go?"

"I can only stay a minute, Denny. Elise . . ."

Elise is a big girl. Maybe a lot more grown-up than you know. "Maybe just once around the block, then?"

Sophia nodded, and they stepped out of the alley and onto the sidewalk of the next street over. Here there was sound and noise again; people, other lovers strolling by, also holding hands. The traffic was thick; nothing like Los Angeles, of course, but then the streets here were narrower. It was a nice, typical Riverside Friday night in May, but it was spectacular to Denny.

Sophia was spectacular. He held her hand and smiled at her. He didn't say anything; he just looked at her. She was beautiful.

Sophia liked the feel of Denny's strong hand in hers; she liked the way he smelled when he walked close to her. She liked his smile and the way the streetlights danced in his green eyes. She liked the way he looked at her and she liked looking back at him. But it was a short block. Soon they would come around to the bar again, and she would have to scare up her wayward sister, and like Atlas with the weight of the world, Sophia would again have to shoulder the burden of trying to keep Elise out of bars and away from rock stars.

"My sister has a crush on you," she told Denny.

"That's putting it mildly. Your sister tried to . . . to seduce me."

Denny thought that he might as well get it out in the open. Elise meant nothing to him; he would just as soon forget that she was even alive. But he knew that wasn't going to happen. Little lying Elise was Sophia's sister, and Denny wanted more than anything to continue to *just look at Sophia.* He couldn't think of anything else past that yet, but whatever would happen between them, he was resigned to the fact that Elise would always be hovering in the background.

"Jesus!" Sophia stopped abruptly and dropped Denny's hand. She ran her hand through her hair in exasperation. But she wasn't really surprised.

"My brother told me she was only sixteen. So I told her to go away."

"Is this something that happens to you a lot? Little girls, trying to . . ."

"Seduce me?"

Denny found that he liked the word. It was lyrical, almost airy. He thought he could build a song around it. It was far less harsh on the ear and tongue than the common, vulgar, four-letter word for which it was a euphemism; that other term, the one that they were both thinking.

Denny shrugged. "All the time." His arrogance was endemic; it was the truth. But his smile was almost apologetic. "Girls like guitar players."

"So I've heard," Sophia replied neutrally. *Elise especially.*

Denny liked that, too. She was displaying her own arrogance. Whatever it was about guitar players that made them so attractive was lost on her. Sophia was immune.

"So, there are plenty of girls. I don't need any underage ones."

"Plenty of girls," Sophia repeated softly.

Denny grabbed her hand again. "But I've never met anyone like you, Sophia."

A small bark of surprised laughter escaped her. "You don't even know me, Denny."

I've got a mindless, dead-end job, and the responsibility for the care and feeding of a wild, devious, underage, attempted-seducer of guitar players. And it's going to be that way for quite a while.

He took her other hand, but didn't step any closer to her. Suddenly Sophia realized that perhaps Denny just waited for girls to make the move, then he just went along with it. Maybe that was what he thought was so different about her. Sophia wasn't impressed with the part that he played, she wasn't eager to *seduce* him, solely because he was a musician.

"I'd like to get to know you," he said, with the same serious intensity he'd used earlier. *I'd really like to talk to you.* "Could we maybe have lunch tomorrow?"

Sophia knew that few girls probably ever turned Dennis Whitly down if he asked them to go to lunch, or if he asked them for anything else. But there was nothing arrogant about him now; he wasn't really even flirty. He was just a guy, asking her out, not knowing for sure if she would accept.

Again Sophia saw that the rock star persona was all an act. If a girl treated him like he was the sexiest thing that had ever picked up a Les Paul, then Denny would act exactly the way such a person would be expected to act. If a girl wanted to play willing, compliant fan to his egotistical guitarist, then he would accommodate her.

Rod Stewart's timeless ode to groupies suddenly played through Sophia's mind:

So in the morning
Please don't say you love me
'Cause you know I'll only kick you out the door
Yeah, I'll pay your cab fare home
You can even use my best cologne
Just don't be here in the morning when I wake up

He was so gorgeous, but now, he was so . . . Well, Sophia really couldn't call him *unsure*. Dennis Whitly would never be unsure. He didn't need to be conceited, because he was convinced. At twenty-one, he had already had an army of girls like Elise to assure him of his appeal. But at the moment, he wasn't playing Denny Whitly, rock god, and with the switch to that guy turned off, he was so . . . serious.

Rod shouted, *Hey, what's your name again?* in Sophia's head. "Sure, Denny. I'll have lunch with you. What time?" She smiled and was pleased at the answering smile that bloomed across his beautiful face.

He released one of her hands, and they started walking again. "Anytime. If you want to come to my place, I'll cook for you. It's actually Lenny's turn this week, but he's a terrible cook."

"I'll be there at one. You rock stars need your sleep."

Satisfied that he would be seeing this stunning woman again, Denny changed the subject. "There was a guy from Sony Records in the crowd tonight. He wants to sign us."

Sophia stopped again, just as they rounded the corner, not far from the crowd on the sidewalk in front of the bar. "Oh, my God, Denny! That's great!"

"Ain't it, though?" He grinned crookedly; the egotism of a successful musician flickered across his face. *"If you ever get annoyed, look at me, I'm self-employed."*

Sophia narrowed her eyes. She wanted to kiss him right then. He was gorgeous, talented; he was gonna be famous. But the arrogance and conceit were just an act, something he could turn on and off at will. He didn't want a girl that worshipped him because he was in a band. He wanted to be just a regular guy to Sophia.

"Where do you live?" she asked.

"Ask your sister," Denny said and winked at her. Sophia's smile evaporated and he said, "I'm just kidding, Sophia. Nothing happened. She's too young. I would never . . ." Denny let the thought die, and took her other hand. *I would never, because she's too young. I would never, because of you.* "You gotta trust me."

The rock star was gone again. Once more, he was plain ol' serious Dennis Whitly. How could she not trust such a beautiful face?

He spied Elise marching up the street toward them, so he told Sophia his address, then quickly dropped her hands and dashed across the street. He turned back, waved, called, "See you tomorrow!" And then he was gone.

****

Elise noticed her sister talking to Denny, then disappointment dropped upon her when she saw him take off in the direction of his apartment. How worthless was Sophia, anyway? She couldn't even keep his attention long enough so that Elise could get up the street to talk to him again.

Elise was confident that, if she was persistent, she could make Denny forget that she was underage. Sammy had been a little reluctant, too, had told her some tiresome story about a friend of his who had actually been prosecuted for messing around with a teenage girl.

It was such a silly thing, this idea that she was forbidden to do what she wanted to do – that she was forbidden to do the things Sophia could do – just because a few years had not yet been lived. She had changed Sammy's mind with a whisper, a kiss and a caress. She had promised him that she wouldn't tell, that it would be their little secret. That was a laugh – everyone that worked at The House of Ale knew that Elise was, for all intents and purposes, Sammy's girlfriend. The only secret was that she was sixteen, and Elise doubted that was still a secret from the waitresses and the bartenders. They didn't care. Only the manager had a stake in it, and that was only if she got caught in his club. But he didn't concern himself with who his employees dated. He didn't concern himself with his employees at all, as long as they showed up on time and did their jobs. He hadn't noticed Elise in his bar.

Sammy had taken little persuading to overlook this stupid law. It was artificial, after all, arbitrary, unfair. Was Elise not woman enough? Did she not have the same cycles, did she not have to take the same precautions as older girls? She made that all seem logical to Sammy. The idea that some sixteen-year-olds were not as knowing and forward as Elise, the idea that some of them did need protection from influences such as his own, did not occur to him.

Elise was sure it would be the same with Denny. All she'd have to do would be to get him alone, to talk to him a little bit more, to kiss him again. But it wasn't going to be tonight. Her uptight sister had bored him. She had let him get away.

But Elise knew where Denny lived. She was nothing if not determined, and tomorrow was another day. *Tomorrow, I'll be that much closer to eighteen.* And she aimed to get that much closer to Denny Whitly.

She joined Sophia on the sidewalk, and accompanied her back to the car. Sammy expected her to come back to The House of Ale, to go home with him when his shift ended. But Elise was tired of Sammy. He had served his purpose. She knew where Denny lived now, so she didn't need Sammy anymore.

Besides, she had promised Sophia that she would be a good girl. No more staying out all night, no more hanging out at over-21 bars. Sophia would be pleased that she was going home now. She would believe that Elise was conforming to her commands. She would relax, her vigilance would subside. Then she might not notice, at least not immediately, anyway, when Elise eventually started staying overnight at Denny's place.

"Well?" Elise said when her sister didn't even speak of Sonic Daydream's singer. "What did you think? Is he not awesome?"

"He's all right."

Sophia thought Denny *could be* awesome. She liked him very much, after just a few moments of his intense, serious conversation. But she didn't know him well enough to make such a judgment yet. Sure, he was adorable, he was a great musician, but the real question had not yet been answered: what kind of a person was he?

"All right? He's . . . He's *amazing!"* Elise shook her head, appalled at her sister's incredible lack of perception. "I swear to God, Soph, your taste is in your mouth."

Sophia felt a small, painful pang. That had been their mother's expression, delivered with patient amusement whenever her daughters' opinions of clothes or music or anything else differed from her own. *Your taste is in your mouth.*

Sophia wondered fleetingly what Elise would be like now, a scant eight months after Mandy's passing, if their mother hadn't given up all hope, if she hadn't simply wasted away and died once her beloved husband was gone. Sophia doubted if Elise would be the bar-hopping, musician-chasing, *wild* thing that she had become. She still would've been crafty and manipulative, but she wouldn't have taken her act to the street already. She'd still be an innocent-appearing high school kid. She would still be Daddy's little girl.

As they got into the car, Sophia decided to lay her cards on the table, or at least on the dashboard. "I know you've been to Denny's place, Elise. He told me."

Who would've pegged Dennis Whitly for a chickenshit narc? But still Elise's affection for him didn't dim, her determination to *have him* didn't waver. He was incredible, and he going to hit the big time, and he was going to take her with him. She knew she could show him the error of his ways. He was just a guy, no different from Sammy, and Sammy hadn't taken much persuasion.

"Did he tell you that he kissed me? That the only reason that we didn't do it was because his idiot brother pounded on the door and told him I was sixteen?"

Sophia marveled at the child still resident in her sister's grown-up body. What mature, adult woman would use the term *do it?* Here was the reason that age of consent laws existed. Elise was old enough, biologically, to engage in these types of activities, but she was not ready, not socially, not emotionally, not intellectually. *Doing it* with Denny was just a game to her. Elise had no idea of the responsibilities, the ramifications of such things.

As usual, Denny was not a person to Elise, a human being with his own wants and needs and desires and rights. The idea that he might be horrified at the prospect of any type of involvement with a schoolgirl did not enter into her way of thinking. Denny was an object to Elise, nothing more than another plaything she wanted to have, that she wanted *to do.*

"Yes, he told me," Sophia replied. It was just a little fib. Denny had confessed the gist of the encounter, if not the details, and the important thing that he had communicated to Sophia was, "Denny's not interested in you, Elise."

"He told you that?" Elise would not believe it. All she had to do was *talk* to him a little bit more.

Her sister nodded.

"And did he tell you why? Just because I'm too young?"

"There's that, and . . . Denny already has a girlfriend."

Another small lie. But maybe it would dissuade Elise, maybe it would make her give up this silly obsession. Sophia thought that if Elise thought Denny had a girlfriend, it would make her stop chasing after him, and in the back of her mind, Sophia thought that it might ease the bruise to Elise's adolescent ego that might lie just over the horizon. If she thought that he was already spoken for, then maybe it wouldn't hurt so badly if *Sophia* wound up being Denny's girlfriend.

That all depended on how lunch went tomorrow . . .

Elise laughed derisively. "He wasn't thinking about his girlfriend last week when we were about to—"

"You're gonna have to let this go, Elise," Sophia interrupted flatly. "You're making a fool of yourself. Be as grown up as you pretend to be. Face the truth. He doesn't want you."

Elise didn't want to argue with her sister, didn't want to incite her to further parental watchfulness. She wanted Sophia to return to her former complacency, to get up and go to her boring job every day, to make dinner and watch television and go to sleep at 9:30 every night. Elise wanted Sophia to go back to not worrying about what Elise was doing.

"Whatever you say, Mom."

The House of Ale was yet only a block behind them, and Elise decided that she wasn't going to go home with Sophia after all. It was still *the shank of the evening,* as their father used to say. When they pulled up to the next stoplight, she said suddenly, "Oh, shit! I left my purse at the bar! It's behind Sammy's seat."

Elise didn't carry a purse when she went to The House of Ale. She preferred to travel light when she was at places she wasn't supposed to be. Just her driver's license, not even a year old, and some cash, tucked into her back pocket. She put her house key under a rock in the front yard. Nothing to get left behind if she had to cut out by the back way in a hurry.

She opened the car door and jumped out. "I'll be right home, Sophia. I'll just run back and get it. I saw Andy parked in front of the bar. He'll bring me home."

Sophia was stuck. Elise was already out of the car, the light had changed, and the car behind her honked. "Who's Andy?"

"He's a cabdriver. He'll give me a ride. I'll be home in half an hour." Elise slammed the car door and turned back up the street.

Sophia decided to let her go. She had lectured the kid enough for one night: *no more bars, no more rock stars.* It might do Elise a little good to see that her sister trusted her. If she wasn't home in a half hour, then Sophia would know for sure that her trust was again misplaced, and she would have to take some other steps besides just words to pull her sister back into line. Sophia wondered idly if such a thing as military school still existed.

****

The whole band had assembled at the Whitly brothers' apartment. They had no time for groupies tonight. Tonight they wanted to hear what the guy from Sony had said. Tonight was for slapping each other on the back in congratulations and wonderment, for drinking a few beers, for planning the unbelievable future that now loomed in front of them.

"You know, we could've gone on tour on our own," Lenny stated with a grin. "Without Sony."

Calvin rolled his eyes. "No, thanks. Been there, done that."

The previous summer, Calvin had taken a break from Sonic Daydream, because he had been offered the opportunity to tour with another band, Scranton. Their frontman's girlfriend was a rep for *Pernod Ricard*, owner of *Chivas Brothers*, producers of the world-renowned, blended Scotch whiskey. Part of her job was to travel to bars up and down the West Coast, selling the liquor she represented. She used her connections to secure a series of gigs for her boyfriend's band.

Afterwards, Calvin had referred to it as the *1987 Fire-Trap Tour.*

Not too many large or successful places were willing to exhibit an unsigned band, sight unseen, but Allie was pretty and perky, and she had faith in Scranton, so a number of the smaller bar owners had allowed themselves to be charmed, and had booked her boyfriend's band to play.

Calvin had been unsure at first, but he, too, had been persuaded by Allie's enthusiasm. So what if the pay was crap? It was *exposure!* Who knew what kind of important people might see them in LA or Portland?

The tour lasted three weeks; eighteen rinky-dink little clubs from San Diego to Seattle. The band scraped together enough money to stay in a hotel five or six times, but mostly, they slept in Allie's van, beside their bandmates, beside their instruments.

"You get to know people, crammed next to them, practically 24/7, for almost a month," Calvin had proclaimed upon his return. "You get to hear them fart and belch and cough and snore, get to hear the same stupid jokes, the same complaints, repeated over and over. Plus, Allie's a terrible driver. I was in fear for my life on those hilly, narrow-ass streets in Frisco."

"But you were on tour!" Ernie exclaimed. Sonic Daydream had never been on tour.

Calvin shook his head. "It was the road trip from hell. It was a nightmare. Not a single meal that wasn't fast food, not too many beds or showers, no action whatsoever. Except for Peter – we had to listen to him and Allie whenever they thought the rest of us were asleep." Calvin shook his head. "Never again. Not like that."

"It's not gonna be like that now. We're gonna have our own little bus. A nice hotel every night." Lenny smiled at his brother. *"Johnny looked around him and said . . ."*

"'Well, I made the big time at last.'" Denny grinned back.

They all sang, *"Don't you know that you are a shooting star, and all the world will love you just as long, as long as you are a shooting star . . ."*

"Here's to the big time!" Ernie declared, and they all clinked beer bottles.

There was a knock on the door and the band fell silent. No one else was expected. Denny asked, "Who is it?"

"It's . . . Sophia."

It was a shot in the dark. Denny had no reason to have told her sister where he lived, but Elise had seen them talking, and she figured he was more likely to open the door for someone who was *of age*. If she could just see him, just talk to him for a *second*, then Elise was sure she could convince him that it didn't matter, that age was just a number.

Ernie wiggled his eyebrows at his frontman; Calvin and Lenny grinned wolfishly. Denny smiled, shrugged, and got up to answer the door. He was surprised. From their brief interaction, he wouldn't've thought that Sophia was the type to just show up at his door in the middle of the night, but if she was here, he couldn't be more stoked about it . . .

Denny's welcoming smile fled when he saw Elise standing in the hallway. He didn't have to glance over his shoulder to know that his bandmates were rolling their eyes. Calvin and Ernie had laughed heartily when Lenny had told them about little brother Dennis's unfortunately persistent, unfortunately underage Number One Fan.

Denny frowned. His Number One Fan or not, Elise was most assuredly *not* Sophia, and he just as assuredly didn't want to see her. He stepped into the hall and closed the door behind him.

"You're a liar, Elise." *A clever, conniving . . . child.*

"I just want to talk to you, Denny."

"I'm sorry, kid. I'm glad you like my band and all, but you can't come over here anymore. You're gonna get us in trouble."

"I've got some trouble for you." Elise attempted to embrace Denny, but he grabbed her wrists and gently pushed her away from him.

"I'm not playing with you, Elise. Like they say in those bars you're too young to be in, you don't have to go home, but you can't stay here."

Denny was interested in Elise's sister – he had discovered in a very short time that he was *extremely interested in her sister* – all the talk about the big time with his band tonight had more or less passed him by, because Denny could think of nothing else besides his scheduled lunch with Sophia tomorrow. He would whip up a little feast, make a pitcher of mimosas. Lenny had already agreed to stick around, just so Denny could demonstrate that he wasn't just trying to pick her up, that he looked at her differently, that she wasn't just *any* girl to him. . .

And Elise was trying her damnedest to ruin everything. When she didn't move, Denny's patience expired. "If you don't leave this minute, I'm gonna go back inside and call Sammy. I'm sure that he'd be interested to know where you are."

"I broke up with Sammy." *He just doesn't know it yet.* "It's none of his business where I am."

"Then I'll call your sister." It was a chickenshit threat, empty. Denny didn't want to be a tattletale, and he sincerely didn't want Sophia to know that her little sister couldn't seem to take no for an answer. He didn't have her phone number, anyway.

The warning didn't faze Elise. She smirked, and remained rooted in the hall.

"All right. I'll call the cops then."

Elise blinked, unable to hide the fear that this new promise engendered, and Denny caught the look immediately. Elise wasn't afraid of Sammy or her sister, but she was afraid of the law. He thought perhaps she had run afoul of them before, what with her penchant for sneaking into bars . . .

"I love you, Denny!" she blurted out.

He remembered Sophia's words. "You don't even know me, Elise."

And you've already shown yourself to be a lying, scheming little brat. Even if I wasn't already halfway in love with your sister . . . I could never trust you.

"I'm sorry you feel that way," Denny said, "but I'm too old for you. There's guitar players aplenty your own age. Go find one of them to love."

A thought struck Denny. He shouldn't be cruel to her, because he would be seeing her again, if God would only smile on him and allow him to make something happen with Sophia. So he added gently, "We can be friends, Elise. I'm sure you're a great kid." The teenager winced at the word. "But you can't come over here anymore. Goodnight."

Dennis Whitly turned the doorknob and stepped into his apartment without a backward glance. His heartbroken Number One Fan heard low, murmured voices, questioning; then a burst of laughter.

The tears started – Elise was sure that they were laughing at her – and she ran down the hall, then outside into the always-comforting darkness.

By the time she walked back to the bar and talked Andy the cabdriver into giving her a free ride home, Elise's tears had stopped. Rationalization for all the ugly truths of life had always come easily to her. Nothing was ever lost; there was always an angle. This time, Elise told herself that Denny's dismissal was just a temporary setback. She would look at it as a sterling aspect to his character. He was just demonstrating that he was a good guy.

He thought she was just a kid because she was only sixteen. There was no way for him to know that her journey around the block had begun right after her mother had passed, when she had allowed the captain of the football team to comfort her sorrow in a new and different, *physical* kind of way. The comfort had not lasted, nor had the football player's sympathy, but Elise had discovered that it was not difficult to find similar comfort from similar sources, about the same time that she found that she enjoyed this style of comfort. She was not hardly a kid anymore.

But Denny didn't know that. He was just looking out for her. Elise reasoned that Denny had to like her. It was just this stupid, temporary, age thing. He couldn't help it that she was underage, any more than she could. He had said that they could be friends, had he not? That would have to do for now.

Elise's sadness lifted. She wouldn't be a kid forever, not in Denny's eyes nor the law's. And once she turned eighteen, a friendship with him could expand, it could bloom. He would be willing to give it a try with her then. He would become her boyfriend, he would love her as much as she loved him . . .

****

It took a month of lunches and dinners and movie dates for Sophia to get to know the real Dennis Whitly, the regular guy that lived just below the take-it-as-it-comes, musician's façade.

Sophia didn't like him *because* he was a musician, yet she accepted that it was a big part of him. She discovered that he had studied more than just the six-string in the five years that he had sequestered himself in his room with it. Denny knew rhyme and meter; he had absorbed the ephemeral smoke of a hundred poets and distilled it again, through the mirror of rock and roll, into his lyrics and music. His familiarity with bands and their tunes was encyclopedic.

Denny knew that he was attractive, and he knew he was talented, and because this knowledge was second nature to him, he didn't possess the need to constantly point it out. He neither commanded nor demanded. He got what he wanted with a soft word, backed up by that killer smile. And what he wanted more than anything in the world was Sophia.

But Denny was patient. In a month, he hadn't even made a pass at her. He'd only held her hand or put his arm around her, given her friendly, quick good-night kisses. She was so much more to him than another beautiful girl. There were a million of those. Sophia was one of a kind.

He enjoyed her wit, her determination to raise her sister in the wake of their parents' passing. Sophia never dwelt on the tragedy of that, the unfairness that she should have to take on the difficult and unforeseen role of looking out for Elise. She didn't whine that her life, college and her own future, had had to be put on hold because of it. Denny admired her loyalty, her sense of responsibility, and he complimented her on it. He let Sophia know that he was fond of her beyond just her beauty, that he cared about her thoughts and ideas. He *listened.*

In that same month, Elise had been seeing a kid from school. Without realizing that she had done so, she had taken Denny's advice and found a guitar player her own age.

It wasn't like it was love. Sammy, and now Carl – that was the guitar player's name – they were just placeholders, just amusements to Elise. There was no sense in being a nun. Boys were fun, and eighteen was still a long way off.

In the blink of an eye, Elise had resigned herself again to the role of schoolgirl. No more sneaking into bars and frat parties. No more drinking with guys that would buy her beer just to get to know her better, and no more getting to know guys old enough to buy her beer. She became a one man woman.

She had decided that it was the part that Denny wished her to play. He had enough slutty groupies hanging around the gated loading zone at The House of Ale, throwing themselves at him after the show. It had become clear to Elise that Denny wanted a nice girl, so she decided to go back to being one for him.

She showed her sister, too. She didn't cut school anymore; she quit smoking. And while Sophia might've been appalled at the things that Elise and Carl did at his house when his parents weren't home, she always returned from their dates by nine on school nights and eleven o'clock on the weekends, so Sophia didn't have cause to ponder what they might be doing.

Elise had tasted the grown-up life. She knew it would be waiting for her again when she was chronologically grown up. In the meantime, she would demonstrate to Sophia that she could be mature and responsible, all the qualities that she wanted in a sister.

All the qualities that Denny would want in a girlfriend.

She immersed herself in school, and hanging out with Carl and his band when they rehearsed and played high school parties. Carl was no Dennis Whitly, and never would be, but he had talent enough. Elise enjoyed being the lead guitar's girlfriend, saw it as practice for later, when she would appear on the arm of a far better musician. She smiled smugly at the baby groupies that came to hear Carl sing. They could cheer and whoop all they liked, they could try out their inexperienced some-hither smiles and winks on him. Elise knew that Carl would always leave the party with her.

The girls' attentions to her new boyfriend didn't bother Elise because she didn't love Carl. Before the first week was out, he'd declared that he loved her, and Elise was confident that he believed that he did. But she knew that it was just what they *did together* that he loved. He was just a boy. He couldn't differentiate between the thrill of sex and the height and depth and breadth of feelings and emotions that one felt when one was truly in love.

Sex was great and all, most usually a means to an end for Elise, but it wasn't love. Love was when your heart soared upon seeing the other person, or even when just thinking about him. Love was when you got all breathless and light-headed, just with the anticipation of talking to him. Elise knew what love felt like because she experienced these things whenever Denny crossed her mind.

Elise knew that she would never love anyone but him. Once she was legal, her life would really begin. Her life with Denny.

Elise's return to acting her age had one significant drawback, however. Removing herself from the bar and the stage door meant that she didn't get to see this irresistible person whom she loved. But that was okay, too. Denny became an ideal in her mind. The future that they would have together was easier to plan, easier to daydream about, when he wasn't standing right there with an annoyed look on his face, telling her to get out of the bar, to get out of his apartment, to leave him alone.

Elise was patient. Her time with Denny would come, once she was of age. They would begin afresh, become friends, then lovers. It was just a matter of getting these pesky, adolescent years behind her.

Elise was so busy being Carl's girlfriend, so busy being a teenager again, that the fact that her sister had been seeing her one true love on the down low for the past month had completely passed her by. If she had been less self-absorbed, Elise might have marked the extra time Sophia spent in front of the mirror before she uncharacteristic disappeared for a few hours, damn near every night. Elise figured she was probably just visiting with the other girls from her office. Had she cared more about her sister's life, then Sophia's bright eyes and thoughtful smiles when she returned home might have told Elise otherwise.

Sophia had dated in high school; Elise had never noticed any of her boyfriends. Steve, the college kid that she'd been seeing when Mom died – he had dropped by the wayside when Sophia had dropped out of school to support them. Since then, Sophia had not gone out on a single date. She was so responsible, so adult and parental, so *boring*. The possibility that her sister had found a new man did not occur to Elise.

Reality would unload like the oft-mentioned ton of bricks once the calendar turned from May to June, however.

It was Sunday morning, and Elise had overslept. She had been looking forward to going to Newport Beach with Carl, had chirped happily about it to her sister all week. She was supposed to meet him at eight, but Elise knew that Carl would wait for her to call him. So when the alarm went off, she hit the snooze button. Then she hit it a couple of more times. Now it was almost nine thirty, and she thought it was time to be getting her tail in gear.

She donned her bikini and a modest cover-up, grabbed her striped beach bag, containing her sunscreen and her big red towel, and a trashy novel to read at the beach. She breezed out of her room and down the stairs. She paused at the phone in the hall, gave Carl a quick call, told him she was sorry she was late, she had overslept, but if he'd like to come pick her up now, she was all ready to go. Carl didn't even mutter in annoyance – he thought he was in love with the bubbly, vivacious blonde, who was always down for whatever he wanted to do, especially behind closed doors – he said he'd be there in ten minutes.

Elise thought she'd have a quick bowl of cereal, but eating and the beach and Carl and every other aspect of her life up to that moment were forgotten when she strolled into the kitchen and beheld Dennis Whitly, shirtless, flawless, sitting at her kitchen table.

Sophia was sitting across from him, dressed in the light blue camisole and shorts that she wore for pajamas. Wisps of blonde hair had come loose from her ponytail. She and half-dressed Denny were chatting happily, giggling with each other. When the cheerful smile that she had been sharing with him froze on Sophia's face, Denny turned and looked at Elise.

Elise felt as though she had been punched in the mouth. Denny had not just shown up here at nine o'clock on a Sunday morning, shirtless. He didn't even know where she lived. He had been here all night, with Sophia, they had been . . .

Oh, my God! She's stolen Denny from me!

A white flash of hatred burst in Elise's mind. Like a spotlight set off by a motion detector in darkness, it blinded her for a second, made her eyes water. Her mouth dropped open.

"I . . . I thought you went to the beach."

Even if Elise hadn't grasped the situation for what it was immediately, the guilty tone to Sophia's surprised words would've made it clear to her. They were caught. Busted.

Just because she's older, just because she can go where he goes, just because he's so awesome . . . She's taken him from me! Just because she can!

Elise struggled to form polite words in response, but Sophia's blinding treachery overwhelmed her. All she could think of were harsh, hysterical pejoratives. *Whore! Bitch! Thief!*

Denny expression was the same as the little boy caught with his hand in the cookie jar. It wasn't guilt, per se, that colored his beautiful eyes to a darker shade of green. He wasn't ashamed of what he had done: he'd steal another cookie if the opportunity presented itself. He was only waiting to see what Elise's response would be, now that she had apprehended him in his crime.

They were waiting for Elise to speak, to react. Before allowing her to do so, her agile mind produced a quick assessment, a guide, a plan to dictate her next move. Rationalization, the thing that had gotten her through an oft-times tragic existence, stepped in to moderate.

It was clear now that her sister was more of a tramp than Elise had ever imagined. When Sophia had pronounced that she had found Denny to be merely *all right,* that had obviously been a lie. Sophia had found him to be just as spectacular and irresistible as Elise had herself, and because she was of age, she had taken the initiative and waited around behind the bar last night until he was done playing. She had simply picked him up, like the slut she so clearly was, and then had gone right on ahead and brought him home.

Elise had been being a good girl on a Saturday night – she had been studying with Paula from Chemistry class until nine – and then she had gone to sleep, to be well-rested for her day at the beach. Elsie remembered wondering again where her sister had been last night, and now she knew. Sophia had been living the lie of don't-do-what-I-do-

do-what-I-say. She had been whoring it up on the boulevard, picking up strange men and keeping them overnight.

Elise reckoned it could be nothing else but that. Before she had managed to talk to him that first time, before she had herself caught his tomcat's roving eye, Elise had seen Denny leave the bar with many girls. A different one after every set, as a matter of fact. Once upon a time, Denny had left with Elise, too, and if his brother hadn't narced her off . . .

That Denny's-got-a-girlfriend line that Sophia had fed her, that had also clearly been bullshit. Elise realized that maybe her sister had been interested in Denny even then. How devious she had turned out to be! Sophia had just bided her time all month, working up her courage. And when her low-life sister had at last propositioned him last night, of course Denny had gone for it.

Therefore, it only followed that Sophia meant no more to Denny than had all the other girls that had offered their of-age goods and services to him in the past. Sophia was just another groupie to him, to be forgotten and replaced by the next eager fan after the next show.

Elise herself was through with all that. She was a good girl now, and as soon as she turned eighteen, Denny would appreciate her for it. He was just marking time with her slutty sister, in the same way, really, that Elise was just marking time with Carl. It was strictly a physical thing. There was no way that Denny could be in any way interested in Sophia beyond that – she was so averse to going out and having a good time – hell, he might not even *like* her. But it was all the same in the dark, and she had no doubt come on to him, so Denny had done what comes naturally.

It couldn't possibly mean anything to him, so Elise figured that there was no reason for her to flip out about it. There had been many girls before Sophia, and there would no doubt be many more afterwards, until such time as Elise was of age, and Denny would give all that up so he could be with her.

Elise didn't call her sister any of the nasty names that populated her mind. She didn't run out of the house in an outraged fit of betrayal. Instead, she said matter-of-factly, "I overslept. Carl's gonna be here in a few minutes." Her only acknowledgment of their sleazy situation was a wink at her sister. "You kids have fun."

Before Sophia could formulate a response, Elise left the kitchen, left the house.

Denny grinned, leaned across the table and kissed Sophia quickly, with a shade of what could only be termed relief. "That went well."

Sophia smiled back, much more relieved that he was. "I would've thought she would've freaked out. She has quite the thing for you. She talks about you all the time. *Denny's so cute! Denny's so great!*"

The rock star flashed in his eyes. "It's the general consensus."

Over the past month, Sophia had begun to believe it herself, and after last night, she was convinced. Denny had made her feel as if she was the only woman in the world, the only woman he would ever see again. He had put her upon a pedestal, above the sea of wistful fans that would soon be clamoring for his attention and affection.

"Elise found another guitar player. That happens, too." He took Sophia's hands across the table. "So now we don't have to sneak around anymore, like we're the kids. You can come on tour with me."

"Let me think about that for a minute, Denny," Sophia said quickly. "Okay?"

He nodded, changed the subject, asked her what she would like to do with the rest of the day.

Sophia arose and sat in his lap. "Whatever amuses you, Rock Star."

****

Three months after his sixteenth birthday, Dennis Whitly had been sitting on the porch swing at his parents' house, strumming his guitar and making notes for his first song. It was dusk; his brother was at Calvin's place, practicing with the rest of the band. It was a Saturday night, and Denny could've been out with a girl from school, or any girl that struck his fancy, actually. They had been noticing him, and he had been noticing back, since he had been about fifteen. He had even started to return their attention, had kissed a few of them . . .

But then Lenny had given him one of his cast-off guitars, and Denny's mind had turned to music. *Didn't know how to play it, but he knew for sure, that that one guitar, felt good in his hands . . .*

But Denny would not be permitted to forget about the opposite sex just because he had decided to emulate his big brother and teach himself to play the old Ibanez. He was just sitting on the porch, minding his own business, writing a song. Then Marcia Goodman from two houses down was standing at the gate, calling his name.

Denny and Marcia had gone to grade school together, and they attended the same high school, but didn't have any classes together this year. Denny didn't think he had said more than a passing hello to Marcia for months, yet here she was, smiling shyly, asking him what he was doing.

"Play me something," she suggested, settling in beside him on the porch swing.

Denny noticed that Marcia was exceptionally pretty, round and curvy in all the right places. And she smelled good, too. He asked himself why he had not noticed these things before, then asked Marcia what it was that she would like to hear.

Her shy smile widened a little bit; her dark brown eyes glittered in the half-light. "How about a love song?"

Denny immediately thought, *Come on baby, make it hurt so good,* and grinned to himself. John Cougar's raucous anthem, released the previous year, was one of his brother's favorites, always a hit at parties. But then Denny considered Marcia's soft, expectant gaze for a second, and thought she might like something a little slower.

He remembered another one of Lenny's favorites.

"It's a cautionary tale," the bass player would tell Denny with a sly grin. "It lays it all out, the sad life of those of us dedicated to our craft." Calvin would do a rim shot on the snare. "It's a warning to the young ladies, but it still never fails . . ."

Denny strummed, sang, *"Beth, I hear you calling, but I can't come home right now. Me and the boys are playing, and we just can't find the sound . . ."*

He never got to tell Beth that he knew she was lonely, or Marcia either, for that matter, never got to hope she'd be all right. Long before Denny got to the sad truth of a musician's lot – *me and the boys will be playing all night* – Marcia leaned over and kissed him.

Denny had not played all night with the boys. He had not played with them at all yet, because he considered himself to be an amateur. He would not bore Lenny and the other guys with his fledgling licks. But Denny learned the inescapable truth of being a musician that evening. It wasn't necessarily how well he played – just the fact that he *could* play was enough for some girls. John Cougar would sum it all up later that year: *All women around the world want a phony rock star – who plays guitar.*

In between kisses, Marcia murmured that she had heard him out on the porch before, and had just decided to drop by tonight and see how *good* he really was. Apparently, he was good enough.

Marcia had never paid a whole lot of mind to Denny in the past, but before he was even half-way through Kiss's whiny old ballad, she was on him like ugly on a bulldog. For the first time, but not hardly the last, Denny discovered that he had his hands full with a girl, eager and passionate, almost forceful in her willingness. All because he played the guitar.

He knew that it was the music that had put Marcia's motor into overdrive, and Denny held on to the old Ibanez, fearing that if he set it down, the spell would be broken. Marcia would stop kissing him, stop tangling her hands in his hair, cease trying to climb into his lap. But the instrument was preventing her from doing that, so she took it from him and quickly leaned it against the porch railing.

Denny waited. The thing that had suddenly made him so charming to Marcia was no longer in his hands. Would she return to her senses? His guitar set aside, he was just plain ol' Denny Whitly again.

"I really like the way you sing, Denny," Marcia said, returning immediately to his arms.

Denny heard Lenny's voice in his head as she started kissing him again. *It works every time, little brother.*

Denny's relationship with his first Number One Fan would last for only a couple of months, however. Her initial infatuation with the fact that he was a musician eventually wore off, and then Marcia started to make demands on his time. She pouted, she railed. "You never want to go anywhere, or do anything! All you ever want to do is sit around and play your stupid guitar! You're not even in a band!"

His *stupid* guitar and his still-learning ability to play it had ceased to be of any importance to Marcia. She wanted Denny to pay attention to her now, exclusively. She wanted to take the place of the music in his life, the thing that had so completely fired her imagination in the first place. His talent had turned her on, but then she expected him to turn it off and devote himself to her.

Beth, what can I do?

Kiss's paean to a musician's lot proved prophetic for Denny and Marcia. When he wouldn't give up practice to go to the mall or to the movies with her, Marcia broke it off with him.

Denny was philosophical about the ending: *easy come, easy go.*

He didn't waste his time with another girl during all the years before he revealed his talent to his brother. *You know you can't touch that stuff without money or a brand new car. Let me give you some good advice, young man, you better learn to play guitar.*

But Denny's self-imposed exile had been worth it, because in the five months since he'd started as frontman for Sonic Daydream, there had been more women than he ever would've dreamed, far more than enough to make up for his monkish years of study. As Lenny had not failed to observe, they lined up around the block to hear his little brother sing, and Denny availed himself of his eager fans whenever the mood struck him.

Yet even on the very doorstep of fame – it wasn't only enthusiastic young women telling him that he was great now, it was Sony Records – Denny hadn't forgotten the lesson he'd learned from his brief time with Marcia. The girls that wanted him because he was a musician – none of that was real. Just like Lenny said: *Don't be surprised when they go home with the drummer from some other band next week.*

The groupies were fun – as long as he made sure that they were of age – and Dennis Whitly was surely not averse to allowing them to exercise their fantasies upon him. But he never lost his belief that it wasn't really him that they wanted. As soon as the sparkly-eyed beauty said, "You're great, Denny! I love how you sing!" he put her into the *fan* category, wrote her off as a candidate for any kind of real relationship. He wasn't interested in a real relationship, anyway. Music was his sole passion.

It was all like a blue fiction: not real life, but how the groupies wanted real life to be. He was Denny Whitly, incredibly sexy musician, and they were there to show their appreciation for his talent. He gleefully allowed them to do so, but he expected nothing more than sex from them. He would not give anything of himself, of his emotions, to it. That drummer from that other band might be taking the stage right after his next set.

But Sophia was different. She'd listened politely while he ran a few new tunes by her. She gave honest feedback, said she liked this one more than that one, and so on, but she didn't beg him to sing to her. His talent was not the thing that most interested her about him.

They talked about his big future. But they also talked about all the other things that made up their lives at twenty-one: how she didn't really miss college; how he had never even considered it. Sophia told him about her happy childhood, her loving parents. They discussed how Elise was coping with their loss, speculated about how she might turn out. Sophia talked about her secretarial job.

Denny learned that Sophia was a world-class movie fan. They had actually gone out to the movies a few times during the month, but mostly they sat on the couch at his apartment and watched rentals from Blockbuster. There weren't many that she hadn't already seen, and it amused Denny that she always took a lesson from each of them.

Movies were a truer reflection of real life to Sophia; they helped her to fine tune her perceptions. They showed life how it was, how it used to be, how it might be, how it should be, distilled, without all the inanities of meals and commuting, going to the grocery store, getting enough sleep, having a boring job. For almost any real life situation, Sophia could think of a movie that refined it, made it clearer, predicted its inevitable outcome. To her, movies were guideposts, shorthand for all the foibles of mankind, all the triumphs and joys and tragedies that could befall them.

Denny considered Sophia's enjoyment of cinema to be a benign escape from the boredom and sadness that had happened in her life, especially in the last couple of years. But he was here now, and he aimed to make her happy, every day, just to see her smile, because her smile had become like a candle in the darkness to him. In a short thirty days, Denny discovered that he was now ready for a real relationship: he had fallen for Elise's sister. He felt for her as he had for no other woman. He tuned himself to the nuances of her moods. It was the most enjoyable study he had taken up since the guitar, because Sophia was a finer and more delicate instrument.

****

The night before had been Sonic Daydream's farewell show at The House of Ale. Denny thanked the hometown fans for their support and invited them all to come out and see his band on tour. The applause and cheers were deafening. Like Sammy, they would be able to say they knew Sonic Daydream when.

Denny thought Sophia lingered in his light embrace a little longer when he came up beside her at the bar after the show. He smiled and downed her drink in one gulp, as he had the night they'd met. But before he could again say, *Let's get out of here,* fans came up and shook his hand, slapped him on the back, told him congratulations.

Sophia waited patiently for a break in the stream of well-wishers. It was several minutes in coming. At last there was a lull when no one was begging for Denny's attention, so she said, "Let's go back to my house."

This was a first, but Denny wasn't overly surprised. He had sensed her affection growing commensurately with his own. It was time.

He tried to skip out on the load out again – he was as eager as any groupie to go home with Sophia – but she would hear none of it. Murmuring something about Yoko Ono, she went outside to the loading zone and waited patiently by the truck. Girls called to Denny and he waved absently as he quickly helped the rest of the band with their instruments.

Sophia realized suddenly that it would probably be the last time they ever had to do the task themselves. Sonic Daydream was signed now. They were going to have their own tour bus, and she reckoned that their equipment would be on a truck. There would now be roadies to load in and load out, and the crowds would be so much larger than at The House of Ale. Backstage passes would be required for her to see Denny after the show. Sonic Daydream had hit the big time.

It was past eleven when Sophia and Denny arrived at her house. Mom-like, she went upstairs and peeked in on Elise, found her in full good girl mode, home and asleep on a Saturday night, probably dreaming of her age-appropriate guitar player and their day at the beach tomorrow.

Sophia went through the motions of loading a cassette into the VCR; watching movies together was what she and Denny did. But Denny knew that there would be more tonight. He didn't fail to notice that Sophia dimmed the lights this time, and cuddled up a little closer to him than she had in the past. Someone less familiar with women's signals might've missed the subtlety of Sophia's increased affection; she didn't throw herself into his arms, after all. A less experienced young man might've figured that Sophia was just being quiet so as not to wake her sister.

Denny waited, as he always did. A few minutes into *The Princess Bride*, Sophia kissed him, and when he felt her ardor rise to a new level, still he waited. He was in no hurry. As was his modus operandi with all women, Denny would allow Sophia to make the decision. He was fairly sure it would be tonight – already she murmured appreciatively under his mouth and hands, more fervently than ever before – but if she changed her mind in the middle of it, that was okay, too. If not tonight, it would be soon. Denny was patient. He loved her.

But Sophia didn't change her mind. She believed that she knew Denny now, after the month they had spent together. He was kind, caring, insightful, intelligent. He was easy-going, funny, witty. He had all the qualities that she had ever looked for in a partner.

And he was a rock star.

Tonight, as Sonic Daydream bid farewell to their small-town roots, Sophia had allowed herself to see Denny as all the other girls saw him. She had decided that she could love the quietly confident man that she had found him to be on the inside, so tonight she had paid attention to the performer that he became once on stage.

Denny noticed her studied interest, and because of it, he was even more incredible than usual, the very personification of a thousand groupies' fevered fantasies. He was sly, alluring . . . *available*. As always, he held the crowd in the palm of his hand, responding to their adulation with smiles and a few clever words. When he winked at her towards the end of the set, Sophia's mind was made up. Tonight, *she* would seduce the lead singer from Sonic Daydream. Tonight would be her turn, and she hoped that it would continue to be her turn for a long, long time.

As they sat on the couch, the movie forgotten, Sophia felt that Denny's attentions were of a different sort than they'd been in the past. Before, he had seemed to hold back. His quick kisses and brief hugs had seemed almost only a friendliness, a simple fondness. But no longer. Now he kissed her slowly, lingeringly. He teased her, tempted her.

After thirty days (exponentially, the longest period of time Dennis Whitly had ever waited for any woman), Sophia gave in to the guitar player's temptation. She stood, took his hand. They quickly tiptoed to her room at the back of the house, with only a few giggles to mark the momentous journey.

****

Now the musician smiled at the beautiful, slightly disheveled woman sitting in his lap. They had said *I love you* in the throes of passion, and again before they drifted off to sleep, and again upon waking. Denny felt as though his life was now complete.

He was the lead singer for Sonic Daydream, newly-signed with Sony Records. There had already been a fat advance. His band was scheduled to go to a studio in LA tomorrow and record, and they were supposed to shoot a video the following week. Then they were headlining a short West Coast tour at the end of the month to promote album and video. He had just spent the night (finally!) with the sweetest, most beautiful girl he had ever known. Denny felt unstoppable, on top of the world. He had every single confidence: he was sure Sophia would go on tour with him.

****

Elise was quiet at the beach, deconstructing the scene she had left back in Riverside. Carl tried to engage her in conversation a few times, but received only monosyllabic replies. He persisted; he liked talking to Elise almost as much as he liked everything else she allowed him to do.

He told her how nice she looked in her bikini, he commented on how cool it was to be hanging out at the beach. Elise only nodded and stared out at the surf, and Carl soon realized that she had something on her mind. She didn't want to talk.

"Didn't you bring that thing for a reason?" She nodded at his Boogie Board lying in the sand.

Carl took the hint. In the short time that they had been together, he'd discovered that Elise could be moody. Laughing and loving and affectionate one minute, she could turn into an ice cube the next, with no obvious provocation. So he picked up the board and headed out into the surf. No reason to annoy her. Let her think about whatever it was that was preoccupying her. There would be time to talk on the drive home.

Elise watched Carl hit the waves and smiled to herself. He had been as easy to train as Sammy.

Elise had not yet met a member of the opposite sex who hadn't acquiesced to her whims immediately. She instinctively understood the power that she held, and already wielded it as well a woman twice her age. Even if some of them had been too old to qualify for the term, they had all been *boys* to her, easily manipulated. If she showed them not much more than her little finger, the next place they inevitably found themselves was wrapped around it.

Except for Denny.

Her favorite musician would've fallen into line, too, Elise was sure of it, just like all the others. The captain of the football team had once quoted a famous coach to her: *In my entire career, I never lost a single game. I just ran out of time,* and that was how Elise figured it with Denny. He'd been well on his way to doing exactly what she wanted on the night they'd met, and she was completely sure that he would've joined the ranks of her infatuated admirers, if she'd just been granted a little more time alone with him. If only she'd gotten the chance to demonstrate how much she loved him.

But that was water under the bridge. When Denny found out that she was underage, the spell had been broken. His curiosity, his anticipation, had evaporated.

Damn Leonard Whitly, anyway. Damn him straight to hell.

Now Elise would have to win Denny's love with something more than just her body and the promise of continued access to it. He was not like all these other *boys*, to be used and discarded as she saw fit. That was part of his charm, was it not? His aloofness made her want him even more.

Elise believed that she was up to the task of winning Denny to her way of thinking, even without the easy tool of sex. There was more than one way to skin a cat. There was flattery, there was seeming-obedience. Elise realized that she might just have to visit the bar again, after all. She might have to keep an eye on Denny, once he was through with her sister. Elise consulted an imaginary watch on her wrist: *that'll be by the time I get back from the beach, no doubt.*

77

Elise thought about how she would comfort Sophia, once the guitarist dumped her. It was an occurrence that Elise had witnessed enough times – Denny took a different girl home after every set. *I need a lover that won't drive me crazy, some girl to thrill me and then go away.* Sophia would be hurt at his sudden indifference, whereas Elise knew the score. She had never personally experienced being dumped, by a musician or any other, because she had always been the one doing the dumping, and Carl was the only musician she'd ever snagged. And Carl was loyal, because he was in love.

But Elise had heard a few stories from Anita, another notorious chaser of guitar players, and she had observed Denny and other musicians' cavalcade of different women ever night. *Some girl that knows the meaning of, "Uh, hey, hit the highway."* Elise considered herself educated, philosophical about the whole thing. It wasn't difficult to catch a guitar player – especially if one was of age – but it was decidedly difficult to keep one. How could boring Sophia ever believe that someone like Dennis Whitly – awesome, sexy, talented – would ever so much as give her a second go?

Elise would be gentle with her sister, soothe her hurts. She would explain: *A musician's just not the guy for you, Soph. Maybe you should go to some college bar, somewhere like Mickey's, where they don't have live bands. Surely, you can find yourself a nice boy there.*

And leave Dennis Whitly to me.

Elise thought she would drop by The House of Ale and see Denny again next week, let him know that she had no hard feelings, just because he had taken advantage of, and then summarily dropped her sister like Third Period French. She would tell him that she understood the ways of rock and roll, she would remind him that she had given up all that decadence, even if he had not. She would reiterate again for Denny that she was a good girl, the kind of girl that he really wanted, and she would remind him that it was less than a year and a half before she was legal. She would remind him that she would be waiting for him then.

Sure, it might be a little prickly when she started seeing Denny, what with Sophia's broken heart and all, but by the time Elise's eighteenth birthday rolled around, Sophia would be over it. She might even have found herself a nice college boy by then. Hell, she might even be married by then.

Elise was patient. She would just drop by the loading zone next Saturday and have a word with Denny. She wouldn't even try to go into the bar. She would just remind him that she was still around, being a good girl. Waiting for him.

****

Elise would not have to wait until the following weekend to see her favorite musician. She would not have to hang out by the chain-link gate in the alley behind The House of Ale to try to catch a word with him. Sonic Daydream would never play The House of Ale again, and Dennis Whitly was sitting on the couch in her living room, drinking a beer and watching a movie with her sister, when Elise returned from the beach.

The two of them were sitting very close together, holding hands even, when she walked into the house. It was an affectionate scene. Apparently Denny had had nothing pressing to do on a Sunday, so he had remained in the company of his latest pick-up all day. *No doubt anticipating another quickie before he takes off for good*, Elise thought.

But maybe that wasn't fair. Denny was basically kind-hearted, after all. Hadn't he demonstrated that by refusing to take advantage of her because he thought she was just a kid? Elise saw the glint of love in Sophia's eyes, and Denny had no doubt seen it there, too. He wanted to let her down easy, so he had stuck around, watched movies with her, held her hand. This kind of affection meant nothing – Elise was affectionate with Carl, was she not? She was fond of him. Perhaps Denny, nice guy that he was, was fond of Sophia, and this outward PDA was his way of confirming it to her.

But all that physical stuff was fleeting. Night was coming, and Denny would do a fade then. He no doubt had to rehearse, to fine tune the talent that would allow him to pick up some other infatuated groupie next weekend. Sophia had made a grave error. She had proved herself to be just another slutty fan, the type of girl with which Denny was all too familiar. He could never love someone like her. He wanted a good girl, not just another one-night-stand. Sex was just sex. True love – what he would come to feel for Elise someday – that was in the heart.

Elise smiled kindly at her obviously love-struck sister. *Oh, there are going to be tears.* Elise thought again how she would comfort Sophia when Denny didn't call back.

Sophia returned her sister's smile. She clicked off the TV and gestured for Elise to have a seat in the armchair beside the couch. "Denny has some incredible news."

I've got some incredible news for you, groupie-girl. He's not gonna be your boyfriend. You're never gonna see him again, unless you decide to be pathetic and hang out at the bar when he plays. Then he'll just ignore you.

"Sony signed us," Denny said simply.

"I heard something about that," Elise replied. "My friend Anita told me." Just because she had gone back to being a teenager, did Denny think that she didn't know what time it was? The news was all over town. Riverside's own Sonic Daydream now had a record contract. None of her high school confreres could quite say what that meant, but it wasn't hardly a secret.

"We're going to a studio in LA tomorrow, and then, something about a video. For *Tomcats.*"

Denny shook his head dismissively. His brother was the businessman. All the details of the video, the recording, the contracts, the tour – Lenny would take care of all that. Denny was in love. The particulars of his incipient fame were inconsequential to him. He only wanted to make Sophia happy, and to be happy with her.

He had not again brought up the subject of the tour, but now an inspiration struck Denny. Sophia had not wanted to discuss it, and now he kenned the reason for her hesitation. He didn't know why he hadn't seen it before.

Sophia didn't want to talk about going on tour with him, because even though she loved him – that was clear to Denny already – she was going to have to say no. She had responsibilities. She couldn't leave wild Elise to her own devices and flit up the coast with him and his band. Sophia hadn't wanted to talk about it because she hadn't wanted to disappoint Denny by turning him down. But of course, there was no way she could go with him. Unless . . .

"We're going on a little tour. Up the coast."

Just like Calvin's 1987's Fire-Trap Tour with Scranton, Denny thought. But not exactly. No stadiums this time, not yet, but concert venues, nonetheless. No tiny clubs or bars.

There was no money in playing the bar scene. The places were too small, and the customers had to be of age. The money was in the jailbait, teeny-bopper fans' pockets. Big concert venues, big bands, catered to all ages.

"I want you guys to come with us." Denny put his arm around Sophia, but looked expectantly at her sister.

"Both of us?" Sophia squawked in surprise.

It was the only solution.

"Sure, why not? It's just a short tour. Three weeks, I think Lenny said. I figure . . . You could get vacation from work, right? And Elise is gonna be out of school for the summer. Why not?"

Denny had not discussed this with the rest of the band. When Lenny said *tour*, all he could think about was that he wanted to take Sophia. He didn't think that he could bear to be out of Sophia's company for the three weeks it would take them to climb the West Coast, and that was even before they had spent the night together. Denny had not thought out the details, had not considered that she couldn't or wouldn't take off of work for all that time. He didn't know what the record company stipulations on girlfriends might be; he hadn't cared. He'd figure out a way to put her up nearby as they toured. He'd figure it all out some way, if she would just say she'd go . . .

Now Denny knew that he'd have to make arrangements for Elise, too. He saw his cut of the band's advance going up in hotel rooms and meals for Sophia *and Elise*, but he didn't care. He wanted Sophia by his side, for just as long as it could be managed.

Elise considered them. This had to be some kind of joke. Sophia had a dumb, shocked expression on her face, so she obviously wasn't in on it. Denny was just messing with Elise, showing her what she might have someday, when she was old enough: going on tour with Sonic Daydream. The crowds, the noise, the heat, and Elise above it all, backstage, waiting for Denny . . .

He was just teasing her. He knew it was what she had always dreamed – what fan didn't dream of going on tour with her favorite band? But she was too young to go with him now. Hadn't he harped on that in every one of the three or so conversations they'd ever had? *Go away, Elise, you're too young. Leave me alone, Elise. You're too young.*

It had to be a joke.

"You want me to go on tour with you."

"Yes." But he squeezed Sophia to him, said to *her*, "Both of you."

Sophia smiled back at him. Denny saw that she was up for it. As long as Elise could go too, as long as she could continue to keep an eye on her little sister, Sophia wanted to be with Denny as much as he wanted her to be with him.

Elise scrutinized their shared gaze, but then disregarded it. Whatever had been going on between them all day . . . It couldn't mean anything to him. It just couldn't. Sophia was just another pick-up to him. This thing about the tour . . . It had to be some kind of joke.

"On the bus," Elise said, to make them look at her again.

Now Denny backpedaled. "I don't know about that. You'll probably have to drive your own car–"

81

"I can rent a car!" Sophia hugged him enthusiastically.

Elise raised an eyebrow at this. *She's falling for it. She doesn't realize that this is some kind of joke. 'Yeah, Denny, we'll meet you at the bus, in our rented car.' But when we get there, the bus will be gone.*

"So you're saying you want us to trail behind your tour bus. Like some kind of convoy. Like groupies. Like *camp-followers.*" It was ridiculous. Denny was having them on.

Elise expected Sophia's eyes to widen at the derogatory terms, but instead she just smiled serenely. "You would've camp-followed Oingo Boingo after Mom died, if I would've let you."

Elise ignored her. "What's your deal, anyway, Denny? This is bullshit. You're not serious about taking us on tour with you."

Sophia squeezed him; they shared another smile. Then she told her sister, "It's real Elise. Do you want to go or not?"

****

On Elise's much anticipated eighteenth birthday, on October 15th, 1989, she was again on tour with Sonic Daydream. But Dennis Whitly was not her boyfriend. In the year and a half that she had known him, her desire for him had not subsided, however.

In that same short period of time, Sonic Daydream had become famous, sought-after chart-toppers, as the astute A & R man from Sony Records had known that they would. He had gone out on a limb, signing an unknown group, immediately booking them as headliners for a West Coast tour. Local bands had opened for them, had brought in the fans, curious to see new material. But Sonic Daydream had won them all over. The A & R guy was good at his job: he had seen it all, in that little beer-smelling tavern in that backwater California town. When he'd heard Dennis Whitly sing, he'd been put in mind of a famous critic's review of a then nobody named Bruce Springsteen: *I have never been so overwhelmed by totally unknown talent.*

His risk had paid off in spades. Sonic Daydream had pretty much been on tour constantly ever since, throughout the States, raking in the money for him, for Sony, and for themselves.

Now they were about to go to Europe.

Elise was going with them.

She had swallowed her dislike for Leonard Whitly, and had slowly wormed her way into his confidence, making herself indispensable on the road. Lenny had been savvy enough to act as the band's manager, their *road dog,* from the moment they'd been signed, but even though the record company booked the venues and the accommodations for the band, and signed their paychecks, as well as the bus driver's and the truck driver's and the crew's, there were still a million administrative details that needed to be answered in every town. Sometimes Lenny felt a little overwhelmed.

Elise had always been shrewd and inventive beyond her years, and despite her youth, she was always Johnny-on-the-spot with a solution when the truck was late or if the merch didn't arrive at the venue or if they came up a roadie short or if the promoter was being an asshole. Lenny welcomed her help; in fact, he came to depend on it.

Elise could not possibly have cared less about the bass player's gratitude. She loathed him, would always blame him and his big mouth for the fact that she had missed her initial chance with his brother. Elise stepped and fetched for Sonic Daydream, she got on the phone and took names and kicked ass on their behalf, for no other reason than to remain close to Denny.

Sophia was there with them, too, of course, but Elise wasn't entirely upset about that. She was sure that Denny's infatuation with her sister would run its course eventually. Surely, he wrote songs about her; three to be precise. The tunes had wowed the fans on the road, and they would be on the next album.

And surely, Elise overheard him say how much he loved Sophia, all the time.

But seriously, what good was she? She didn't do anything, she didn't help in any way. She was just there, like any other groupie, like a camp-follower. Elise was part of the team, and Denny told her frequently how much he appreciated her help. She was indispensable, irreplaceable, and what was Sophia? She was just Denny's current squeeze, an expendable hanger-on that could be interchanged with any girl from any town.

Elise was convinced that Denny would tire of Sophia, especially now that she was eighteen. Now it was no longer necessary for her to be under Sophia's legal and parental thumb. Elise was free now, an adult at last. Sophia no longer needed to feel any obligation to look after her. Now that Sophia's parental responsibilities were ended, Denny would send her sister back to Riverside, and Elise would finally get her chance.

It couldn't last, Elise was convinced, if for no other reason than the way it had started. Elise had shown herself to be a good girl since her initial thwarted attempt to bed Denny. She had not so much as looked at another guy since they had gone on that first tour. Carl was a memory. When he'd heard she was leaving town with newly-signed Sonic Daydream, he'd made the fatal mistake of asking Elise if maybe she could perhaps get them to listen to his band's demo. Carl had even been so bold as to suggest that maybe Denny could be persuaded to put in a good word for them with that A & R guy from Sony.

"Why do you think Dennis Whitly would waste his breath mentioning a talentless amateur like you to his label?" Before Carl had time to recover from the shock and insult of that question, Elise had delivered the coup de grace: "Really, Carl, this just isn't working out. I might look you up when school starts in the fall, but don't hold your breath."

Her senior year in high school had passed in a flurry of anticipation for Elise, the day-to-day desire to just *get it over with* and get back on the road with *her band*. Sophia had stayed in Riverside with her, had even kept her stupid typist job, even though Denny sent her money and presents from the road. He had bought her a new car.

Sophia had at last quit her job when Elise graduated last June, and Elise thought that had been premature, presumptuous of her. Sophia was acting like this thing with Denny was going to last forever, while Elise was sure that it would not. Any day now, now that she was eighteen, Denny would send Sophia back to Riverside. Hadn't she just picked him up that first night, just like any other trampy fan? Any day now, Denny would see that Elise was the kind of girl he wanted, sober-minded-but-still-fun-loving, loyal, indispensable.

He hadn't sent her sister home yet because he probably just wanted to let Sophia see Europe with them. He was a nice guy, after all, and it was obvious how much Sophia loved him. But she had proved herself to be nothing but an easy pick-up at the start of their . . . *thing*. Elise was sure that Denny would never forget that. He would send Sophia packing as soon as they returned from overseas. And then Elise would take her place beside him.

****

Lenny valued Elise's managerial assistance. She was a dynamo, a pit-bull, when it came to the band's interests. Venue owners and hotel managers were always surprised to discover that the virago that had been yelling at them on the phone about something lacking in Sonic Daydream's backstage or overnight accommodations was just a slip of a teenage girl. Lenny often played good cop to her bad cop. She bullied successful promoters and snooty concierges alike, and seldom failed to get whatever it was that she thought the band needed.

Because she had proved herself to be unbelievably competent and professional, Lenny trusted Elise implicitly on all matters concerning business. Sometimes, all that would be needed would be for him to show up and sign off on a contract or bill – Elise couldn't do that in the past because she was a minor. Most days, the bass man couldn't believe his luck: his band was a solid hit, he was making money hand over fist, and his brother's girlfriend's amazing little sister was everything that he could've asked for in a co-manager.

Elise's loyalty to Sonic Daydream seemed unshakable, but the bassist knew instinctively that if they should for some reason change singers . . . Lenny knew that Elise's allegiance was in reality to Denny alone. He saw the way the kid looked at his brother when she thought no one saw her: that predatory, cheetah-like determination to *get at* Denny, present from the first night, had never gone away. Even with Sophia around, and she and Denny so obviously in love – Lenny knew that Elise still harbored some kind of insane hope, some kind of crazy fantasy that it was going to be her and Denny someday.

Her selfless devotion to his band, her chutzpah and drive – that was all great, but Lenny was still unsure of Elise, because at the core of it all was her groupie's obsession with Denny. As a helper, she was wonderful, but as a human being, he didn't trust her any more than Denny did. Lenny thought that Elise could do absolutely anything in her pursuit of his brother; she was smart and devious and manipulative. And someday, when she at last realized that it wasn't ever going to happen – Christ only knew what the fallout from that awakening might be.

Denny himself made a concerted effort to never find himself alone with Elise, because he often caught the blank, nearly mindless adoration that still dwelt in her eyes. He was used to it by now, having seen it on the faces of legions of young women in a hundred cities. Denny Whitly didn't hang around and sign autographs after the show, so he left each and every one of those young women behind to sulk, to dream afresh, to wait eagerly for the next tour. *'Cause when that morning sun comes beating down, you're going to wake up in your town. But we'll be scheduled to appear a thousand miles away from here . . .*

But Denny couldn't leave his Number One Fan behind. Sophia's little sister was always there, backstage or on the bus or in the hall outside his hotel room. Waiting.

Denny's mistrust of Elise lessened somewhat as the tours progressed. It never disappeared completely, because that longing in her eyes never faded. But she had become businesslike, professional; nothing suggestive had ever again passed her lips to him. And Denny had other things to occupy his mind besides the unwavering worship of one teenage girl. He was in love with her sister, for one thing. His band was unstoppable. But still Denny made sure he and Elise were never alone.

Lenny was all business – Elise hated his guts, anyway. He had stymied her in her conquest of Denny, and for what? Some stupid, arbitrary age restriction, now expired? But Elise respected the bass player. He kept the operation running smoothly (with her help), and he was an awesome musician. This respect, coupled with the fact that she knew he would always be around – he was her beloved's brother, after all – made it effortless for her to keep her hatred for Lenny hidden.

Elise talked to her sister, of course, was friendly, but it was all an act, just as were her always-sunny exchanges with Lenny. They'd never had a trusting, tell-all-their-secrets-to-each-other kind of sibling relationship in the first place. Sophia was too boring to have any secrets, and Elise's secrets – well, they wouldn't have been secrets if she'd blabbed them to her sister, now would they? The last thing that could be even remotely considered a secret that Elise had confided to Sophia was how wonderful she'd found Dennis Whitly to be, and look how that had turned out. Her only blood kin in the world had betrayed her.

Elise had never had a whole lot of respect for Sophia. She'd always seen her as strait-laced and uptight, anti-fun. And when Elise discovered that her sister was actually a traitorous, slutty groupie, what modicum of respect she had once encompassed drained away to nothing. Nowadays, Elise found her interactions with Sophia to be positively tiresome – couldn't she see that this thing with Denny wasn't ever going to work out, that it was never going to last? Elise no longer felt that she would comfort Sophia when Denny eventually dumped her. She just wanted her sister to *be gone already*, to go back to Riverside and resume her narrow little life, and leave the road and the world of rock and roll to those who knew what it was about, to those who were cut out for it.

Lenny was too busy with business to waste time with a different girl in every town, and Sonic Daydream's irresistible frontman avoided all comers by practically running and hiding on the bus after every performance. So it was Ernie LaBelle, the second guitar, who became the de facto groupie-slayer in the band. It was not a difficult role for him to assume: Ernie had always been a player. He had even gone so far as to wink at Elise a few gigs into their first tour, to give her that *hey-ya-wanna?* raised eyebrow. Like Sammy, Ernie would not have cared that she was underage.

Elise had felt the urge to cut Ernie's legs out from under him then, to laugh in his face. *Why would I even give someone like you the time of day when Dennis Whitly stalks the earth?*

But it wouldn't do to insult Ernie. He was also a fine musician, and he was another person that was always going to be around, as long as the band existed. So Elise had turned him down without hurting his feelings. She had resurrected long-forgotten Carl, telling Ernie that while she was indeed flattered by his proposition, she had a guitar player of her own waiting for her back home in Riverside.

That satisfied Ernie. If he and Elise got together, she might think that they were exclusive, like Denny and Sophia, and that would've precluded him sampling the fans in each new town. That would've definitely killed all the fun of being on tour.

So Elise's prospects for companionship and conversation had been somewhat limited during the days and nights that she had spent touring with Sonic Daydream. But life on the road was lonely. Elise needed to talk to somebody, so by the process of elimination, Calvin became her buddy, her pal, her confidante.

He hadn't ever made a pass at her, because he shared Denny's distaste for underage girls. Calvin even took it a step further. He claimed – to Elise, if not his bandmates – to be disgusted by the whole sex-crazed-fan phenomenon. He hadn't gotten into music to take advantage of this undeniable perk, he told Elise. His father had once been a jazz drummer, and little Cal had had a pair of sticks in his hands almost before he was out of diapers. Calvin considered himself to be a musician's musician. Drumming was an art form to him, something more than just a tool to pick up women. At least this was the story that he told Elise.

From her own father, Elise had learned to appreciate music, long before she had ever discovered the itch to chase musicians, and guitar players in particular, and then one specific guitar player. So she saw Calvin as an aficionado of music for its own sake, like herself, a vast storehouse of lyrics, history and trivia; a bit of a snob. Because he had studied the art since childhood, Elise believed that the drummer felt himself to be above Ernie and Lenny and even Denny.

Surely, his bandmates' skills matched his own, but there were the small things, little careless inaccuracies that irked Cal. Even though he could do a dead-on Bob Dylan impression, Ernie always referred to *Rainy Day Women #12 & 35* as *Everybody Must Get Stoned.* And Denny never failed to call *Baba O'Riley Teenage Wasteland,* as if he was any commoner who had perhaps once heard the song and liked the famous intro. The fact that Denny could not only play it but could also hit

87

Townsend's high notes on the middle eight – *Don't cry, don't raise your eye, it's only teenage wasteland* – was immaterial to Cal. Denny always got the title wrong, and that lent a whiff of the peasant to the world-renowned frontman, as far as the drummer was concerned.

Elise thought Denny did it on purpose, just to annoy Calvin. The singer had sequestered himself for five years, had taught himself to read the dots and squiggles on a scale that would forever remain a mystery to musicians even more famous that he would become. His and Lenny's record collection rivaled her father's. The brothers Whitly *knew music*. Yet still Calvin saw them, and Ernie, too, as possessing a certain lack of purity regarding its history and nuances.

Elise loved Cal for this tiny spot of disdain that he felt for his bandmates. Flawless musicians all, she still had a reason to disdain each of them herself: Lenny was a narc, Ernie had dared to make a pass at her, and Denny – well, Denny had dared to turn her down.

Denny and Lenny and Ernie never had a single bad thing to say about each other, or their drummer, for that matter, but in Calvin, Elise found a kindred spirit. If she grumbled about any of the other members of his band, Calvin would always smile and agree with her.

And Elise believed, to her delight, that Calvin just flat out didn't care for Sophia. The vibe that she got was that he considered her sister to be just another guitar-player-infatuated groupie, even if she did seem to be a semi-permanent one. Sophia personified the reason that Ernie and Denny and Lenny – but not Calvin – had become musicians in the first place: an endless supply of women. He was above all that.

Elise had given up her own groupie ways, and when she talked to Calvin of the love she'd had for music since childhood, Elise was almost able to convince herself that she toured with Sonic Daydream for deeper reasons than just her yen for Denny. She was along for the ride for the same reason that Calvin was, basically: because of her enjoyment of the music.

Calvin wasn't buying it, but he allowed Elise to attempt to sell it to him. He was impressed with her *Name That Tune* ability to recite lyrics to damn near any song he could name. She was definitely knowledgeable about the art, as much as any non-musician could be, he had to give her that. But he knew that she wasn't along on tour with them simply to appreciate their sound. She was there because she *wanted Dennis Whitly*, in the worst way, just like all the other little girls (and big girls, too) that saved up their lunch money to buy a ticket to see him. But if Elise wanted to lie to herself, it was all right with Calvin.

Like the brothers Whitly, Calvin was aware of Elise's deviousness, her determination to get what she so obviously wanted. This facet of

88

her personality led Lenny and especially Denny to mistrust the teenager, to be wary of her, but it fascinated Calvin. He suspected an instability in her mind – how could Elise not see that Denny was in love with her doting, colorless sister? How could she not see that she didn't stand a snowball's chance in hell with him?

How could Elise not see? She refused to allow herself to see, that was how. It wasn't every day that Calvin got to witness a living, breathing delusion played out in front of him. Elise's obsession was an amusing diversion from the boredom that made up ninety-nine percent of his life on tour. *The only time that seems too short is the time that we get to play.*

It wasn't as if Elise had simply confessed the depth of her obsession to the drummer, however. Calvin had had to coax it out of her: a little admission here, a few telling words there. He'd had to gain Elise's trust first. They were just two followers of Euterpe, the Muse of music, above the Dionysian bacchanal that raged around them nightly. They were simpatico. *Do you need a friend, would you tell no lies? Would you take me in? Are you lonely in the dark?* How could Elise not pour out her heart to him?

By the time that they were ready to go overseas, Calvin had become like Lord Scroop, notorious traitor to King Harry: he didst bear the key of all Elise's counsels; he knew'st the very bottom of her soul. But Calvin was not a turncoat. He kept all of Elise's pathetic yearnings to himself and would not *coin her into gold* for many years. By then, Elise would be beyond the reach of any pain that his revelations might have inflicted.

****

On her nineteenth birthday, Elise Carlin, diehard music fan from the little town of Riverside, California, found herself in the cosmopolitan city of Berlin. Sonic Daydream was in the middle of their second, sold-out tour of Europe.

Dennis Whitly was still not her boyfriend. Quite the contrary: after all the toasts and happy birthdays had been paid to Elise at dinner, Denny had stood and made a stunning announcement, news that Elsie had suspected for a few weeks already. Sophia had been pale and drawn in Paris, she had missed the show entirely in Munich. *Pink isn't well, he stayed back at the hotel.*

Grinning sheepishly, with a somewhat astonished look of *I-can't-quite-believe-the-wonder-of-it-all* in his eyes, Denny had told his band and his girlfriend's sister the incredible truth: Sophia was pregnant. Dennis Whitly, frontman of one of the hottest acts on God's green earth, was going to be a daddy.

There was a second of shocked silence, then all was congratulations and back-slapping. Lenny, his German a little better than everyone else's, ordered another round of beers. A toast to future baby Whitly was called. But after a few moments of joyful exclamations and wishes for happiness, Calvin at last got down to brass tacks. He asked the question that was on everyone's mind.

"What does this mean for the band?"

Denny smiled. He had anticipated that it would be his drummer that would voice this most pressing of concerns. Calvin had always been in it for the money. "The baby's due in May. We'll be back home by then—"

"We'll be on tour in May," Calvin reminded him. "Again."

"Still," Elise added neutrally.

"Lenny's already talked to Sony. We cancelled the dates for the end of April and all of May and June, and added them back on at the end of the tour. A little break isn't going to hurt us. Nobody's going to forget us in three months."

"And after that?" Elise asked.

Calvin knew that she meant more than just after the end of the tour. Her question, like her sister's womb, was pregnant with all the myriad, divergent possibilities for the future. Calvin smiled to himself at his own poesy. Elise wanted to know more than just what was going to happen after this ill-timed baby was born. She wanted to know what its arrival meant for her continuing fantasy of someday being with Denny.

Denny ignored the implications inherent in Elise's question, if he even recognized that they were present. "I figure that we'll take some time off from touring."

Of course you do, Calvin thought. *You're the front, the singer, the face of the band. The rest of us . . . Well, we just have to go along with whatever Dennis Whitly wants.*

"I thought we might go back to the studio. I've got a few ideas. Some new songs . . ."

More paeans to your love for your milquetoast woman, no doubt, Calvin sneered to himself. *And then, odes to the joys of fatherhood. Christ save us from the Sonic Daydream versions of* Isn't She Lovely, *or* Stay Up Late, *a la Denny Whitly's legendary songwriting skills. Songs about babies do not rock and roll make.*

"That sounds great, little brother," Lenny said, his eyes unreadable. "We could use a break."

****

Dinner ended and they all went back to the hotel. Calvin caught Elise's eye in the lobby, so while the mommy-to-be and the rest of the band retired to their rooms, she paused to have a word with her confidant.

"We had joy, we had fun, we had seasons in the sun, but the wine and the song like the seasons have all gone," he suggested.

Elise arched an eyebrow in mild surprise. "You think so? I see this as just a momentary lapse of reason on Denny's part. You're not suggesting that he'd quit the band?"

Calvin shrugged, assumed his best Topol impersonation, and belted out: *"Is this the little girl I carried? Is this the little boy at play? I don't remember growing older. When did they?"*

Elise smiled fondly at him and added, *"Swiftly go the days."* Then her expression hardened. "Seriously, Cal. You don't think that he's gonna—"

"No. There are lots of bands with families, even if the fans don't realize it. They're mostly older than us, but . . . Besides, what's Denny gonna do for money, what with a new mouth to feed? Get a job at Guitar Center?"

This comment surprised Elise. There was plenty of money. Sonic Daydream was on top. They had the potential to tour forever, even if Denny did insist on this tiresome hiatus. There would always be royalties, and Lenny had already made a few sound investments, at least for his brother and himself.

It was a silly statement for Calvin to make – world-renowned rock star Dennis Whitly having to get a job – he was already set for life, even if he quit today. Elise figured that perhaps Calvin didn't know all this. Maybe he hadn't had a peek at the books like she had.

"I wasn't thinking about Denny quitting the band, Leesy."

It was his pet name for her, and hearing him say it never failed to bring a smile to her face. Her father had called her *Leesy* on occasion. Calvin wasn't like a father to Elise – he was not quite ten years older than her, and he made too many blue comments. He drank too much. But he *was* like a big brother. He was her best friend.

"What then?"

"I was thinking . . . Denny's kinda stuck with your sister now, don't you think? It doesn't look like you're ever gonna get together, and I'm sorry about that."

He moved to give her a comforting hug, but Elise held up her hand. *"I don't need no arms around me, and I don't need no drugs to calm me."*

Elise wasn't upset in the least. Calvin was amazed, but he hid it immediately, realizing that she was simply ignoring *the writing on the wall.* She was just as crazy as she wanted to be. He waited for her explanation. He waited to see the parade of her delusion once again.

"I figure it this way. This is the last tour Sophia will ever accompany him on, now isn't it? She's gonna have to stay at home, raising her baby. Denny and me . . . and you . . . we'll be on the road alone."

This was a true statement, Calvin had to give her that. But just because the mother of his child wasn't on hand, didn't mean Denny was going to all of a sudden give it to her sister. The possibility of that occurrence wouldn't just logically proceed from the truth of the first statement, to anyone but Elise. The girl was nuts.

"No. Don't think I need anything at all." Elise smiled and pinched the drummer on the cheek. Then another thought struck her and her smile fled. "You don't suppose he'll marry her, do you?"

Calvin shook his head. "Why should he? He hasn't yet. There's the whole cow and milk thing, and it might hurt records sales. All the hopeful young girls . . . They're not as interested in paying to see a married singer."

Dennis Whitly was Calvin's brother musician and all, and he felt a little prick of disloyalty at bad-mouthing him. But just a little prick. He liked Elise, felt sorry for her, trapped as she was inside this impossible dream from which she refused to wake up.

Even though he would miss her, Calvin thought that the most upstanding and adult thing that Denny could do would be to banish Elise from touring with them. Denny knew of her love; everyone knew. They were only able to ignore it because she never mentioned it to anyone but the drummer.

Calvin thought that Sonic Daydream's multi-platinum singer/songwriter was taking advantage of Elise's devotion, as surely as if he gave her a tumble in the back of the bus some night, and then kicked her to the curb in the morning. The honorable thing to do – and hadn't Denny become all honorable since he'd met Sophia? The honorable thing would be for him to send Elise back home. She might be hurt for a while, but it would give her the opportunity to move on, to forget this obsession.

But Denny wasn't going to get rid of Elise. Sophia still wanted to keep an eye on her, and as long as Sophia was around, Denny was able to hide behind her, was able to ignore the fact that Elise forever had her hopeful eye *on him.* And Lenny used her for her topnotch managerial skills. It all just struck Calvin as unfair. Elise was bat-shit crazy for Dennis Whitly, and all of them just let her go on with it.

Calvin thought that her sister or Denny himself should apply a little tough love to Elise. Sit her down, tell her how it was, how it was always gonna be. Denny and Sophia were going to be parents, for Christ's sake. If that didn't cement their already fairy-tale romance . . . But Elise didn't see it that way. All she could see was Sophia out of the way, at home with the baby, and Denny alone on the road, at her disposal.

Somebody should make her see reality, Calvin thought. *But it isn't going to be me.*

****

When they returned to the States, Denny took some of his rock star megabucks and bought a house in Malibu, on Pacific Coast Highway, near the foot of Decker Road. Sam Elliott, who would go on to star in *Tombstone* a few years later, was their neighbor.

"Good money squandered," Calvin said in an aside to Elise. "What's wrong with Riverside?"

Elise looked out at the crashing surf, then back at her friend in amazement. "No beach in Riverside, Cal."

"I hate the beach," he informed her.

But the band did go back to Riverside, in secret, immediately after Denny and Sophia and Elise settled into their new digs. It wasn't so they could play a gig at The House of Ale, for old times' sake. That would've blocked off downtown, closed streets, caused a riot. Sonic Daydream had filled Wembly Stadium. Dennis Whitly couldn't even show his face in the little hometown bar where he and his band had gotten their start, nonetheless play there. It would've almost been like Mick Jagger and his mates dropping in for a pint at a tiny London pub.

Despite what Calvin had theorized and what Elise had hoped, the band accompanied their singer back home for his wedding. It was a small ceremony, held in the bride's house. At a time before the internet dominated the world, it was easy to keep the event off the radar, out of

Rolling Stone. Only immediate family and a few good friends were invited.

When Calvin looked askance at Elise in her maid-of-honor finery, she had simply shrugged. "He has to give his baby a name. Divorces happen all the time."

She'll never give up, the drummer said to himself.

Lenny paid off his parents' mortgage and then took up residence in Sophia and Elise's old house in Riverside. Somebody had to look after it, since they were now beach dwellers. Ernie purchased a large, secluded place on Victoria Avenue, not far from where they'd all gone to high school.

Sonic Daydream was due back on the road by mid-November, another tour crisscrossing these great United States. They would be gone through April, so Calvin thought it would be foolish to be picking out real estate like his bandmates. If he bought a house now, he'd just need to find someone to look after it while he was gone, as his bandmates would have to do.

And who knew what would happen after May, after Dennis Whitly's heir made its appearance? Calvin stayed with his parents until the tour resumed. He'd decide what to do for a place to live when he found out if there was still going to be a band, after Denny's kid was born.

****

Almost three years to the day that her parents met, Valerie Denise Whitly arrived, on May 7th, 1991. Her mother and her well-known father were both twenty-four, and her Aunt Elise was not quite twenty. Sophia checked into the hospital under her maiden name, so the news of a daughter being born to the famous singer never made the papers. Married-daddy rock stars didn't sell a lot of records.

James Brown might've been the hardest working musician in show business, but the young men of Sonic Daydream weren't far behind. When his baby was six weeks old, Denny took his show back on the road, to make up the tour dates canceled due to his brief paternity leave. His wife and daughter stayed at home in Malibu. Auntie Elise packed her kit and got on the bus with the band.

In Kansas City, Calvin noticed an increase in her wistful, longing stares at Denny. He hardly would've thought such a thing possible, yet there it was. The tour was almost over; three more shows and they'd be catching a big bird back to California. Elise's time alone with Denny –

except that Denny made doubly sure never to be alone with her – was running out.

Calvin decided to sneak up on the situation. "Didn't you used to date a guitar player once?"

Elise wondered where this factoid of ancient history had come from. "Yeah. But not the one I wanted."

"Why don't you look him up when we get home?"

Elise barked laughter. "Why would I ever want to do that? He's in college by now, I'm sure. He probably doesn't even play anymore, and if he does, it's probably the same kind of boring frat parties that you guys used to play. Carl is no Dennis Whitly."

Calvin ignored that remark, shrugged. "We all gotta start somewhere."

"Why would I ever want to . . . That would be quite a step down for me, don't you think? I'm co-manager of the greatest band in the world. I draw an obscene salary from Sony Records."

It was true. Lenny had insisted that the label put Elise on the payroll, the moment she turned eighteen. He was not much more than a figurehead manager nowadays. Not even twenty yet, Elise did damn near all the work, and made bank as long as Sonic Daydream was on tour.

"It's the good life, huh?" Calvin said, and studied her closely. "Always on the road, with the greatest band in the world – that's a laugh."

"You must be too busy to count your money, my friend."

"Making money doesn't make us great, Leesy."

"It sure beats playing frat parties." Elise eyed him curiously. "What are you trying to say, Cal?"

"I dunno. I'm gonna sound like a hypocrite, but . . . Maybe this isn't the life for you. Maybe, when we get back home, you should . . . I dunno. Stay there. Go to school. Find somebody . . . Find somebody that's gonna love you back."

There. He'd said it.

Elise was silent for a minute. "Life is long, Cal. Denny . . . All you guys. You need me right now. The tour–"

"The tour's almost over, Leesy. We're taking a year off, remember? To record? So Denny can get a chance to be a daddy, to dandle his daughter on his knee?"

"That won't last."

There it was, the insanity that she spoke aloud to no one but him. "Why won't it last, Elise? Surely, you have to see that Sophia and the baby aren't gonna just disappear—"

"Denny's stuck now, Cal. He's saddled with these . . . *responsibilities*. But what use are they to him? She can't even come with him anymore. Life is long. Someday, he's gonna see—"

"He loves her, Elise! When are you going to realize that?"

Elise smiled slyly. "Maybe. Maybe not. He's stuck with her now, true, but . . . Love can be a tricky thing, Cal."

Calvin couldn't contain his pity. He asked quietly, "What do you know about love, Leesy?"

"You love me, don't you, Cal?" Elise said brightly. She touched his cheek, and the drummer flinched. "You're just trying to look out for me."

"I would love you, Elise, if I thought it would make you forget about Denny."

Calvin was shocked at his own words. *Now I sound just as crazy as she does. I don't love her, and she's never gonna forget about Denny.* It was a stupid, ridiculous thing to say. It wasn't love, it was pity that he felt for Elise, and he suddenly hoped that she wouldn't transfer all her mindless, obsessive, insane groupie love to *him* at his thoughtless words. *Don't you step, step too close; you might catch it.*

But of course, that would never happen.

Again that sly smile. "I love you, too, Cal. You're the only friend I've got. Like I say, life is long, and I've got this hope inside me . . . What do you want me to do, sit around in that big house on the beach? Babysit?"

"You could take some of that record label big-money and you could—"

"I could what, Cal? Go back to Riverside? Scare up no-talent Carl and his garage band?"

"We were a garage band. My garage, as a matter of fact."

"You were a *good* garage band." Elise paused. "You can't honestly expect me to go back to the old boring life, now that I've toured with—"

"The greatest band in the world. I know."

Calvin saw the futility of it all. He wasn't Sigmund Freud. He couldn't *talk* Elise out of her delusion.

Elise hugged him, kissed him noisily on the cheek. *"How ya gonna keep 'em down on the farm, after they've seen Paree?"*

Here was another layer to her craziness, another lie Elise told to herself. It wasn't just Denny that kept her with the band. It was the road. It was the biz. It was rock and roll.

Calvin sighed. Elise would never stop. He wouldn't bring it up again.

****

When Elise at long last turned twenty-one, she was again, *still*, on tour with Sonic Daydream.

Dennis Whitly had been true to his word and had taken a year off to watch his baby grow. The band had recorded and released two new records in that year. Denny discovered that he had a lot of time on his hands, about the same time that he discovered that babies don't do a whole lot, and the studio was just up the road in LA. On top of all that, Sonic Daydream's frontman was nothing if not a prolific songwriter. Both albums went platinum. The fans clamored to hear them performed live.

Valerie turned a year old on May 7th, 1992, and by the end of July, her daddy and his band were back on the road.

By Elise's birthday in October, the tour was almost over. They had just played another sold-out show in San Diego. Sophia had planned to bring Denny's daughter down from the beach, to meet up with her husband and watch him perform, but Valerie had a little sniffle, so mother and child had stayed home. One more show in LA the next night, and the tour would be concluded. The next one wasn't scheduled to start until the new year. Denny had demanded the time off. He wanted to spend the holidays with his family for a change.

Denny was bummed that he hadn't been permitted to see his wife, and even though it would be just another twenty-four hours or so before they would be reunited, his disappointment led him to have a little too much to drink at Elise's birthday celebration. The party took place at the Hotel Del Coronado, that playground of presidents and celebrities, far away from the flocks of fans that had come to hear him sing that night.

Elise had booked the accommodations personally. The hotel was historic, secluded, romantic. She hoped she might persuade Denny to take a walk on the beach with her after the festivities. No one would see them if she requested that he give her a little kiss for her birthday . . .

But Denny was drunk, and would not be budged from his seat in the banquet room Elise had reserved for her party. He gave her quite the thrill, anyway, even if he refused to take a walk on the beach with her. Egged on by Ernie, Denny plopped Elise down in his lap and sang *Happy Birthday* to her. A million young women, worldwide, would have thought themselves died and gone to heaven at such a treat.

Elise took full advantage of Denny's drunken, unaccustomed friendliness, this always dreamt-of closeness to the man she loved. She wrapped her arms lightly around his neck, gazed into his eyes as he sang. The tune completed, Calvin and Lenny and Ernie cheered, and Elise kissed Denny, right on the mouth. Everyone was drunk, so she figured that no one would either notice or care. Denny just smiled good-naturedly at her, startled at the intimacy.

Uncharacteristically, Calvin was the least drunk of the celebrants, and he read the truth behind Denny's smiling surprise: Elise had fooled him. He had let his guard down, and she had used his momentary inattention, his simple brotherly friendliness on her birthday, as an excuse to lay one on him. Nothing had changed. His marriage to her sister, the birth of their child; none of that mattered to Elise. She still wanted Dennis Whitly, and if he had ignored it before, here it was, once again in his face, in his lap.

But before the singer could look around for one of his bandmates to remove this now embarrassing burden, before Elise could make a fool of herself and whisper, *I love you, Denny!* into his ear – Calvin could almost see the words forming in her mind – the drummer grabbed her by the hand and pulled her to her feet.

"Let's dance, Leesy." Calvin nodded at a waiter waiting nearby. They had such good service here. The uniformed kid hit a button on the sound system, and the timeless guitar riff to *Johnny B. Goode* poured out of tastefully hidden speakers. Calvin spun the birthday girl out to the length of his arm, as if either of them knew how to dance.

They made a game try of it anyway, and when Chuck sang, *His mother told him, 'Someday you will be a man, and you will be the leader of a big ol' band,'* Elise glanced over her shoulder at Denny. He was yukking it up with his brother and Ernie. Elise was ignored, their brief kiss forgotten.

But Elise had not forgotten it. She had at last been near Denny again, after five years of touring with him. She had at last kissed him again, just like on that long-ago night in Riverside, when he had so obviously wanted her, before his despised brother had narced her off. Before Sonic Daydream was signed, before they had toured the world, before they had made millions. Before Denny had met, knocked up and married her dumb-luck sister.

Elise could still taste Denny on her lips. He had sat her in his lap, had sung to her! He wasn't thinking about Sophia any more. Elise was elated. This was the best birthday ever!

She turned and smiled at her dance partner. "Still love me, Cal?"

The drummer had not missed Elise's glance at the singer. He could see the insane light of her obsession dancing in her eyes. *She's never gonna give up.*

"Of course, Leesy. Happy birthday." Cal stood still for her exuberant hug. He knew he was playing Denny's stand in.

****

Elise's elation persisted through the next day and night, because Denny continued to be inordinately friendly to her. He had even given her a hug after the show in LA, had thanked her, had told her how important she was to him, told her that the band couldn't exist without her. The idea that his good mood might be because he was looking forward to seeing Sophia and Valerie did not occur to her.

Denny had a God-given talent for the guitar, and God had also gifted him with another talent that his bandmates envied. Denny could drop off to sleep immediately on the tour bus, stay asleep for the entire trip, awaken refreshed. Not even stiff.

Lenny would do paperwork until sleep overtook him. Calvin would stare out the window until he nodded off – *we got time to think of the ones we love, while the miles roll away* – although he didn't have a love at the present, at least not one anyone had ever heard about. It seemed like Ernie hardly ever slept on the bus, instead playing *Tetris* on his GameBoy, relentlessly, until Lenny would yell at him to turn that *mindless, electronic, Russian shit* off.

Elise was like Denny: she could also curl up and fall asleep effortlessly on the bus. He sometimes came to her in her dreams, and these same dreams always seemed more real, more frequent, when he was sleeping just a few seats over from her. It was the nearest, really, that she ever got to be to him.

The praise that Denny had given to her after the show still sung in her heart as she gazed at him now, asleep across the aisle. They were going home; it was just a short trip down Highway 1 to Malibu, but Denny was getting a little catnap in, anyway. After the bus dropped him and Elise off, it would take Lenny and Calvin and Ernie back to Riverside, like a chartered Greyhound. Elise had booked it that way.

Elise would miss the thrill of the road until the next tour started, and she would miss standing backstage and hearing Denny sing. As for the rest of the band – *Here come the jesters, one, two, three, it's all part of my fantasy* – she would miss Cal. She knew he loved her, but because he knew it could never be, he had settled for being her best friend. The other two – suspicious, loathed Lenny, and horndog Ernie – they could go straight to hell as far as Elise was concerned.

Elise considered Calvin, seated beside her as always, staring out the window at the darkness. She wondered again if he had a girlfriend in Riverside, someone he loved in addition to herself. Maybe she was another snooty music buff like he was. Or maybe she was also a musician, beautiful and talented, above mention to his peasant, rock and roll bandmates. Elise often imagined what Calvin's perhaps fictional girlfriend must be like – maybe she was a concert pianist; maybe she played the violin in a string quartet. Maybe she was a ballerina. If she existed at all, he had never spoken of her.

"Are you looking forward to seeing your parents?"

Calvin turned from the window, and his eyebrows went up in mild surprise. Was Elise asking him a question about him? Was she talking about something besides herself for a change, something besides Denny and her depthless love for him? *My God, she must be getting . . . what? Sentimental? in her old age.*

"It'll be good to be home."

"For a little while."

"What about you? Are you looking forward to seeing your sister and your niece?"

Are you looking forward to Denny immediately forgetting your existence in favor of showering his affection on them? And after the baby is put down to sleep, are you looking forward to imagining what he and your sister'll be doing then? Surely you can't hear them in that giant cave of a house, but you'll know, nonetheless, won't you? Looking forward to that, are ya, Leesy?

"Actually, I can't wait to see Valerie. I bought her a teddy bear in Dallas. She loves her Auntie Elise."

At least one of them does, Calvin thought sourly. His pity for her choked him. It would be good to go back home for a while, to get away from his best friend – *Christ, how did I wind up with a love-sick kid as my best friend? It's not even me that she loves.* It would be good to get away from Elise's sad, fruitless obsession. Until the next tour.

Calvin went back to contemplating the silent freeway, and Elise took out her compact, checked her look. Satisfied, she closed it, and peeked over at Denny again.

Elise had always been confident in her attractiveness. Not unlike Sonic Daydream's frontman, she'd had her own besotted fans over the years. There had been Sammy and Carl, and before them, all the other boys back home. There had been the tattooed roadie in Germany that had given her a small bouquet of flowers after the show, had stammered, "Du bist schön, Ich liebe dich!" *You're beautiful, I love you!*

"Danke, aber ich habe einen Freund," she'd replied with false shyness. *Thank you, but I have a boyfriend.* The inked *Deutsch Mann* had not been her only admirer overseas. Elise had learned the phrase in several languages.

If Ernie lacked a groupie, he still smiled hopefully at her. Elise knew that Ernie wanted her, that all she would have to do was return his smile. And she knew that Calvin loved her.

She was grown now, finally twenty-one, finally come into the stunning beauty that she had inherited from her mother. Yet she was still young, fresh; not worn out by the tribulations of motherhood like her sister. Elise told herself that Denny had become more appreciative of this fact during the last leg of the tour. Hadn't he been friendlier, more . . . *available,* sitting her in his lap and singing to her? Hadn't he let her kiss him? Hadn't he told her how much he appreciated her?

Elise was sure that Denny was just about through with the albatross around his neck that waited just down the road. How many singers had left their boring wives for their managers or girls in their band? Springsteen had done it, just a couple of years ago, dumped his actress wife and took up with the hometown girl that sung back-up for him. Once Denny was confronted with the reality of his tiresome old wife again, Elise was sure he would also come to his senses.

She was confident that they would get together, as soon as the next tour started. Then he would divorce Sophia, provide her with – what was it called? *Alimony.* Denny would send Sophia back to Riverside with *alimony* to pay her way, and then it would be the two of them together in the big house in Malibu. Denny and Elise, together at last, in love, on the beach, on tour. Just the two of them. And Valerie.

Elise began to picture Valerie as her own. She was sure that Denny was tiring of Sophia; she was old, and old news, as well, was she not? Elise was vibrant, alive, and Denny was noticing that. Hadn't he given her a hug after the show tonight? Hadn't he told her how important she was to him and the band? Weren't they already friends? He would divorce Sophia soon enough. He didn't need her. She wasn't there on tour with him like Elise was.

But Denny would always love his daughter, so Elise planned to shower her niece with all the love of which she was capable, all the love that wasn't held in reserve for Denny.

Denny didn't divorce Sophia when they arrived home, but Elise still clung to her fantasy of her and Denny and Valerie together someday, a little, happy, rock and roll family.

The years passed, and Elise became the best aunt a little girl could've wished for. She sent Valerie presents from the road. Almost every mail delivery was like Christmas morning for Sophia and Denny's daughter. When the band was at home, Elise took Valerie on shopping trips, took her to Disneyland.

When Sonic Daydream played locally, Elise would take the time out of her busy schedule and hire a limousine, especially to fetch Val from the beach. She would take the little girl backstage and show her around, make sure that she had earplugs when the band performed.

"Isn't your daddy great?"

Someday, it would just be Elise and Denny. And Valerie.

****

In May of 1999, Elise Carlin was twenty-seven years old, would be twenty-eight in October. She'd been touring with Sonic Daydream for more than a decade. She'd become besotted with Dennis Whitly as a sixteen-year-old girl at a frat party, the moment she had heard him sing. It was not an uncommon occurrence: a million girls, worldwide, had fallen in love with Sonic Daydream's frontman over the years. He was mesmerizing: incredibly sexy, yet boyishly adorable, awesomely talented.

But he was also utterly unachievable, and while he would always have a special place in all their hearts and memories and fantasies, his legions of admirers would go on to find their own, in-real-life loves. Not so his Number One Fan. Dennis Whitly would remain the only man Elise would ever want. She knew it, and somehow, deep down, she was sure he knew it, too. She would love Denny until she died.

Sonic Daydream came off of their latest tour on May 7th, Valerie's eighth birthday. The day before had been their last show, in Frisco, and now the band was in LA, finishing up some business with the record label. Denny and Elise cut out of the meeting early and took a limo home.

The sun was on its way down when they arrived. They had not been expected until the next morning, but early in the tour, Denny had decided that come hell or high water, boring meetings with Sony or not, he would be back home in time to surprise his little girl on her birthday.

Valerie was indeed surprised. She squealed and joyfully hugged her daddy and her beloved aunt. Sophia, on the other hand, was not as impressed.

"I wish you would've let me know," she replied flatly to her husband's I've-missed-you hugs and kisses. "We're having a birthday party for Valerie in a little while."

Denny glanced around questioningly at the lack of cake, presents, decorations, or guests.

"It's at the club. It was Sondra's idea."

The club was the Malibu Golf Club, a few miles up the hill off Decker Road. Sondra was the wife of one of their famous neighbors, an actor or director or some such. Denny couldn't remember exactly which. He seemed to recall that Sondra had a little girl – or maybe it was a little boy – about Valerie's age.

"But I wanted to spend some time with you guys tonight–"

"That's why I wish you would've told me you'd be home early," Sophia snapped. Elise blinked at her uncharacteristic churlishness.

"It's been planned for weeks. We have a life besides just waiting for the band to come home, you know." Denny's eyes widened at this remark. "Val wants to go to this birthday party, Denny. She wants to see her friends. Don't disappoint her."

Not wanting to deal with his wife's pique, Denny leaned over and said to his daughter, "Do you want to go to the party, Valley?"

"Yes, Daddy. But you'll still be here when we get back, won't you?"

The little girl's question stung Denny. *'When ya comin' home, Dad?' 'I don't know when, but we'll get together then. You know we'll have a good time then.'* That was why he'd made sure to be home a day early. He'd wanted to surprise his baby on her birthday.

"Yes. Your auntie and me – we'll be home for a while." He hugged Valerie and coaxed a smile out of her mother.

That's a lie, Elise thought. The next tour was scheduled to begin in about six weeks.

"I'll see you when we get back, Daddy. Come on, Mommy, let's go!"

Valerie tugged on Sophia's hand, and Denny thought, *He walked away but his smile never dimmed, it said, 'I'm gonna be like him. Yeah, you know, I'm gonna be like him.'* Denny had a flash of fear. He didn't want his daughter's life, his life, to be like Harry Chapin's cautionary tale about busy fathers and neglected children.

"Take the limo," Elise suggested. "It's still waiting outside."

LM *Foster*

Denny had planned to take them all down the coast to dinner, had slipped the driver a $50 and asked him to wait. Now those plans were shot. Elise reveled in this little spot of trouble in paradise. She saw that Denny was miffed, although he hid it well.

Sophia kissed him perfunctorily on the cheek, told him that she would see him later, took Valerie by the hand. Elise went outside with them to instruct the limo driver on his new destination. Sophia said he didn't have to wait through the party; that would cost a fortune. She would get a ride home with Sondra.

As she went back into the big house, Elise had a revelation. It made her stop short. She and Denny were alone. No band, no promoters, no roadies, no fans; no Sophia, no Valerie. After all these years, alone at last.

Can you break away from your alibis, can you make a play, will you meet me in the dark?

Elise thought she would soothe Denny now, *right now*. She'd make him forget all about Sophia, troublesome, suddenly head-strong, getting-long-in-the-tooth . . .

She found him still standing in the kitchen, where he had surprised wife and daughter with his early arrival. He still had a confused, slightly put-out, somewhat worried expression on his face.

Oh, Denny, I love you so much! I'm gonna make it all better!

His next words thrilled Elise, convinced her that everything she had ever dreamed was indeed finally going to occur.

"I guess it's just you and me then. What do you want for dinner?"

Besides being a splendid musician, Denny was also a great cook. He'd often missed dinner in high school, what with his solo practicing and all, so he'd learned to feed himself as well as he'd learned to play the guitar.

"Whatever you want to make, Denny," Elise replied softly.

She was still a little bit awed that it was going to be just the two of them tonight, that he'd be cooking only for her. She knew it would be a labor of love for Denny. He spent a great deal of time on the road, so it was always a joy for him to come home and cook a couple of meals for Sophia and Valerie. But they were gone. It was only him and Elise now, the way it was soon going to always be.

After dinner, they would consummate this new relationship that was to come. Sophia had been snappish, rude. She was obviously tired of the life of a rock star's wife. Denny had seen her boredom. She didn't love him anymore, and in the morning, after he'd spent a little quality time in bed with Elise, he'd tell her he wanted a divorce. Sophia would go back to Riverside, evict Lenny from their old house, and then

104

it would be just Elise and Denny – Valerie would visit on the weekends, when they were in town – it would be just Elise and Denny and Valerie. Forever.

Elise said, "I'm just going to go take a quick shower first."

Denny was peering into the giant, stainless steel, side-by-side refrigerator, deciding what he would make. He waved absently without looking at her.

****

Elise took more than a quick shower. She shaved her legs, then powdered and perfumed. She quickly changed the sheets on her bed – Denny wouldn't want to take her to the one that he had formerly shared with his wife. She put on a little makeup.

Elise pawed through the second drawer to her dresser, the one that contained the exotic lingerie she'd purchased while they'd toured the big cities in the States, the grand capitols of Europe. No lucky young man had ever seen her in any of it; there had been no lucky young men. There had only ever been Denny, if just in her imagination, and Elise had purchased all the barely-there negligees, the garter belts and silk Mandarin robes for him. Now she would at last get to model one of them.

She chose a shiny, lacy black camisole and shorts set. She admired herself in the mirror, decided that Denny couldn't help but love it. She was about to skip down the stairs and claim her long-awaited prize, when another thought occurred to her. Maybe she was being a trifle premature.

There was still dinner to be served. Denny had volunteered to cook for her, something he enjoyed. Maybe she shouldn't rush him through that. She pulled a pair of jeans and a T-shirt on over her unmentionables and went back downstairs.

****

After *Happy Birthday* was sung and her daughter had opened all of her presents, Sophia took Sondra aside.

"Thanks again for throwing Valerie this great party."

Sondra laughed, a high, carefree, tinkling sound, stuffed full of money. "It was nothing. It's fun to amuse the little ones."

Sondra certainly didn't have a lot else to do. Her director husband was on location; she had a staff to keep up her grand house, down the beach from Sophia and Denny's. Her devotion to amusing her son

Markie, eight years old, was her life. Sophia thought Markie was a bit of a spoiled brat, and she hoped that Valerie, daughter of a famous entertainer, child of wealth and privilege, wouldn't turn out the same way.

Sophia marveled, as she frequently did, that she even had to worry about such things. She remembered rides her family had taken along PCH when she was a child. Tourist-like, she had been awestruck by the mansions, never dreaming that she would someday live in one of them. She had not yet met Tom Cruise, but she had met other famous Hollywood types, actors and actresses, screenwriters and directors like her friend's husband.

Like Sondra, Sophia's biggest decisions of a day revolved around how to spend Denny's money. Gone forever were worries about whether there was going to be enough of it to cover even the basics. Sophia was wealthy now, and quite so, and sometimes how her life *might have been* made her feel like Eliza Doolittle. *All I want is a room somewhere, far away from the cold night air, with one enormous chair, ow, wouldn't it be loverly?*

And then the supreme joy of how her life *was* would hit her: *Someone's 'ead restin' on my knee, warm an' tender as 'e can be, who takes good care of me* . . . More important than the money and the big house and the Mercedes, more beloved than even her darling baby girl, there was Denny.

Sophia sometimes sensed a ghost of loneliness in Sondra, a scintilla of resentment, of mistrust. Her husband was seldom at home, and his frequent absences left Sondra to speculate, after Markie was asleep, after her elegant parties were over and her sparkling and prominent guests had gone back to their own beach houses: just what exactly did her husband get up to on location?

He was surrounded by hungry starlets, as well as established divas – did he ever sample their charms? Sondra hid her suspicions well, but she had shared them with Sophia. Sondra loved her husband deeply, and as far as Sophia knew, there had never been as much as a whiff of scandal. The famous director had never given his wife any reasons to doubt him. But infidelities happened every day in show biz. Late nights in discreet hotels, the thrill of that day's shooting, a future starring role; a famous director, loyalty forgotten at a few whispered words, a momentary lapse in judgment . . .

Dennis Whitly was a world-renowned rock star, and Sophia knew that his life on the road presented him with far more opportunities for intrigue than a film director. While actresses and script girls might eye Sondra's husband as a ticket to further their own careers, all the groupies wanted was a chance to *love* Sophia's husband, if only for one night. And there were thousands of them, worldwide, after every single show.

But the possibility of Denny cheating on her with nameless fans had not once crossed Sophia's mind. Denny wasn't the sex-god with a guitar that he portrayed to the world. That was Ernie LaBelle's shtick. For Dennis Whitly, it was all just an act, the part he played, and his wife knew it. She knew who he truly was. She had never doubted him for a split second, from the very night they had met.

****

Elise had eaten dinner with Denny thousands of times, in hotels and restaurants around the globe, at her ancestral home in Riverside, as well as in this very house. But upon reflection, Elise realized that she and Denny had never dined alone. She couldn't recall one single time.

She sat at the kitchen table and watched him cook. The room was brightly lit: there was neither seductive candlelight nor soft mood music. Dennis Whitly, rock god, sang, *No sugar tonight in my coffee, no sugar tonight in my tea, no sugar to stand beside me, no sugar to run with me*, softly to himself, as he moved between fridge and counter and stove. Yet it was the most romantic moment Elise had ever encompassed.

Denny made steak and eggs. It was an odd selection for dinner, but Elise was grateful for the hearty choice. She intended to *devour* Denny in a minute, to release the swirling storm of a decade of pent up desire. He would need all his strength just to keep up with her.

They made small talk about the tour just past, the new tour that would soon begin. Elise noticed that Denny purposefully avoided mentioning his wife. *That's because he's already forgotten about her. He's thinking about me now.*

When dinner was over, Elise dutifully helped to load the dishwasher. When the task was almost completed, she darted out of the kitchen, quickly doffed her street clothes. She returned to pose in the doorway in her lacy finery.

In the middle of some comment about the band, Denny happened to glance in her direction, and the statement died on his lips. His train of thought disappeared into a dark tunnel and was forgotten.

Long ago, in their hometown, when she was just sixteen, Elise had offered this same seductive smile. *"Let's get together*, Denny, *before we get much older. What I'm dying to say is that I'm crazy for you."* When he didn't speak, she thought, *Eye to eye, we need no words at all* . . .

Denny shook his head: *Elise and her song lyrics.* He considered it an odd pairing – The Who and Madonna – but he had to admit it was one of the most original come-ons he'd ever heard. It beat the hell out of *Oh, Denny, I just love the way you sing,* or *You must get so lonely on the road.* But he had no time to admire his sister-in-law's originality, because she was as serious as the oft-mentioned heart attack. She stepped out of the door frame and closed the distance between them.

Elise tenderly caressed Denny's cheek. He took her wrist. Next, he would kiss her hand, then he would say, "Let's go upstairs, Elise. You've waited long enough."

But Denny didn't do that. When she tried to lean into him, to kiss him, his grip tightened on her wrist. He gently pushed her back a step, then dropped her hand. He took a step back himself.

"We need to talk, Elise."

She giggled prettily. *"There's nothing left to talk about 'les it's horizontally."*

Now, I have heard that one before. If she says, 'Let's get physical,' I might just laugh in her face.

"Seriously. You need to go put some clothes on. This is just . . . silly."

"I love you, Denny," Elise said softly. Her blue eyes sparkled; the pupils were huge and black with desire, with anticipation.

"I know you do," he returned, just as quietly.

Denny had ignored that look in her eyes for all the years he'd known her, at home, on the road, in a thousand towns. He had hidden from it behind his bandmates and his wife, and by doing so, for all these years, he'd managed to avoid just such a repeat of wild Elise's attempts at seduction.

But it was only the two of them now, alone, and Denny couldn't avoid the elephant in the room any longer. He was going to have to tell her no, just like he'd done when she was sixteen, the one thing that he'd never wanted to have to do again. She was a great kid, an invaluable asset to his band. She was his wife's sister, his daughter's aunt, but . . . "You're being ridiculous, Elise."

Like a petulant child, she stamped her bare foot on the kitchen's tile. "Why am I being ridiculous? I love you, Denny!"

"And I love you, too," Denny lied. She had never been anything but an embarrassment to him, despite her business prowess. His wife's kid sister, always hanging around, mooning over him. When the brothers Whitly were alone, Lenny still made fun of him about it.

The time had come for it to end. Elise had to *stop.*

"I love you like my little sister. But look at yourself, Elise. You're standing in *your* sister's kitchen, trying to seduce her husband. That's not a very lovable thing–"

"I don't care, Denny–"

"That's just it. You've never cared. *I love you, Denny, I love you* – but what about everyone else's feelings? What about Sammy and Carl? They loved you. What about Sophia and Valerie? Your niece loves you more than anything, Elise. And Sophia . . . I tried to tell her – maybe you'd be better off at home, away from the road, away from me – but she always said, 'No, take her with you, she enjoys it so much.'

"Sophia trusts you, Elise. She loves you. She's always looked after you–"

"I've always looked after myself."

"Still, is this any way to treat your only sister? How would she feel if she came home right now and saw you standing here in your underwear, alone with me?"

Elise only tilted her chin up defiantly. Denny sighed. Elise didn't care about her sister's feelings. There was no other way. He was going to have to tell her, once and for all. He was going to have to hurt her.

"This is never gonna happen, Elise. Not in a thousand lifetimes. Not even if your sister dropped dead tomorrow. You're a great kid. You're the little sister I never had. But it's never gonna be . . ." Denny gestured at her lingerie. "It's never gonna be like that. We'll always be friends, but that's all we're ever gonna be. You have to stop, honey. You're embarrassing yourself, you're embarrassing me . . . You're embarrassing the band.

"Go on, now. Put some clothes on, and we'll just go on like this never happened. You've gotta see reason, Elise. You've gotta accept the way things are." And then Denny delivered the coup de grace: "Can you do that for me?"

Can you face the fire when you see me there, can you feel the fire, will you love me in the dark?

No. Denny would never love her. She'd finally asked, and in no uncertain terms, he'd told her.

Elise felt as if some kind of controlled demolition was occurring inside her. The explosions were like sparks behind her eyes, making them water, as floor after floor collapsed. All that she was: competent manager, Dennis Whitly's loyal, Number One Fan – had she ever been anything more than that, really? – all of it fell into ruin in Elise's mind.

Reality shoved Rationalization out of the way like a linebacker guarding his quarterback. Reality played for a team called The Truth,

109

and Elise saw all at once that she'd lost the game. Rationalization, now on injured-reserve, had always been her star player.

Elise nodded slowly. She would not let Denny see her cry, would not give him something else about which to have a good chuckle with his loathsome brother. *You shoulda seen her, Lenny, just like any other sobbing fan. 'No' was definitely not the answer she expected.*

Hardy har har.

Elise took a deep breath. "I would like to get some air, though. Maybe take a little drive. Can I borrow the car?"

Denny studied her. Not for a second did he believe that it could be that easy. Elise had spent her entire adult life *in love with him.* She wasn't going to give up her enduring fantasy with a simple nod of her head, just because he had finally made things clear to her. But what else could he say?

Denny opened a drawer, located the spare set of car keys. He arced them through the air to her.

Elise caught them deftly. *I've always been so perfectly in sync with him . . .*

They stared at each other for another moment, while Elise watched all the dreams of *what could have been* circle the drain. At last, she cleared her throat. "Well. I'll just go change first."

She bolted from the kitchen and bounded up the stairs to her room, wiping away the hot tears of pain and embarrassment. She tore off her clothes and viciously stuffed the lacy underthings back into the drawer with their fellows. They were all worthless. Denny would never love her.

It was all Sophia's fault.

Denny looked at the place Elise had stood, then he sighed and pushed the button on the dishwasher. He looked out the window at the darkness, sorry that he'd had to hurt her. But she had left him no choice. There had been no other way.

A few minutes later, he heard the muted slam of the front door.

****

As she watched Valerie and the other children play musical chairs in the country club's brightly decorated banquet room, Sophia considered that, despite the fact that she loved Denny, despite the fact that she was now and believed that she would always be *in love* with him, she had been a little short with him tonight. She felt a pang of guilt about how she'd treated him.

"Could you do me a little favor, Sondra? Denny came home a day early, and I was wondering if you might keep Valerie tonight." This same plan had already been in place for tomorrow night, when Denny had been expected to arrive. Sophia had also agreed to do the same for Sondra, to keep Markie when her husband's latest blockbuster concluded.

Valerie had seen her daddy. The fun of spending the night at Auntie Sondra's house would make up for any disappointment that she might have over not seeing him again until tomorrow. Mommy and Daddy needed an evening alone.

Again, Sondra's tinkling laughter. She *was* happy, most of the time. "Of course, Sophie. I'll keep her for as long as you like. Markie'll be thrilled to have her. He's got quite the little crush on her, you know. Who knows? Maybe we'll be related someday!"

Of course Valerie'll marry into money, Sophia thought. *After all, she was born into it, unlike her mother or her father. Lots of choc'lates for Val to eat, lots of coal makin' lots of 'eat. Warm face, warm 'ands, warm feet, ow, wouldn't it be loverly?*

Sophia thanked Sondra and took out her phone to call Denny, to tell him that she was sorry that she had snapped at him, to tell him how much she'd missed him. To tell him that she'd be seeing him very soon. She was surprised when the Nokia rang in her hand.

"I'm out in the parking lot," Elise said. "I thought I'd give you guys a ride home."

****

On the drive up Decker Road to the country club, Reality-with-a-capital-R sneered in Elise's mind in a cackling voice, thick with sarcasm and false sympathy. *Was it worth it, honey? All the great, fantastical imaginings, the excited hopes; the limitless possibilities and the contemplation thereof . . . Will they keep you warm at night now that Denny has shown you the stark concreteness of* This is never, ever, ever gonna happen? *Were all the miles and days and nights and wasted years worth it?*

Just what the hell are you going to do now?

****

111

Denny decided to take a nap on the couch while he waited for his family's return. How long could a little kid's birthday party last? It had to be over soon. He would just catch a few Zs, forget about the unpleasantness with Elise. Soon, his beautiful wife and darling daughter would be home, and after Daddy's happy birthday girl went to sleep, he and her mommy would at last get a chance to demonstrate how much they'd missed each other . . .

He was awakened by the doorbell, ringing repeatedly, insistently. Denny felt cold and stiff. The couch wasn't as comfortable as it looked, and apparently he'd been asleep for quite a while. Greg Ham's inimitable sax played in his mind: *Who can it be now?* Denny thought briefly of his sister-in-law. *It's not the future that I can see. It's just my fantasy.*

Denny opened the door. There was a black and white police cruiser in the driveway, its lights splashing the house, alternately red then blue. There were two solemn cops, their long faces like clichés.

Sophia probably could've named a hundred movies where the sad, hushed dialogue played out in exactly the same way. A sample script would've read:

```
EXT. MALIBU BEACH MANSION - NIGHT

                FIRST COP
           (consulting notebook)
          Are you Dennis Whitly?

     SECOND COP looks at him in disbelief. Of
    course it's Dennis Whitly, the rock star.
              DENNY nods.

                FIRST COP
     Do you own a 1998 Mercedes, license number
                    -?

                SECOND COP
      (interrupting his clueless partner)
       I'm sorry, Mr. Whitly. There's been an
                 accident.

                  DENNY
                (blanching)
                My wife?
```

```
                    FIRST COP
            (consulting notebook again)
        She's on her way to the hospital. But the
        driver, Elise Carlin . . . I'm sorry, Mr.
                      Whitly.


                      DENNY
                  (chokes out)
            What about my daughter?


                   SECOND COP
        There wasn't anyone else in the car.
```

Denny recalled that Valerie had been scheduled to spend the night at the neighbor's, tomorrow, the day he was supposed to come home. Relieved, he reckoned that Sophia had sent her along after the party tonight instead, so that the two of them could be alone . . .

"Where did they take my wife?"

The first cop turned over another page in his notebook, and told Denny that Sophia was at Cedars-Sinai, hospital to Hollywood's elite. The second cop gave him further details about the accident, then, again like in a movie, he handed Denny his card. Their unpleasant task completely, the cops quickly fled into the darkness.

Denny found his cellphone in the kitchen where he'd left it. Elise had insisted on everyone in the band having one. *So I can keep track of you,* she'd said. Denny had never used it much, except to mostly ignore his sister-in-law's frequent summons, and to call Sophia from the road. But it would come in handy now. Denny pushed the button that would call his brother.

"What the fuck, Dennis? It's one o'clock in the morning!"

"There's been an accident, Lenny. Elise is . . . Elise is dead."

There was silence on the other end of the phone, then Denny heard a woman's questioning voice, her actual words inaudible. He knew it meant that Lenny was still in LA.

The astute A & R man that had plucked Sonic Daydream out of obscurity had moved on to discover other bands. Lenny had a little thing on the side with the gal from the record company that had taken his place. *Barbara. That's her name.* The one that collaborated with Elise on booking their tours. The one that cut their checks.

"What happened, Denny?"

That's the million dollar question, now isn't it?

113

"Elise and I . . . We had a fight. She was upset . . . I shouldn't have let her go . . . She must've gone to pick up Sophia at the golf club. There was a party for Valerie's birthday . . ."

"Are they all right?"

"Sophia's at Cedars. Valerie – Christ, Lenny! What's that woman's name, the one that lives down the beach? I think Valerie's with her. The cops said she wasn't in the car–"

"What happened, Denny?"

Lenny gathered his clothes from the hotel room floor. His sometime girlfriend watched him silently from the bed. Barbara gleaned that something had happened to Lenny's brother Dennis, the front for his band, the band that she represented. Barbara hadn't spoken much to the singer over the years, because he always did a fade as soon as he could whenever she met with them, if he showed up at all. She couldn't imagine any good reason why he'd be calling at one in the morning, and from Lenny's tone, she could tell that it was bad. All bad.

Barbara liked the sexy bass player. He was fun and discreet, and they never failed to have a good time whenever he was in town, so Barbara listened to his side of the conversation with a lover's concern. But her worry was also coupled with a businesswoman's more professional apprehension. If something had happened to Sonic Daydream's singer, it would affect the band's bottom line. And Sony's. And hers.

"I'll find out that woman's name and check on Valerie. I'll meet you at the hospital."

Barbara saw the agony in Lenny's eyes as he ended the call. She waited.

"There's been an accident. Elise and my sister-in-law . . . They went over the side on Mullholland Highway. Elise is dead."

Barbara covered her mouth with her hand in speechless shock. She knew Elise Carlin quite well. She was one of the best road managers in the business, and Barbara talked to her all the time when the band was on tour. She had been sitting in a meeting with Elise, just this afternoon . . .

Barbara leapt up and hugged Lenny, told him how sorry she was. Elise was more than just his road manager. She was his sister-in-law, too, Denny's wife's sister, and this blow had to be devastating. *Jesus, Denny's gotta be a mess, too . . .*

"Do you know the guy's name, the one that lives down the beach from Denny? He's an actor or a director or something?"

Barbara nodded. "Frank MacPherson." She knew quite a few of the rich and famous that lived in Malibu, up and down PCH.

114

"Could you call his wife for me? Denny's daughter is supposed to be with her."

Barbara dressed quickly, all business now. Lenny needed her to make a few phone calls. That's what she did best. "I'll get in touch with her, one way or another."

Lenny said thanks, kissed her. "They took Sophia to Cedars."

"I'll see if MacPherson's wife — her name's Sandra — no, it's Sondra. I'll see if she can keep your niece for a few days."

Lenny smiled at her through his shock and pain. "Thanks, Barbie. You're the best."

"I'm so sorry about this, Lenny." And she was, sorry for his loss, sorry for the fact that she was going to have to find a new road manager for Sonic Daydream. And where was she gonna find another Elise Carlin? The girl was a wunderkind. "I'll give you a call, as soon as I talk to Mrs. MacPherson."

Lenny nodded, kissed her again. Then he headed out into the brightly lit Los Angeles night to meet his brother.

****

Through the pain and the anesthesia, Sophia dreamed.

It was daytime, and she was standing on the side of Mulholland Highway. She glanced over the side at the rocks and scrub; she could smell the hot asphalt, the dusty sage. She looked back up the shimmering road as a school bus approached, and when the brakes huffed and stopped it on the shoulder, Sophia saw that it wasn't just any ol' school bus. It was the Partridge Family bus.

From each window, a young girl sneered out at her. Blondes, brunettes, redheads; thin, fat, big, tall and small, all wild-looking, heavily made-up: Sonic Daydream's groupies. Then the faces disappeared from the glass and became part of the distinctive, black-outlined squares of the iconic bus's famous paint-job. Twenty, a hundred of Denny's nameless fans, frowning at her, were suddenly airbrushed into the side and roof of the Partridge Family bus.

The door opened with a squeak, and Sophia looked inside. With the logic of dreams, Denny was wearing a bus-driver's hat; Elise was sitting on his lap.

Sophia's sister frowned. "You think he loves you, but where has he been, almost from the moment you met? He's been on tour with me. I've always been there for him. Maybe he loves you, but I'm his road dog. And now, after all these years . . ."

115

Elise looked at Denny with that familiar love-light in her eyes. It was an expression that Sophia had always seen there. But she had ignored it, because Denny had always ignored it.

Now, in her dream, he just smiled blankly back at his wife with that crooked, rock star's grin.

Elise kissed him on the cheek, then glared at her sister again. "This is our tour bus, Soph. You don't belong on it."

Denny moved the lever and the door snapped shut. With a wheeze and a cloud of gritty dust, the bus trundled back onto the asphalt, leaving Sophia standing in the heat on the gravel shoulder.

Then it was night, and Sophia was again sitting in the plush, snug seat of the Mercedes. It wasn't raining – the sound of thunder and rushing water and the tinkling piano were coming from the car's sound system. *Riders on the Storm.*

There's a killer on the road, his brain is squirming like a toad . . .

Elise was crying. "And now, after all these years . . ."

Sophia screamed, but couldn't quite awaken from the anesthesia, as the car again plunged through the guardrail.

****

Life changed abruptly for Valerie after the accident.

The loss of her aunt brought utter devastation to the eight-year-old's world. No more smiling, perfumed, loving hugs. No more presents, no more trips to Disneyland. No more happy conversations in which Auntie Elise gave Valerie her full attention, wherein she acted as if her niece's rambling, childish thoughts were as important to her as the proclamations of presidents. Elise had always made Valerie feel bright and clever and beautiful. And now that light in her life was gone forever.

While this life-changing hurt was still fresh and bewildering, Valerie couldn't turn to her mother for comfort, either. Sophia was at first bedridden, trapped in her room at the top of the stairs, in pain, mostly sedated. Then she was in a wheelchair, but still she never left her room. A nurse moved into Aunt Elise's old room, and brought meals and medication to Valerie's mother, helped her in and out of bed, helped her to dress and bathe. Valerie just felt underfoot.

Denny did all the things for his daughter that her mother used to do. He made her breakfast and dinner, he packed her a lunch. A cheerful, frizzy-haired lady name Cindy was hired to drive Valerie to and from school. She was Valerie's own private chauffeur, her babysitter and friend for these trips. Denny played with his daughter when she came home in the afternoons. He watched movies with her, and helped her with her homework. He sang to her, played old songs for her on an acoustic guitar.

And while Valerie was thrilled to have Daddy home all the time, she sensed that there was something different about him. He was not the same Daddy she had known before Mommy's accident. He was quieter now, distracted. He would sometimes stare out at the ocean while he was cooking dinner; he had even burnt it a few times. Denny was worried about Sophia, and he unconsciously communicated his worry to their daughter.

And then, after about six months of this sad, static lifestyle, Valerie's world suddenly changed again. Denny packed wheelchair-bond wife, uncomprehending child, and the entire earldom of Whitly and the movables thereof and returned without fanfare to his hometown.

Valerie's Uncle Lenny stayed on for a few days at Mommy's old house, until the family was settled in. Her Uncle Calvin, white-faced and silent, dropped by for a short visit, as did her Uncle Ernie.

Uncle Ernie brought her a Barbie Dream House and a Barbie Porsche Boxster and a Barbie and a Ken. Valerie thanked him and gave him a big hug, all the while thinking that the gifts were not really something that she was going to play with too often. Valerie had never had much use for dolls.

She liked to watch movies, like her Mommy. She would've preferred a poster from one she'd seen recently, such as *The Matrix* — that one was very strange and Val wasn't sure she'd completely understood it — or perhaps a poster to remind her of *The Mummy*, starring Brendan Fraser. Valerie had liked that one very much. Rachel Weisz was so beautiful, and there were scary parts and yucky parts and thrilling parts. And Valerie thought Brendan was strong and brave and pretty in his own right, just like her daddy.

Valerie visited with Sonic Daydream for a few minutes: her daddy's real brother and these other men that she had also always called *uncle*. Ernie was funny and laughing as always, but the little girl noticed that Uncle Calvin never even smiled, not once.

Valerie had not seen them all together like this for a long time, since before the accident. A pang of loss struck her young heart, and she felt the tears start again. She realized that she had *never* seen the members of Daddy's band gathered together like this, never in her short life, without Aunt Elise also being present. And Aunt Elise would never be here again.

Valerie took Nurse's hand and turned her face into her side, so Daddy wouldn't see her cry. Nurse took her back to Sophia's room so that they could watch a movie together.

Uncle Lenny soon moved out. He'd purchased a house and a big spread in Anza, California. Valerie remembered the long drive she took with her daddy up there to see it for the first time. Mommy, still confined to a wheelchair, stayed in Riverside. Uncle Lenny promised to buy Valerie a pony someday, if she wanted one.

****

From the accident that had claimed her sister's life, Sophia had sustained lacerations and contusions, had broken both legs and her left arm in three places. Elise had not been wearing a seatbelt, and had been ejected, while Sophia had remained in the vehicle while it rolled over and over down the scrubby hill. Elise was pronounced dead at the scene, but LA County's crack rescue team had saved her sister's life, had airlifted her to Cedars-Sinai.

Sophia was in surgery for several hours, and afterward it was speculated that she might never walk again. But she would not settle for that. She wasn't paralyzed, now was she? There were just a bunch of bones and muscles and tendons, damaged, that had to be taught to do their jobs again. She had to look after Valerie – it wasn't fair that Denny should become both mother and father to their daughter, while she hid in her bedroom and had dark conversations with her own self-pity.

After a year and a half of grueling physical therapy, Sophia was again on her feet. There was still pain and she would forever use a cane, like an old woman. But she returned again to the lives of her husband and child.

Denny had the Carlin's garage remodeled, enlarged, turned into a small recording studio. For the first couple of years that they lived back in Riverside, Valerie saw Ernie and Calvin and Uncle Lenny regularly. She was even permitted to sit in the studio – as long as she remained very quiet – while they recorded. After his wife's accident, Denny and Sonic Daydream released three new albums. But they never toured again.

Eventually, Calvin and Ernie stopped coming to the house. Valerie saw Uncle Lenny on holidays, and when her family visited him at his ranch, but Calvin and Ernie faded from her life. Denny told her that Ernie had started another band. He played a few of their tracks for her, but these sounded the same as the tunes she'd heard all her life. Ernie's new band sounded just like Sonic Daydream to Valerie.

When she asked if Uncle Calvin had found a new band, too, Denny said something about *a little studio work,* then shrugged. The drummer didn't keep in touch.

The sacks of fan mail still came in, and the royalties, although Valerie wasn't aware of how any of that worked. All she knew was that her dad didn't leave for weeks and months at a time anymore. He and Uncle Lenny sometimes jammed in the record-lined room upstairs, or in the converted garage in the backyard, and other bands sometimes recorded there. Her dad sometimes wrote songs for them, and even played and sang on a couple of their records. But Sonic Daydream was no more.

The calliope crashed to the ground.

****

Valerie attended the best private schools that her father's rock and roll money could buy. As she went through the grades, fellow students and even teachers eventually ceased saying, "You're Denny Whitly's daughter? I love his music!"

The new records sold well. The fan mail still came in, but it dwindled as the years passed. Sonic Daydream had been a huge act with a worldwide following, but since they no longer toured, they didn't garner too many new fans. By the time his daughter was sixteen, Dennis Whitly was seldom recognized in public anymore. Valerie and Sophia no longer had to stand patiently by while he signed autographs.

Eventually, Valerie forgot about her childhood at the beach. At first she was glad that Denny stayed home all the time, but after a while, that became second nature to her as well. Even though her mother and father didn't get up and go to jobs every day, Valerie saw her family as run-of-the-mill, just like everyone else's.

Yet Valerie sensed there was something missing, that things were different from how they'd been when she was little. There was more to it than just the inland heat, the absence of the cool beach breeze and the crashing surf. There was the gaping hole left by her aunt's death – into her teens, Val would still feel Elise's loss. Whenever she would hear one of Sonic Daydream's songs on the radio, she would remember driving in the car with her aunt. She would remember her bright smile, her happy words: *Isn't your daddy great?*

Valerie discovered computers early, and from about the age of twelve or so, she avidly pursued the solitary, somewhat lonely activity of writing code. But she didn't sense any loneliness while enmeshed in the processes: making the machine walk and talk and conform to her slightest whim was more than its own reward.

But sometimes, when she would emerge from her room to see what her parents were up to, Valerie would be struck by how much things had changed since Malibu, since Aunt Elise had passed, since they'd moved back to Riverside. Sure, Dad was always there, and that was great, but he wasn't the perfectly wonderful, always smiling and gleeful Dennis Whitly that had once joyously picked her up and threw her into the air whenever he returned from tour. He was still a great dad. He gave her his full attention whenever she asked for it, which was more than could be said of other, busier fathers, and Valerie knew that.

Valerie loved him, and she knew he loved her, but the happy-go-lucky rock star he had once been was gone. Denny had never lost the quiet distractedness that had come upon him after the accident. He would glance with sadness and pain at Sophia sometimes, when she didn't know he was looking. But Valerie saw. When she arose stiffly from a chair, or took a little extra time getting in or out of the car due to her cane, it seemed to his daughter that Denny felt the lingering aftermath of her injuries himself.

Valerie observed changes in Sophia that were even more profound.

Her mother had never been as loud or flamboyant as Aunt Elise. If her younger sister would say some blue remark in front of the tender ears of young Valerie, Sophia had never failed to hiss in shock and scold her.

Aunt Elise would just smile, unapologetic. "I'm road dog for the greatest band in the world, Soph. I spend my days and nights with Calvin Bascomb, SoCal's answer to Keith Moon; Dennis Whitly, guitar-god; *God's bass player;* and Ernie LaBelle, God's gift to women. Verily, am I blessed." Elise would grin at her niece. "Not to mention, there's an army of roadies, all out to see what they can get. An occasional four-letter word is bound to slip out." Then Aunt Elise would noisily hug and kiss the little girl. "Never mind your auntie, Val. You'll understand it all someday, and then you'll see that your mommy is just uptight, and like Cindi Lauper, your auntie just wants to have fun."

Valerie was unsure exactly what *uptight* meant, and she thought that her mother knew how to have fun. She always took Valerie to the mall and out on the beach; she went to all her school functions. Sophia always had a bright, sunny, happy, loving smile for her only child, and for her husband when he came home, and even for naughty Aunt Elise.

But then there was the accident, and there was the pain, and the loss, and the long road to recovery. Even after she was walking again, after she was again part of the family, Sophia didn't smile as much as she once had. To her daughter, she seemed more austere, less likely to see the humor in life. As she grew up, Valerie noted that Sophia seldom laughed anymore.

Denny would look at his wife with worry, and similarly, Valerie would sometimes see her mother staring fixedly at her father, not smiling, when he was unaware that she watched him.

These moments passed quickly, however. It was not as if Denny and Sophia argued, or as if they were cold to each other. On the other hand, Valerie would have had to have said that they were definitely *cooler* than they had been before the accident.

At sixteen, Valerie didn't dwell on her parents' little melancholies. She believed that they were happy enough, and if the beaming affection that they had expressed for each other when she was little had mellowed, Valerie reckoned that these things happened. They were still married, were they not, which was more than she could say for the majority of her school friends' parents. Valerie was sure that they still loved each other, and she had no doubt whatsoever that they loved her.

The workings of their relationship were really none of her business, and Valerie had other things to occupy her mind besides the intricacies of her parents' marriage, anyway. She had school to think about, and making any computer that crossed her path submit to her will. And there was Darren Silver, her . . . Yes, she would say it! *Her boyfriend!*

Tall and well-built, Darren played on their school's water polo team. Valerie had not noticed boys too much before beholding Darren, because the ones with which she interacted were either scrawny or fat, pale, unattractive code-monkeys. It was a worn-out stereotype – wasn't Steve Jobs cute? But unfortunately, in Valerie's high school world, it was the truth. There were a few fellow geeks whose skills she respected, but not a single one of them looked even remotely like Steve Jobs.

But on the first day of school, Valerie had immediately noticed good-looking Darren in English class. Some new little bell had gone off in her mind for the very first time ever, the moment she saw him. It made a pleasant little tinging sound in her mind, and it was followed by Paul Rodger's voice: *I said, 'Hey, what is this? Now maybe, baby, maybe she's in need of a kiss.'*

Valerie had not kissed anyone yet. Her aunt Elise had always cranked up Free's old standard whenever it came on the radio, however, and it continued to play in Valerie's head as she appreciated

121

the athlete sitting across the aisle from her. *I said, 'Hey, what's your name, baby? Maybe we can see things the same. Now don't you wait, or hesitate. Let's move before they raise the parking rate.'*

"Hi. What's your name? I'm Valerie."

Darren introduced himself. There was an insignia stitched into the letter on his jacket, so Valerie gleaned his sport. She off-handedly told him that she'd once played water polo herself, but had unfortunately had to quit because her horse drowned. *I slay me*, she thought and giggled.

Darren had smiled indulgently, as if he'd never heard *that one* before.

They'd started hanging out after school, and then started holding hands, and then kissing. Darren had spent most of his life in the pool, so he was almost as sheltered and inexperienced as Valerie, the solitary code-writer. They were both a little late in discovering the chief joy of adolescence. But at a school dance, Darren had asked her if she would be his girlfriend, and in the months since then, they had caught up. They had become quite adventurous in their explorations of each other.

Despite an unabashed eagerness to explore the new world of physical intimacy with the water polo player, Valerie knew that she wasn't in love with him. She didn't think of him every waking moment, didn't long to talk to him and kiss him and touch him all the time. That was the way some of the girls at school acted about their boyfriends, but Valerie also had a computer waiting at home, a slave which waited, cursor blinking, to do whatever she had a mind to tell it to do.

Growing up, Sophia had always told her, "Make men a sideline, Val, not your sole occupation." Valerie had not really paid attention to this pearl of wisdom; her mother often made pronouncements or quoted movies on subjects that Valerie was not quite old enough to understand yet. But now she saw thought that perhaps she had taken her mother's advice after all, without even realizing it.

She certainly liked Darren. He was muscular, with that flawless, wide-at-the-shoulder, narrow-at-the-hip swimmer's body, the physique that would ever-after be Valerie's type. Darren was pretty, blue-eyed, with a fall of straight, dark hair that he was always (adorably!) shaking out of his eyes. Valerie did like to look at him and kiss him when he was around; she very much enjoyed all the new things that they did together.

But love? No. Valerie had seen enough movies to comprehend that she would know love when it happened to her. And this wasn't it.

It would be Darren, star water polo player, however, with or without a swimming horse, who would bring the past lives of her parents once more back to the forefront of Valerie's mind.

It was April, 2008; Valerie would be seventeen in another month. Spring break had just ended, and she was waiting for Darren at their accustomed spot in the cafeteria. He had gone out of town for the holiday week with his family, and Valerie missed him. Still, she glanced at the clock on the wall with mild annoyance. He was late; there was only twenty minutes left 'til next class started.

Finally, she saw him hurrying across the crowded room, and then at last he was standing before her, a look of surprised, questioning confusion pasted across his good-looking face.

"What?" she asked, when he didn't speak.

"Is any of this true?"

He handed her a thin paperback. Its front cover was a garish red, and the words *Sonic Nightmare* were embossed in black across the top. Valerie recognized her dad and her uncle and the rest of the band from a grainy and unflattering black and white photo below that.

"Calvin Bascomb explores a darker, though not unfamiliar side to rock and roll," said the blurb from *Rolling Stone.*

Valerie glanced up at Darrin. He still looked surprised, questioning. *Is any of this true?* She turned the book over. The back cover was black, and in large, stark, white lettering it said, *An obsessive Number One Fan, suicide – the real reason why the world's premier rock band called it quits.*

In smaller font: Leonard Whitly's phone call woke me out of a sound sleep on the early morning of May 8th, 1999. He told me the awful news: Denny's wife was in the hospital, barely clinging to life. There had been an accident. Her sister, Elise Carlin, Sonic Daydream's road manager, had driven her car over the side of a dark, twisty, California mountain road. Elise died in the crash.

I told him I would get to LA as soon as I could and hung up. You have to understand, this was in the days before texting. Even having a cellphone at all was a new thing to me. I didn't notice the missed call or the voice message until right before I left to meet Lenny and the rest of the band at the hospital.

But after I listened to Elise's message, I knew that what had happened had been no accident.

Valerie dropped the book as if it was a filthy thing. She looked up at Darren again; not a word came to her mind. At last she stammered, "You read this?"

"My mom picked it up in the airport. Before we went to Oregon."

123

"What does it say?"

Darrin sat down and leaned across the table toward her. Quietly, he replied, "He's saying it wasn't an accident, Val. He's saying your aunt killed herself. Because . . . because of your dad."

"WHAT?"

Heads turned in the cafeteria.

Darren lowered his voice further. "He says your aunt was in love with your dad. He insinuates that there was something going on between them. That's what I got out of it, anyway. Something went wrong in their relationship, and she couldn't handle it, so she drove her car off a cliff. She killed herself, and she tried to take your mom with her." He paused, then asked again, "Is any of it true?"

"You've got to be kidding."

Darren blinked, unsure of what she meant. "So, you're saying–"

"I'm saying, how the hell am I supposed to know about something that happened when I was eight years old?" She gestured at the book. "That isn't the story I was told."

An obsessive Number One Fan . . .

A memory played in Valerie's mind. Aunt Elise had brought her to a show in LA, to see her daddy sing. She couldn't have been more than seven years old, because when she turned eight . . .

There had been a small crowd gathered backstage, in what Valerie would in later years learn was called a *green room*. She remember a long table filled with food, a couch, a TV monitor.

"Stand right here a minute, Val," Aunt Elise had instructed. "Don't go anywhere. I'll be right back." Valerie watched her slip quickly around the other grown-ups.

"Are you Denny's little girl?"

Valerie looked up to see two young women, dressed in black: tight pants, boots, Sonic Daydream T-shirts. They were very pretty. Valerie nodded.

One of them smiled at her. "Aren't you just adorable?" Then conspiratorially, she said to her friend, "Let's hope her mother isn't around. Come on, let's see if we can find him." The girl patted Valerie on the head and she and her friend scanned the chatting crowd.

Valerie heard a man's voice say, "Hey, who let you back here?" and the girls skittered way.

Aunt Elise returned then and took Valerie's hand, asked her how she was, if she wanted something to eat, if she was looking forward to hearing her daddy sing.

The little girl wasn't concerned with her daddy at the moment. The young woman had said *mother* with the same venom that she might've used to say *viper.*

"Why do those girls hate Mommy, Aunt Elise?"

Elise watched a security guard escort the interlopers out of the green room. She echoed his earlier question. "How did they get in here?" Valerie tugged on her hand, repeated her own question.

Elise laughed. "They hate your mommy because they want *to be* your mommy, Val." She hugged the child. "We all do."

It didn't make sense to Val then. Why would all the pretty girls want to be her mommy?

It wouldn't be until years later that the import of her aunt's words would click in Valerie's mind, not until recently, in fact, since she and Darren had been exploring their adolescent curiosities together.

The child of a rock star, Valerie had never been much of a follower of bands. But she knew an attractive singer when she saw one, and she'd always recognized that there was something special about how women looked at her dad. And since Sonic Daydream had recently released a two CD greatest hits compilation, some of her school chums' own mothers had again recalled that their kids attended school with the singer's daughter. A few of her friends had brought copies of the new CD to Valerie, but more often, it was an old copy of Sonic Daydream's second disk, the one with a young, shirtless, devastatingly attractive, grinning Denny Whitly on the cover. *Could you ask your dad to sign this for my mom? She says she used to just love his band.*

He was her dad and all that, but Valerie could see what his fans had seen back in his touring days. At almost seventeen, Valerie understood what Elise had meant all those years ago. It had been a rather mysterious way for her aunt to put it, but what else could she have said to a seven-year-old kid?

Elise had said that all the pretty girls in the audience – and especially the ones that managed to slip backstage – they all wanted to be Valley's mommy. That was just a nice way of saying that they had all wanted *to do her daddy.*

Valerie had felt the jealousy, the envy and dislike coming off those two groupies, even if she hadn't understood the *why* of it at the time. "They hate your mommy because they want *to be* your mommy, Val." Then Aunt Elise had added, "We all do."

Jesus, could it be true?

****

125

Apparently, Brett Cooke had never heard of Calvin's tell-all, which was not surprising. It had been a quickie, sensationalistic exposé, and to the Whitly family's relief, it had soon faded into obscurity.

Brett didn't ask Valerie for any further details about the end of her dad's career. Instead, he asked, "That's when you got into movies? While your mom was recuperating?"

"Even before that." Valerie again quoted Quentin Tarantino. *"When people ask me if I went to film school, I tell them, 'No, I went to films.'"*

Valerie's ability to liberally sprinkle her conversation with lines from movies struck Brett as a little odd, but just a little. Mostly, he found it clever: she came up with just the right one at just the right time, and he usually got the reference, although sometimes her quotes were obscure. Valerie's appreciation of cinema stretched back to the Golden Age of Hollywood, to black and white films, almost to the silent era.

Brett had a similar skill himself, and at times he believed that it was the primary thing that Valerie liked about him. It was a lot of fun, impressing each other with the talent. To what other girl could Brett quote *Sin City*, and not get laughed at? *"My warrior woman. My Valkyrie. You'll always be mine, always and never. Never. The fire, baby. It'll burn us both. It'll kill us both. There's no place in this world for our kind of fire. Always and never. If I have to die for you tonight, I will."*

"Are you not entertained?" Valerie would reply. *"Are you not entertained? Is this not why you are here?"* And then she would squeeze him to her and kiss him.

Brett liked Valerie, but saying that Valerie *liked* him in return was perhaps too vague a term. Valerie *loved* Brett. He knew it because she told him frequently, using all the famous lines: *You had me at hello*, and *Today, I consider myself the luckiest man on the face of the earth*, and *I never knew it could be like this. Nobody ever kissed me the way you do.* She frequently called him *My precious*.

Perhaps Brett would have been disconcerted with Valerie's abject affection for him – *I promise to love you forever, every single day of forever* – if it wasn't for the fact that *everybody* loved him. Or he might've worried about it if Valerie was clingy or possessive or jealous, or if she talked about plans for their future together. The only future Valerie ever talked about was a career at 20th Century Fox. Her buddy, Greg Castro, had graduated early and was already working there. He told her that he was sure that he could get her on as a programmer in the motion capture division, as soon as she graduated.

Valerie never brought up the dreaded term *marriage;* she never even talked about moving in with Brett. They never discussed commitment at all, never said that they were *going together,* or that they were *exclusive.* Brett didn't cheat on her, not in any physical way, but he still talked to any girl who smiled at him. And that was just about any girl. Just as Joyce had surmised, Brett was not yet ready to contemplate a future with just one girl. He liked Valerie well enough, and he remained physically loyal – who knew, maybe someday – but he was not ready to settle down now. There were too many things in life yet to experience.

Valerie had never brought up the idea of commitment with Brett because she believed that was just something that was simply understood. *Love is passion, obsession, someone you can't live without. I say, fall head over heels. Find someone you can love like crazy and who will love you the same way back.*

These words summed up how Valerie felt about Brett. Anthony Hopkins had said it all. She didn't need other words, humdrum, ordinary ones, promises about the future. Who knew what the future would bring? Whatever it was, Valerie knew that Brett would be there beside her.

We're like a lock and key.

****

During college, her fellow code-monkey Greg would drop by and say hello to Joyce and Valerie, if he saw them at Q's. Valerie didn't fail to notice that he only seemed to do so if Brett hadn't yet arrived, and then he always had some sly insinuation as to where Brett might be, what he might be doing. To her irritation, Joyce always agreed with Greg's theories.

He would ingenuously ask Valerie where her boyfriend was, then answer his own question. "Probably helping some young thing study. I took a few business classes." Greg would grin at Joyce, and she'd grin back. "They have test questions like: *When he spies a pretty business major studying for her Principles of Management exam, Brett Cooke routinely shows skills in supporting her ideas and shows sensitivity to her fear of decreased performance caused by fatigue. He is exhibiting which of the following types of group roles? A. Task. B. Mentoring. C. Trying to get in her pants . . .*"

Joyce would giggle, then both of them would look at Valerie to see what her reaction would be to their commentary on Brett's popularity, on his legendary way with the ladies.

Valerie would shrug, say, "I didn't take too much business, but I would have to guess that the answer to that one would be *B. Mentoring.*"

Then she would ignore Greg and Joyce when they'd share a glance, communicating pity, embarrassment at their friends' naiveté.

Valerie didn't care if Brett was, *had been,* a player. Audrey Hepburn once said, *Everything I learned I learned from the movies,* and it was true of Valerie as well. Concerning Brett and his many lady friends, she likened him to Julian from *American Gigolo.*

"This movie helped stimulate women's educational efforts, and the whole economy, Val, did you know that?" her mother had told her, as they prepared to screen the classic Richard Gere film.

Val, maybe eighteen at the time, shook her head.

Mom nodded, grinned. "It inspired a whole generation of young women to go out and make enough money so they could pay Richard Gere for sex. He is absolutely stunning in it."

But paying Richard Gere for sex had just been the vehicle for the story, the *setting,* Valerie reckoned. What she had come away with from *American Gigolo* was that it was a story of true love. When Julian desperately needs Lauren Hutton to alibi for him, she does, because she loves him. She gives up everything for him; she saves him because she can't live without him.

Brett was certainly no gigolo, but it was impossible to ignore the fact that he knew a lot of girls. They were always walking up and flirting with him at Q's, as if Valerie wasn't even standing there. Complete strangers, as well as ones Brett had known before he'd met Valerie.

And that was all right with Brett's current girlfriend. There was the smugness that she felt, being with such an attractive man. She didn't have a line from a film for it, but it came down to *you bitches can look all you want, and I know you envy me, because he's mine.* Valerie had not a jealous bone in her body because she was utterly sure that Brett was indeed hers. There were simpatico, copacetic.

****

Brett and Valerie had been — for lack of a better word — *a couple* for six months on graduation day. Valerie met his mom, a small, very pretty woman, from whom Brett had inherited his adorable blue eyes.

Because many UCLA graduates came from big money, there was more than one parent-transporting limo in evidence at commencement. Joyce's mom and her dad, the former district attorney, had so arrived, and no one noticed Denny Whitly and his wife when they stepped out of a slick, blacked-out, stretch Cadillac. Mr. and Mrs. Vinson were not at all star-struck: they had met Valerie's dad before. They shook hands and greeted Denny and Sophia like old friends. But Brett, even though he thought he would be prepared for it, was momentarily speechless, and his mother . . .

Geri Cooke's mouth fell open. *Oh, my, God, it really is Dennis Whitly!* He was older now, of course, as was she, both of them with college-graduated children. His daughter made introductions, and when the rock star smiled at her, Geri was carried back in time to that night, a million years ago, when she had stood at the rail with a couple of her girlfriends and gazed up at Denny Whitly on stage. After the show, she'd sworn up and down to Mona and Crystal that he'd looked *right at her* as he sang the chorus to *Tomcats. Kitties and cats wanna do their thang,* and like all the other girls in the crowded Forum that night, young Mrs. Cooke had wanted to do just one thang with Sonic Daydream's frontman. Geri's friends had been too busy singing along to notice, but Geri was sure. Incredible Denny Whitly had made eye contact. He'd *looked right at her.* He'd smiled.

Unexpectedly, the heat of her long-forgotten youth suddenly flooded through Geri. She'd been probably twenty-one when she'd seen Sonic Daydream; her soldier husband had been deployed somewhere. She'd left Brett, still in diapers, with her grandmother for the evening.

The excitement she'd felt watching Denny sing all those years ago returned like it had all happened yesterday. It was like the first time Lori Petty saw Keanu Reeves in *Point Break.* She stared at him in open-mouthed appreciation.

Geri hadn't felt that kind of aliveness in years. Her marriage to Brett's dad hadn't lasted, and the life of a single mother hadn't always been a bed of roses, but seeing Denny Whitly, standing right there, offering her that crooked, rock star's grin, caused all the hurts-so-good fire of a fan's unrequited desire to blaze through her once more. *Mercy, when did the weather turn so hot?*

The guitar-god's hair was shorter; the exquisite fall of brown shagginess that used to cover one eye when he played had been cropped back, as befitted a man his age, and Geri couldn't see his big green eyes behind his black Ray-Bans. But he was definitely still just as breathtakingly sexy as he had ever been.

Geri realized that she was staring at him. She quickly closed her mouth and shook his proffered hand, said it was nice to meet him. She glanced guiltily at his wife, the lucky Mrs. Whitly, and Sophia featured Geri with a slightly curious smile. Brett's mother wondered suddenly if the woman could see the lust that Geri had once possessed for her husband, remembered, reimagined in a heartbeat. *Well, what if it does show? Surely, she's met her husband's fans before?* Geri hid her discomfiture by quickly telling Sophia it was nice to meet her, too.

The proud mothers shook hands, then words again failed Geri.

But Denny was notoriously charismatic, utterly charming, and he seamlessly dissipated the awkward silence of fan meeting famous. He slapped Brett on the back, and congratulated his mother on a son well-raised. Soon the parents were chatting together almost normally, as if Valerie's dad hadn't once toured the globe and headlined at mega-venues. As if his daughter's boyfriend's mom hadn't once upon a time, and frequently, imagined Denny beside her in bed, naked, glistening . . .

As they went to find their seats for the ceremony, there were only momentary flashes of further silence, when Geri would again realize, *Oh, my God, it's really Dennis Whitly!*

****

Valerie brimmed with joy. Her beloved parents had made the trip down for graduation; she had an interview scheduled at Fox in two weeks; she was in love with the most wonderful guy in the world. They were heading to Las Vegas immediately after graduation to celebrate. The last six months had been the happiest of her entire life.

But *all good things gotta come to an end,* as it was once said in an ancient novelty tune.

Joyce got the text while attending a party, several hours after commencement had ended. Or begun, depending upon how one looked at it. She figured that Brett and Valerie would be yukking it up in Las Vegas by now, but such was not the case.

He's still on Plenty of Fish, Jo, Valerie's text said. *And okCupid, & Tinder. I saw his phone. He's still looking, talking 2 all those girls. He doesn't luv me. It's all a lie.*

"*Houston, we have a problem,*" Joyce said out loud. She immediately tried to call her friend, but Valerie wouldn't pick up, so she texted, *May b he just forgot the apps r on there, honey.*

He's got 100s of messages. Some from 2day.

Ah, honey! That doesn't mean he's cheating on u! He's just talking.

He's obviously never stopped talking, so I kno what else he's been doing w/them.

Ah, honey! I'm so sorry!

Purple in the morning, blue in the afternoon & orange in the evening. Just like that, 1, 2, 3, 4!

That didn't make any sense to Joyce. It must be from a movie.

This is Ripley, last survivor of the Nostromo, signing off. I luv u, Jo. Adieu, adieu! Remember me!

Oh, Christ! Joyce ran out of the party without even saying goodbye to anyone. She jumped in the car and texted, *Don't do anything stupid, Val! He's not worth it!*

Amazing tradition. They throw a great party for u on the 1 day they kno u can't come.

Joyce quickly Googled *movie quotes about death*. She would speak to Val in her own language until she could get back to the house. Keep her talking, until she could save her.

A man's legacy is determined by how the story ends. It was from *J. Edgar,* starring Leonardo DiCaprio. *Don't make it end this way, Val! Not over stupid, fucking Brett!*

For in that sleep of death what dreams may come, when we have shuffled off this mortal coil, must give us pause, Valerie texted.

Christ! I'm in The Twilight Zone. Valerie was quoting *Hamlet,* she was planning to *snuff it,* because she had at last come to the realization that she wasn't going to be the ladies' man's last lady. *Where did you think he was, whenever he wasn't with you?* Joyce thought. *I'd always hoped you were smarter than this, Val.*

But Joyce knew her hope had been in vain. She'd seen it from the beginning. Val *loved* Brett. All her flirty, out-for-a-good-time, bad-girl self-control had evaporated, the moment that she'd seen him. *You can't deny love.*

You don't throw away a whole life just because it's banged up a little, Joyce texted. It was from *Seabiscuit.* They were probably talking about a horse. Joyce thought it was weak.

Lightbulbs die, my sweet. I will depart, Valerie texted back.

I'm coming, Val! Please wait 4 me, honey!

Don't u be afraid, sweetheart. Death is just a part of life, something we're all destined to do.

Joyce looked at the Google search again, all the while trying to maneuver through traffic.

You can be mad as a mad dog at the way things went. You can swear and curse the fates. But when it comes to the end, you have to let go. That was from *The Curious Case of Benjamin Button.* Joyce decided against sending that one. She didn't want to mention letting go.

Instead she chose one from *Man of La Mancha: There's a remedy for everything except death, Val. Please wait 4 me. I luv u!*

Funny how gentle people get with u once ur dead.

Joyce almost rear-ended a Mercedes that stopped suddenly in front of her.

Oh, honey, ur not dead yet! Hold on! I'm almost home!

Dave, this conversation can serve no purpose anymore. Goodbye.

****

Brett had betrayed her. The love of her life was carrying on with other women via the modern convenience of his cellphone. *Nothing in the history of mankind has allowed infidelity to proceed with such ease,* Valerie reflected.

Ah, yes. Infidelity. The assassin of true love. Valerie discovered that she had become rather mushy in her present state of mind. Mushy, maudlin, suicidal. Before she'd met Brett, these feelings had each been totally unknown to her.

Infidelity. Betrayal. Death. Valerie was suddenly put in mind of a similar tale: her Uncle Calvin's exposé, *Sonic Nightmare,* which purported to reveal secrets never before told about *the world's premier rock band.*

Valerie clearly remembered: she had been almost seventeen, had taken the scandalous paperback home with her after school, had retired to her room to read it.

Her boyfriend Darren, homework, coding; all were forgotten. Valerie wanted to hear this new take on her family history, from Uncle Calvin's point of view.

First she'd thumbed through the pictures bound into the middle. There was her dad and the other guys, impossibly young, their instruments set up in the grass, tiki torches burning nearby. The caption read, *Alpha Epsilon Pi House Party, University of California, Riverside, 1988.* The next one showed the four of them, smiling, arms linked together, in front of some establishment called The House of Ale. The caption said, *House Band, 1988.*

Valerie felt the light touch of history upon her shoulder: that bar was downtown. This picture was from before she was even thought of, yet the bar's sign had not changed. She knew Dad's band had started here in his hometown, but she'd never known the name of the establishment, never realized that she'd passed the place a million times.

There was a professionally done headshot of a smiling, insouciant Elise Carlin. The credit said, *Courtesy of Sony Records.* Valerie traced her aunt's smile with her fingertip. *God, how I miss her!*

There was a shot of her parents' wedding. Sophia was ethereally beautiful in her lacy gown; Denny, still long-haired, proud and gorgeous

132

in his tuxedo. Valerie had seen a similar photo in their family album, or perhaps it was the same one.

Once Valerie had understood where babies came from, Sophia used to like to point at her still flat belly in the snapshot and tell her daughter, *You were already on the way that day, Valley. So in a sense, you're in this picture, too!*

Valerie studied the other faces in the wedding party: Ernie and Lenny grinned, as happy as the happy couple. Valerie had not read the book yet, but based on the horrible allegations splattered across the back cover – *I knew that what had happened had been no accident* – she considered. Did the smiles of her aunt and Sonic Daydream's drummer seem a little bit forced?

Valerie flipped through the remaining photos. A few more shots of the band performing, one of Calvin and Elise sitting across a table from each other, having lunch. *My best friend,* the caption read.

A few shots of Aunt Elise walking beside Denny, gazing adoringly at him . . .

Isn't your daddy great?

Valerie turned to the last page of the book. It said *About the Author,* and showed a concert shot of a young drummer. *Calvin Bascomb had a pair of drumsticks in his hands almost before he could walk. He is a founding member of Sonic Daydream. Currently, he lives in Temecula, California.*

So close, Valerie thought in amazement. *Temecula's just down the road, really. But I haven't seen Uncle Calvin in years . . .*

I guess people just drift away. It was a melancholy realization for someone not quite seventeen years old, and Valerie sighed. *But they're never really gone, are they? Unless they die, like Aunt Elise, they're still around, maybe just down the road, living their own lives, playing for other bands . . .*

And then some of them come roaring back into your life with outrageous allegations . . .

Valerie skimmed the first chapter, which detailed the origins of Sonic Daydream as a three-man combo: the lean years of practicing and recording demos of their own material in Calvin's garage, with Lenny or Ernie singing lead. The days of playing covers at frat parties. It was old news. Valerie had heard the story before. She skimmed, too, over the details of the first six months of her father's tenure as front for the band. Again, that was all a part of her family history.

After the first sentence of the next chapter, however, Valerie read Calvin's supposedly true story word by word.

I was appalled that Denny was allowing his girlfriend's sixteen-year-old sister to accompany us on our first tour. Elise Carlin had once tried to seduce Denny – that was his word – and her attempt had failed only because he had discovered that she was underage before the act could be consummated.

Valerie frowned. She didn't notice the bombshell as much as its phrasing. *Consummated. That's a big word for a drummer.*

Denny's life soon changed forever, as did mine and Lenny's and Ernie's. And of course, Elise's life also changed. Denny met and fell in love with her older sister, Sophia. Elise had brought her along to The House of Ale to see her favorite band, her favorite singer, never guessing in a million years that the two of them would click. That very night, Sony signed Sonic Daydream, and not long after, we made a record, shot a video, and went on tour.

Because he was in love, Denny insisted that Sophia accompany us on the road. And because she was her sister's legal guardian, Elise had to come along, too.

Elise showed a business savvy beyond her tender years and by our third tour, she had pretty much entirely taken over the reins as our road manager. It was a job that Lenny was not opposed to relinquishing, mostly because Elise was so much better at it than he was.

Uncle Calvin's down to offend everyone, now isn't he?

She became indispensable to us, whenever we were on tour, which was most of the time. Sony loved her. They knew that there would be no hassles with their headlining cash-cow as long as Elise Carlin was in the driver's seat.

Elise was so good at her job because it was the only thing that kept her where she most wanted to be, which was at Denny's side. She loved the responsibilities: bitching at stingy promoters, yelling at tardy concierges for more towels and faster room service. She loved the road: the endless highways, a different town and venue and crowd every other night. She loved to stand backstage and listen to us perform. But most of all, above all other things, Elise loved Dennis Whitly.

"She loved rock and roll," Valerie protested aloud.

A memory from childhood: Valerie listening to her dad talk about an especially receptive crowd somewhere in Texas, not being exactly sure what *receptive* meant, or exactly where Texas was. So she'd asked her aunt what it was like for *her* on tour.

Elise had grinned at her niece, the delight shining from her big blue eyes. She summed it up for Valerie using Jackson Browne's famous lyrics – *We just pass the time in our hotel rooms, and wander 'round backstage, 'til those lights come up and we hear that crowd, and we remember why we came . . .*

"What do you like to do most of all, Valley?" Aunt Elise had continued. "Concentrate now. Is it going to the mall? Or running on the beach with your mommy?"

"I like watching movies with Mommy," the child had replied. "It's my favorite thing."

"That's how I feel about touring, Valley. It's my favorite thing, what I like to do most of all."

Even as a little girl, Valerie had been aware that Elise considered Sonic Daydream to be *her band*. She considered herself as much a part of it as if she was another musician. There was nothing more exciting and rewarding to her than to be on the road with them – these sentiments had always come through to her niece. So Valerie knew there was much more to her aunt's desire to accompany Sonic Daydream than this mythical crush that Uncle Calvin was ascribing to her.

So far, he had not backed up his shameful insinuations enough to convince Valerie that some secret – what was the word that Darren had used? That some secret *relationship* had existed between her dad and her aunt.

Then she heard Elise's sorely missed voice in her head. "The thing I like most in life is to hear your daddy sing, Valley."

Valerie frowned. But she remained unconvinced.

The next chapters of *Sonic Nightmare* detailed Aunt Elise's alleged confessions of her love, as supposedly related to the band's drummer.

135

Calvin mentioned that he believed Elise's mind was unstable, that her life was just one non-stop delusion.

> She ignored every aspect of Denny's love for Sophia. She refused to see that there would never be another woman in his life, and certainly never her.
>
> For the decade that we toured, like Annie, Elise always believed 'the sun'll come out, tomorrow.' Tomorrow, Denny would decide he was tired of his wife. Tomorrow, Denny would finally acknowledge his sister-in-law's constant, unwavering, obvious love for him. He would return it. He would send his wife and daughter away, and he and Elise would be together, in love, forever.
>
> The most tragic thing about Elise's obsession with her sister's husband was that no one ever tried to talk her out of it, no one ever tried to make her see the truth. Everyone knew about her love; the light in her eyes whenever she looked at Denny was undeniable. But everyone pretended it wasn't there.
>
> No one ever attempted to talk Elise out of her love for Denny, no one ever sat her down and explained reality to her, except for me, and I only tried once. But Elise was entrenched in her fantasy, and she refused to be shaken awake from her dream world, not even by her best friend. Someday, Denny would send his wife packing, and he and Elise would be together then. If I didn't believe it, all I had to do was be patient and wait, just like she was. Someday it would happen.

Jesus, how he does go on! Valerie struggled to remember the expression they had recently learned in English class. She didn't pay too much attention there, mostly because the subject bored her – why should she have to *read* all these supposedly timeless, classic stories, when she could watch their movie adaptations? Also, she spent a lot of time in English class shooting sly glances at Darren and receiving them in kind. It was the only class they had together, the one in which they'd met.

Valerie remembered the term that Mrs. Latimer had taught them, for when a story was overwrought, full of heavy, flowery emotions:

purple prose. Uncle Calvin's descriptions of Aunt Elise's supposed love for her dad was like something out of a gothic romance: her impossible longings, her delusional certainties, all confessed to no one but him. Valerie looked at the spine of the book, to see if it had been published by Harlequin Romances. It had not. The designation was *Nonfiction.*

Valerie still remained unconvinced. Calvin had to be making this stuff up, or at least inflating it to sell books. No one pined for an unachievable man for ten years, not even one as attractive and talented as her father. Valerie couldn't imagine having emotions as strong and all-encompassing as these inescapable feelings that Uncle Calvin attributed to her aunt.

"If a man doesn't want you, you're a fool if you don't just give up," Sophia's mother had always told her, and Valerie agreed, even though she had only had experience with one man. She liked Darren, and Darren liked her, but if he changed his mind, if he suddenly failed to appreciate Valerie for her awesomeness, then she figured that it would just be his loss. If things soured between them, Valerie knew that she'd never waste any time pining for Darren, especially not ten long years. There were other water polo players in the world, just as cute as he was.

Uncle Calvin's *purple prose* about Elise's undying passion for her dad – it was just too far-fetched. It was ridiculous. Such things didn't occur in real life.

Valerie at last got to the climax of the drummer's allegedly nonfiction tell-all, the part where Calvin related the contents of the voice mail that his road manager, *his best friend,* had left for him, shortly before the accident that claimed her life.

> I took out my phone to call Lenny, to tell him that I was on my way to LA. I noticed I had a missed call from Elise. It was a shock. Lenny had told me that Elise was dead. Wild hoped surged in me. Maybe I'd misunderstood him somehow; maybe she wasn't dead at all. But then I saw that the call was from the previous night.
>
> Elise was dead. I thought about just erasing her message. Whatever she'd had to say to me – it didn't really matter anymore, did it? If she'd wanted reassurance about something, I had been unavailable to provide it. If she'd wanted a question answered . . . it was all too late now.

But Elise had wanted neither reassurance nor answers. She had just wanted to say goodbye.

She and I frequently spoke to each other in song lyrics. It was our thing. The words written by the great legends of music were our shorthand, almost like our own secret way of communicating. A lot of meaning and emotion could be packed into a few short verses.

She sighed heavily into the phone. *"This is the end, my only friend, the end. Of our elaborate plans, the end. Of everything that stands, the end. No safety or surprise, the end. I'll never look into your eyes, again.*

"I really wanted to talk to you, Cal. It's chickenshit to do it like this, but you would've just tried to talk me out of it, anyway. You would've said, *there's still time to change the road you're on.*

"I guess I've been kind of a one trick pony for as long as you've known me, huh? All I ever talked about was Denny, wasn't it? I want to thank you for listening.

"I finally got to touch him again, after all these years. *All you touch and all you see, is all your life will ever be.* We were finally alone . . . Then he told me that things couldn't go on like they had been. He told me that it would never be just the two of us." She sighed again.

"I have seen the writing on the wall, Cal. Denny showed it to me, so now, I *don't think I need anything at all. No. Don't think I need anything at all.*

"I know you'll miss me – you'll be the only one – and for that, I'm truly sorry. *But I don't need to fight to prove I'm right. I don't need to be forgiven.*

"I saw him first. He would've, *should've* been mine, all along. She doesn't deserve him. She never has." Elise sighed a third time.

"Just what you want to be, you'll be in the end. Goodbye, Cal."

The message was over, but the next line of the song played in my head, Justin Hayward's plaintive, lamenting, haunting voice: *And I love you, yes, I love you, oh, how, I love you. Oh, how I love you.* I felt Elise's unendurable pain.

I don't know for sure what happened between them that night. Maybe Denny at last gave in, then had a fit of conscience. Whatever it was –

Valerie stopped reading. *There it is. The accusation. Just one sentence, but it's quite damning, isn't it?* It had gotten Darren's mind to thinking: "There was something going on between them. Something went wrong in their relationship . . ."

Uncle Calvin had insinuated a myriad of sins in only twelve words. *Maybe Denny at last gave in, then had a fit of conscience.* The entire book up until that point had alleged that Aunt Elise had possessed a crush, long held, on Valerie's dad, but this one sentence had transferred the concrete crime of infidelity, of adultery, onto him.

Darren had ignored the disclaimer of the first sentence – *I don't know for sure what happened between them that night* – and so would anybody else that read this tripe. They would take for gospel Calvin's next assertion, that *Denny at last gave in,* that he broke his marriage vows, that he cheated on his wife with his sister-in-law. And then he *had a fit of conscience* about it.

Valerie read on.

Whatever it was, whatever he said to her, it was the final straw for Elise. For ten years, no one could talk her out of her dream. But in one night, Denny shattered the illusion, completely. Elise's voicemail to me had said, *She doesn't deserve him. She never has.* It was identical to the lethal cliché: *If I can't have him, no one will.*

Elise drove up Decker Road to the Malibu Golf Course to pick up her sister. Sophia was attending a birthday party there for her eight-year-old daughter, Valerie.

Valerie blinked to see her name in print.

The little girl was slated to spend the night at a neighbor's house – perhaps if she had been along for the ride back home, Elise wouldn't have taken her fatal step. She wouldn't ever have done anything to hurt her niece. But Valerie remained behind at the party in the neighbor's care, and distraught, heartbroken Elise turned Denny's slick black Mercedes out of the parking lot and onto the dark asphalt, with only Sophia along for the ride.

But she didn't take Decker Road back down the hill to the beach house. It would've been the shortest route home, and it was curvy enough. But instead, Elise got onto Mulholland Highway. Full of twists and hairpin turns, it has forever been the road of choice for daredevil motorcyclists out to prove their nerve. Taking Mulholland instead of Decker would've put Elise and Sophia miles out of their way up PCH, when they at last reached the bottom of the hill.

But Elise didn't intend to make it home.

She drove straight through the guardrail. Investigators found no skid marks. She had not tried to brake at all, yet they put it all down as simply a tragic accident. A young woman had lost control of a big, powerful car on a dark, twisty, California highway. Many such heartbreaking events happened yearly in the area.

But I knew better. The heartbreak had come earlier in the evening for Elise. Whatever had occurred between Denny and his sister-in-law –

There it is again, Valerie thought, *the black, shameful insinuation.*

Whatever had occurred between Denny and his sister-in-law, he had rejected her in the end, and it undid her. If Elise couldn't have the object of ten years' desire, then her sister wasn't going to have him any more either.

I'll never look into your eyes again.

Oh, for crying out loud! In disgust, Valerie flung *Sonic Nightmare* across the room. It made a satisfying *flak!* sound when it hit the wall.

It was all just patently ridiculous. Uncle Calvin's purple prose, the maudlin gravitas of Elise's doomed, unrequited crush. The slyly worded insinuations that her father had at long last requited it for her, had then been stricken with remorse, and had thereafter immediately spurned her. It was as if the drummer had taken the rejected screenplay for some incredibly bad sob-story of a romance, substituted Valerie's family's names for the screenwriter's characters, and then went right ahead and peddled all this nonsense as fact.

To use Calvin's own expression, Valerie *knew better.*

Valerie had *known* her aunt, had loved her. She had been brazen, loud. Elise had been *one tough cookie,* like Jennifer Jason Leigh's girl-reporter character in *The Hudsucker Proxy, a fast-talking career gal who thought she was one of the boys.* Elise spoke her mind, and didn't suffer fools lightly.

She was not some obsessed groupie, pining away within some impossible dream of making it with a rock star, as Uncle Calvin would have the world believe. She was a professional, a businesswoman. She had never had a boyfriend that Valerie could remember, because she was too busy with managing the band. *No time for love, Doctor Jones,* she would tell her niece with a grin.

Darren's voice again spoke in Valerie's mind: *Is any of this true?*

She shook her head. *No. Just because Aunt Elise never had a boyfriend, it doesn't mean that she was in love with my dad.*

The way Uncle Calvin had portrayed him was just ridiculous, too. Dennis Whitly was a good man. He would never cheat on his wife, not with anybody, and certainly not with her own sister. Valerie knew that her dad loved her mom. She knew it as certainly as the sun would come up tomorrow. Sure, maybe things between them had cooled after the accident, but hadn't he given up touring? For all intents and purposes, hadn't he given up his career in order to look after his injured wife? If that wasn't love . . .

Valerie remembered the teaser on the cover of Calvin's book: *the real reason why the world's premiere rock band called it quits.* She looked with dread at the glossy, garish, black and red covers of the paperback, splayed out on the floor beside her dresser. Then she sighed. She had followed Uncle Calvin along through all this ridiculousness so far. She might as well see it through to the end.

The question of *why the world's premier rock band called it quits* had puzzled fans and family, promoters, Sony Records, and the other members of the band. It had puzzled *Rolling Stone,* too. They had interviewed Denny after the release of Sonic Daydream's second, post-accident CD, and Valerie knew that the reason Denny had given in the interview was the true one. He'd quit because his wife (and his daughter, too), hurt and grieving after their devastating loss, had needed him. Touring, rock and roll – they had been just a job, easily set aside. Helping to heal his family had meant everything to him.

The healing had been incomplete, spotty at best, Valerie now reflected. Sophia had grown cold, austere, and Denny himself had become quiet and introspective after his touring days ended.

"Whatever," Valerie said aloud. *Let's see what Uncle Calvin's take on it is.*

She retrieved *Sonic Nightmare* from the floor and turned to the final chapter. As might've been expected from Calvin's mawkish style throughout the book, the epilogue was entitled *Aftermath*.

And because of what had come before, Valerie was not surprised by her uncle's explanation of why Sonic Daydream had ended. The idea that Dennis Whitly had sought to comfort his wife and child, the concept that he himself might've been saddened by the loss of his road manager, his sister-in-law – these simple human emotions didn't fit in with Calvin's tale of theatrical pathos and undying delusion. Valerie saw it coming a mile away. At least the drummer was brief in his summary.

Dennis Whitly, legendary front for *the world's premier rock band* had *called it quits* out of guilt, you see.

He was in a biz where women threw themselves at him constantly, perennially, eternally. But after Elise's death, Denny decided that his wife had put up with this inescapable fact of a rock star's existence for long enough. If he quit touring, there would be no more legions of lusty fans clamoring for him after every show. No more danger of crazy, obsessed, suicidal stalkers, like her own sister had been.

His undeniable appeal had caused a generation of women to fall in love with him, to make him rich. He didn't need any more money, and it had become obvious that he couldn't control the affection of his followers. His Number One Fan had killed herself out of love for him, and his wife and his child had suffered immeasurably because of Elise's inability to let go of her fantasy. The idea that such a thing could very easily happen again appalled Denny. So he quit.

Elise Carlin lived and died for her love of rock and roll, her love of the road, and her love for Dennis Whitly. She was never a musician, only a

142

fan, yet she joined the same club as the great ones she revered. Hendrix and Joplin, Morrison and Cobain never saw their twenty-eighth birthdays, and neither did Elise.

Rest in peace, my friend.

Valerie threw the book at the wall again.

Damn Uncle Calvin, anyway.

Valerie had her own life to lead. There was school, thoughts about college in the near future, how she planned to take the IT world by storm. All the programs and processes she planned to create. And there was Darren, her respite from the sterile environment of the computer, her favorite thing to *do* IRL.

Now there would have to be a pause. She would have to get to the bottom of all this. It might be unpleasant for Mom and Dad – allegations of adultery, and suicide! Yes, it would be painful to her parents, but the suspense was killing Valerie now. She had to know: *Is any of this true?*

****

Valerie hopped into the gently used Volvo that her parents had given her for her sixteenth birthday and drove quickly to the Borders in Riverside Plaza.

In what could only be termed the *Tell-All Section,* Valerie discovered a large display for Barbara Walter's newly published hardcover memoir, *Audition.* There was *Tom Cruise: An Unauthorized Biography* on the shelf below it. Valerie considered picking that one up for her mom, as she'd always been a Tom Cruise fan, as much as she was a fan of any particular movie star. But Valerie decided against it. Sophia cared more for the parts the actor played; a recitation of his marriages and divorces and religious beliefs would only bore her.

The rest of the biographies and autobiographies had some years on them. She found Janice Dickenson's 2002 tale of her career as the first supermodel, *No Lifeguard On Duty,* flanked by Pamela Des Barre's notorious, *I'm with the Band: Confessions of a Groupie.* Originally published in 1987, it had been rereleased in 2005.

There was Karrine Steffen's *Confessions of a Video Vixen.* Surprised that a second, more modern groupie tale had been published, Valerie picked it up. It wasn't that modern: it was also from 2005. There was *Little Girl Lost,* Drew Barrymore's saga of a child in Hollywood, beside

143

Tina Turner's life story, published twenty years before, and there was the bombshell that had started the genre, Christina Crawford's *Mommie Dearest*.

Twelve copies of *Sonic Nightmare* were sandwiched in between the other groupie exposés. Valerie chose one and took it up to the cashier.

The smiling young woman looked at her selection and commented, "Did you know that they're from Riverside? I hear Dennis Whitly still lives here."

Valerie figured the talky cashier would see her name on her ATM card anyway. "I know. He's my dad."

The Borders' clerk's mouth fell open as Valerie took her purchase and headed for the door. As Valerie was about to exit the store, she called, "Is any of it true?"

Valerie ignored her.

Her motivation for buying a second copy of Calvin's book was simple. Valerie tried to remember the word for when someone convicted of multiple crimes served all their sentences at once. As she started the car, she had it. *Concurrently*. She would have her parents read this perhaps fictional tale of their lives *concurrently*, as opposed to *consecutively*.

Valerie wanted to hear the real story. She wanted the answer to *is any of it true?* But it wouldn't be fair if one parent got to read the book while the other one wondered about what it contained. And there would be a further delay in the business of getting back to her own life, if Valerie had to wait while first one, then the other one read it.

Valerie sighed, again thinking that this was all going to be painful to them, the dredging up of the accident that had claimed Aunt Elise, the tragic, pivotal event that had turned them off of the path of famous rock star and famous rock star's wife.

Valerie thought about how different her own life might've been. She'd be going to high school at the beach, would know all kinds of famous people. Movie stars, maybe, or at least their kids.

But Valerie wasn't unhappy with her life in Riverside, and it wasn't *her* life that was important at the moment, anyway. It was unfortunate that Calvin's book and her question – *Is any of it true?* – would be uncomfortable to her mom and dad. But Valerie had to know.

She waited until after dinner, until after the dishes were cleared away. She waited until right before Denny would go upstairs to Valerie's never-met grandfather's music room, where he might put on the old leather headphones and spin a few discs, or maybe even write a new song. Denny still did that, although none of them ever saw any kind of release these days.

Valerie waited until right before she usually went to her room to write code, before Sophia retired to her own room to watch a movie.

"Have either of you seen this?" From the identical looks of speechless surprise on her parents' faces, Valerie knew that they had not. She handed them each a copy.

After a moment of silence, Denny said, "Well, I'll be goddamned." He traced his finger over the grainy black and white picture of his younger self.

Sophia read the back cover, then thumbed through the photos in the middle of the book. "Jesus, Denny! Our wedding picture's in here!"

The guitarist shook his head. He was amazed at his drummer's betrayal, that he was parading the band's dirty laundry before the world. But on the other hand, such a thing was not totally unexpected. "I'm actually surprised it took Calvin this long. He never did save his money. He tried for years to get another good gig, but drummers are a dime a dozen." Denny grinned crookedly at his daughter, with a ghost of his old rock star's smile. *"If you ever get annoyed, look at me, I'm self-employed."* He looked at the garish red cover, at the book's title, a dark play on the band's world-famous name. "I guess he'll make a few bucks off of this."

Valerie made her demands in a gentle, even voice. "I want you guys to read it. I want you to tell me if any of it's true. I have a right—"

"Or at least you think you do," Sophia said coldly. "Things that happened when you were just a little girl really aren't any of your—"

"I loved Aunt Elise, Mom," Valerie said softly. "It's mostly about her. I want to know if any of it's true."

"All right." Dennis Whitly had once brought sold-out stadiums to their feet, simply by walking out on stage, and even though it may have been subdued by tragedy and sadness, the confidence that had allowed him to so thoroughly entertain his fans had never really left him. He displayed it to his daughter as he plopped down right there at the dining room table, and flipped his drummer's book open with a flourish. "I'm sure none of it's true." He winked at Valerie. "Cal didn't even get the name of the band right."

Sophia was expressionless. She took her copy of *Sonic Nightmare* and retired to her room.

****

145

The next afternoon, Valerie was surprised to discover that she couldn't concentrate on the program she was writing. It was an electronic update on a card trick her Uncle Ernie had taught her as a child.

Out of sight of the mark, the trickster would pick a card, place it on the top of the deck and put the deck back in the box. Then he would call the sucker's attention – "I'm psychic, Valley. I can read your mind. First, name the four suits of cards for me."

"Clubs, hearts, spades, and diamonds."

"Ok, now pick two."

"Clubs and hearts."

"That leaves spades and diamonds, right?" Valerie nodded. "Pick one."

"Spades."

"That leaves diamonds, right?" Valerie nodded again, and Ernie grinned at her father. "So our suit is diamonds."

By a clever process of elimination, Ernie had gotten Valerie to believe that *she* had chosen diamonds, not him. By the same process, he got the child to believe that she had chosen the denomination of the card that he had already hidden at the top of the deck. "If ace through ten is low, and the jack, queen, and king is high, pick high or low."

"Low."

"That leaves high, right? If the jack and queen are low, and the king is high, pick high or low."

"High."

"So your card is the king of diamonds?"

Valerie again nodded. Denny rolled his eyes when his bandmate miraculously, *psychically*, produced Valerie's card.

Valerie decided to work in concert with the computer to accomplish the trick. It would be easy enough to make the machine do all the work, but she thought it would be so much more clever to have an actual, physical deck of cards on hand to present to her dupe. She would hide the king of diamonds at the top of the deck as her uncle had done, then she would take the added step of typing *KD* into the computer before calling her sucker.

The algorithm skipped the first step of asking the player to name all four suits. The prompt said, *Pick two suits of cards. H, S, C, or D.*

Whatever suits the mark typed, the next question would include *D* as a choice, until the only choice left was *D*, thereby establishing the suit. And the same would happen with the numbers, until the computer at last said, *The card you've picked is K of D. My human counterpart will now extract that card from the deck.*

It should've been a simple fall-through program, elementary if-then-else loops, but it was giving Valerie a hard time. The suits worked, but she was having trouble with the numbers, and after an hour or so, she realized that the reason the program wasn't behaving was because she wasn't giving her full concentration to writing it.

She had slept through family breakfast, but at lunch, both Denny and Sophia had ignored her and each other, immersed in their copies of *Sonic Nightmare,* even as they dined. But it was late afternoon now, and Calvin's volume was slender. Valerie knew that both parents had to have completed it, yet neither had come to her to offer an explanation.

That was why she couldn't concentrate on the card trick program. The truth was nigh, but neither parent had knocked on her door to tell it to her.

Valerie sought her mother first. If Calvin's scandalous assertions were true, then Sophia was the injured party. She was the victim of an adulterous husband, and worse: according to the drummer, Denny had not only cheated on his wife, he had driven her sister to suicide behind it. If what Uncle Calvin had written was true, it was no wonder to Valerie that her mother had grown so much cooler to her husband after the accident. If it was true, Valerie wondered why Sophia hadn't divorced him.

Sophia was in her room, watching *The World According To Garp.*

Valerie stood beside the bed and looked at the television. Garp and his two sons sped down the hill. *Make it fly, Dad!* Garp shut off the headlights . . . There was the clang of metal, the blare of a horn, as the car crashed into another car in the garage, wherein Garp's wife was performing a sex act upon her young boyfriend . . .

Sophia shut off the television and glanced at her daughter. Valerie returned her gaze expectantly.

"You remember this movie, Val?"

Valerie glanced at the darkened TV, nodded slowly.

"One of their little boys dies in the crash, the other one loses an eye. All because Mom's in the garage, doing some college kid."

Sophia had perennially used movies to teach life lessons to her daughter, and Valerie saw the connection now: adultery, a car accident, life-changing disfigurement, death . . .

Valerie blinked in disbelief. "So you're saying that what Calvin said about Aunt Elise and Dad . . ."

"Men get away with adultery all the time, Val. Remember how, earlier in the movie, Garp screws the star-struck babysitter?" Valerie winced at her mother's language, so uncharacteristic of her. "But

147

nothing ever comes of that, does it? It's all okey-dokey. Adultery is condoned, almost expected, especially if a man is famous.

"But adultery on a woman's part . . ." Sophia gestured at the blank screen. "That is a sin unforgivable. According to Irving, it's akin to murdering your children."

Valerie remembered the piles of fan mail, addressed not to the band in general but to its singer specifically. She remembered the screams of the girls in the audience, deafening, even from backstage. She remembered the two groupies looking around in the green room for her father, like predators, as if they might eat him. She remembered Elise's words. "They hate your mommy because they want *to be* your mommy, Val. We all do."

Did you cheat on Mom, Dad? With her own sister?

"Why didn't you divorce him?" Valerie asked softly.

Sophia shrugged. "I love him. Elise was gone. He quit the road. Just like Cal said, it wasn't ever gonna happen again."

Valerie's shock made her unable to speak for the span of several seconds. "So you're saying it's all true?"

Sophia's expression hardened. "You're a big girl, Val. You . . . You and Cal, you brought all this up again. You figure it out."

But then Sophia sighed and began to tell her daughter what she'd never told another soul.

"Elise came to pick us up at the country club. I left you there with Sondra and got into the car."

To the police and Denny, Sophia had claimed to be unable to remember anything that happened afterward, until she woke up in the hospital. The doctors said such memory blanks were common when life-threatening injuries were sustained; they called it *pre-trauma amnesia.*

This memory loss was actually just a lie Sophia repeated to get everyone to stop asking her about the accident. In reality, she remembered every second of her last ride with Elise; she'd gone over every detail of it a million times in her mind since it occurred.

"Elise put *Riders on the Storm* on the stereo. It was always one of her favorites. I can't stand to hear it anymore.

"Your dad and Lenny were playing it one night, not long after we moved back here. I was asleep downstairs, but the music got into my dreams. It all happened again, and I screamed myself awake. Your dad came rushing in, and Lenny. They asked me what was wrong, but I couldn't . . . I just couldn't verbalize it. I just said I'd had a bad dream." Sophia took a deep, shuddery breath.

"Morrison was singing, and out of nowhere, Elise started to cry. She said, 'I've loved him since the moment I saw him, Soph.'

"I knew she wasn't talking about dead Jim Morrison. I knew she was talking about Denny, even though she'd never spoken to me about him, not once, not since we got together, not since before you were born. But it had always been there. In her eyes. I said, 'I know, Elise. *He* knows.'

"She screamed at me to shut up. She said I didn't know anything. She said, 'We were alone tonight . . . and then . . . And then he told me that it was never gonna be just the two of us. I can't handle it, Soph. It's so unfair. After all these years . . .'"

And then, Valerie thought. *It's a loaded phrase. It could mean everything — we were alone tonight and then he* gave in *and then he changed his mind. Or it could mean nothing — we were alone and then he told me it would never be just the two of us.* What her mother was telling her wasn't precisely a confession . . .

"*And then,* she stomped on the accelerator and drove us through the guardrail." Sophia tossed her copy of *Sonic Nightmare* to her daughter. "So you tell me, Val. *Just what the truth is, I can't say anymore.* But I don't think people just decide to go with murder-suicide over nothing."

Sophia put her head in her hands, and Valerie quickly left the room.

****

Valerie found the famous rock star upstairs. He was sitting in the record room, with his guitar and a small amp, wearing her grandfather's ancient headphones.

The record jacket for *Synchronicity* was leaning against the shelf below the turntable. Valerie picked it up, curiously, as always. How big records were! In the yellow, blue and red stripes of the cover, she could clearly make out the photos of the trio, with Sting in the middle, shirtless, Hamlet-like among skulls and skeletons.

"Hey, Valley, you remember this one?" Denny always said that, even if the tune was from before she was born. He spoke loudly, because of the headphones. He played the unmistakable licks to *Every Breath You Take,* sang snatches of the lyrics:

Since you've gone I've been lost without a trace
I dream at night, I can only see your face
I look around, but it's you I can't replace
I feel so cold, and I long for your embrace
I keep crying baby, baby, please

149

Oh can't you see
You belong to me?
How my poor heart aches with every step you take

Valerie felt a surge of love for her parents and she smiled. Her mother had always sought to show her the truths of life via the silver screen, and here was her dad, communicating through the medium of music. He was discussing Elise's obsession through Sting's unforgettable lyrics.

But then Valerie's smile fled. Sophia had said that it was all true. Not just her sister's fixation, but all the rest of it. Dennis Whitly was an adulterer, a chickenshit monster.

Denny saw his daughter's icy expression. He stood his guitar against the shelf, removed the headphones and placed them on top of the closed turntable – couldn't leave it open and allow any dust to settle upon one of grandpa's old records. Valerie could still hear Sting's plaintive voice, tinny and far away.

"You can't imagine what it was like, Valley."

"What's that, Dad?" she rejoined harshly. "The constant temptation? The groupies throwing themselves at you every night? Aunt Elise–"

"Is that what you think of me?" Denny's voice was soft, incredulous. "Just because a jealous drummer said so?"

Valerie remained silent. She didn't want to believe it, but her mom had said . . .

"It ain't necessarily so, Valley." Denny shook his head, still not believing that his daughter could think so poorly of him. "There was no temptation. Not from your aunt or anyone else. I've loved your mom from the moment I saw her."

He sighed. "When I said, *you can't imagine what it was like,* I was talking about your aunt." He gestured at *Synchronicity,* still in her hands. "I lived Sting's song for ten years, Val. Constantly, every step of the way, there was your aunt, staring at me, *watching me.*

"It's true that before I met your mother, I . . . *dated* a lot of girls. Your aunt was almost one of them. But only almost, Valley. She was way too young for me. If it hadn't been for your mom, I never would've spoken to Elise again. She would've become just another fan . . ."

"But that didn't happen."

"No. She introduced me to Sophia, and I never wanted another woman after that. But Elise was still there. Every night, every town, with that lovesick look on her face . . .

"I tried to tell your mom that Elise would've been better off if she stayed home, but she said that leaving her behind would break her sister's heart. Your mom trusted me, Valley. We were so much in love."

"Not so much anymore, Dad," Valerie whispered.

"I can't believe that, Val. Just because Calvin said Elise committed suicide? It's all so ridiculous. Sure, Elise loved me, but there was absolutely nothing I could do about that, was there? It had been like that for as long as I'd known her. Nothing had changed, so why would she all of a sudden decide to kill herself, and Sophia, too? His theory doesn't make any sense, Val."

"What happened between you guys the night of the accident? Calvin said that you . . . that you and Aunt Elise . . ." Valerie just couldn't say it out loud, couldn't form the words that spelled out his unforgivable sin.

Denny's eyebrows went up in surprise. "That we what?"

"You read it, Dad!"

"What? I don't remember reading anything – what are you talking about, Val?"

Apparently, Calvin's one damning sentence had passed Denny by, had failed to make the same impression that it had upon his daughter, and Darren, and everybody else that would read his dreadful book.

Denny's copy of *Sonic Nightmare* was lying on the couch. Valerie gently set *Synchronicity* down against the shelf and snatched it up. She pawed viciously through its pages. "Right here, Dad. *I don't know for sure what happened between them that night. Maybe Denny at last gave in, then had a fit of conscience. Whatever it was, whatever he said to her, it was the final straw for Elise. For ten years, no one could talk her out of her dream. But in one night, Denny shattered the illusion, completely.*"

Valerie turned a few pages. "And then he says it again, Dad! *The heartbreak had come earlier in the evening for Elise. Whatever had occurred between Denny and his sister-in-law, he had rejected her in the end, and it undid her. If Elise couldn't have the object of ten years' desire, then her sister wasn't going to have him any more either.*

"Uncle Calvin's saying that you and Aunt Elise . . . that you guys . . ." Valerie still couldn't say it.

"That's not true, Val. Nothing happened."

"That's not what Mom thinks. She thinks that you and Aunt—"

"Because of what Cal says?" Denny showed anger now, for the first time since his daughter had presented him with his drummer's traitorous exposé. "Because he made up some voicemail to back it up? It's bullshit, Val! We'd never been alone together in all those years. I made sure of it, just so the kind of thing that happened wouldn't happen again—"

"So now you're saying it did happen!"

"No, Val. Your aunt made a play for me once, a long, long time ago. And I would've gone for it – that's no secret. Your mom knows all about that. But I didn't, because I found out that Elise was just a kid. In all the years after that, she never made a pass at me again. But on that night . . ."

Denny considered his baby girl for a second, and decided that she was old enough. It was Valerie who had brought all of Elise's insanity back into his life again, Valerie who was demanding explanations, so *she* certainly thought she was old enough to hear them. So he spelled it out, as if he was talking to another adult, someone that was not his daughter.

"We ate dinner, then Elise disappeared for a minute. She came back half-naked in this lacy, teddy thing. She tried to kiss me. I told her no, Val, just like I did when she was sixteen. I told her it was never gonna be like that. She said she accepted it, and asked if she could take the car to get some air."

Denny shook his head again. "Your mom doesn't know anything about that part of it, so I don't know how she can believe this bullshit that Cal wrote. I just don't get it."

"Elise told her, Dad. Before she drove off the road—"

"WHAT?"

"Aunt Elise told Mom that you guys were alone . . ." Valerie tried to remember what Sophia had said, then she realized that it wasn't so much *what* she'd said, as how she'd said it.

"It was the pause, Dad. Mom said that Aunt Elise told her that you guys were alone, and then . . . Mom paused, just like Aunt Elise must have. You were alone . . . *and then* . . . and then you told her that it was never gonna be just the two of you. She made Mom believe that something had happened between you guys, with that pause, something . . . *physical*. Then Aunt Elise told Mom that she couldn't handle it. She said, 'It's so unfair. After all these years . . .'"

"So your mom has *always* thought . . ." Denny's eyes widened in stunned disbelief. "Even before Calvin's bullshit book. Your mom has always believed that we . . ."

152

Denny arose to go and find his wife, to confront her. As Valerie followed him, she remembered a scene from a play they'd recently covered in English: Shakespeare's *Henry V*. She remembered the begging insistence of the king as he prayed, pleading with God not to be set against his army because his father had come to the crown through the death of the previous king. He promises to build more churches, and

> *More will I do;*
> *Though all that I can do is nothing worth,*
> *Since that my penitence comes after all,*
> *Imploring pardon.*

All the pieces slid into place for Valerie. Her mother's coldness to her father after the accident: of course she would be cold. From her sister's words and deadly actions, Sophia believed that her beloved, always-trusted husband had betrayed her.

She had forgiven Denny because she loved him, but his own actions had sealed the truth of it in Sophia's mind. Dennis Whitly had not given up touring because he wanted to heal his wife's loss and see her through her devastating injuries, as he had told *Rolling Stone*, as Valerie had always believed.

No. That wasn't it at all. Sophia had always believed what Calvin had stated in his book, that he'd quit out of guilt. She believed that he'd slept with her sister, so the damage, irrevocable on so many levels, had already been done. Sophia believed that Denny's selfless gesture, like the king's prayer, had come *imploring pardon*. Sophia believed that Denny had given up his career to make amends for messing around with Aunt Elise.

Father and daughter found Sophia watching another movie, in the living room this time.

"How can you believe that any of this is true?"

Denny's bride, the mother of his child, the love of his life, looked up at him expressionlessly. She clicked off the TV. "Of course it's true. It's all true. Elise loved you. There's no denying that. And after you . . ." That damning pause again. Sophia couldn't say the words, either.

"Then you told her you'd never be with her again. She lost her mind. If she couldn't have you—"

"Stop quoting Calvin's stupid fucking book, Sophia!" Denny thundered savagely. "Can't you see that he's just trying to make a buck off a tragedy?"

153

"Elise told me, Denny!" Sophia sobbed.

He sat beside her on the couch, moved her cane aside and took both of her hands in his. "I don't know what she told you, Soph. I don't care. Whatever it was, it was a lie. Nothing ever happened between us. Not ever.

"That night, she asked me again. It was the first time she'd ever brought it up in all those years, and I told her no. I told her that you loved her, and that what she was suggesting was a terrible thing, a horrible, disloyal thing. I told her once and for all that it was never going to happen. She said she wanted to get some air, could she borrow the car. I had no idea that she was going to go and pick you up, that she would . . ."

Valerie was appalled to see the tears fall from her father's eyes. She had never seen him cry before, not ever, not at her injured mother's bedside, not at her aunt's funeral. Dennis Whitly had always been stoic in his grief. But now he cried. The idea that his wife had suspected him of infidelity, and that she had suspected him for all these years — whilst she dealt with her own pain and grief — that she had suspected him to be the cause of it all — it was too much for Denny to bear. It undid him. He cried.

"I would never hurt you, Sophia, I would never . . . Jesus, how could you think that? That I would . . ." Denny suddenly turned his agonized face toward his daughter and Valerie jumped. "How did Cal put it? That I . . . *gave in?*" Valerie was relieved when he looked at his wife again. "Jesus, Sophia! What kind of a man did you think you married?

"Your sister . . . Your sister was as crazy as a shithouse rat, Sophia. She always was. She was delusional. Calvin got that part right. She convinced herself that she was in love with me when she was sixteen, and when I finally made it clear to her that it was impossible, she just—"

"She just gave up. Like Mom did."

A realization dawned on Sophia. Her face went slack at the wonder of it. She glanced at her silent, shocked daughter, then back at her husband again. "My mom . . . Dad was always the most important thing in her life, and after he was gone, so was her reason for living. She just gave up, just wasted away.

"And Elise . . . *Oh, my God, Denny!* She was just a little bit quicker about it. Once she finally saw the truth . . . She just couldn't go on, just like Mom!" Sophia threw her arms around her husband and squeezed him to her. "I'm so sorry! How could I have ever doubted you? It was never you — you always tried to tell me. Elise would never give up. I

154

should've realized that. She was crazy, just like Mom . . ." Sophia sobbed into his shoulder. "I'm so sorry, Denny! I love you so much!"

"I love you, too, Sophia. I've never loved anyone but you."

The crisis past, Valerie rolled her eyes at her parents' soppy declarations of devotion, and as they kissed, she slipped silently from the room.

****

A glorious change came to the Whitly home after that. It was again filled with joy and laughter and love, just like Valerie remembered from her childhood at the beach. That her parents had always loved each other had never been in doubt to their daughter, but now they once again expressed it with smiles and hugs, quick kisses and frequent *I love yous*.

The discussion that Valerie had demanded after reading Calvin's book had cleared away the solemn clouds that had hung over the family for half of her life, and her parents frequently thanked her for forcing the explanations. All suspicions were swept away. Everything was again as it should have always been.

The whole incident colored Valerie's perception of the relationships between men and women, caused her to look at all inter-gender interactions in a new and different light.

First, there was the whole sex thing. She and Darren had tripped the light fantastic on that score, and Valerie enjoyed it very much. But there was little emotion attached to it for Valerie. She couldn't quite imagine it as the basis of home and hearth and a life with another person.

She knew that if she wasn't careful, the act would produce a baby, but she couldn't quite connect the two in her mind. If was like the idea that she knew that if she dropped the hairdryer in the bathtub with her, she would be electrocuted. She understood the processes of conductivity and electrons seeking ground and all that, but the *why* of the thing eluded her. Sex produced babies – but why would anyone want to use it for that purpose, why would anyone want to saddle themselves with their baby's daddy for a lifetime – as her mother and father had done, as most people did? It didn't quite jell in her mind.

Valerie enjoyed sex, so much so that she often found herself eyeing Darren's teammates and even men she passed on the street. She already had a type – pretty, dark-haired, confident – and if the men she saw met these simple criteria, she wondered what they would be like. She understood, intellectually, that she and Darren had an arrangement.

She had agreed to be his girlfriend, so that meant that monogamy was expected. But the idea of breaking their unspoken high school vows – Valerie reckoned that if she liked Darren and the things they did, she would like it just as much with his buddy Aaron, or the cashier at the grocery store – and what would be wrong, really, with sampling someone else? It wouldn't mean anything to her. She would still have lunch with Darren, they would still go to the movies and hang out. She would still be his girlfriend.

Valerie knew that to act on such impulses was wrong. The words were ugly – *cheating, infidelity, adultery*. She would be considered a *whore*, a *slut*, a *bitch*. She would of course never do such a thing. If Valerie discovered that there was someone who might be more fun than Darren, well . . . she would just tell Darren goodbye before she endeavored to find out.

Eventually, that's just what would happen.

Valerie completely understood the groupies' attraction for her dad, now. If one was attracted to a man, of course one would want to sleep with him, and all the other societal strictures be damned.

But the idea of being a groupie was foreign to Valerie, besides its basic motivation. An obsession with one man – be he singer or actor, race car driver, pro quarterback or hockey goalie – if he was unachievable, then why bother? Valerie was loyal to Darren, but she looked around her and saw a world of attractive men. She couldn't imagine wasting her time in the fruitless pursuit of any particular individual one of them. She had only had experience with Darren so far, but Valerie imagined that men were no doubt interchangeable. Why pine for just a single, unreachable one and only?

There were a thousand hobbies in the world for which Valerie had absolutely no interest: traveling to exotic, third-world countries, places where they didn't even have electricity, nonetheless an internet connection. Hanging from cliff faces by one's fingers, jumping out of perfectly good airplanes. Valerie could picture the thrill and excitement that these activities held for others, without ever once feeling it herself.

And so it was for her with the idea of love everlasting, the concept of one's other half, one's soulmate. She had seen enough movies to know that the perfect union between two people, forsaking all others and all that, could exist. I love you, you love me, 'til death do us part.

Valerie knew that true love was out there; her parents had achieved it. But their love story had not been all roses and lollipops, now had it?

Somewhere in the back of her mind, Valerie feared such an overpowering emotion. What must such an absoluteness of feeling be

156

like? What heights, surely, might it lead a girl to, but also, what depths? From the absence of the love of her life, her grandmother had just wasted away. From the constant presence of a love she could never have, Valerie's aunt had been driven to suicide. Sophia mother had lived with the painful certainty of Denny's betrayal for eight years, would have gone on carrying that burden forever, all because of love. Denny had given up his career, not out of guilt for something he had not done, as her mother had believed, but because he loved her and wanted to be by her side.

O, that way madness lies; let me shun that.

And this lack of communication that seemed to exist in these true love situations also puzzled Valerie. Why hadn't her mother discussed all her suspicions with her father at the earliest opportunity? If she thought Denny had cheated on her, why not just accuse him of it, accept the truth, whatever it was, and move on? Why live in pain and sorrow for eight years, knowing in her heart but not really knowing, because in the end, she threw off her suspicions when she at last heard her husband's side of the story? Why not ask him for it in the beginning?

Once he did explain, Sophia had just gone right ahead and accepted Denny's tale. That was the oddest part of all to Valerie, although she thought she understood why Sophia had abandoned her agonizing suspicions all in one fell swoop. It was because, all along, Sophia had *wanted to believe* that her husband was above reproach. She had wanted to believe that none of it had been true, none of it had been his fault, because she loved him. Her mind had accepted the ugly, probable possibility that Denny had slept with her sister, and her spirit and emotions had warred with her intellect for eight years over it. The suspicion was not as painful as the truth would be.

Sophia reveled in the cinema because she could effortlessly suspend disbelief. She accepted the rules of vampire life or space travel without a moment of doubt, in order to enjoy the story completely. And just as effortlessly, once Denny had told his side of the story, Sophia had decided to believe him. His truth was no more likely than what she had believed before, but because she saw that it would allow her to be happy once again, Sophia had let go of all the old suspicions. She accepted the (possible) fantasy of his explanation because *she wanted to.* She had wanted to all along.

After her parents' happy reconciliation, Valerie's perception of her father also changed. He was beautiful, sexy, talented, adored by millions, and she still loved him for all that. But after Calvin's book and the emotion-wrought showdown that led to her parents again being happily-ever-after, Valerie saw Denny as silly. He was unable to control the ramifications of his own charisma. He should've shut Elise down immediately, but apparently he hadn't wanted to hurt her feelings. He couldn't help it if she loved him, and he wasn't even willing to try.

Valerie liked pretty men, but after her parents finally made up again, Valerie believed that she could never get too attached to any of them. *Consider the lilies of the field, how they grow; they toil not, neither do they spin.* What possible purpose could they serve, other than a passing amusement?

Her aunt, her mother – all the grave emotions they had wasted on one pretty man! Such a one track preoccupation was just pointless. There were so many pretty men! Throughout her high school and college years, Valerie perceived the world as just one big toy store, filled with attractive playthings, all at her disposal. She could not imagine devoting her life and energy, her spirit, *her love,* to just one of them.

But the Valerie that felt that way had yet to meet Brett Cooke.

Brett had made her understand true love, the perfect congruence with another person who thought just like you did. Just like her mother loved her father, Valerie had loved Brett. Just like Sophia had been unable to confront Denny with the seeming proof of his infidelity, Valerie could not hold up Brett's phone and demand, "What is this?" It would just hurt too much to hear the words come out of his beloved mouth. Valerie now understood how Sophia could've existed in doubt for eight years. It was better to hurt a little then to hurt forever.

But unlike her mother's doubts, Valerie had seen the proof irrefutable, in text form. Denny had never cheated on Sophia, but Valerie had seen the evidence of Brett's duplicity. The business major had never given up his own horde of groupies.

And at last, Valerie understood her aunt's pain. To think of the man you love with someone else, to see it, all the time . . . Valerie did not know how Elise had coped with it for ten long years.

Valerie knew that she could never cope with seeing Brett with someone else. Not for ten years. Not for ten minutes. She was not the tough cookie that her aunt had been. Better to end the pain sooner rather than later.

****

158

Joyce slammed her car into park and leapt out. She left the keys in the ignition, her purse and phone on the passenger seat. She ran up the walk. Fortunately, the front door was unlocked.

She burst into Valerie's bedroom. All the curtains were drawn; the room was in shadow. The only light came from the television. Valerie was huddled on the bed, against the wall, holding a remote control. She was alive, awake, but accoutrements of suicide stood grimly on the nightstand: two prescription bottles filled with fat pills; a large plastic bag; a pen and pad for the note.

Valerie's bottom lip trembled and tears rolled silently down her cheeks.

"What did you take, Val?"

"I didn't take anything yet."

"You wouldn't lie to me would you?" Joyce picked up one of the prescription bottles. The first pills were Oxycodone. The patient's name and any other identifying marks had been removed from the tan plastic. The label on the second bottle was similarly defaced – *generic for Vicodin* was all that Joyce could make out.

Valerie shook her head, quoted *Fight Club*. *"This isn't a real suicide-thing. This is probably one of those cry-for-help things.* Not yet, anyway." She gestured at the TV with the remote. "I made some clips." She pushed the button.

Bogie, in black and white, riding in an open car with a blonde. Joyce didn't recognize the blonde or the movie. Bogie said, "I was born when she kissed me. I died when she left me. I lived a few weeks while she loved me."

Cut to Jennifer Grey, pre-nose job, strident in her adolescent confession: "I'm scared of walking out of this room and never feeling the rest of my whole life the way I feel when I'm with you."

Travis Bickle, driving through the teeming streets of New York, looking at the people, apart, alienated: "Loneliness has followed me my whole life. Everywhere. In bars, in cars, sidewalks, stores, everywhere. There's no escape. I'm God's lonely man."

Cary Elwes, as the Dread Pirate Roberts: "Life is pain, Highness. Anyone who says differently is selling something."

The Wizard of Oz, revealed as just a man, cautioning the Tin Man: "Hearts will never be practical until they are made unbreakable."

Rutger Hauer, in the rain, from *Blade Runner*, his face gashed, his incredible blue eyes aglow with madness and sorrow: "I've seen things you people wouldn't believe. Attack ships on fire off the shoulder of Orion. I watched C-beams glitter in the dark near the Tanhauser gate.

All those moments will be lost in time like tears in rain. Time to die." And while Harrison Ford looked on, he did just that.

Joyce had seen enough. She took the remote from her friend, and killed the power to the television. The room faded immediately to black.

Val was despondent, suicidal – how many hundreds of sad movie clips might she have compiled? This might go on for hours. Besides, Joyce wasn't here to wallow with Val in this dangerous adolescent melancholy, *over worthless Brett Cooke*. She was here to snap her out of it, if it was the last thing she ever did.

But she loved Val, so Joyce would attempt to do it slowly, kindly, gently. She switched on the lamp atop the nightstand, sat down on the bed and gathered her heartbroken friend into her arms. "Tell me what happened, honey."

Through incoherent sobs and wails, Joyce got the story. Valerie and Brett had driven his mother home after graduation. They were going to visit for a minute and then head off to Vegas. Brett had excused himself to use the facilities, so he was not present when an alarm went off on his phone – time to get on the road. Mrs. Cooke picked it up and started pushing buttons, but being unfamiliar with modern contrivances, she couldn't figure out how to make the noise stop, so she handed the phone to Valerie.

Somehow, Brett's mother had called up one of Brett's dating site apps. Valerie couldn't help but see!

"It was like that scene in *Animal House,* Jo. Boon goes to visit Katie; she's surprised to see him. Then he hears a man's voice in the background. We see Donald Sutherland in the kitchen, looking for something. He reaches up and we realize he's not wearing pants . . ."

Joyce blinked as though slapped. She had not seen *Animal House,* seeing as it had come out about ten years before she was born. *Donald Sutherland's not wearing pants?*

"Boon realizes Katie is cheating on him. We see the betrayal on his face. He runs away. Brett's cheating on me, Jo. I'm as sure of it as Boon is in that scene."

Valerie sobbed. "All those apps are still on his phone! His mom was chirping at me, saying how lovely it was that her son had found a nice girl, and I was seeing just how many *nice* girls he'd been talking to. Some as recently as today, before graduation!"

Joyce couldn't overcome her curiosity. "What did they say?"

"One girl said, *It was nice seeing you at Q's the other night,* and another asked, *Are we ever going to have dinner again?* He doesn't love me, Val! I'm just a place holder! A . . . *a prop to occupy his time,* while he keeps looking!" Valerie buried her face in Joyce's shoulder and sobbed.

"That doesn't seem too damning, Val." A trace of annoyance tried to edge out Joyce's compassion. Valerie was overreacting, as if this was some bad rom-com, where an innocent text message on her boyfriend's phone sends the heroine fleeing into the night, convinced of infidelity. Can't have a make-up if you don't have a break-up. "It's not like he's talking dirty to them–"

"How do I know that?" Val cried shrilly. "There were *hundreds* of messages! I didn't read them all!"

It's a slippery slope, Joyce thought, *all a matter of degree. Surely, Val couldn't expect charming, good-looking Brett to give up all his legions of female friends. That would be unfair, jealous, controlling, things that Valerie is not. But, on the other hand, she could (and obviously did) expect him to stop talking to women on dating sites . . .*

"Then what happened?"

"I got a text. It was just my uncle saying congratulations, but I told Mrs. Cooke that it was important. I closed all the apps on Brett's phone and handed it back to her. I told her that I had to make a quick phone call – I'd be right back. I went outside and took my suitcase out of the car and called a cab."

"You didn't say anything to Brett?" Joyce was incredulous. This was still like some film, where the couple breaks up over nothing, without meeting face to face. That kind of thing never happened in real life – there were always tears, recriminations, an argument – but here was Val making it happen, making her life into a scene from a bad movie.

"I texted him. I told him something had come up. I told him to go to Vegas without me."

"Something came up?"

"He called, but I didn't pick up. I had the cab drop me at the bar. Brad was working." Valerie gestured at the pill bottles.

Joyce knew that Brad was the best kind of drug dealer, the ask-no-questions, tell-no-tales kind. Valerie had requested narcotics, and Brad had supplied them. It was graduation day, after all, and he probably figured that she was looking to have a good time. Her and a battalion of her friends, from the amount she had purchased. The idea that Valerie wanted all the pills for herself, that she was contemplating suicide, hadn't entered his mind, crowded out, as it no doubt was, by the dollar signs inherent in the transaction.

"I took another cab home and texted Brett. I told him that I didn't want to see him anymore. I told him that he obviously had enough online friends waiting in the wings. He could take one of them to

Vegas. He wouldn't miss me. He called, but I didn't pick up." Valerie sobbed again.

"Why didn't you talk to him, Val? Give him a chance to explain?"

"*The greatest trick the devil ever pulled was convincing the world he didn't exist,* Jo. I didn't want to hear him explain. *Words! Just words!* He'll never stop. I'm not gonna spend the rest of my life being suspicious every time he gets a text. He doesn't love me, Jo."

"But what did he *say* about it?"

"He said that they were just his friends, and that he hadn't gone anywhere or done anything with anybody but me since we'd met. He said that in a voice mail, when I wouldn't answer his calls. Then he texted and said he was coming over here. I told him that I was on my way to Riverside to see my parents. I told him to go to Vegas. I told him to leave me alone."

Joyce was amazed at the unyielding black and whiteness of Valerie's mindset. There was not a single nuance of gray; it was like the demarcation on the sun during an eclipse. Here was darkness, here was light. Brett was suddenly irretrievable to her. The idea that maybe he would've stopped talking to other girls if Valerie had simply asked him had apparently not occurred to her, or if it had, she had discarded it. Her mind was made up. He would never stop. She would not live her life in suspicion.

It was over. Valerie had dismissed the love of her life over *nothing,* and was so broken up about it that she had contemplated – no, she had *planned* – to kill herself. She had taken all the requisite steps, the drugs, the plastic bag.

Joyce's annoyance ratcheted up a notch. Valerie was ridiculous, she was maudlin. She would consider suicide because pretty Brett was talking to a few girls online? She would do herself in without even giving him a chance to explain? She was absurd. She'd seen too many movies.

"I blocked him," Valerie was saying. "I made myself a little drink." She picked a bottle of vodka up from beside the bed. Joyce had not seen it there, but suddenly realized that Val had to have something on hand with which to wash down all those deadly narcotics. "I got a big freezer bag from the kitchen, and brought it in here with my pills. I was gonna do it, just like Auntie Em."

"What?"

"The actress that played Auntie Em in *The Wizard of Oz.* She came home from church, and arranged all her mementos and stuff in her room, got all dressed up, took a handful of sleeping pills, and tied a bag over her head. She was going blind, Jo, and had arthritis. Her note mentioned that she couldn't take the pain anymore. I also wrote a note." Valerie nodded at the pad and Joyce picked it up.

"Goodbye, cruel world, I'm off to join the circus?"

"It's an old James Darren song. My dad used to sing it sometimes. *I'll tell the world that woman, wherever she may be, that mean, fickle woman made a cryin' clown outta me."* When Joyce remained dubious, Valerie added, a trifle defensively, "I thought it was apt.

"Since I didn't have any mementos to lay out, and I didn't feel like getting dressed up, I strung together a few clips that express how I feel. Then I called you."

"Tell me you're better now, Val," Joyce said evenly. "You sang your song, you wrote your note. You cobbled together some weepy clips. You bought enough drugs to kill every self-pitying, washed-up nobody that ever felt sorry for themselves in Hollywood.

"But you're not a nobody, Val, and there are a lot of people that love you. Jesus! What would your mother say, how would she feel, after what her sister did . . ." Valerie's eyes widened and Joyce let the thought die.

"You're sad and you feel stupid. I understand. I get it. But tell me you're over this now, Val. No more talk about killing yourself." Joyce's anger seethed, and she added softly, through gritted teeth. "Over stupid, worthless Brett Cooke."

Valerie nodded, chastised. *"We all go a little mad sometimes. Haven't you?"* Now she looked down at her feet, embarrassed. She realized that she had been behaving childishly, selfishly. She knew now that she would never have gone through with it. She never could've hurt Jo that way, and not her mother and father, not over some man, like Aunt Elise . . .

"Permanent solution to a temporary problem and all that," Valerie said. She tried a smile, failed, and the tears ran down her face anew. "But it's a permanent problem, Jo. I'm not going to kill myself, and I'm so sorry that I made you worry." She sobbed once more.

Joyce hugged her, said it was okay. "I'm just glad that you've realized that Brett's not worth—"

"But you have to do me a favor, Jo. You have to keep him away from me. Make something up. Tell him I moved back to Riverside . . . *Yeah, that's the ticket . . .*" Valerie flashed a sly smile, and Joyce believed that the danger of suicide was passed. Then her friend sobered again. "You tell him I left town, and that you haven't heard from me. Say I went to visit Lenny. With Dad."

"Who?"

"Leonard Whitly. *God's bass player*, as *Rolling Stone* once said. Dad's brother. He was in the band. He owns a big piece of ground in Anza now. Up there in the middle of nowhere. Tell Brett I went to visit Uncle Lenny."

"Brett knows you're going to interview with Fox in two weeks, Val–"

"In two weeks, Brett will have forgotten that I ever existed, Jo. I was never anything special to him." *Just like Aunt Elise was never anything special to Dad. It was all in her head, just like the love I thought Brett had for me . . .*

Valerie hitched a long, shuddering sigh. "I can deal with this. It'll take a few days, but I can deal with it." Her eyes pleaded with Joyce. "As long as I don't have to see him."

All at once, Joyce felt responsible for Val's pain. She'd known that Brett was different from the run-of-the-mill college boy; he was special, beautiful, incredible. And he knew the movies, too.

Joyce should've seen that Valerie wouldn't have been able to resist such a combination. All of her nonchalant appreciation for pretty boys as nothing but *props to occupy her time* – that all fell by the wayside when she met Brett. Valerie had at last discovered love. Unfortunately, she had also discovered that it *hurt*.

Joyce should've known that Valerie would fall for Brett – hell, Joyce was half in love with him herself.

But Joyce had always been smart enough to view Brett like a character in one of Valerie's movies: gorgeous, flawed. He was like a sexy fiction that she just happened to see, with whom she was lucky enough to interact. But she knew that she couldn't get involved with him anymore than she could get involved with Butch Cassidy or the Sundance Kid. A relationship with Brett was fun to think about, but Joyce knew better than to love such a man. It would only bring heartache. Yet she had allowed Valerie to go right ahead and do something that she herself would never do.

Valerie thought life could be like a movie, that there could be happy endings with cads and ladies' men, at least this one. Joyce should've seen it all coming. She should've tried harder to dissuade Valerie from the rom-com, the ride into the sunset, the happily-ever-after fade to black that her friend had envisioned with Brett.

So Joyce made up her mind on the spot that she would protect Val from this sort of thing in the future. She would look after her quirky friend. She would shield her from the world that was not like the movies.

"I'll handle Brett, Val," she promised. "You just rest for a while. Think happy thoughts. Here." Joyce clicked the television back on, called up Netflix. "Let's find a good movie for you to watch."

Joyce paged through their voluminous Netflix queue. Love stories, adventures, thrillers. But nothing very new, nothing Val hadn't already seen.

Joyce wanted to take her friend's mind off her heartache. She wanted Val to become engrossed in her familiar fantasy world of cinema, but she didn't want anything too familiar. If Val had seen it before, her mind might wander back to her troubles.

She clicked through *Popular on Netflix,* read a few descriptions.

There was *The Beekeeper – A sexy lady cop, a forensic scientist, and the beekeeper (Jake Franklin) make for an unusual love triangle while solving crimes in this quirky Canadian import. 36 episodes.* Joyce had never heard of Jake Franklin, and the series was several years old. She wondered when Netflix had begun co-opting old, *quirky Canadian imports* starring unknowns, and decided to give it a pass.

But the idea of a television series appealed to her. Something longer than a movie, something that would last more than two hours. She clicked down to find the TV list. Binge-watching a series would definitely get Val's mind off of Brett.

She found new episodes of *CSI;* no, that was too depressing. Something lighter. *Always Sunny in Philadelphia?* Too light. Too much silliness would bore Val. Busy with school, Joyce didn't watch a lot of television, so she wasn't sure of any of the new titles that she saw. She passed the old and new *Star Trek,* and *MacGyver.* Val had seen all of those.

Joyce clicked past *Hoarders.* Val was as neat as a pin. The only thing she hoarded were movies, and they were not even visible. No piles of DVD cases or disks. Val kept all of Hollywood on her computer. *And locked in her memory.*

She paused at *Coupling,* the original British series upon which *Friends* was based, then decided against it. Perhaps too much romance for Val's delicate state. She also considered *Black Mirror – This sci-fi anthology series in the vein of "The Twilight Zone" reflects on the darker side of technology and human nature.* No. Val pretty much lived in *The Twilight Zone* as it was, her vocation was technology, and she'd had enough of the darker side of human nature lately.

Joyce noticed out of the corner of her eye that Valerie was becoming fidgety. She wanted her friend to *pick something, already.* Joyce read the description for *Sonny's Diner – An eccentric former high school teacher*

165

(Edison Forbes) dispenses wisdom, humor, and ham-on-rye from behind the counter of the diner he runs with his equally eccentric grandmother. 36 episodes.

"How does this one sound?"

Valerie shrugged. "Okay, I guess. Bunch of unknowns . . ."

Joyce clicked the remote and the pilot episode of *Sonny's Diner* began. She paused it, handed the remote to Valerie, and turned to go.

"You're not going to watch with me?"

"I've gotta make a phone call, Val." Joyce eyed her friend significantly, and Valerie understood.

"Thanks, Jo. Tell him I'm out of town."

Joyce went into the living room and made herself a drink. She wasn't much of a drinker, but she thought she needed one now. She most assuredly deserved it. It had been quite an exciting day: she had graduated from college, had saved her best friend from suicide. Now all she had to do was deal with Brett. A glance at the clock amazed her. It was only seven o'clock.

Joyce gulped her Scotch, and glass in hand, she went out to the car and retrieved her phone. She hesitated. What did one sane person say to another sane person about someone who lived in the fanciful realm of rom-coms and happily-ever-afters? Someone who made life-altering, snap decisions from the Land of Oz? Joyce sighed and pushed the button. She would make it up as she went along.

"What the fuck, Jo?" the newly graduated business major said in greeting.

"Where are you, Brett?"

"I'm in Las Vegas."

Joyce was a little taken aback. She had always thought that Brett had cared about Val, at least as much as he was capable of caring for one woman at this point in his life. She thought that he would've stayed in town, upset over the guillotine-like swiftness and finality of Valerie's decision to break up with him. Joyce thought Brett would've been at least a *little bit* distressed about it.

But apparently she was mistaken, apparently Brett had just chosen the next name on his *okCupid* queue, the next lucky bachelorette on his own personal, electronic version of *The Dating Game*. Joyce had always known he was a bastard, and this move proved just how much of a bastard he really was. Valerie was right, and she was good to be rid of –

"My mom wanted to see The Blue Man Group. Val and I had tickets. She told me to leave her alone, so I figured I'd do what she wants, at least for the weekend. No sense wasting the money."

Immediately, Joyce felt bad about the low-down conclusion to which she'd jumped. Brett was her friend, and sure, he was a player. He was still talking to girls on dating sites, but he wasn't enough of a son of a bitch to forget about Valerie just like that, in the blink of an eye. Joyce reckoned she was getting as bad as her friend, thinking the worst of him with no evidence. Brett was basically a good guy. Maybe Valerie was making a big mistake.

"What the fuck, Jo?" Brett repeated. "Everything was fine, then all of a sudden she starts texting me about Plenty of Fish? Telling me to go to Vegas without her? Telling me she doesn't want to see me anymore?"

"You know how . . . high strung she can be."

"*High strung?* She's nuts, Jo. I haven't done anything wrong."

Joyce considered saying, *Val's just an old-fashioned girl, Brett. She thinks that you talking to other women is the same as cheating on her.* The second part was true, in hysterical, relationship-ending spades, but Brett wasn't going to buy the first part. Other than taking incredible offense at his (possibly innocent) texting practices, Valerie was anything but an old-fashioned girl, and nobody knew that better than Brett. Hadn't Val gone right on home with him, moments after they'd met?

"She's stressed right now, Brett." *Yeah, that's the ticket.* "She's got that big interview with 20th Century Fox coming up. That's a huge step in her life, if she gets on with them, right out of school. She's not thinking clearly right now, so she just overreacted, seeing all those messages—"

"They're just friends, Jo. Just girls that like to talk to me. There's nothing wrong with that."

A shadow of Valerie's outrage crept back into Joyce's mind. *Just friendly girls that like to talk, that you meet on* fuck *sites. What do they want to talk to you about, Brett? If they were all just your friends, maybe you'd have their actual names and numbers. Valerie wouldn't have objected to that. But when you're talking to HotTrixie via okCupid, and swiping right and answering messages from ShyKitty on Tinder, perhaps your girlfriend does have a legitimate bitch.*

"Maybe you should've uninstalled the dating apps, Brett."

"I'm not meeting any of them, Jo. It's just a way to pass the time."

Maybe Valerie was right. He would never stop. He didn't see anything wrong with it. But on the other hand, Valerie hadn't *asked him* to stop. If she'd asked him, maybe Brett would've taken the dating apps off of his phone. He didn't think he was doing anything wrong, but he might've gotten rid of them for Valerie. If she'd just asked him.

But that was all water under this melodramatic bridge over the information superhighway now, wasn't it? Jo wasn't on the phone with Brett to discuss the nuances of monogamous boundaries in the modern, wired world. It wasn't her place to debate the merit of

Valerie's perceptions or the hastiness of her decision. She wasn't a relationship counselor, a go-between, goddamn Cyrano de Bergerac, for Christ's sake. All of this was really none of her business. The only thing that concerned her was that Val wanted her to keep Brett away from her, and that's what she would do.

"Maybe you should—"

"I'm gonna enjoy The Blue Man Group and Vegas with my mom. Let Val cool off for the weekend. I'll call her when I get back home."

"That's a good idea, but what I was gonna say was this: maybe you should consider the idea that maybe Val's changed her mind. Her *future's so bright, she's gotta wear shades,* Brett."

Val had played the old novelty tune for Joyce once, telling her that her father had admiringly said that he wished he'd written it.

Joyce continued. "From what Greg says, this interview at Fox is really just a formality. He's talked her up. They know what she did in school. She's got the job. Maybe's she's decided that she just doesn't have the time, anymore, for someone that—"

"Val hasn't changed her mind, Jo. She loves me."

Oh, my Christ, the insufferable ego of a man! The fact that Brett was correct only incensed Joyce further. She had loved Jeremy once, and although the pain of his memory had lessened, had almost disappeared, Joyce did not remember him now with nostalgic joy because she *had* loved him, and it hadn't worked out between then. Brett was right. Valerie loved him, and she always would, but that love hurt. She wanted to forget it now, as best she could.

And Joyce had vowed to shield her from further such hurts.

"Maybe she loves you, Brett. Maybe not."

Joyce didn't want to hurt him either, but on the other hand, he could take it. Everybody loved Brett, did they not? Just like Val had said, he had plenty of other girls to whom he could turn, if he was too broken up about her decision.

"Val's got a lot to think about right now. Her career, her future. My advice to you would be *not* to call her when you get back from Vegas. Wait for her to call *you.* Don't embarrass yourself."

The adorable little boy inside Brett, so intrinsic to his charm, peeped out. She could hear it in his voice, across the airwaves, all the way from Nevada. "Ya really think so, Jo?"

Ah, Brett, you're so damn fine, what I wouldn't give . . . I'd take you myself, if you were just a little less . . . you.

"Let it ride, Brett. What will be will be."

"You know her better than anybody, Jo. If that's what she wants . . ."

"That's what she wants." Joyce turned to see Valerie standing in the doorway, listening. She watched her friend nod resolutely, dry-eyed.

That's what you think you want right now, honey, but what about tomorrow and next week?

The little boy in Brett's voice persisted. "We're still friends, though, aren't we, Jo?"

Maybe he *was* broken up about it. But Joyce restrained her pity. Brett would get over it. Her main responsibility was Valerie. "Sure, Brett. Always."

"Tell Valerie . . ." His voice hardened. "Whatever. Don't tell her anything. If this is how she wants it, nothing I can say will change her mind."

There was the Brett that Joyce knew. Easy come, easy go.

"I'll call you when I get back from Vegas."

Joyce said okay and goodbye. She knew that she'd never hear from him again. Nobody had ever dumped gorgeous Brett Cooke before, and he wasn't going to hang out with the friend of the first girl that had. Especially when she wasn't having any either. There were plenty of other fish in the sea, as close as the app on his phone.

"What did he say?"

"He said, if that's the way you want it . . ."

Valerie frowned bitterly. "What did I tell you?"

Joyce watched the sorrow etch itself across her friend's face again. Val had hoped that Brett would beg for forgiveness, had feared that he might. That's why she'd ask Joyce to keep him away, because she would've relented if he'd just said he was sorry. Then she would've been trapped in a life she didn't want. Every time his phone beeped, the suspicion would've come back . . .

"Val, don't you think that maybe–"

"I can't think about that right now. If I do, I'll go crazy. I'll think about that tomorrow." Valerie took a deep breath, ran a hand through her hair. "Que sera, sera, Joyce. This, too, shall pass. *After all, tomorrow is another day."*

Joyce waited for a heartbeat, and then another, to see if Valerie would break down, beg her to call Brett back, tell him it had all been a mistake, that she loved him. All would be forgiven if he would please come back . . . But to her amazement, none of that happened. Valerie was weak, sad, but she was resolute. She and Brett were through.

After another heartbeat of silence, Joyce asked, "Did you eat anything today?"

Valerie shook her head. "Not since breakfast."

"How does a Mulberry Street pizza sound?"

"It sounds great." Valerie crossed the room and hugged Joyce tightly. "Thank you so much for being my friend!"

"With friends like me . . ." *I'm the one that introduced you to him in the first place.* Joyce smiled, hugged Valerie back. "I want some ice cream, too. I'll pick up the pizza while I'm out. Do you need anything else?"

A heart transplant. The one I've got is broken. Valerie shook her head.

"Okay. I'll be back as soon as possible."

****

As soon as possible turned out to be nearly two hours.

Ever-popular Mulberry Street Pizza was packed on a graduation-day-for-UCLA, Friday night. Joyce saw Greg Castro inside, alone as always. She had often noted that computer techies were a solitary bunch: Valerie had never endeavored to make any other friends besides Joyce herself, except of course for Brett, now summarily, tearfully, dismissed. Greg was the same way. Whenever Joyce saw him at Q's or on campus, he was always by himself.

Greg smiled and waved at her, so Joyce sat down with him until the crowd thinned out and she could order her pizza. She had often speculated upon why he was a loner. For an IT geek, he wasn't unattractive, nor was he shy or socially awkward. But when he immediately asked after Valerie, the thought occurred to Joyce, as it had in the past, that perhaps this was the reason that Greg was always solo. She suspected that the blondie had a thing for her roomie. Maybe the flame from the torch he carried for Valerie Whitly blinded him to the presence of all the other women in the world.

Joyce thought about telling Greg that Valerie had just called it quits with Brett. She thought about inviting him back to their place, as yet another diversion to take Valerie's mind off of her troubles. The best cure for a man was always another man, was it not?

But Joyce decided against it. There was no need to be telling tales out of school, spreading Valerie's business all over town, and there was no need to give Greg a hope that would no doubt come to nothing. He wasn't Val's type. She had never expressed even the vaguest interest in him before. Greg Castro would never be a replacement for Brett.

So Joyce only told him that Val was waiting for her back home. Then she took it upon herself to thank him for finagling the interview at 20th Century Fox for her friend.

"Es nada," he replied. "Facial motion capture is the next big thing. Actors can be anything the director needs – monkeys, dragons. It's so

much more realistic than stop-motion or animation. Fox is on the cutting edge, and they're always looking for new talent. Valerie's brilliant. She's a shoo-in."

"Is that what she worked on in school? Motion capture?"

Law school had been arduous for Joyce. She had never had a lot of time to listen to her friend discuss her IT assignments. That's what she had Greg and her other techie associates for. Joyce had been there for the giggling girl-talk, to be Val's wingman at Q's while she trolled for pretty boys. Again Joyce felt a pang of remorse. She was Val's best friend, the one with whom she chose to spend her free time, once she closed her laptop and forgot about programming for the day. And Joyce had let her down, allowed her to become entangled with the one man that Joyce had known would wind up being no good for her.

"She didn't work on that specifically, but when you're as good as Valerie, programming is programming." Greg smiled. He instinctively knew not to go into the details of his craft with a girl like Joyce. She was no-nonsense, businesslike. Electronic devices were her servants, expected to perform their functions on command. She had no more interest in their inner workings than had an English lord for the life of the charwoman that scrubbed his parquet floors.

"I know she'll go far, Greg. There's something special about Val. I've seen it from the moment we met."

"She's brilliant." *And beautiful.* He realized that perhaps he was allowing his admiration for Valerie to show a little too much. He cleared his throat and changed the subject. "What are you gonna do now that school is over? Are you gonna fight the good fight and prosecute the wrong-doer, like your dad did?"

Joyce grinned. "There's no money in that, my friend. But I am a legacy, so through Dad's connections, I'm going to be starting as the most juniorest of partners at–"

"Dewey, Cheatem and Howe?" Greg grinned. He had no more interest in the nepotistic, good ol' boy system of LA law firm politics than Joyce had in computer programming.

She smiled back. "Something like that."

As always, she found Greg to be clever and witty. He was charming in his own right, if one liked the weather-beaten, I-just-got-back-from-Half-Dome look. He shouldn't have any trouble getting girls. It was a shame that he was always alone. Joyce shrugged inwardly. Just like the Valerie and Brett soap opera, Greg's romantic prospects were none of her business.

The line of patrons waiting for pizzas had lessened, so Joyce got up to order her own. She chatted with Greg further while she waited

171

for it, and when at last they called her name, she told him, "It's always great talking to you, Greg. I'm sure I'll see you all the time, once Val starts at Fox."

"You, too, Jo. See ya around."

****

There was some check dispute in the line at the grocery store. A manager had to be called over for a consultation. Joyce exchanged a glance with the guy waiting in front of her: *Who writes checks anymore?* When it seemed that there would be no quick resolution to the high finance transaction, Joyce stepped out of line and went to another cashier. Her ice cream was melting. The Mulberry Street pizza in her car was getting cold.

"I'm home, Val!" she trilled gaily when she finally made it back. "I'm sorry it took so long. I saw Greg at the pizza place, then some woman was trying to do arbitrage in the line at the . . ."

The living room was dark. No light spilled from Valerie's bedroom, either, and all was silent. A dark wave of fear, of panic, careened through Joyce. There should be light coming from the television, the canned noise from the laugh-track to the sitcom she'd picked out for Valerie to watch. But all was bleak, cold blackness.

Had Valerie changed her mind? Had the sorrow overwhelmed her, had she gone ahead and offed herself anyway, over *stupid, worthless Brett Cooke?*

Trembling, Joyce slowly set the pizza and ice cream down on the coffee table. She took a deep breath, the fear coursing through her like a drug. She took her phone out of her purse, prepared to call the paramedics, although she figured that it would undoubtedly be too late. She had been gone a long time, and Valerie had so many pills . . . *Why didn't I make her dump them out before I left?*

"Oh, Jesus!" Joyce said aloud. She willed her feet to carry her to the dark rectangle that was the door to her best friend's bedroom. She didn't want to see, didn't want to be the one that found her. She didn't want to have to be the one to call Riverside and tell Sophia that her daughter had killed herself, over a meaningless man, just like her sister had done . . .

The door to Valerie's bathroom was ajar; a thin sliver of light peeped out. The pill bottles stood starkly empty on the night stand. Joyce could hear the water running, but no other sound. *Oh, God, not in the bathroom, like Elvis and Lenny Bruce. Not like that guy from Murphy Brown who OD'd on heroin on the cold floor. Not like Jim Morrison, breaking through to*

172

the other side, dead in a Paris bathtub. Goddamn you, Brett, you conniving, cheating bastard, this is all your fault . . .

Joyce softly said her friend's name and pushed open the bathroom door.

When she saw Valerie standing in front of the mirror washing her face, waves of indescribable relief inundated Joyce. She hugged her friend before she could stop herself.

"Sweet, Jesus, Val! Why didn't you answer me? I thought that you'd . . . What did you do with the pills?"

Valerie returned her hug. "I'm sorry, Jo. I must not have heard you over the water. What do you think I did with them? I flushed them. " She turned the faucet off and presented a clean-scrubbed, joyfully smiling face to her worried friend. She held up her arms and mimicked Kevin Bacon in *Animal House: "Remain calm! All is well!"*

The change in Valerie's demeanor was astonishing, and Joyce thought that there could be only one reason for it. "Did you talk to Brett?"

"No. He called, but I blocked him, remember? I'm done with Brett, Jo. He'll stop calling, eventually. His *okCupid* app is right next to his contacts list icon. He'll choose that instead." Valerie turned and winked at herself in the mirror, spoke to her reflection. "No more Brett." She turned back to her friend. "I've discovered the most *phenomenal* actor! He's just . . . Oh, my God, Jo! He's incredible! Come on, *my brother and only friend.* Watch *Sonny's Diner* with me. You've got to see Edison Forbes!"

It had begun.

.

173

ACT III

The headquarters of TTAMS Los Angeles was just around the corner from the bar where he'd serendipitously made the acquaintance of screen legend Mitch Barlo, and Morris Baker, key in hand, let himself into an unmarked door in the alley behind the building. He led the famous actor down a darkened corridor to a brightly lit, glassed-in office. Mitch saw a similar office at the top of a flight of stairs. He glanced curiously at the floor before him, full of small cubicles.

"It's so nice to meet you, Mr. Barlo. I'm Greg Castro."

"My boss," Morris commented, a trifle nervously. All of his *As soon as I finish my beer* bravado had fled. This wasn't just his boss. This was *the boss*, the Director of Technical Operations for TTAMS, according to the sign on the door.

And not a fan, the actor noted from the man's expression. "Call me Mitch." He shook the head tech's hand.

"It's not often we get real movie stars in here." Greg eyed his employee balefully. "What is it that Morris has told you? What is it that you'd like to know?"

Mitch offered his Oscar-nominated smile. "Morris mentioned a confidentiality agreement. He hasn't said anything to jeopardize your secrets, Mr. Castro. Or his job."

"Please, call me Greg."

"I'm fascinated with the whole concept of TTAMS, Greg. If it's possible, I'd like to learn all about it." Mitch had decided that upon meeting pudgy Morris, after he'd said, *I am you.*

He was not a Method actor by any means, but Mitch had always tried to understand the underlying motivations of whatever character he played, although he'd never really been much like any of them. He was neither a party-boy looking for a mentor like Shamus, nor distrustful and money-hungry as he'd played in *Two of Swords*, although as most actors are, he'd always been a bit of a gambler. In his almost-

Oscar turn in *Random House,* he portrayed a man plagued by self-doubt. Mitch wasn't that guy either: the only self-doubt he'd ever known was over his inability to save Janna. That had been a big one, however. It had almost crippled him, but he was slowly working through it.

One of the reasons he'd become an actor was his enjoyment of getting into character, of attempting to see the world through the eyes of those that had experiences different than his own. *Remember that all the people in this world haven't had your advantages.*

And of course there had been the applause, the adulation, *the smell of the greasepaint, the roar of the crowd.* Mitch had first trod the boards as Mortimer Brewster in his high school's production of *Arsenic and Old Lace.* The reactions of his peers in the audience, the girls that were suddenly interested in him: Mitch Barlo never wanted to be anything but an actor after that.

So he wondered – what was it like to be a TTAMS operator, to pretend to be another actor, night after night? Morris was obviously a tech. He had no desire for the spotlight. But Mitch had heard that some of the operators aspired to the craft. What better way to become a better actor than to mimic those that had already made it, and the characters that had given them fame? But was it really acting, since the capture technology lent most of the illusion?

And then there were the fans. What did they say to these simulacrums of him at different ages, playing different characters? What was it that the program prompted the operators to say back to them? What would it be like to share an intimate conversation with one's biggest fans, without the danger of acquiring stalkers, without the necessity of making it quick and moving on in to the premiere? The very real dangers were removed. They couldn't grab him or try to kiss him or kidnap him or any of that tangible-world, physical bullshit. So what did they say?

Greg Castro hesitated. He shot another disapproving glance at Morris. This was new territory, one of the stars just be-boppin' in off the boulevard and asking how things worked.

Mitch caught his caution. "This is just for me, Greg. I'm not a spy." Again, that killer grin. "The studio didn't send me, or TMZ."

Greg rolled his eyes.

"I'm not gonna tell anybody. I'll sign a confidentiality agreement, too, if that would make you feel better. I just finished a picture in Canada. It's in post-production, and I'm at loose ends."

That was the truth. He had not much to do, except kick around the big house up the hill, brood about Janna. He had a few scripts to look at, but wouldn't be starting anything new for months, not until after he'd done the talk-show circuit for *The Erskine Dilemma,* attended the premiere. Mitch was lonely, but was not in the mood for any real company. Learning about TTAMS was the perfect diversion.

He glanced at the rows of operators, each ensconced in a tiny booth, with walls and a door for privacy. He thought, *You don't care about post-production, do ya, Greg? And I bet you're never at loose ends. You're obviously not a fan, and you're wondering in what manner Mitch Barlo, star of stage and screen, intends to attempt to fuck with your operation.*

Mitch decided that the honest, mano-a-mano approach would work best. He had to get this guy to trust him. "I'm just curious, Greg. I promise not to get in the way."

He wondered if the Director of Technical Operations had to check with someone else before showing him around. He'd read the little fluff piece on Variety.com about TTAMS, the interview with the mastermind and her UCLA School of Law graduate *consigliere.* The article didn't say much; it didn't indicate how hands-on the women who ran the place really were. But this was just one installation, Mitch reasoned. There had to be others; no doubt dozens of others. He doubted if the owners were sticking their noses into who was given a tour here, even if he was a famous celebrity.

No, Greg Castro was obviously in charge, at least of this floor of operators. Morris had done Mitch a solid. He had introduced him to the boss, at least the only boss he wanted to talk to.

"Okay," Greg said at last. "I'll treat you like you're applying to be an operator, if you want."

"That would be awesome, Greg!" Mitch Barlo enthusiastically shook his hand again. *Seriously, what else do I have to do right now?*

"Okay, sign this." Greg took a copy of the aforementioned confidentiality agreement out of a drawer in his desk and handed it to the actor. Mitch signed it without reading it. If he ever had a mind to talk about TTAMS, some cookie-cutter gag order wouldn't stop him. The studio had some of the most brilliant legal minds on retainer; surely they could get around this. Mitch wasn't out to talk about TTAMS, anyway. He was just curious.

"I don't imagine that you expect me to actually put you on the trainee payroll. It's not like you could attend training with the rest of the noobs anyway, is it? That would be a disruption."

"Someone would talk," Morris said darkly.

Greg looked at the operator as if he had forgotten his presence. "I'm beginning to think this is just a play for OT on your part, Baker. Didn't you get the email about OT?"

"No more than ten hours a pay period," Morris recited.

"I'll authorize it tonight. Take the movie star over to the simulator." Greg grinned at Mitch and he smiled back. "There's no one over there at night. It usually takes about a week of training before you go live, Mitch, but since you'll be playing you . . ." He looked at the operator again. "If you want to switch shifts, Baker, you can work with him for a few days. In the simulator, at night."

"Do I get instructor pay?" Morris dared.

"No. This is just for Mr. Barlo's enjoyment. He's not gonna be on the payroll, and I'm not giving you a raise. You're not instructing a roomful of Performing Arts refugees. You're showing one actor how to follow the prompts."

"I really appreciate this, Greg," Mitch said quickly, when his operator looked a little disappointed that he wasn't going to be making *instructor pay.* "My father always told me to try to learn something new every day. It'll be fun."

Greg nodded, then smiled at Morris. "Don't look so hangdog, Baker. It's not every day that someone like you gets to hang out with a real celebrity, now is it? Just keep it on the down low. You guys keep sneaking in the back door. I don't need my people noticing you're here, Mitch. Clamoring for autographs."

Mitch donned his shades. *"Mr. Hughes hid in Dylan's shoes wearing his disguise."* Greg's eyebrows went up at the Jurassic Rick Nelson reference and he smiled again. Morris was oblivious. "I'll wear a hoodie," Mitch added.

"I appreciate it," Greg said.

****

The Director of Technical Operations saw a useful angle to this famous guy that fat Morris had dragged in. *Just like the 9 Lives spokescat,* he thought, pleased with his own pun. If this actor could be compelled to keep his instantly recognizable mouth shut . . .

Greg saw how it could go: *Real actors at TTAMS! Attention, ladies! Sign up for the service and you might actually get to talk to the* real *Mitch Barlo!*

It was a shot in the dark, Greg realized. This guy was probably just bored, what with his latest blockbuster in *post-production.* He was probably just slumming amidst the sea of remoras that made money off his likeness, the millions of little people in the aftermarket. It was

probably the high-tech equivalent to hanging out at a *Maps to the Stars'
Homes* stand for Mitch, without all the messy run-ins with his adoring
public. But being an operator wasn't easy. He would probably lose
interest quickly.

A real actor lurking around TTAMS? Greg thought that Valerie
might appreciate that . . .

Greg Castro was in love with his boss. He suspected that Baker
was in love with her, too, to a lesser degree, as well as all the other techs
in the LA facility, a least the heterosexual ones. And maybe some of the
girls who liked girls, too. Valerie Whitly was beautiful. She was brilliant.
She was friendly to everybody.

But Greg wasn't like Baker and all the other techs on the floor. He
actually knew Valerie, had considered himself friends with her in
college, had worked with her at Fox. Hell, he had gotten her the job at
Fox. She had personally chosen him to be Director of Technical
Operations. He had been with her from the very beginning, and liked
to brag that his employee number was a bunch of zeros followed by a
3. Valerie, of course, was number 1, and Joyce, number 2.

Greg Castro was a computer genius in his own right, and his skill
afforded him an outlet for his secret crush on the boss. Greg didn't
have access to the passwords on Valerie's laptop or the files or emails
on it. But from the very beginning, he'd added a couple of extra lines of
code into her TTAMS profile.

Just a few simple commands. Greg had put a keeper on Valerie's
profile. When and if she ever logged on to her own system, that system
would alert him. His motivation was simple: if Valerie Whitly ever
decided to talk to a movie star, her biggest fan aimed to know what was
said.

Conversations between operator and subscriber were archived
individually for a short period of time, so the next time a subscriber
logged on, the system could prompt the operator, remind him of what
had already been said. But these subscriber interactions were also fed
into a main program; the conversations were analyzed to help
streamline the process. Individual subscriber names were not kept
there, only demographic data, thereby avoiding any thorny issues of
subscriber privacy, blah, blah, blah. Valerie's conversations would go in
as a twenty-five-year-old computer programmer from LA, female.

But her sessions would also go directly to Greg's own computer.
Here at the office and at home.

Greg didn't imagine that he could afterward pretend to be some
actor for her. He wasn't an operator; he'd never logged any time in a
motion capture device. He was a tech, and being that, information was

what he sought. He didn't have to be the one that talked to Valerie, but he wanted to know what she said to the one she chose. Greg thought that he could afterwards use that information to his benefit, maybe talk to her about similar things, somehow, only in person, face to face.

Unfortunately, Greg's keeper had never found its quarry. Valerie didn't talk to the simulacrums of actors on the system she'd developed. She didn't even play around on the service. She left beta testing to her battalions of underlings.

But Greg thought that it wouldn't be that way forever. TTAMS was growing by leaps and bounds, gaining more sophistication, more nuance, every day. He was convinced that its creator would decide to explore it sooner or later, and when she did, he would know about it.

****

Greg would bet a month's pay that the first celebrity that his boss would choose to pretend to talk to would be Edison Forbes.

Valerie thought that Joyce was the only one that knew the depth and breadth of her obsession for the Canadian, and for the most part, she was correct. But Valerie had forgotten about Greg Castro, had forgotten that her crush on the actor had already been a full-blown phenomenon when she'd started working at Fox. Valerie had forgotten that she'd shown Eddie's pictures to Greg, had asked him if he'd ever seen any of his movies.

Greg had not seen them. He was on the payroll of one of the biggest studios in the world; he got enough of the movies at work.

He was more of a fan of the old stuff, anyway, from the Golden Age of Hollywood and all that. From the days when the stars endeavored to hush up their scandals, instead of parading them before the entire world and *People Magazine*. Greg had not the slightest interest in Sean Penn's hatred of the paparazzi, or Matt Damon's politics, or the fact that Brad and Angie had a foundation, *building green homes for those in need around the world*. He didn't care about celebrity break-ups and make-ups, births and adoptions. He sincerely didn't give a tinker's damn that Mitch Barlo's high strung actress wife had OD'd.

And Greg certainly didn't care about some Canadian nobody who'd only made a few films in the States, none of which had made any money.

Valerie had forgotten – or perhaps she didn't even know – that Greg had observed her at Fox, had heard her talk up any and all personnel that wandered onto the backlot and said *Eh?* How many times had Greg watched her corner some snowback noob and ask him, "Did you ever work with Edison Forbes?"

She had never received an affirmative, except once, from some sound guy.

****

The Canadian Foley artist was short, sandy-haired, bespectacled. When she overheard him talking to Greg, Valerie noticed his accent immediately. Americans had it all wrong. It wasn't that Canadians said *Eh?* all the time. That was a Bob and Doug McKenzie, comedic stereotype.

What made them stand out to Valerie, after only their response to her brief queries about working with Edison Forbes, was an odd garbling of the short vowels – something about the *o* in *consulate* or the *a* in *what* – she couldn't quite put her finger on it, but it just wasn't American English. *Sorry* was always a dead giveaway. Valerie had watched enough of Eddie's movies and television shows – *Sonny's Diner* alone was 36 episodes – that she could pick out his countrymen by their accent alone, as easily as if they'd had a maple leaf tattooed on their foreheads.

Valerie frequently amazed Joyce with this peculiar ability. If they were watching an American-made film, sometimes her friend would cock her head, birdlike, at a certain turn of phrase. Then she'd quickly Google the actor. "Did you know Michael Ironside was Canadian?"

Joyce had seen most of these actors for years, always believing them to be American. She was always surprised when Valerie outed them as Canucks. Joyce would say, "They're taking over, aren't they? Just slipping on down here, appearing in our flicks, and no one even realizes it."

She liked to imagine the scenario for Val, how she could put this otherwise worthless talent to use. "Suppose we were at war with Canada. They look just like us, so you could get a job with the CIA or the NSA, spotting the infiltrators. Do your patriotic part.

"I can see you – you've got a cigarette between your second and third fingers. Maybe a monocle. You're pointing one of those funny square pistols at the hapless captive."

"It's called a Broomhandle." Valerie didn't know much about firearms, but she had seen the iconic German weapon in enough movies: Turkish officers carried them in *Lawrence of Arabia;* James Bond's foreign foes in *From Russia with Love* were fond of them. She'd been curious as to what they were called, so she'd Googled it.

180

"'Ve haff vays of making you talk, Canuck,' you'd tell him. 'So *sore-y* to send you back to the commonwealth.'" Joyce would dissolve in a fit of laughter.

"You slay you." Valerie would grin sheepishly to herself, thinking that she would be the first in line to collaborate with the enemy if Edison Forbes was leading the fight. She'd switch sides in a heartbeat, defect, become his own personal spy. How unpatriotic would that be?

Valerie was always Googling Canadian things she saw in Eddie's movies, so Joyce had learned more minutia about the Great White North than she'd ever wanted to know.

"Did you know that Grolsch beer is a sponsor of the Toronto International Film Festival?"

Joyce shook her head. *Nor do I care.*

But Valerie's obsession with Edison Forbes and all things Canadian didn't annoy Joyce too much. It seemed to have completely cured her romantic troubles, extinguished utterly the torch she could've carried for Brett, as if it had been dunked in Alfred Creek Falls. That was in British Columbia, one of the tallest waterfalls up there. Because Valerie had told her so, Joyce understood that they had a lot of spectacular natural landmarks in the Great White North.

Joyce often thought that she'd be a frontrunner if she ever got on *Jeopardy!* and the category was *Things About Canada that Nobody Cares About.*

This black-haired, blue-eyed, Alberta native has totally besotted your best friend.

That would be Edison Forbes, Alex.

I'm sorry, Joyce. You didn't give your answer in the form of a question.

****

When Valerie initially asked the sound guy if he'd ever worked with Eddie, he'd blinked stupidly for a split second. She'd quickly explained, "What with you being in the biz and all and both of you being Canadian, I just thought I'd ask."

The statistical logic of the fact that there were probably hundreds of thousands of Canadians in the biz, at home and abroad – who called it *the biz,* anyway? – and that only a handful could've worked with Edison Forbes, had not deterred her optimism.

The Foley artist was amazed at his luck. He smiled at the beautiful blonde. "As a matter of fact, coincidentally, it's a small world after all, I have worked with Mr. Forbes."

He watched Valerie's eyes grow big and round. He opened his mouth to tell her more, but at that moment, some production assistant with a clipboard appeared, and Valerie's job intervened.

Before turning back to her monitor, she smiled winningly at the sound guy. "I'll talk to you again soon, –?"

"Liam." He shook her eagerly outstretched hand.

"I'm Valerie."

I know.

Liam had noticed the shapely tech, hurrying from the parking lot to the motion capture studio, a stand-out among the other plain-Jane computer geeks. It was probably the third time he'd been in the building, because he only came over here to speak to Greg Castro as an excuse to catch another glimpse of her. He'd say a few words to Greg – the tech worked a little with sound – look at Valerie, then leave. Their jobs didn't really overlap. She was always busy, and Liam hadn't as yet thought up a viable reason to introduce himself. He'd never dreamed that she would speak to him first.

O, Canada! Who could've guessed it would be his homeland that attracted her attention? If he would've known she'd be interested in that, he would've worn his Maple Leafs' jersey.

"So nice to meet you," he said.

The production assistant frowned, a look of *What are you doing over here?* pasted on her fat features. She glanced at the clock on the wall and Liam took his cue. He reluctantly walked away.

"See you soon!" Valerie called after him. Liam smiled, waved. Valerie turned her attention back to the annoying assistant and he scuttled out of the studio.

Liam grinned to himself in delight. *What d'ya know? Eddie's got an American fan, right here at Fox.*

What Valerie couldn't have imagined was that the Foley artist had so much more than just *worked* with Edison Forbes. They were practically lifelong buddies. They had shared a locker in high school, had lived down the hall from each other in college. Before Liam immigrated to the States, he and Eddie had worked together *in the biz* for years.

****

As he left the studio after work that afternoon, Liam spied Valerie already sitting in her car. He smiled when she waved, motioned him over, told him to get in.

He noted the disbelieving but infinitely hopeful gleam in her eyes, lips parted slightly in anticipatory wonder. Without preamble, she said, "Is it really true? You worked with Edison Forbes." A statement now, but clotted with doubt.

Liam nodded humbly. "On *Undercover Homicide.*"

He'd also worked on the effects for *The Silvery Moon* and *Desperate Caper.* But Liam didn't show all his cards at once. He didn't mention these other Edison Forbes vehicles to his buddy's fan, nor did he talk about high school and college. He answered the question that he'd been asked and did not elaborate. No need to reveal his friendship with Eddie, if just the idea that they'd worked together on one movie would do the trick.

Liam had parlayed his friendship with Edison Forbes into getting into girls' pants before, in Canada, but Valerie was the first woman he'd met in the States that had ever even heard of his friend. And Valerie had definitely heard of him. He could tell from the look on her face that she was an obsessed, rabid fan, and Liam wondered how *that* had happened. Eddie was big back home, God love him, but his inroads into the American land of milk and honey had been limited.

But this girl – it was like being in Toronto again, at the height of *Sonny's Diner.* In those days, Liam had had a picture on his phone of he and Eddie together, smiling, arm in arm, and it had worked like an all-access backstage pass. Liam got as much action from Eddie's fans as Sonic Daydream's most charming roadie once did upon displaying Denny Whitly's axe.

"If you ever get to Toronto, look him up. Tell him Liam Cote sent you."

"Liam Cote. The Foley guy."

He nodded, waited; he knew it wouldn't be long. He watched Valerie work out the possibilities in her mind. Even though she was an up and coming computer geek nobody at 20th Century Fox Studios, Hollywood, California, USA, how likely was it that she would ever get close enough to famous Canadian actor Edison Forbes to say, "Hey, Liam Cote sent me?"

Damn unlikely, that was how likely. When Valerie's lip curl craftily, Liam blinked guilelessly and continued to wait. Valerie had hit upon the solution, the most original solution in the world, a foolproof way that she could actually *meet* the object of her obsession. Liam was her Golden Ticket.

"Do you think you could introduce me to him?" Surely the Foley guy had never before heard such a request.

"Wherever Eddie is these days, it's a long way from here, Valerie." He pointed over his shoulder, northward.

"I need a vacation. I know we both just started working here, but – you need a vacation, too." She leaned closer to him, ran her fingers lightly over his shoulder. "Will you go to Canada with me, Liam? Be my guide?"

The time for hesitation was past. "All right."

Liam took out his phone matter-of-factly, like it was absolutely *no thang*. He pushed one button – Valerie's mouth dropped open when she realized that the short, nondescript Foley guy had Canada's favorite son *in his contacts list*. Liam smiled at Valerie while the phone rang.

"Hey. Eddie."

"Hey, Liam! How the hell are you?"

Valerie was absolutely flabbergasted to hear the familiar, beloved, honey-dark and sexy voice come out of the Foley guy's cellphone speaker. She blinked rapidly, positively speechless with astonishment.

"I'm at 20th Century Fox these days. What are you doing?"

"As little as possible." Eddie Forbes laughed, and because she had seen nearly all his movies, the sound was as familiar to Valerie as was Joyce's laugh, or . . . Brett's.

"I'm starting the revival of *Born Yesterday* in Toronto next month."

Valerie incompletely suppressed a squeal. Liam grinned. She knew Eddie would be playing journalist Paul Verrall in the play, hired to give a little couth to a tycoon's ignorant girlfriend. She gets smart, sees the tycoon for what he is, falls in love with the newsman. William Holden had played the part in the original movie, Don Johnson in the remake.

Eddie said something, but it was muffled because the sound guy had clicked his phone off speaker. Liam replied, "Second row center has always been my favorite." There was a pause while Eddie spoke again. "All right. I'll see you then." Liam hung up.

Valerie was holding her breath. Liam let her wait. He counted to five in his head, then said, "If you've got the plane fare, we've got two seats for–"

"Oh, Liam! Is there any way we can get three? We've gotta take Joyce!"

Liam tilted his head doubtfully, but another quick call to the Great White North secured a seat for whoever the hell Joyce was. It made no difference to Liam, seeing as how Valerie was footing the bill for the trip. The more the merrier. Perhaps Joyce was a grateful fan, too.

Perhaps, before they all got on the silver bird to Toronto, the three of them could –

"Oh, my God, Liam! This is so awesome!"

Awesome didn't begin to describe it. There was no word in Valerie's vocabulary for how awesome it was. What had started out as just another regular day at work had turned into the best day ever. *I'm going to Canada! I'm gonna get to meet Eddie!*

In gratitude, Valerie kissed the sound guy quickly. The idea of going all the way to Canada to perhaps catch a glimpse of Eddie had never before crossed her mind, but now that it had, now that she was actually going to *meet* him, she wanted the sound guy to get out of her car so she could go home and book plane tickets, find a hotel, reserve a car.

But Liam pulled her against him, kissed her back. Valerie hesitated, but soon, her kiss expanded into something more than just gratitude.

Liam knew precisely what it was.

Valerie was thinking about Eddie now, oh, my God, she was actually going to meet him, oh, my God, who knew what might happen? Liam wasn't Eddie, of course, but he was a man, and he was right here, and he was going to make whatever might occur possible, and oh, my God, what she wouldn't do, and she was already kissing him anyway, so why not just go along with the flow . . .

In this incredible state of aroused anticipation, Valerie had climbed over into the passenger seat and completed the act with Liam almost before she was aware that she had done so, right there in the car, right there in the employee parking lot on Fox's backlot, under cover of late afternoon, in front of God and everybody.

She was a little surprised at herself. She was not ashamed – Valerie was never ashamed of sex – just surprised, because Liam wasn't really her type. He wasn't as tall as she liked, he wore glasses. But he was going to introduce her to Edison Forbes, and the prospect of that, coupled with the fact that she hadn't been with anyone since Brett had betrayed her, well . . . Valerie had just lost control of herself a little bit at the prospect of meeting Eddie.

Liam had been surprisingly good, however, for a short guy. The possibility that it could've been her inflamed imagination in overdrive that had made it seem so did not occur to her.

Afterward, Valerie kissed him again, and before any awkwardness could intrude into the torrid-scene-now-cooled, Liam asked her if she'd like to have dinner later that evening. She smiled and said okay. She'd just nailed the guy; the least she could do was have dinner with him.

185

They went back to his place after dinner to watch a movie. In the interim between their encounter in the car and dining, Liam had dashed out to the nearest Best Buy and purchased a copy of every single one of his *colleague's* features that they carried in stock, plus the boxed set of *Sonny's Diner*.

Always in the mood for Eddie, Valerie chose the two hour pilot to that one, but fifteen minutes into it, she leaned over and kissed Liam again. He had been sitting innocently next to her on the couch, not with his arm around her; not even close.

Again Valerie was thinking about Eddie and wanted it quick and hard and immediate, and Liam accommodated her.

He didn't mind it in the least that Valerie was pretending he was his old friend. Not in the slightest. Eddie was up North in the cold, counting his money and being famous, about to do theatre, and Liam was here in the always-sunny entertainment capital of the universe, working for a great studio, doing hot, blonde, sexy Valerie Whitly, who was a positive wildcat in bed. So what if she kept her eyes closed throughout the whole thing, because she was pretending he was Eddie?

The weeks that they dated were a cakewalk for Liam. He didn't have to wine Valerie, or dine her. He didn't have be charming or clever. He didn't have to set a romantic mood, he didn't have to kiss her just right to get her motor running.

All he had to do was sit back and be patient. She would get herself halfway there, just by watching one of Eddie's movies, and then all Liam had to do was hold still and let her take her lust out on him. He didn't have to do anything in particular, didn't have to say anything at all. He just had to wait until the desire reached critical mass – Eddie on the screen and the thought that she was going to actually meet him – Liam wasn't Eddie, but he was here, and maybe this time, we could just let the movie play in the background?

Liam had been taking advantage of his friend's fans since Eddie played Romeo in a Toronto Free Theatre production when they were still in college. But Liam wasn't a charlatan or a liar. He kept his promises. In Canada, it had just been a matter of taking the girl up the road to the studio or playhouse to introduce her to Eddie, but if Valerie wanted to foot the bill for a trip all the way back home, Liam was game. He hadn't been home for a while. It would be great to see his famous friend again.

And if the actor was down for a little action with his biggest fan (this week), hand-delivered, American – Liam didn't mind sharing. That was the least a guy could do for his buddy. There was that old joke: this guy's such a good pal that if he got two blow jobs, he'd come home and give his buddy one, and after a fashion, that's how Liam's friendship with Eddie was. The anticipation of an introduction made the girls settle for Liam in the meantime, and if Eddie wanted to take over once the introduction was accomplished, well . . . hell. That was his due.

After all, if Liam hadn't known Edison Forbes, Valerie wouldn't have given him the time of day. She was too beautiful and he was just the Foley guy. Once they got to Toronto, Eddie might not even be interested, but if he was, that was okay. They'd only be in Canada for the weekend, and Valerie would be coming back to Hollywood with Liam.

****

Greg Castro didn't care for the Canuck sound guy. He was always hanging around at the motion capture division, seemingly from the moment Fox had put him on the payroll, and soon office gossip informed Greg that Valerie had actually started *dating* this refugee from the Great White North.

If he admitted it to himself, Greg had felt more than just a little jealousy and resentment over Valerie's relationship with the sound tech. No looker was Liam Cote: he was short and bespectacled, no Brett Cooke, and certainly no Edison Forbes, even if he was Canadian. The Foley guy was surely no better looking than Greg himself. If Valerie had decided to give up pretty boys, why hadn't she looked in his direction?

Then Valerie took off early on a Thursday afternoon in December – where to, Greg didn't know. The Foley guy was MIA at the same time, and Greg worried that perhaps Val had run off with him. A week or so later, the sound guy came back to work, pale and quiet. But Valerie never did come back, and Greg wondered if it was because she had had some kind of fight with him. She simply quit Fox, without even giving two weeks' notice.

Greg barely had a chance to miss her – not a month passed before she was calling him, asking him to come onboard and help flesh out her idea for this revolutionary, never-before-seen-in-the-history-of-Hollywood service. Through performance capture, subscribers would seem to be actually *interacting* with movie stars . . .

Greg hadn't given Fox two weeks' notice, either. Not long afterward, they'd launched TTAMS.

****

187

Joyce Vinson's rolling-in-it, ex-DA daddy had floated the loan for all the equipment and this very facility, and from the beginning, Greg had dropped by Valerie's office at the top of the diamond-stamped steel steps as often as he could think of an excuse to do so. He'd loved her since college, after all.

On the morning they went live, with great ceremony, Greg had personally typed the command that linked Valerie's laptop into the system for the very first time.

"We'll call this *Day One*," Joyce had commented.

Then she and Greg had watched their new boss add her own personal touch. Valerie Whitly was the greatest programmer since Gates and Wozniak and Jobs to Greg Castro. To him, she was more brilliant than a CeBit full of Mark Zuckerbergs and Larry Pages and Susan Wojcickis. So he was amazed when she didn't run a security check, when she didn't even log on to her new, ground-breaking service.

Valerie's actions were the same as any housewife or student with a brand new computer. She stuck a red thumb-drive into the USB port of her brand new, best-that-money-could-buy laptop, downloaded a folder. She clicked the desktop, chose *Personalize* from the menu, and created a background slideshow from the folder. A photograph appeared, and that black-haired, blue-eyed, Canadian nobody smiled at Greg.

"Prettiest man I ever saw," Valerie said with an adorable giggle. *"Never seen eyes so blue."* She grinned at her friends. Her employees.

She was still obsessed with Edison Forbes.

So Greg had Googled him, had read his Wikipedia and IMDb pages. He had familiarized himself with the Canuck's filmography, read the reviews of his movies. Greg had even downloaded a copy of *Undercover Homicide* from Pirate Bay – he couldn't find it anywhere else – and slogged through it, just because Valerie had raved about Forbes' performance. He played a dirty cop who inevitably got his comeuppance at the end, as dirty cops always do in the movies. Greg had been unimpressed. He found Forbes to be an okay actor, and the foreign production values were pedestrianly ho-hum. *Undercover Homicide* was no *Bad Lieutenant*.

But on the other hand, Greg didn't feel that Edison Forbes was God's gift, like Valerie did. Greg wasn't obsessed with the so-so performer, like Valerie was.

Greg was obsessed with Valerie.

It wasn't a burning, passionate preoccupation that the Director of Technical Operations had for his boss. He didn't long to sweep her off her feet and carry her back to his little apartment and ravish her. He considered himself too old for such fantasies, although he'd felt the sting of jealousy in college when she'd been dating that asshole Brett Cooke, and when she'd taken off with that Foley guy for the weekend.

But neither of those relationships had lasted for Valerie, and these days, Greg hadn't heard of her dating anyone, not since they'd launched TTAMS. So he didn't have any cause to be jealous.

Greg believed Valerie Whitly to be above romance. He thought it was because she was too brilliant, and it was because she was too busy counting the money that she was making for herself, for him and Joyce, for half of Hollywood.

Greg was obsessed with her in a gentler way. Surely, he'd like to hold her in his arms, have her smile only at him. He would like to hear her adorable giggle, close in his ear. But above all that, Greg longed to have a friendship with Valerie, to pal around with her, to know the inner workings of her mind, the way Joyce did. If Greg could be friends with Valerie the way Joyce was, then he *just knew* that a physical culmination would come along eventually.

Greg's primary motivation for giving Mitch Barlo an all-access backstage pass to TTAMS was this gentle though infinitely persistent fondness he felt for Valerie. He had discovered that he liked the actor, and would've been surprised to realize that it was Mitch's extremely well-paying job to make people like him, and that he was exceedingly good at it. Mitch seemed like a regular guy to Greg, despite his looks and his fame, because that was precisely how Mitch had decided to come off.

Greg reflected that he couldn't recall having seen a single Mitch Barlo film, although he'd seen his pretty face plastered up on enough billboards, all over town. Yet Greg was sure that he'd be able to parlay this bored actor's curiosity to his advantage, nonetheless.

The thought never crossed his mind that anything personal would ever come to pass between Mitch and Valerie – that would certainly not serve his interests – but Greg knew that *People's* once upon a time *Sexiest Man Alive* was Valerie's type. Brett Cooke, Eddie Forbes, Mitch Barlo – all black-haired, blue-eyed pretty boys, the exact opposite, unfortunately, of Greg's own fair, tow-headed blondeness.

Not to mention the fact that Greg had always resembled a rugged, outdoorsy type, like a sailor or a lumberjack, even though he hated the great outdoors. Greg's idea of roughing it was being at the wrong end of the hall from the ice machine without an internet connection. Regardless, no one would ever mistake him for a pretty boy.

Greg thought Valerie would never be interested in Barlo, however, despite his looks. She was too busy to date, and Greg had never perceived her as star-struck, except of course for her thing for Eddie Forbes. There had been many famous types in here for tours and photo ops, sound bites and free publicity, and Greg could tell that she'd not been in the least impressed.

Valerie was beautiful, true, but she was not a starlet, so Greg didn't think Barlo would ever be interested in her, either. Celebrities tended to gravitate toward other celebrities, and this one had been married to that big-eyed redhead that has overdosed. Valerie was not his type.

But Greg thought it would behoove him to bring Valerie and Barlo together, nonetheless. The pretty boy was interested in the system, which would flatter Valerie's professional ego.

But there was another little detail, and Greg saw it as far more important, much more useful than mere flattery. While he'd never seen a Mitch Barlo movie, Greg had seen the actor's name in one specific cast list. While he'd been researching the movies that Valerie raved about, he'd discovered a most advantageous tidbit of film trivia: Mitch Barlo had once co-starred with a certain big-in-Canada, unknown-in-the-States actor.

Valerie couldn't help but be grateful to Greg for introducing her to someone who had actually *worked* with Edison Forbes. Valerie would definitely want to be friends with Greg after he introduced her to someone who could answer that eternal question, the one that Greg was sure burned within her: *What was Eddie Forbes really like?*

So Greg would allow the actor to hang around, to dabble in TTAMS for a while. If he didn't get bored and take off right away, then Greg would present him to Valerie. They would talk about Forbes for a while, she would learn all the fun facts she longed to know. Then she'd drop by Greg's office to thank him for the introduction to Eddie's co-star.

Greg would tell her it was nothing, *es nada,* a mere bagatelle. He would tell her that she could make it all up to him by having a drink with him, or dinner, or by going to the movies – she would love that – not like a date or anything, just as friends . . .

****

The Operator Preparation Center at TTAMS was mostly dark. It consisted of a bank of ten booths, similar to the ones on the live floor down the hall. The difference was that the training booths had doors at both ends, unlike the system booths, and there were two monitors instead of only one, separated by a soundproof glass partition. There was a little sliding window in it, so the instructor could speak directly to the trainee.

After they passed their psych tests, but before arriving at these booths for training, the operator-to-be hopefuls learned how to wear a facial motion capture device in a large classroom in the basement. Some never made it any farther than that. They were cut because they couldn't get the hang of it, or they quit because they didn't like it. Some liked it so much that they quit and put their training down on resumes when they applied at the studios as motion capture extras.

Mitch Barlo never saw the big classroom downstairs, because the actor didn't really need to learn the intricate art of motion capture. He didn't need to wear a device at all. He *was* Mitch Barlo, was he not? Why should he wear a facial device in order to pretend to be himself? It was unnecessary. If a subscriber wanted to talk to today's Mitch, she would actually get today's Mitch.

But he still needed to learn the interface, how to go with the system prompts. What to say, what not to say. So the Operator Preparation Center was dark, except for the fluorescents over the booth at the farthest end of the line, against the wall. Mitch sat behind one monitor, and on the other side of the glass was Morris Baker, who up until that evening had pretended *to be* Mitch Barlo. Now he was going to train the actor to talk to subscribers, although Greg had refused him instructor pay.

The blue strip on the left side of Mitch's screen would contain the system prompts; at the bottom of it was a rectangle, grayed out now, that would've shown Mitch how he looked in a device, how he appeared to the subscriber. The voice synthesizer was also turned off. On the right side of the screen was a green strip, not present on the live monitors, where Baker could type commentary and instructions to his famous student.

Morris slid the glass aside and peered in at Mitch, grinning. He didn't really mind about not getting instructor pay. He loved his job, and this would be good practice for when he did get promoted to instructor.

"Okay, Movie Star. Let's start with a shy one. She's gonna talk to you via text. Just answer naturally, Mitch, like it was a normal conversation with a fan. If it goes south, the system will help you out."

"I'm going to be talking to a real—"

"No, Mitch. This is a simulator. You're talking to me."

Mitch nodded. Baker closed the soundproof glass, and after a moment, a line of text appeared on the screen.

Hi, Mitch. My name's Tammy. I'm your biggest fan.

Mitch read the fake stats that appeared in the blue strip. The tech was pretending to be a twenty-two-year-old female, a college student from Milwaukee, Wisconsin. When the actor hesitated, Baker slid the window open again. "Type hello to Tammy, Mitch."

Hello, Tammy, he typed. He slid the glass window open. "Why can't I just talk to her?"

"Tammy's a shy one, Movie Star. She grew up with IM's and texting. It's her usual way of conversing. You don't get too many, but some of them won't even turn on their mikes. Tammy's that way. She doesn't really want to talk to you. Not yet. She just wants to look at you. Just smile at the screen every now and then, as if you can see her. Don't pick your nose." Morris slid the window shut.

Mitch typed, *How are you?* He couldn't think of anything else. He felt silly. He didn't have to ask real fans how they were. They usually just giggled and asked him for an autograph, mostly too star-struck to say much else, so he'd never had to actually converse very much.

He'd met enough shy Tammys in real life, fans that were struck dumb by being face to face with their favorite celebrity. They didn't see just an actor, a fellow human being; they saw the cowboy, the gambler, the tortured writer from *Random House*. They saw the man of their dreams, and having lost the ability to speak, they just stared at him.

I'm just as thrilled as I can be, Mitch. I can call you Mitch, right?

Yes. Certainly, Tammy.

A prompt popped up on the blue strip. *What would you like to talk about?*

So Mitch typed that.

Well, you know, I've seen all your movies, and there's something I've always wanted to ask.

There was a seven second timer on Mitch's monitor; if Tammy didn't ask her burning question by the time it counted down, the system would prompt him to again ask her what she wanted to discuss. Mitch gave it five seconds, then typed, *Ask whatever you'd like, Tammy. That's what I'm here for.* He smiled at the screen.

Why don't you do more nude scenes? appeared immediately, faster than Tammy could've typed it, or even Morris, for that matter.

Mitch grinned. The operator was fucking with him. Tammy's girlish hesitation was all part of the act. Baker had had the question already queued up and then had simply pushed *Enter.*

A prompt appeared on the blue strip. *Nude scene, Shamus Alive. View y/n?* Mitch was amazed at the system's resources. It had taken keywords from the subscriber's question, searched its database, and provided the appropriate film, all before the seven-second timer ran down. There would be no artificial pause in the flow of the conversation. Mitch could mention the movie, then review the clip in order to discuss it further, if, as an operator, he was unfamiliar with it. As he was himself, he surely did not want to view it.

There was the skinny-dipping scene in Shamus Alive, Mitch reminded Tammy. *You didn't like that one?*

(*Easy, big fella,* Morris warned from the green strip.)

That one didn't show much. You do have a nice ass, though.

Thanks, Tammy. Mitch thought about again typing, *That's what I'm here for.* This was silly. Morris was fucking with him. Fans didn't talk like this.

I'd like to see all of you, Mitch. Christian Bale ran around naked with a chainsaw in American Psycho. And Marky-Mark showed everything in Boogie Nights.

(*It was a prosthetic,* Baker advised.)

Why not you, Mitch? Tell me a secret. How big is it? Maybe you could send me a selfie to . . . The phone number came out as asterisks.

Mitch slid the glass window open. "Are you gay, Baker?"

Morris grinned. "I most assuredly am not."

"Then why are you asking me this stuff? No twenty-two-year-old girl from Milwaukee is gonna ask me how big my dick is."

"Maybe not in person. But people will say anything online. This is a fantasy for the subscribers, Mitch. After a while, you can get more familiar with them. But not right away."

"It's not just random? You talk to the same subscribers?"

"It works better that way. You get into a rhythm, how you talk, how they talk. Even though the computer does most of the work — there's a bunch of women out there that think my speech patterns are how you talk."

"Do you tell them how big my dick is, Morris?" Mitch grinned at the operator, and he shook his head. "What else do they ask?"

"They're liable to ask damn near anything. They ask you to send them selfies, because they forget they're not really talking to you, but to an operator. But you can't break character and remind them of that. You just tell 'em to take a screen shot of their device. They really think they're talking to a movie star, Mitch. That's the beauty of it." Morris's grin widened. "Don't tell me you don't know that getting naked with you is the kind of thing your fans think about."

Mitch shrugged. "But they're not going to ask me—"

"Trust. We get this kind of shit all the time. Look at the prompts." Morris closed the window.

The prompts were red now; the timer had run down.

No selfies permitted. Question too personal.

Mitch put on an embarrassed face and typed, *We're not allowed to send out selfies, Tammy. And if I sent you a picture like that, it would be count as pornography, and that would be illegal.*

Unless I call it art, Mitch thought. *Put it on the big screen at Cannes.*

(It would be too big to fit on her phone, Baker commented.)

Are you sure you're not gay, Tammy?

(Follow the prompts, Movie Star.)

Besides, that's kind of a personal question, don't you think, Tammy? We've just met. It makes me uncomfortable. You don't want me to be uncomfortable, do you?

(Very good, Baker praised.)

No, I don't want you to be uncomfortable, Mitch. You're too cute. How about this – are you still single?

Yes.

I was so sorry to hear about Janna.

Me, too.

Mitch waited to see if Baker was curious about that sad subject. If he was, then Mitch would tell him to consult the interview in *Rolling Stone.* He didn't want to talk about Janna. This thing was supposed to be fun.

What kind of girls do you like, Mitch? Are you partial to redheads, like Janna?

The prompt said, *Request webcam.* Mitch thought that the command was a trifle abrupt, so instead, he typed, *I like all kinds of girls.*

(Ask her what she looks like, Morris instructed. *Then tell her that she sounds like your type.)*

But a memory came to Mitch's mind, of Janna, after she'd returned from rehab. He'd walked into the bedroom to find her sitting before her vanity, staring fixedly at her reflection. "I'm so ugly," she'd said.

"You're just a little tired," he'd told her. Any other response might've brought on a flood of tears. Janna only thought she was beautiful, that she was anything other than worthless, when she was

194

acting or when she was high. Mitch had discovered that within a few months of marrying her.

It's what's inside that counts, Tammy, Mitch typed. *How people look on the outside doesn't matter.*

Tammy probably believed she was ugly, too, or she would've shown herself via her webcam. Mitch knew it was only a simulation, but it was supposed to mimic real subscriber interactions. If Tammy had wanted to show herself while she talked to a movie star, she would've done so from the outset. She didn't want him to see what she looked like, so there was no use asking her to describe herself.

The timer was ticking down again. Mitch didn't want to see another red prompt, so he typed, *What else did you want to ask me?*

Which one of your movies is your favorite?

Morris figured he'd run the actor through the standard prompts now. The system would say *Yours?* so Barlo would ask the subscriber which of his movies was *her* favorite, and so on. The goal was to let the subscriber do most of the talking. Or so it seemed.

Morris realized that Mitch hadn't gone through the psych tests for TTAMS, or even the basic orientation. He didn't have the slightest clue that it wasn't anything even remotely like a real conversation.

Morris remembered sitting in the big classroom downstairs, after he'd been cleared to train in a facial device. The candidates from an acting background that hoped to be operators were greeted by Joyce Vinson. But it was Greg Castro, Director of Technical Operations, who spoke to the techie types.

He'd stood behind a podium, in front of a giant screen. It wasn't just a laptop blown-up and projected onto the wall so that the trainees could view it. It was an actual *screen,* like at a press conference for a new Apple launch.

There's some money here, Morris had said to himself, impressed.

"Welcome, Noobs," Greg began. A titter ran through the class.

"As you are already aware, Talk To a Movie Star is the most sophisticated entertainment-themed information processing system in the world. Its programmer, Valerie Whitly, is brilliant." A picture of their founder flashed on the screen. *And beautiful,* Morris thought.

"I won't bore you with statistical details. All of that's in your handbook. What I'm here to tell you is that all of you aren't going to make it. It takes a special type to be a TTAMS operator.

"But when you get frustrated in training, when your instructor laughs at you, when you feel like perhaps a job working for the most fascinating, most original service in the world might not be for you after all, I want you to remember what I'm going to show you now.

"Despite its intricacy, the program is actually deceptively simple. Before you learn the complexities of motion capture, before you memorize the encyclopedic history of Hollywood and its stars . . ." Another titter of laughter. The trainees already knew that they'd have to memorize nothing. All the info they would need to interact with subscribers would be at their fingertips.

"I want to show you one of Ms Whitly's first programming attempts. It's incredibly simple. I would expect that any one of you could write it in an hour or so. But you're techs. You know how this kind of stuff works, or at least you think you do.

"But to the average person, this simple little program, like TTAMS itself, seems like magic."

Greg produced a deck of cards from atop the podium, shuffled them theatrically, returned them to their box. He asked for a volunteer. Morris, sitting in the front row, was picked as the dupe. A prompt appeared on the screen, writ large, *Pick two suits of cards. (H, S, C, D)*. An ordinary cursor blinked beside it.

On its most basic level, TTAM's worked the same way as the old card trick program that Valerie had written as a senior in high school. Morris realized that while all the trained operators knew this, Mitch Barlo had not a clue.

A TTAMS session wasn't just a random conversation, as it appeared to be to the subscriber. It was stage-managed, controlled from start to finish. Sure, a subscriber could ask whatever she wanted, if it wasn't too dirty (at least at first), but the operator's responses were designed to lead her in a specific direction. *Pick two suits of cards. Which of my movies is your favorite?* The subscriber was led to talk about what the TTAMS operator was trained to discuss, in the precise way he was trained to discuss it, and she never even realized it.

Follow the prompts, Movie Star.

Mitch had told Tammy that it didn't matter to him what women looked like. Morris doubted that seriously, but much more importantly, it wasn't the kind of thing that appeared in the TTAM's script. This wasn't supposed to be a philosophical discussion on beauty or the lack thereof. It was fans telling their idols how much they loved them, how much they liked their movies. It was the movie stars humbly saying thanks, telling a few anecdotes about their films and maybe a few (perhaps fictional) details from their private lives. It wasn't psychotherapy. It wasn't real. It was *all in good fun.*

But on the other hand, Mitch's thoughtful response had meshed well enough with the program. After telling Tammy that beauty was only skin deep, he was able to get right back on track, asking her what else she wanted to know. That had led to the *Which one of your movies is your favorite?* question, part of the regular scheme.

Sure, Morris had initiated that one, but it was a common subscriber query. The system had taken over after that, prompting *Yours?* Morris let the program run on autopilot, let it ask Mitch the subscriber questions that most commonly followed. He was doing fine, leading Tammy by the nose, as if he were a more seasoned operator.

Morris considered. Maybe TTAMS had more subtlety to it than he gave it credit for. Maybe there was room for a few off-script, philosophical questions. After analyzing thousands of hours of sessions, maybe TTAMS was getting to *know* its subscribers, like some fictional AI juggernaut. Even this simulation was more nuanced than when he'd trained on it.

Tammy, the fake subscriber scenario that Morris had chosen, *was* shy. If Mitch had asked her to turn on her webcam as the system had prompted him, Morris would've told him no. It was a little *Kobayashi Maru* exercise for the noob. The self-conscious subscriber wouldn't show herself, nor would she describe herself, but she wanted the star to tell her what kind of women he liked. He couldn't say, *Women like you,* because that was just dumb. He couldn't see her. He couldn't really describe any type of women at all, lest he risk offending the subscriber. It was a no-win situation, designed to get the trainee to think fast enough to ask a new question and quickly turn the conversation back to his control.

Mitch hadn't even fallen into the trap, hadn't even bothered to try to get reluctant Tammy to reveal herself. He'd skipped the entire inquiry loop. Morris felt a new respect for the movie star. He obviously knew more about women than the team that had designed the shy Tammy scenario.

(Okay, Mitch. Let's try one that you can see.)

TTAMS sessions lasted for forty-five minutes at the longest, unless the operator deemed that the subscriber would be best served for a particular session to continue. They were trained to begin to guide things to a close at about the thirty-five minute mark, and most times they were successful. Training sessions were shorter; each conversation lasted from five to fifteen minutes.

(Say goodbye to Tammy.)

I'm glad you liked Random House, Mitch told the simulation. *If here's nothing else you want to ask me right now, I'll say goodnight.*

Okay, Mitch. It's been great talking to you.

The prompt in the blue strip said, *Return. Anyone. Waiting.*

197

You, too, Tammy. And be sure to come back anytime you'd like to chat. With me or another actor you like. We'll be waiting for you.

Bye, Mitch!

Bye, Tammy.

Before Mitch had a chance to collect his thoughts, the screen displayed a woman, perhaps thirty-eight or so. She looked a little worn, tired, maybe, but she had a girlish twinkle in her eye. Mitch knew that she was also a simulation, that whatever words came out of her mouth would be put there by Morris Baker, but he was amazed at how lifelike she seemed. The only indication that her image was computer enhanced was the fact that she stared blankly at the screen, blinking at appropriate intervals. Mitch thought the blinking was a nice touch, but a real person would've glanced away from the screen by now.

The prompt told him that she was Sarah, age thirty-six, a stay-at-home mom from Cleveland, Ohio.

Mitch looked at the keyboard, then realized that he could just speak to this one. He clicked the blue mike icon, instead of the red one for the voice synthesizer. Morris had told him the actual mike was built into the console, into the booth; he didn't have to speak in any particular direction. The operator had forgotten that he was talking to a professional actor, of stage in addition to screen. Mitch knew how to find his light, as well as how to project naturally as though no microphones were present.

"Hi, Sarah. What would you like to talk about?"

The simulation came alive. Sarah giggled. She actually blushed. "I'm not really sure, Mr. Barlo."

The prompt said, *First time?*

"Please, call me Mitch. Is this your first time on TTAMS?"

"No. But it's my first time talking to you . . ."

Sarah blushed again, broke eye contact, fidgeted. The prompt said, *Weather?*

Mitch thought that was just stupid. He said, "Tell me what you like best about going to the movies, Sarah."

Again the simulated woman blinked blankly. Mitch grinned. Morris hadn't been ready for that one, but a real woman would've had *some* response.

Sarah repeated, "I'm not really sure, Mr. Barlo."

Mitch saw the simulation for what it was. Sarah indeed didn't know what she wanted, and it was his job as operator to get her talking.

"Do you like gladiator movies, Sarah? Ever seen a grown man naked?"

(Follow the prompts, Smart Guy. Ask her about the weather in Cleveland.)

Mitch considered the weather in Cleveland to be a dead-end topic. Nobody paid $9.95 a month to talk to a movie star, even a simulated one, about their hometown weather. Mitch said, "Your profile says that you're a stay-at-home mom. How many children do you have?"

Morris had no comment to make on this line of questioning. He had Sarah say, "Two," and then nothing more. Mitch had guessed correctly: this simulation was designed to teach an operator to get the subscriber talking.

Mitch wasn't following the prompts, but that was okay. Morris had dealt with enough tight-lipped subscribers; he could easily answer the actor's off-script questions with monosyllables. He would show his pupil that however clever he thought he was, it would behoove him to follow the prompts. The system knew best.

"Are they boys? Girls? How old are they?"

"A girl and a boy. Six and four."

Mitch watched the timer count down. Morris/Sarah wasn't going to offer more details unless he said something else. His prompt said, *Favorite movie?*

But that would lead to just another short response, or even another *I'm not really sure, Mr. Barlo*. He had to get the subscriber to relax, to talk. Everyone's favorite subject was themselves, so Mitch said, "I see from your profile that you're thirty-six. So you decided to have children a little later than average?"

It was a great question, a gently probing question, one that a real person would perhaps feel compelled to answer. But Sarah was not a real person, and Morris wasn't falling for it. Sarah simply said, "Yes."

"What do your children want to be when they grow up?"

"I'm not really sure, Mr. Barlo."

"You're a terrible mother, Sarah," Mitch said and giggled. "Everyone should know what their children's ambitions are."

Simulated Sarah didn't react with outrage to the insult. She just blinked blankly. Morris slid the window aside and said, "I see you get the point of this one."

Mitch featured his operator with his world-famous, killer smile. "What's next?"

Morris brought up Cara. She was in real life a TTAMS employee, who had started out as an operator like Morris, but was now an instructor. She'd made a video and then it had been enhanced by the training staff as another educational tool. But Mitch didn't know any of that.

Cara's simulation was of a curious, technically savvy subscriber, who wanted to know how the system worked. She wanted to know who she was really talking to. Mitch followed the prompts, offering to send Cara an email detailing all of TTAMS's specs. He reminded her that a description of how the system worked was included with her sign-up package. If she wanted to know more than that, he offered to switch her over to Morris Baker, Operator Extraordinaire, who was not making instructor pay, but who would answer any further questions she might have, face to face, just like he was talking to her now.

Morris grinned. The prompt had said *Customer Service,* but as he had done throughout the evening, Mitch Barlo had made the direction his own.

When the prompt said, *Anything else?* Mitch grinned. The system wanted him to get rid of pushy Cara, but he went in another direction.

"After you speak to Customer Service, maybe you'd like to come back and talk to a movie star, Cara. You like movies, don't you? That's why you logged on in the first place, right?"

Like Sarah, Cara blinked blankly. This time, Morris took the bait. He wanted to see where the Oscar-nominee was going with this.

"Well, yes . . ."

"And you like my movies? That's why you picked me to talk to?"

"I really just wanted to know how it all works," Morris had Cara say, just to be difficult.

"It works like this. Whatever question you had in your mind tonight – whatever you thought you might like to hear from me, right from the horse's mouth – you just go ahead and ask it. Then, in your imagination, you can say to yourself, 'It must be true, because Mitch told me so himself.'"

"How big is your dick?"

"I'm sorry, Cara. That's another question I'm gonna have to refer to Morris Baker."

The screen went black. After a moment, the door on Mitch's side of the booth opened, and his grinning instructor said, "Come on, Movie Star, let's go get something to eat. You pass."

Mitch was surprised. "Already? That's it?"

"We could run Ultra-Feminist Flora. *This whole service just reinforces the patriarchal system that women are second-class citizens, that we should worship all men, as our culture worships male movie stars.* Or something like that. But I figure that you'd have her number, too. And my gut would hurt from laughing."

"What does the system prompt for Flora?"

"What would you say?"

"I'd sympathize with her feelings of inadequacy," Mitch replied, trying to keep a straight face. "Then I'd tell her, *It's just a job, lady*. Then I'd tell her that if she wanted to tell me what . . . *parts* . . . of my movies she liked, that it would be just between the two of us."

"That's not in the script, Lover Boy."

Mitch shrugged. "Maybe not. Maybe it wouldn't work. If it didn't, I'd tell her that Jodie Foster or Sharon Stone would probably be more sympathetic to her cause. I'd recommend that maybe she might want to commiserate on the patriarchal state of society with one of them."

Morris shook his head in amusement. "Another satisfied customer. Maybe. Come on, let's hit the cafeteria. No one's there this time of night, but there are vending machines."

"That's really it?"

"Time for immersion, baby. You've got the gist of it. You shut down the ones that talk smut right away. Ms Vinson's got it in her mind that they're not real subscribers, that they're reporters or something."

"She could be right. No one's ever just come up to me and started talking dirty."

"You don't spend a lot of time online, do you?"

"I do not."

"I don't think they're reporters. You don't get many dirty-talkers that show themselves. If you can see them, it's usually a bunch of drunk girls gathered around the screen – let's call up Mitch Barlo and tell him, 'Nice shoes, wanna fuck?'"

Mitch grinned.

"You do the ol' humble, *that makes me uncomfortable* shtick with them, too. They usually get bored and log off, to go look for IRL men to proposition. But like I say, the ones that ask you sex shit, but don't show themselves – I don't think they're reporters. It's the anonymity of the interface. People will say damn near anything when they can't be seen." Morris paused. "You'll get the Sarahs to talk, and maybe even the Caras, too. The rest are just fans, down for the fantasy. They want to hear you talk about behind-the-scenes movie stuff. They want to tell you they're your biggest fan. They might get around to wanting you to say how pretty they are, eventually, how much you like talking to them. Maybe a little romantic stuff. Tell them you love them, if you think that's what they want to hear, that if you could meet them IRL, you'd ask them out.

"You obviously already know how to talk to women, Mitch, so I don't think you're going to run into any trouble. Castro might want to monitor a few of your sessions, but I think you're ready."

"Do you know how to talk to women, Morris?"

201

The chubby operator lifted his chin with techie pride. "I do all right. But if you want to throw any starlets my way, I won't object."

"I'll have you over to the set, the next movie I do in town."

"I will appreciate it. In the meantime, let's go get some M&Ms."

****

Mitch discovered that he sincerely enjoyed "working" at TTAMS. It sounded clichéd, even to him, but there was something refreshing about talking to regular folks. His family and the people he grew up with were all back East; he had no friends in LA that were not in the business. And since it was a 24/7 business, the idea of the next job was always in the back of people's minds. How might their acquaintance with Mitch Barlo help or hinder their ambitions? He was admittedly the same way; trust and companionship were single serving in Hollywood. When the picture was done, most people immediately became competitors again.

His interactions with his fans through the interface was different than in real life, too. Better. There was none of the rush of the red carpet, nor was there that self-conscious awareness – *maybe I'm bothering him* – which occurred when they approached him on the street in LA. Added to that was the fact that the subscribers didn't know that they were talking to the real Mitch Barlo. It was a game, a fantasy, a simulation to them, and consequently they were relaxed, friendly, altogether not as star-struck as they would've been if they were talking to him in person.

Mitch frequently ignored his prompts, went off-script. *You may do it extempore, for it is nothing but roaring,* he'd think with a grin. He talked to his fans about more than just which one of his movies was their favorite.

The system told him what they had included in their profiles: ages, locations, occupations; whether they were married, single, or divorced; whether they had children. After a few innocuous questions, he discovered that his fans would open up to him about their lives and loves and jobs, their ambitions and dreams. Mitch found that listening to and discussing the lives of strangers was pleasant, often interesting. It took his mind off of his own troubles, his own loneliness.

Concerned that Morris Baker had passed him too quickly, Greg Castro monitored Mitch's first few live sessions. But once satisfied that the actor wasn't giving away the company secrets, that he was indeed pretending to be someone pretending to be him, Greg let him go on his own. Baker was right: the actor was a natural.

Mitch enjoyed the game. He arrived promptly at 6:15, damn near ever night. If for some reason he couldn't make it or was going to be late, he called in to Greg or Baker, like a conscientious employee. No one knew he was there. Shift change was at 4:00, and Greg had set him up with a live feed in the Operator Preparation Center, in the booth in which he had so briefly trained.

Greg alternated shifts. Sometimes he was there in the morning, when he might think up an excuse to exchange a few words with Valerie. Sometimes he worked afternoons and attended meetings. Mostly, he worked the four to midnight shift, where the bulk of the Pacific Standard Time subscriber interactions occurred. It wasn't like he had anything else to do with his nights.

Sometimes he would catch a cup of coffee with his solitary undercover operator. Mitch was true to his word, always wearing a hoodie or a hat and shades when he entered the building, always through the back door. No one had as yet spotted the real movie star in their midst. Morris Baker would join them sometimes, and the three of them would sit together in the deserted cafeteria and talk about TTAMS, or Mitch would tell them stories about Hollywood and the movie business.

Greg enjoyed the actor's company. He seemed like a regular guy, as comfortable discussing current events as he was laughing at Baker's raunchy jokes. After a few months of his prompt attendance, Greg and Morris each forgot that Mitch was a famous celebrity.

Quite by accident, Greg saw him on television one night, yukking it up with Jimmy Kimmel and plugging *The Erskine Dilemma*.

I just split a stale ham sandwich with that guy, not three hours ago, he marveled.

****

Joyce entered Valerie's office, stood in front of her desk and theatrically flashed open a copy of the *Los Angeles Times'* Entertainment Section.

"Have you seen this?" she demanded.

Valerie was reminded of the scene in *Helter Skelter* where Manson shows the jury the newspaper bearing the banner headline: *Manson Guilty, Nixon Declares*.

This headline was smaller, but considerably more germane to Valerie's interests. *How Talking to a Movie Star Saved My Life*. Joyce deftly spun the paper onto the desk in front of her.

203

Valerie said, *"On the twenty third day of the month of September in an early year of a decade not too long before our own, the human race suddenly encountered a deadly threat to its very existence, and this terrifying enemy surfaced, as such enemies often do, in the seemingly most innocent and unlikely of places . . ."*

Joyce pointed at the second headline. *Marianne Jackson Discusses Divorce, Depression, and Hollywood's Best Talking Cure.*

Valerie looked up at her business partner in astonishment. "Marianne Jackson? Really?"

"I told you a reporter would get through someday."

"But didn't you say she does political commentary or whatever? She's not an entertainment reporter. Is she?"

Valerie could not be bothered overly with the world outside of Hollywood in general and TTAMS in particular. Her workload was stupendous, and she liked it that way. Work kept her mind focused, so she didn't have time to think about anything superfluous, such as the fact that Brett was back in town. For fun, she read about the misfortunes of the stars on TMZ.com, as well as usually better news about them on People.com. She consulted Variety.com for all the skinny on the biz they called show. *The Los Angeles Times*, dot com or print version, was not high on Valerie's reading list. But she had heard Joyce mention Marianne Jackson and her views on world and local events.

Valerie didn't wait for Joyce to reply to her question about the reporter's usual beat. The world was at her fingertips. She Googled *LA Times reporter bios.*

There was a photo of a graying woman in her late forties, with kind brown eyes and a reluctant, somewhat world-weary smile. Valerie read aloud, *"Marianne Jackson is the assistant Op-Ed editor at The Times. A native of San Bernardino, she studied journalism at USC before a five year stint at Rolling Stone."*

Valerie wondered briefly how long ago that had been. She wondered if Ms Jackson had ever interviewed her dad.

"She was later an editor of the Los Angeles Times Magazine and has edited several books on the food, music, art, and cultural history of Southern California. She has been a part of several Pulitzer Prize nominated news teams." Valerie again looked at Joyce. "So why is a Pulitzer Prize nominee writing about us?"

"I'll let you read it. She does go on. I'm going to go fire Marvin for not letting me know that this was coming out."

On cue, as if beamed down from the *Enterprise*, Marvin materialized in the doorway. Valerie nodded over Joyce's shoulder. "Don't fire him. He's got a lot on his plate."

Valerie wasn't sure of Marvin's precise title – something to do with public relations, she thought – but he was a nice guy. He always smiled shyly at her whenever they passed in the office. He'd been instrumental in scheduling the interview they'd done with *Variety*, but now what-have-you-done-for-me-lately Joyce wanted to can him because he was late telling her about this piece in *The Times*. It wasn't as if either of them could've stopped it.

"It's six o'clock in the morning, for Christ's sake, Jo. Go have your coffee. Don't fire anybody."

Valerie leaned back in her imported, ergonomically wonderful leather desk chair and snapped open the Entertainment Section with a flourish. She felt like J. Jonah Jameson, barking orders from the helm of the *Daily Bugle*. All that was missing was a cigar and a visit from Peter Parker. Valerie Whitly, reading a *newspaper*. What was it, 1946?

At 42, I had it all: exciting career, trendy downtown LA digs; brilliant, successful, loving husband. My life was perfect. I had achieved all the things of which I had dreamt in high school and college, and missed none of the things at which I had sneered then: dogs and kids and a house with a lawn in a quiet suburb.

At 44, I had become a cliché. My job felt like a soul-sucking nightmare. My apartment was a tiny, obscenely overpriced cubicle, a fire-trap just steps away from the crime and all-around danger of LA's mean streets.

My brilliant, loving husband had left me for a 25-year-old intern, and not the medical kind, either. He had gotten her pregnant, probably on one of the nights I was working late at the office, perhaps in the bed we had shared. Being an upstanding kind of guy, before the ink was even dry on our divorce decree, he made an honest woman out of her, marrying her and taking her on a honeymoon to Niagara Falls. They live in a nice house in the suburbs now, with a lawn and a Golden Retriever named Oscar. I hear a second child is on the way.

In two years I had become what my mother had always feared I would: lonely, childless, over-the-hill, with nothing but my job, now grown tiresome,

205

to keep me company. "You're going to die all alone," Mom had told me once. That memory ushered in tears and insomnia to keep me company. Depression soon followed, and with it, thoughts of suicide. I was alone. Nobody would miss me, except maybe my editor, and the Pulitzer Committee.

"That must be newspaper humor," Valerie said aloud to her empty office.

She sighed. *Same song, second verse.* She had seen *Kramer vs. Kramer* and *An Unmarried Woman; Sliding Doors* and *Closer* and *Diary of a Mad Black Woman,* and then she'd stopped watching divorce and infidelity movies. Although she'd never caught Brett red-handed, *in flagrante delicto,* Valerie understood the pain of betrayal. And the rest of it didn't apply to her. She was never going to get married, so she'd never have to get divorced. The suspension of disbelief it would take for Valerie to identify with these characters was too much for her to sustain.

Marianne Jackson's whiny navel-gazing was crammed with a little bit too much regretful, mid-life bitterness, too. In the reporter's words, Valerie had already caught a whiff of the cautionary tale of choosing career over motherhood, and as usual, the admonition stunk. Valerie needed neither husband nor children. She was the creator of the freshest, hottest service in the world. She had Joyce for company. She had Eddie. She would never look back and bewail that she had wasted her life, as this reporter was doing.

What did all of it have to do with TTAMS, anyway? Valerie sighed again and read on.

Marianne talked further about her deepening depression, how therapy hadn't worked for her. She told of the scattered, absent-minded thought processes engendered by Prozac and Zoloft, how both had made her forget where she put her car keys, but neither had made her forget about her husband's happily-ever-after, *sans* her. She described how the feelings of worthlessness and loneliness only increased. She talked about how suicide looked better every day.

"A permanent solution to a temporary problem," Valerie said. Why, if she had gone ahead and killed herself, the world would've been deprived of TTAMS. Again, she toyed with the idea of calling Brett and thanking him for pushing her to the brink; she reminded herself to again thank Joyce for pulling her back.

Joyce had kept Brett away from her, allowing her the necessary freedom to discover Eddie. And it had been Eddie who had suggested the idea of TTAMS.

This reporter was just feeling sorry for herself. Valerie flicked away an imaginary tear in false sympathy.

Marianne talked about nearing the brink, as Valerie had once neared it. The reporter was more literal, however: she actually considered jumping off the balcony of her apartment as her way of ending it. Valerie yawned. She had contemplated suicide and was over it. Ms Jackson's mawkish recitations bored her, and she wondered when the woman was going to get to the point.

At last it arrived, and Valerie was surprised, thrilled. She realized that no amount of money could buy the kind of publicity that Pulitzer-nominated, girl-reporter Marianne Jackson was giving her for absolutely nothing.

> One day, I dragged myself into the office, thinking that it might just be the last. That short step and long drop to oblivion stood out in my mind so clearly as a viable alternative. Some of the young clerks were gathered around a secretary's desk, giggling. One shrieked laughter, and another looked up to see who might be observing them goofing off. She saw me, and figuring that the best way to keep the old woman from reporting them to their supervisor would be to include her, she said, 'Look, Ms Jackson! You can talk to Marilyn!'

And that was the start for poor, sad-sack Marianne. The first step on her return to the world of the non-self-pitying. Her road to recovery, her climb back from the depths of despair to functioning, current events-scouring, op-ed writing newshound had begun right then. Some nameless young clerk at *The Times* had shown her that she could pretend to talk to Marilyn Monroe on TTAMS.

Valerie grinned in delight.

> I couldn't talk to a therapist. The two I had tried had come off as insufferably smug, judgmental. They let me know that my problems were by no means insurmountable, because they had all been described, analyzed and solved in the *Diagnostic*

207

and Statistical Manual of Mental Disorders, Fifth
Edition. I was a healthy and successful, intelligent,
contributing member of society. I had no underlying
mental condition, no schizophrenia, no paranoia, no
bipolar disorder. I was just sad.

Someone as capable as I was should be able to
throw off a little betrayal. A little disappointment. I
should realize how good I had it, look on the bright
side. They had heard my name, knew my
accomplishments. Surely, a little emotional bump in
the road couldn't keep me down.

But here was Marilyn, shy, delicate, as beautiful
as she had ever been. Marilyn, who had had it all,
much more than I would ever have. And she had
suffered so much more than I had, at the hands of
presidents and athletes and writers, men far more
brilliant and successful than my ex-husband had
been.

I took the day off and went home and talked to
Marilyn on my computer. It really seemed to *be* her:
the *Talk to a Movie Star* interface is stunningly
lifelike.

"Fucking A Skippy, it is!" Valerie whooped. From the floor below,
heads turned, looked upward.

Marianne went on to describe how talking to the simulacrum of
the world's most famous dead starlet did for her what all of the high-
priced shrinks in Los Angeles could not. The conversations simply
made her *feel better about herself.*

Marilyn didn't try to tell her to get over it, Marianne related.

She commiserated. She wallowed with me. If I
said that all men were heartless, cheating monsters,
Marilyn agreed. When I suggested pay-per-view
castration as the penalty for running off with the
intern, she said it would make millions.

But when I said I felt that I would be better off
dead, Marilyn told me that dead was definitely not
better. She pointed out the simple truth: killing
myself would not kill my ex-husband. Hating myself
would not hurt him.

Marilyn pulled no punches: my ex-husband was a bastard, and in an imperfect world peopled by men like him, shit happens. She followed that with the famous line, the one that no mental health care professional had been smart enough to tell me: Living well is the best revenge.

I took her advice. As the doctors had told me, I had the building blocks to put my life back together: health and brains, a great job. But it took a computer simulation to show me that I could do it, that I *should* do it. Living well is the best revenge.

Just like Marilyn pointed out, did I want to be changing diapers, or did I want to be chasing Pulitzers? Did I want to be saddled with a middle-aged man with incipient prostate problems, or did I want to see what LA's world-infamous nightlife had to offer?

Valerie pushed the button that rang Joyce's office. "I want you to give all the Marilyns a bonus!"

"I'll be right up!" Joyce trilled back.

Valerie read the rest of the article. Marianne said she talked to a few more of the tragic, tortured starlets of yesteryear: Vivian Leigh and Judy Garland. She bemoaned that Carole Landis was not available.

Valerie was surprised that she could not place the name and quickly Googled the actress. She had been a beautiful blonde, not unlike Valerie herself. On July 5, 1948, at the tender age of twenty-nine, she had committed suicide because actor Rex Harrison would not divorce his wife for her.

Aunt Elise came immediately to Valerie's mind. To banish the sad memory, she quickly closed the web and returned to the article praising TTAMS.

Marianne said that each of the tragic Hollywood sob-sisters of yesteryear had told her the same thing as Marilyn: the best revenge was getting back on that fast-track horse, again going after the Pulitzer. They told her to stop missing the kind of life she'd never really wanted. Find a sexy, slick, disposable man or two. Or three.

They'd told her exactly what the shrinks did not: what she wanted to hear.

The article ended on an upbeat note. There had been no Pulitzer as of yet, but the reporter loved her job once more. She was dating again; she was having the time of her life. And on the rare nights that she relaxed at home these days, she spent a few hours on TTAMS, talking to Robert Downey or Mitch Barlo or Clive Owen.

It occurred to Valerie that Marianne Jackson must be one of those fans that never tired of hearing famous actors say *I love you.*

With Marvin hovering a step behind her like an overly-respectful shadow, Joyce reappeared in the doorway to Valerie's office. The two women had identical ear-to-ear grins; dollar signs flashed in their eyes and cash registers clinked in their heads.

Marvin dared a smile. "SoCal subscriptions are up fifteen percent since this hit the newsstands."

Hit the newsstands. Valerie again thought of Jonah Jameson.

"Hot damn!" Joyce said.

"New car, caviar, four-star daydream, think I'll buy me a football team." Valerie grinned crookedly and for a second, Joyce saw her rock star father in her. *"Waiter! There are snails on her plate! You would think that in a fancy restaurant at these prices you could keep the snails off the food!"*

Joyce and Marvin looked blankly at her, and for a numbing split-second, Valerie missed Brett, disconsolately, utterly. Brett would've gotten the reference.

Marvin cleared his throat. "In the wake of Ms Jackson's . . ."

"Awesome free publicity," Valerie prompted.

"Yes, well . . . In the wake of Ms Jackson's article, I thought it best to add another disclaimer to the subscriber agreement. We've been mostly protecting the personalities – *all opinions expressed by TTAMS's performers do not reflect the views, beliefs, opinions, etc.* I thought maybe we should start protecting ourselves, too." He consulted his tablet. *"All conversations between subscribers and TTAMS's performers are for entertainment purposes only. If you feel you are experiencing a medical or psychological emergency, please go to the nearest hospital or dial 9-1-1. The National Suicide Prevention Hotline number is–"*

"Really?" Valerie looked from Marvin to Joyce. Was this guy public relations, or was he part of the legal team?

"I don't think we have to put the hotline number in the disclaimer," Joyce told her underling. "If they want to off themselves, they're not gonna be reading the fine print." She flashed a smile at Valerie. Then, businesslike, she said to Marvin, "Schedule some kind of suicide awareness training for the operators, though. Bill it to Risk Management."

His task assigned, Marvin quickly offered Valerie his shy smile and left the office. Joyce wasn't going to fire him today.

"When did TTAMS get to be an alternative to psychotherapy?" Valerie asked in amazement. "When did we get to be a *talking cure?*"

"It's something different every day."

"Curiouser and curiouser." Valerie grinned.

"I knew a reporter would get through someday."

"She didn't *get through,* Jo. She came to the service just like anybody else."

"Maybe a little sadder."

"Maybe not. Maybe just single. If you look at the demographics, we don't have a lot of married people . . ."

"Or at least not happily married. Just lonely hearts, looking to spark it up a little bit with Brad Pitt."

Valerie tilted her head curiously at her friend's phrasing. "What's wrong with that?"

"I just don't want the next headline to be: *TTAMS – Suicide Prevention or Phone Sex Service?*"

"I think you're paranoid about that, Jo. Seriously." Valerie grinned, nodded at the newspaper. "Apparently, we're *Advice to the Lovelorn* now. If fake Marilyns are telling sad old ladies what they want to hear, what's wrong with that? By the same token, if people want to talk dirty to a fake movie star, why do you care?"

"I just don't want–"

"Oscar Wilde said, *The only thing worse than being talked about is not being talked about.* I say, there's no such thing as bad publicity."

"Who said that originally?"

Valerie shrugged. "PT Barnum, maybe."

"Your hero."

Valerie whistled *Entry of the Gladiators,* the classic tune of all circuses. When Joyce didn't smile she said, "It's not called *Talk to a Saint,* Joyce, for God's sake. This is Hollywood. Sin City."

"Vegas is Sin City."

"Whatever." Valerie again gestured at *The Times.* "Apparently, people are getting more emotional on TTAMS then I would've thought. When Eddie and I–" Joyce's eyes widened almost imperceptibly. Valerie caught it, so she began again. "When I imagined TTAMS, it was as a way for fans to fancifully get to know the stars that they were the most curious about. And part of getting to know someone is maybe, after a while . . . talking dirty to them. None of it is even remotely real, Jo. You know that. You know how many men we have, paying to hear Brad Pitt say he loves them?"

"If that gets out–"

"If that gets out, we'll be able to buy two football teams. It's already out, Jo. What's your advertising budget?" Joyce opened her mouth, but Valerie cut her off. "I don't really care. *I'm a doctor, Jim, not an accountant.* But I do look at the monthlies. Sometimes.

"When we launched, we had spots everywhere. Everywhere the fans are. TMZ, Entertainment Tonight, HBO, TMC, TvGuide.com. But I noticed you've slashed the advertising budget. Why is that?"

"Subscriptions are up."

"Way up. Fifteen percent here in town, overnight. Thank you, Marianne Jackson. But they were up even before she told the world that talking to a fake Marilyn Monroe got her life back on track. We don't need advertising anymore, Jo."

"Everybody needs advertising, Valerie."

"Our best advertisers are those girls Marianne mentioned in her story. It starts out with two or three of them logging on together, then, eventually, they log on alone. And if they talk dirty to Chris Hemsworth, they're not going to broadcast it to the world. It's a little secret, just between them and Chris. That makes it all the more fun."

Joyce remained unconvinced, so Valerie changed the subject. "I couldn't have done any of this without you, Jo."

"That's not true, Val—"

"It is. You believed in me. You got your dad to lend us the money. You run the place. But I wish you were a movie fan. I wish there was some actor that just *did it for you.*"

"Like Eddie."

"Exactly. If you were somebody's fan, then you'd understand. There's no bigger thrill in the world then a chance to talk to that one actor, the one that gets your motor running."

Head out on the highway, Joyce thought. *In your case, straight to Crazy Town.*

"That one actor, the one that makes you feel like a teenager again," Valerie was saying. "What you wouldn't give, just to say hi to him, just to have him smile at you . . . But how likely is that? Especially if you live in that oft-mentioned, well-known town in Egypt somewhere? TTAMS makes it all possible, even the dirty parts. It's not real, but it's real enough."

Joyce's phone beeped. She looked at it and frowned. "Brett wants me to ask if you want to have lunch with him. Again."

Valerie's every-present smile evaporated. "I told you. I don't wanna see Brett."

Joyce thought about Marianne Jackson and her rebirth. The reporter had managed to get over her betrayal by the novel method of talking to a TTAMS operator posing as Marilyn Monroe. Regardless of the method, the important thing was that she had gotten over it. She was living life to the fullest again. And her heartache had certainly been far worse than what Valerie had suffered.

Valerie no longer trolled bars for pretty boys like she had done in college. She told herself that she was above all that now. She was a successful entrepreneur, too busy for romance, and she buried herself in work to prove it. But the truth was obvious to her best friend. Valerie had never let go of the painful memories of stupid Brett Cooke.

Joyce thought that perhaps it was time for Valerie to throw off her own demons. It was time for the brilliant mind behind TTAMS *to get over it.*

"Ah, come on, Val. It's only lunch. I'll be there with you. He's just gonna keep asking, so—"

"*I don't wanna see Brett, Jo!*" Again, heads looked up from the operations floor.

"Okay, Val." Joyce's voice was soft after Valerie's shrillness. "I just thought . . . It's been a long time—"

"You have lunch with him."

"All right, Val. I understand." Joyce looked at her phone again. "I've got a meeting. I'll see you after . . . I'll see you this afternoon."

Valerie nodded, and Joyce left her office, taking all thoughts of Brett Cooke with her. That was because Val put him firmly from her mind. She reread Marianne Jackson's glowing testimonial again.

"We're *Advice to the Lovelorn,* now," she said to the picture of the Canadian actor on her laptop. "Christ, Eddie! *What hath God wrought?*"

Eddie's picture smiled back smugly.

****

That evening, Morris cut out for break a few minutes early. Joyce had posted Marianne Jackson's article in the cafeteria with a handwritten caption that said, *Way to go, Marilyns! To all operators: keep up the great work!* The floor was abuzz.

Beside the article was a printed memo, again directed *To All Operators: Openings Available for Prompt Overhaul Team. Submit your suggestions to your supervisor by noon on Friday.*

Mitch always *overhauled* his prompts, live, on the fly, off the cuff, as he saw fit. Morris ducked into the Prep Center to ask the actor's opinion of Marianne Jackson's article. He'd printed a copy off the newspaper's website.

Mitch was frowning at a blank screen.

213

"What cracks, Movie Star?"

"Audrey quit."

"Who?"

Mitch gestured at the blank screen. "Audrey. From Cincinnati."

"Your biggest fan?"

"I talked to her every day for a week, Morris. She told me goodbye. She said her subscription was almost up—"

"Oh. A regular."

Mitch's frown deepened, creasing his famous face. "I hate that word, Morris. It makes us sound like—"

"Whores?" Morris raised one ginger eyebrow. "If the shoe fits, baby."

"I'll miss Audrey. She's getting married. We talked about her wedding plans. Her colors are gold and crimson."

Morris made a face. "That's downright ugly, Mitch."

"She was nice. I'll miss her." Mitch sighed and switched on his monitor.

Morris considered the actor. "It's a service, Movie Star. Don't forget that."

"I know. Some of them are just more fun to talk to than others—"

"It's not real, Mitch. They know it. You know it. It's just a way for them to pass the time until life picks up. They love you excruciatingly – it hurts so good – for $9.95 a month. But then an IRL man comes along and they forget all about talking to a movie star. Most of them don't even bother saying goodbye. The subscription runs out, and poof! One less regular. There's always another one to take her place."

"Sometimes they come back," Mitch returned a little defensively.

"Oh, yeah. If things don't work out, they're back, talking about movies again. You're their escape, Mitch. I've got several that check in a few times a month, every month, to ask a few more questions about whether you did all your own stunts in *Shamus Alive* and stuff like that. Like you're their old friend. Some of them prefer the fantasy to reality, a fake famous friend to real, boring ones. Some of them never leave."

"Thanks for bringing me over here, Morris. It's a lot of fun."

Baker was surprised at the actor's genuine gratitude. "It is no problem at all, my friend. Did you see this article in *The Times*? Apparently you're not the only one that talks to them about more than just the movies."

****

Valerie was working late again. Joyce was long gone, probably out on a date, hitting a club with some guy she'd met through work. Being the CEO, the public face of TTAMS, Joyce had plenty of opportunities for romance with hardware vendors, and agents and reps from the studios. With other lawyers.

None of her beaux lasted long, however. Since her break up with Brett, Valerie had become leery of men, but Joyce had always been so. It could be said that success had made the two friends exchange lifestyles. In college, Joyce had been immersed in her studies and didn't date much, whilst Valerie had picked them up and dropped them as might a baby with a toy, when another toy caught her fancy. Now Joyce was enjoying serial, non-serious affairs, and Valerie was still sitting behind her desk at 9:30 on a Friday night.

Valerie supposed that Joyce might even be out on the town with Brett. They had lunch a couple times a week these days, so why not dinner and a movie? One part of Valerie's mind was grateful: Joyce was keeping her ex-boyfriend away from her. That part thought that perhaps it would be best if Joyce and Brett became serious – if that occurred, Valerie would forever be free of him.

But another part just wanted Brett to go away once more, back to Modesto or Oxnard or whenever he'd been working since graduation. If he and Joyce became serious, then sooner or later, Valerie would have to see him again, and then all the feelings would come back: how much she'd loved him, how cruelly he'd betrayed her. Those feelings came back anyway, if she so much as thought of him.

The photo changed on Valerie's laptop. The previous one had been of Eddie from *Undercover Homicide:* cool, haughty, malicious, sexy. The one that succeeded it was a still from *Two's a Crowd.* Valerie smiled, all thoughts of Brett leaving her mind, as they did any time she saw a picture of Eddie.

****

The first time Valerie had shown Joyce the shot of Eddie from *Two's a Crowd* had been long ago and far away, before 20th Century Fox, before TTAMS, before they had gone to Canada with the Foley guy and actually shook hands with the Canada-famous thespian. It had been before other, never-dreamt events had occurred, and long before Brett Cooke had returned to LA, clamoring to see Valerie again.

It had been the day before Valerie's successful interview and immediate employment with the big studio, actually. Valerie had shown

215

Joyce the picture when her obsession with Edison Forbes had still been fresh.

"Look at this one," Valerie had instructed her friend. "I think this is my favorite. This and the next one."

The picture was in stark black and white, showing Eddie and another actor. Eddie had his back half turned to the camera. He was leaning over toward the other guy, as if they'd just been speaking closely; whispering perhaps. Now Eddie was looking over his shoulder, right at the viewer.

Valerie explained, "It's like the three of us are standing in a bar, and I see him there across the room, talking to this other guy. This guy says, *'Look, Eddie, that woman's staring at us.'"*

The other actor's face was neutral. Watchful.

"'Oh, yeah?' Eddie replies."

Eddie's expression was curious, expectant, his big eyes interested, expectant, maybe even intrigued. A shadow limned one perfect cheekbone. Just the ghost of a smile curved his lips.

"The other guy says, *'What do you think she wants?'"*

Valerie pulled up the next photo. Eddie's smirk was complete in the second picture, arrogant. His curiosity had been satisfied. He was smug.

Valerie spoke for him. *"'Oh. I know what she wants.'"*

In the second shot, the other actor had adopted his best smoky stare. *"'Maybe she wants it from me this time,'* he says."

"Eddie says, *'I don't think so, my brother and only friend.'"* Valerie grinned wickedly.

Joyce was incredulous. "You get all that from just two stills?"

Valerie nodded. "I like to make up little dialogues. What he would say, what I would say . . ."

"Your imagination is . . . staggering." Joyce considered her friend's smiling face. In a less brilliant mind, there might be another term for Valerie's imagination. *Delusional,* maybe. Just like her doomed aunt.

But unlike Elise's lethal obsession with Dennis Whitly, Joyce reckoned that Valerie's instantaneous fascination with Edison Forbes was harmless enough. Elise had actually known Valerie's dad. Her conversations with the rock star were real, concrete. Unfortunately, irrevocably, the last one had not been to her liking.

Conversely, Valerie *made up* her conversations with Edison Forbes. She didn't know him; she couldn't ever know him. *What's Eddie Forbes really like?* would forever remain a mystery. Never married, the actor might be gay for all Valerie knew.

Just like Elise with her brother-in-law, Valerie would never get to be with Eddie, but more importantly for Valerie's mental health, Eddie would never turn her down, either. He would never dash her fantastical hopes, never break her heart. The infinite, wonderful possibilities of *what could be* sustained her, but Joyce knew that it wasn't a real world hope for Valerie, like poor Elise's had been. Valerie was never going to even meet Eddie Forbes, and she knew it. Therefore, he would always remain the perfect man to her, a fantasy man that never disappointed.

Brett's seeming betrayal had delivered quite a shock to Valerie's emotions, her ego. She had *loved* him, and the realization that he didn't love her back quite as completely as she'd wanted, as she'd thought he should . . . Like Elise Carlin's last recognition about her sister's husband, Valerie hadn't taken her own realization about Brett and his love well. Not well at all.

Like her aunt, Valerie had contemplated the unthinkable. But she hadn't done it in the end, and if she'd come out of the experience a little nuttier than when she'd gone in . . .

Such disappointments happen to the best of us, Joyce thought. If crushing on some unknown Canadian movie star like she was fifteen years old made Valerie happy again, Joyce figured that it was okay. Edison Forbes was never going to hurt her like Brett had.

"Isn't he just *the sexiest* man you've ever seen?" Valerie demanded with that schoolgirl enthusiasm.

Joyce studied the pictures. Both Eddie and the other actor were dressed in black, or maybe it was dark blue. Joyce couldn't tell because the stills were in black and white, but Valerie had already shown Joyce enough color pictures of Eddie, had made her sit through that terrible sit-com, so she knew that he had coal black hair and blue eyes. The other guy's hair was also dark, probably black as well. Joyce again understood that her friend had a type: either one of these attractive actors could've been Brett's brother.

Joyce had to admit that Edison Forbes was looking good in the shots. But the sexiest man she'd ever seen? She wouldn't go that far. He was attractive, but then the other guy wasn't too shabby either. Joyce asked Valerie who he was.

"I have no idea. These are from a movie called *Two's a Crowd.* I haven't seen it yet. Something about two guys in love with the same woman. Probably not very original, but–"

"You haven't seen it yet? I thought you'd watched all of–"

Valerie shook her head.

"You couldn't find it on Pirate Bay?" *The best place on the internet to search for obscure Canadian nobodies and their films . . .*

"Oh, it's on Netflix."

Joyce recalled that Netflix had become all cosmopolitan lately, with their collection of Canadian television and movies. Maybe they'd always been that way, but it had only been recently that she'd become aware of it, since Valerie had made her sit through all three seasons of *Sonny's Diner,* and two of Edison Forbes's movies. Apparently there were at least three of them on Netflix.

"Why haven't you watched it then? This other guy's cute, too."

"I haven't watched it yet because, well . . . Eddie's got only six movies. He did a couple TV shows, but . . . Well, let's just say . . . I'm saving *Two's a Crowd.*

"You're saving it."

Valerie smiled shyly. "Yeah. Like for a rainy day."

Joyce had to say it this time. "You're nuts, Val."

But her friend's thing for Edison Forbes and the peccadillos that apparently accompanied it weren't hurting her or anybody else. *She's saving it.*

"Well, tell me when it rains. I'll watch this one with you. That other guy's fine." Joyce studied the picture again. "Wait – is that Mitch Barlo?"

At Valerie's behest, Joyce had been paying more attention to Eddie Forbes than the other actor in the picture. But now that she looked at it . . . He was very young, and the haircut was a lot different than he'd worn it in more recent films. "How old is this movie?"

"Oh, it's an oldie. Eddie's third, I think. He's so cute in it, it hurts to look at him."

"How would you know, if you haven't . . . Whatever." Pictures were enough for Valerie. "That *is* Mitch Barlo!" *He's sure come a long way since playing second fiddle to some Canadian nobody.*

Valerie grinned, thinking Joyce might be a kindred spirit after all. Maybe she did appreciate movie stars, if not movies themselves. She'd always scoffed before, rolled her eyes when Valerie talked about the value of movies, the truths they taught. But it only took one actor to turn a girl into a fan.

Valerie had always been a fan of cinema, but once she'd seen Eddie . . . The root word of *fan* was *fanatic,* and that was what she'd become. A fanatic, Edison Forbes's Number One Fan.

"You like Mitch Barlo?"

Joyce shrugged. She certainly found him more attractive than Edison Forbes, even if they were the same type. That lame Western he did, *Shamus Alive* – now there was somebody *so cute it hurt to look at him. Two's a Crowd* must've been from about the same time.

Joyce also considered Mitch to be a much better actor than Valerie's Canadian. "Did you see *A Random House Is Not a Home?* It was great. It was nominated for an—"

"Yeah, but *A Perfect Woe* won that year."

"Mitch was great in *A Random House Is Not a Home,*" Joyce insisted.

"He was all right. I thought it was a little farfetched. If the guy he played was such a great writer, why didn't he have a publisher?"

Eddie was never nominated for Best Actor, Joyce thought.

"That's where he met Janna Langly," Valerie said.

She didn't consider herself a Mitch Barlo fan, Joyce noted, but Valerie knew his history, nevertheless. Daily doses of TMZ.com and etonline.com kept her abreast of all the scandal in Tinseltown, titillating or shocking or just plain sad.

"They fell in love while making that movie."

"He must've been devastated when she killed herself," Joyce opined. *No fairy tale happily-ever-after there. Just another Hollywood trip to the morgue.* Poor, good-looking, talented Mitch Barlo. All the Oscar nods in the world couldn't make up for that.

"It wasn't ruled a suicide," Valerie said, shaking her head firmly. "The coroner called it *an accidental overdose.* There was no note. She had a history of drug use. She'd just returned from rehab. It was just a relapse."

A fatal relapse. Joyce believed that people who did serious drugs had a death wish. She imagined that they probably recognized it, every time they prepared their chosen poison: *Hey, ho, I might not come back from this one, but who cares? So what?*

But just like all of Janna's fans, Valerie didn't want to believe that one of the stars in her firmament could've been so self-destructive. Valerie figured that drugs were just part of the Hollywood culture. Probably all of the big names partook, and poor Janna, she'd just gone a little overboard the last time. She was just a victim of the lifestyle. It was an accident, not intentional. *Not suicide.* Valerie believed the same thing about Marilyn. She hadn't left a note, either.

Like Marilyn, Janna Langly had had it all, a bright career, a stunningly attractive, successful husband who loved her. How could such a lucky woman ever have become so despondent as to see no other way out? The fact that only two weeks ago, Valerie had almost done such a thing to herself, over something as ridiculous as Brett Cooke texting other women, seemed to have slipped her mind.

Not totally without pity, Valerie said, "Shit happens. Shit you can't control. You get over it."

Her dreams and fantasies of Edison Forbes had *gotten her over it*. The little dialogues she made up with him in her mind had totally driven out the real life truths that she believed about Brett, the things that were too painful to think about. Again, Joyce thought Valerie's solution was all right. *Whatever works.*

Valerie gestured at Eddie's picture again. "I never really noticed that that was Mitch Barlo with him. Like I say, I haven't seen the movie, and Eddie eclipses whoever else's in a photo with him."

To you, anyway. Joyce wasn't going to get into a debate on the attractiveness of Eddie vs Mitch, or Eddie vs anybody. There were more than a few black-haired, blue-eyed actors in the world, but to Valerie, *there could be only one.*

Joyce grinned to herself. To Valerie, all the rest were *eclipsed* by his Canadian Majesty's awesomeness, and to attempt to argue with her about it was akin to trying to teach a pig to sing. It makes you look foolish, and it annoys the pig.

****

Sitting behind her lavish desk at TTAMS now, smiling at the still from *Two's a Crowd,* Valerie said aloud, "Why not Mitch Barlo?"

Marianne Jackson's better-than-money-could-buy piece about her service had *hit newsstands* about a week before, and just as Greg Castro had theorized that she eventually would, Valerie had been toying with the idea of logging on to her system. Poking around a mite. Having a little look-see.

TTAMS ran under the Agile theory of software development, *wherein requirements and solutions evolved through collaboration between self-organizing, cross-functional teams,* as Wikipedia explained it. *Adaptive planning, evolutionary development, early delivery, continuous improvement;* each of these actions *encouraged rapid and flexible responses to change.*

Valerie employed the brightest, highest paid cross-functional teams in the world, and through their genius, her baby was growing up. Talk to a Movie Star was evolving. As she'd told Joyce, she and Eddie had originally envisioned the service as pure fun: giggling fans talking to fake actors about real movies, Maisie from Poughkeepsie and Betty from Philly thrilling to the scripted compliments paid to them by simulacrums of their idols.

You're just my kinda girl, Sally, and if I ever get tired of Angelina, why . . . I'd surely look you up.

I love you, Brad!

I love you, too, Sally.

220

But apparently, TTAMS had grown into something more, into psychotherapy, into *Advice for the Lovelorn,* into a life-saving pep-talk for the suicidal. *Curiouser and curiouser.*

Valerie still hadn't watched the movie in which Mitch Barlo had appeared with Eddie. She was so busy, and there weren't too many rainy days in Los Angeles. But Mitch was cute enough, especially back then. Why not see how things were functioning on TTAMS these days by having a session with him?

She called up her never-before accessed subscriber profile. Before proceeding, she edited the information on it, changing her name to *Denise,* her middle name. Last names appeared only on the billing screen, along with addresses and credit card info. Billing was another department; its stats were inaccessible to operators.

Valerie changed her profession to *student,* and changed her location to *Riverside.* She imagined that if she logged on as herself, one of her sharp operators would recognize her statistics and figure out that he was talking to the boss. He would be nervous, self-conscious. The session would become artificial.

Now that she was Denise from Riverside, Valerie called up the landing screen for Mitch Barlo. It showed a cartoonish mock-up of the actor, like the oldie-time graphics from *Money For Nothing.* Valerie clicked, and a list of his movies and the characters he had portrayed appeared. There was *Shamus Alive, Two of Swords, A Random House Is Not a Home.* There was, in fact, all of the actor's filmography, except for *Two's a Crowd.*

Valerie frowned. She figured that Joyce would have a yen to fire somebody from Licensing and Research when she learned about this oversight. *Two's a Crowd* wasn't listed with Mitch Barlo's other works, no doubt because he was an American actor and it was a Canadian film. It was a glaring error. Valerie wondered if any other stars' foreign films were also missing.

Maybe I should've looked into things a little sooner.

Valerie scrolled through the list of the parts Mitch had played. With a click, she could order them alphabetically by film or by character name; she could order them chronologically. She could list his works by genre, then again by film, character, or date. Valerie had seen only a couple of the blue-eyed actor's films. In *Random House,* he had been scruffy, troubled – it had been his *Actor in a Serious Role* part. She had seen *Two of Swords* – he looked good in a tux. He had been cute enough with short hair in her stills from *Two's a Crowd* – he was of course no Edison Forbes, but he was cute enough. He was long-haired and adorable in the shot from *Shamus Alive* displayed on the system

As Shamus, Mitch Barlo had borne a passing resemblance to Brett Cooke. Valerie reflected that it might be therapeutic to talk to somebody who looked like Brett – a baby step, like going up an extra flight of stairs if one was afraid of heights – even if it was only an operator pretending to be an actor playing the part of a fictional cowboy.

Valerie clicked the link that would connect her to Shamus.

****

Greg was at home watching television when a beep went off on his phone and his laptop simultaneously. For a split-second, he blinked in confusion – what was this alarm telling him? He had never heard this particular note from his phone before, especially not in concert with the computer, so what was – *Oh, shit, it's Valerie!*

He leapt off the couch, spilling chips, knocking over his beer. He grabbed his laptop off the desk, plopped back down on the couch. He ignored the crunch of the scattered chips, and clicked the glowing red ball that had appeared in the middle of the screen. He quickly scanned the code that immediately filled it.

"Well, I'll be *goddamned!*"

Valerie had not only finally decided to check out her own system, she had gotten it into her pretty little head to talk to Mitch Barlo, Oscar-nominated star of stage and screen, the one actor on all of God's green earth whom the Director of Technical Operations just happened to know personally. Greg couldn't believe his luck.

Then he frowned. Valerie wanted to talk to his close personal friend Mitch, true, but not the one hidden in the Prep Center. The boss wanted to talk to young Mitch – she wanted to talk to Shamus.

Christ, she's liable to get Baker.

That wouldn't serve Greg's interests. Valerie had at last decided on a movie star, but it was the wrong incarnation. Greg wanted her to talk to the modern Mitch Barlo, the one he had on a no-pay retainer. The one Greg could actually produce for her in the flesh, the one she would be grateful to him for meeting, the one who could tell her everything she wanted to know about that no-talent Canadian nobody.

Greg didn't want Valerie talking to Shamus, to *Baker.* He wanted her to talk to the real Mitch, his buddy, his pal, his *boy.* Greg wanted Valerie to praise him later for corralling a real movie star onto the system, the exact one that could tell her what she wanted to know. He wanted Valerie to be grateful behind it, to agree to go out with him.

Greg typed a command, and it sped across town with the speed of all things electronic, with the speed of magic. It interrupted Valerie's conversation with Shamus almost before it began. Her screen went blue; the message said, *We're sorry, but the star you've chosen is unavailable at the moment. Please try again shortly.*

Greg imagined Valerie jumping up, rushing out and standing on the balcony of her office, hands on hips, Mussolini-like, screaming to everybody and nobody in particular for an explanation as to why her very first TTAMS session had suddenly gone offline. She would demand to know where the Director of Technical Operations was hiding, why he wasn't fixing the problem . . .

Except Valerie wouldn't do any of that. Greg might've done it himself, and such would've been Joyce's reaction, certainly. When her phone or computer failed to perform a task, the CEO took it as a personal insult: one of her myriad electronic slaves was getting uppity with its master.

But Valerie was a code-monkey, and she knew these things happened. The greatest challenge of her life was to ferret out and repair such bugs, to banish the intrusion of reality and restore the computerized illusion, to bring back the magic. Valerie knew that it was a temporary glitch; her system would soon reset itself. It could've been caused by any number of things, perhaps something as simple as her act of changing her profile information and then failing to log out and log back in. She would reason that these actions probably *hadn't* caused the malfunction, but it was a possibility. She would run a diagnostic.

Greg knew the brilliant programmer's methods. Valerie would run a system test, and it would tell her that the break in the function had been caused by an outside command. She would see that it was her Number 3 employee that had sent it, from a remote location, no less. Greg would be busted, his keeper apprehended. The boss would wonder just what the hell was going on . . .

Greg needed a diversion.

He sent another command to Valerie's TTAMS session, causing the one-sentence clip that played first whenever a subscriber chose to converse with today's Mitch Barlo to run on her screen.

"Hi. Before we chat, I just wanted to remind you about my new film, *The Erskine Dilemma*, in theatres this fall. Do you want to watch the trailer with me?" *(y/n?)*

Valerie had finally logged onto her system, but she had attempted to disguise her identity by revising her profile. She couldn't hide from Greg Castro's eternally loyal and efficient keeper, however. She had gone in text-only, so the Shamus operator wouldn't recognize her, and therefore Greg couldn't see her, either. He knew that if he activated her webcam remotely, it would be a dead giveaway. She would know that someone was shadowing her session, because the system never, ever turned on a webcam without the subscriber's permission.

The situation was frustrating to the tech. He licked his lips nervously. Greg needed to know, but he could not see – was Valerie frowning at the screen, wondering why the system had sent her the modern-Mitch movie teaser, instead of resetting and waiting for her to again try to contact a Shamus operator, as it was designed to do in the event of a glitch? Just what in the name of Moore's law was going on with TTAMS's protocols?

Greg reckoned that at this point, Valerie would either run the diagnostic and out him, discover that her session was being remotely controlled, and by whom; or she would take the bait, hit *y,* and watch the trailer for *The Erskine Dilemma.* She would either choose to be the boss and look into her oddly behaving creation, or she would choose to be a subscriber (as she had started out to do) and converse with the modern Mitch. It all depended on her mood, and while her employee could guess at her analytical mind, he knew nothing whatsoever of her moods.

Greg held his breath for a second, then he made his own decision. His choice was a desperate act: he would crash Valerie's laptop, her link into the system, before she could run the diagnostic and discover him.

Very few programmers were without a dark side, and Greg Castro's was more prominent than most. His malicious command and the crash that would follow it would result in several hours of lost productivity at TTAMS. Valerie would order an analytic to be run for the entire system, the granddaddy of all diagnostics, figuring TTAMS could afford the downtime more than they could afford the customer frustration of a service that arbitrarily crashed their lil' ol' home computers.

Valerie would shut down the whole structure while Greg and his staff searched for a bug that didn't exist. He knew that no one would find evidence of his remote command because he would get in there and erase it ahead of time. *Oh what a tangled web we weave . . .*

He typed the command anyway. He would crash the boss, the woman he loved, in order to keep his stalking hidden, and let the chips fall where they may. His finger was poised over the *Enter* key, and it surely would've descended, had Valerie not clicked *y.*

Greg exhaled in relief. He knew that the spiel for *The Erskine Dilemma* would be the full trailer, that it would run for a good two minutes. TTAMS didn't stiff their subscribers on views of coming attractions, and the studios played handsomely to pitch their newest blockbusters. It wasn't much time, but it would have to be sufficient for Greg to communicate to the real Mitch Barlo exactly what he needed to know.

Greg opened a window on Mitch's monitor in the Prep Center. The subscriber to whom the actor had been talking was sent without ceremony to electronic perdition; she got the blue screen and the message that the star she'd chosen was unavailable at the moment. If she tried again shortly, as instructed, she would get another operator masquerading as Mitch Barlo.

Greg grinned. The Director of Technical Operations was now in control of the transmission. He controlled the horizontal and the vertical. With Mitch's assistance, he could shape Valerie's vision to anything his imagination could conceive. For the next hour (or however long it took) Greg would control all that she would see and hear.

"Hey, Mitch."

"What's up, Boss? I was in the middle of—"

"Forget about that right now. I'm about to patch you through to a very special subscriber."

"Who—"

"I don't have time to explain who or what or why or how or any of that happy horseshit." The audacity of secretly guiding his boss's very first TTAMS session made Greg giddy. "She's watching the trailer for your newest right now. She's gonna come in text-only. Just be your normal charming self."

"Who is this girl, Greg? Does she know that I'm—"

"No. She thinks you're just a regular operator. Be that."

"Who—"

"Here she comes, Mitch. You're on."

****

Even though she kept her webcam off, Valerie could of course see the operator. She smugly agreed with Marianne Jackson's appraisal: the interface she had created was stunningly lifelike. She was looking at a Mitch Barlo indistinguishable from the one that had appeared in the trailer she'd just watched.

The operator blinked blankly at the screen. A slight shift of his eyes alerted Valerie that he was reading her bio on the prompt. It also told him that she had opted to chat via text. She waited, and after another moment, he typed, *What would you like to ask me, Denise?*

225

Valerie blinked like a simulation herself, in confusion. *Oh, yeah, that's right. I forgot. I'm Denise.* She typed, *Could I speak to you, Mitch?*

Valerie didn't deal with her operators directly. That job belonged to Greg Castro and a battalion of supervisors and instructors. So while she knew that the employee playing Mitch Barlo would recognize her face, she was willing to take the chance that he wouldn't know her voice.

Yes. Just click the picture of the microphone in the upper right corner of the screen, and we'll be able to hear each other.

Mitch was glad that whoever Greg's special subscriber was in the real world, at least she wasn't a shy Tammy. He'd encountered several who wouldn't show themselves, but not another one that had refused to speak to him, too, as in the typed-only conversation he'd had in simulation. He'd felt silly just smiling blankly at the screen, then. He liked to see their faces, to make eye contact, but if they refused to play it that way, if he could at least hear their voices, it didn't seem quite so artificial to him. It was like talking on the phone.

"Hi, Mitch. I'm . . . Denise."

"It's nice to meet you, Denise. What would you like to ask me?"

Even though it was SOP, evidently this operator didn't want to play the game of suggesting, *It's so much more interesting to talk to someone if I can see them. You can see me. Why don't you click the webcam icon so I can see you, too?*

Sometimes new subscribers didn't realize that they had to click the icon, and would have to click it every time they logged on. It was all part of Joyce's CYA legal policy: in the small print of the subscriber agreement, it read, *By clicking the webcam icon, subscriber acknowledges that subscriber will be visible to the TTAMS operator. . .*

Valerie knew that it wasn't because she'd gotten a noob operator, or that he'd just forgotten. The system had prompted him to ask her to turn on her webcam. He'd just ignored it. Perhaps he was an experienced operator, a just an experienced man, and already knew that if she'd wanted to show herself, she would've done so, or if she was a noob herself, inexperienced with TTAMS, she would've asked if he could see her. But she'd come in text-only, hadn't asked anything. So he'd already recognized that she was self-conscious and didn't want to be seen, although he couldn't know that it wasn't out of shyness.

"Who directed that movie in the trailer?" Denise/Valerie asked.

"That would be David Cronenberg."

"He's Canadian, isn't he?"

"Yes."

"Have you ever done any other Canadian films, Mitch?"

226

Valerie knew that the system would search for *Mitch Barlo Canadian films* and then return *None.* The TTAMS database was usually exhaustive, and if it hadn't offered the subscriber the opportunity to talk to young Mitch Barlo à la *Two's a Crowd*, it was because someone in Licensing and Research had failed to discover that the American Academy of Motion Picture Arts and Sciences-nominated actor had also appeared in a foreign film.

Development wouldn't have had any problem with the character mockup – they would've just used the Shamus wireframe and given it a haircut, taken the cowboy twang out of the voice simulation. No. Valerie was sure of it: Research had somehow overlooked Mitch Barlo's previous not-Hollywood-made film.

But the operator surprised Valerie. He said, "Yes, as a matter of fact, I did one other Canadian picture. It was a long time ago, a comedy, about brothers that fall in love with the same girl. It was called *Two's a Crowd.*"

Maybe I'm wrong, Valerie thought. The system had obviously prompted the operator with the title and the date and the synopsis of Mitch's foreign movie. But that didn't make any sense. If the flick was in the database, why couldn't she talk to the character he'd played in it?

Valerie wondered suddenly if *Two's a Crowd* had also been omitted from Eddie's filmography.

"Hold on one second, could you, Mitch?"

"Certainly."

Valerie opened another window and searched her system's database for *Two's a Crowd.*

Title not found. Search again?

She entered *Edison Forbes's filmography* in the search box. Perhaps this was another goddamned bug. Her system seemed lousy with them tonight. *I should've been more hands-on all along.*

Perhaps the Canadian feature hadn't been properly cross-referenced. Perhaps it didn't appear in the overall movie database, nor on the American actor's list, but it should appear on Eddie's. It was a Canadian film, he was a Canadian actor. He'd been the star, after all.

Two's a Crowd was not listed among Eddie's body of work, either. Valerie thought that if Joyce wanted to fire somebody, she could definitely start in Licensing and Research. It suddenly occurred to her that this might be why so few Americans had chosen to talk to Eddie on TTAMS. *We're not even listing all his movies.*

So how did this operator know about the film?

"I've never seen that one, Mitch. Who was in it besides you?"

Mitch smiled. "Yeah, it was straight to video here. Nobody heard of it."

It's on Netflix, Valerie thought.

"I was the only American in it. My co-star was a Canadian actor named Edison Forbes. You've probably never heard of–"

"Oh, I've heard of him."

Greg Castro was monitoring the session between his beloved boss and his famous good friend, and he would've bet a month's pay – no, he'd bet a *year's* pay – that he could predict what Valerie's next question was gonna be. He patted himself on the back. Everything was going precisely as he had pictured it.

He and Valerie were going to be such good friends. He already knew her so well. He'd thought that she'd ask the question after he'd already introduced her to Barlo, but she was gonna ask it of his simulation, instead, just for fun. Later, when Greg made the big reveal, she'd probably ask it of the actor again, chasing real details about that Canadian nobody. Then she would be so grateful to Greg for making possible all these invaluable co-star insights!

Now, Greg could almost hear the excitement that would color her lyrical voice. She was gonna say, *"Oh, my God, Mitch! You gotta tell me! What–"*

"Did you enjoy making that period piece?" Valerie glanced at the *Two's a Crowd*-lacking list of Mitch Barlo's films. He'd had a minor role in something called, *"The French King's Ransom?"*

The Mitch Barlo simulacrum laughed in surprise. "Wow, Denise, you really are a fan. Nobody's asked me about that one before."

It was true. TTAMS subscribers that wanted to talk to today's Mitch Barlo might've caught *Shamus Alive* on video somewhere, and they'd all adored *Two of Swords,* but they'd never heard of *The French King's Ransom.*

He grinned at the screen, flattered. "Don't tell me you've seen *Stutter and Scream,* too? I wasn't in that one for very long."

Valerie called up Mitch Barlo's TTAMS filmography, and was outraged to discover that this movie wasn't on his list either. Disgusted with her own system, she quickly opened an internet tab and searched for the film on IMDb.com. She looked at the credited cast. She saw a bunch of unknowns, but no Mitch Barlo. She clicked on *See Full Cast,* and there he was at the bottom.

The photo beside his name was not from *Stutter and Scream;* studios wasted neither money nor time on taking headshots of practically-extras. The picture was of the star in his tux from *Two of Swords*, from later in his career, after he'd made it big. Valerie knew that if she clicked on the picture, she would be taken to the now-successful actor's IMDb.com page, where she could read of his many achievements, his well-known flicks, his Oscar-nomination and so on.

Who'da thunk it? Mitch Barlo had started off his stellar career in some forgettable splatter-fest, and it had taken an operator on her own system to inform Valerie of this interesting trivia . . .

"I did see it," Valerie lied. She read from the IMDb.com cast listing. "Your name was. . ."

"Billy. I was the first one to go." Again the operator playing Mitch Barlo laughed.

This guy's good. Either he's got IMDb.com up, just like me, because he knows his TTAMS's dbase sucks, or he's one helluva Mitch Barlo fan.

Valerie decided to see how much of a fan this operator really was. She said, "I was so sad to hear about Janna's . . . suicide, Mitch. It was a horrible shock for those of us who loved her films. I know how devastating it must've been for you."

Valerie was amazed to see a genuine look of sadness cross the operator's face. *This guy is really good!* Then the sorrow changed just the slightest bit, to a resigned look of *I've told this story before.* Valerie was astounded – the operator knew Janna's death hadn't been suicide, as much as Valerie herself did.

The fake Mitch Barlo sighed, again with a startling *realness.* "It wasn't like that, Denise. Janna didn't want to be dead. She just wanted to be high again. She wanted to be someone else, and that's the way she achieved it. The last time, she went too far. Took too much. She'd just landed a great part – the lead in *Angel's Delight.* Her death was an accident."

Valerie was again surprised. She'd read Mitch Barlo's cover story in *Rolling Stone*, wherein the actor had said almost the same words. But Valerie had never seen it mentioned anywhere that the part in *Angel's Delight* had been originally intended for Janna. The lead had eventually gone to Emma Stone. Valerie had seen it: a cute, forgettable little comedy. This operator was good. He'd done his research. He had to be a fan.

Valerie's employee allowed his sad expression to linger. It was so realistic that she was inexplicably moved to feel that she had actually hurt him, not only by bringing up Janna's overdose, but also by so callously assuming that the actress had taken the easy way out.

Valerie felt bad. Sure, it was all a game, a simulation; she hadn't in fact hurt anybody's feelings. But *she* was a real person. She was a real fan – if not of Mitch Barlo particularly, she was a fan of Hollywood and the movies. She knew that fame had its price, that all that money opened the door for easy, dangerous pleasures.

Yet she had behaved like a Philistine, a non-fan, suggesting that Janna Langly had killed herself, when she knew it wasn't true. She had behaved like Joyce.

Valerie felt the need to soothe the simulation, to make amends to him, to erase the cruelty of her words. She marveled again at how adept the operator had been at eliciting real emotions from her.

But before she could apologize to the fake Mitch Barlo for her contrived thoughtlessness, a short snippet of *Eye of the Tiger* played on her phone. It was Joyce.

"Could you hold on for just another second, Mitch? I have to take this."

"Sure," he replied absently. Valerie was again amazed that the operator seemed to be genuinely lost in his own thoughts, as if he was truly reliving the death of a woman he had not actually known. He was good.

Valerie said hello, and was returned with a burst of laughter from her best friend. "Hi, Val! You're still at work, aren't you?"

"Yes."

Valerie watched Mitch Barlo's operator. He stared off into space for another second, then seemed to realize where he was. He glanced down, shook his head, then looked at the screen again. Once more, he was a friendly celebrity on TTAMS, patiently waiting to answer his fan's meaningless questions about his movies. But all those other, more solemn emotions had been there. Valerie had seen them.

"I thought so," Joyce said gaily. "I'm in the lobby with Mortie Fellows, and–"

"Who?"

"Mortie Fellows." Joyce giggled again. "The documentarian."

The name rang not one single bell, so Valerie typed it into the still-open IMDb tab on her laptop. The picture showed a bespectacled, tousled-looking guy, with a curious, challenging smile. He was studiously attractive, like a young Steven Spielberg. Valerie scanned his film credits; she had seen none of them. She wasn't much on documentaries.

"I ran into him at The Conga Room."

Livin' la vida loca, Valerie thought, not unkindly.

"He read the piece in *Variety,* and wants to discuss doing a film about TTAMS," Joyce continued. "A biopic on you, me, maybe even Greg. Come on down, Val. We can talk to him in the big conference room. Then maybe we can give Mortie a little tour." Joyce tittered again.

Valerie thought of her Uncle Calvin's *biopic.* "I dunno—"

"Quit being so suspicious, Val." *Sonic Nightmare* had also come to Joyce's mind. "Mortie's a nice guy. He won't make us look anything but good. Besides, wasn't it you that said there's no such thing as bad publicity?"

"I'm a little busy at the moment, Jo."

"You're always busy," Joyce pouted.

Valerie realized that her friend was ever so slightly drunk. Maybe a little bit more than ever so slightly. They made the drinks strong at The Conga Room, or so she'd heard. But that was okay. Valerie had been ever so slightly drunk and more herself on enough Friday nights, once upon a time, had she not?

"If you don't come down here, Val, I'm gonna bring Mortie up there," Joyce threatened with all the gravity the liquor would allow. "This could be big for us."

"All right. I'm on my way. Just give me a quick second to close what I'm doing. Take him to the conference room, like you said."

"We're waiting for you."

"I'll be right there."

Valerie pushed *End,* again thinking about Joyce's almost Puritan sense of prudishness about the idea that subscribers might be talking dirty to the simulated celebrities on TTAMS. The programmer couldn't understand it – those kind of unachievable-in-real-life, intimate exchanges with their idols were the key to the success of the service. They were the entire point.

Yet Valerie mused that the CEO didn't think it an impropriety to be staggering around half in the bag on the operations floor with some hipster director in tow, however, in front of her hardworking, on-the-clock employees.

It wasn't that Valerie thought herself above her operators, or even that she felt herself to be particularly boss-like. But she had spent a good portion of her life standing politely, patiently by, while fans approached and asked Dennis Whitly for autographs, and thereby, Valerie had learned from childhood that there was an intrinsic difference between people. There were your friends and your family, the people that knew you, and there were those that looked up to you for whatever reason, be it because they admired you as a musician, or because they respected you as the head of the company.

Valerie was acutely aware of the gulf between friends and fans, between employer and employee. It wasn't about superiority; it was about boundaries. You were an idea to them, more than a person, and therefore, there was no reason to be shattering their illusions, to be revealing your clay feet. Joyce ignored this very real distinction. She was the boss and didn't give a tinker's damn about her employees' opinions of her.

But Valerie knew that there was a certain way that these people expected you to act, and if you wanted to maintain their respect, their loyalty, then you didn't roar into the office drunk, as much as rubbing their noses in the fact that they were just rank and file, and you were the CEO and could behave like an idiot if you so chose. To Valerie, such an action was unprofessional. It just wasn't done.

She said to the Mitch Barlo impersonator, "I'm sorry. I have to go. But I really enjoyed our chat. I'd like to talk to you again."

"I understand, Denise. When you log in the next time, and TTAMS asks you who want to talk to, just type in MB426312. It'll connect you right to me."

If you're working. Valerie considered asking her employee what shifts he was assigned, but then thought better of it. That would be asking him to break character, and she had so liked him in character. World-renowned thespian Mitch Barlo didn't have *shifts.*

"I'll be sure to do that, Mitch. Talk to you soon."

"I'll be here, Denise."

Valerie logged off, and hurried down the steel steps to meet her tipsy partner and her *auteur de jour* in the conference room. As she passed the banks of booths, Valerie wondered which one contained MB426312. Perhaps he wasn't even here on the ops floor: TTAMS also had scores of employees that worked from home. It would be a simple enough task to run a trace on the number he had given her; it would direct her right to his assigned booth, or show his home address. Valerie thought that she would like to meet the talented operator, shake his hand, praise him, tell him how good he was at his job. Offer him a raise.

But maybe not, at least not right away. Despite the insufferably buggy start to her first TTAMS session – Valerie reminded herself to tell Joyce to instigate a little shake-up in Licensing and Research, to instill the fear of God in the staff, engendered by the sins of omission and poor cross-referencing – despite the amateurish beginning, the boss had thoroughly enjoyed her session. Valerie would make time to talk to a movie star once more, to chat again with MB426312. Afterwards, she would confront the reality that he was just another operator. And she would give him a raise.

****

Denise's profile disappeared from Mitch's prompt screen, and he waited for the next one to appear. He hoped for no more *special subscribers* tonight.

He hoped that maybe Andrea from San Diego might log on to talk to him. She was always fun. She liked to tell him about all the inner-workings and not-readily-apparent motivations that she imagined for the characters he had portrayed. Shamus had actually been some stripe of warrior-poet. Anders Fresco from *Random House* hadn't actually been tortured by crippling self-doubt about his writing. Not at all. His scruffy, alcoholic, self-imposed seclusion was in fact the result of a latent homosexuality that he was unequipped to acknowledge. Or at least a bisexuality. That was why he had been so reluctant to embrace the love and faith in his talent offered by Corrine, the character Janna had played in the film. Or something like that.

Andrea's character studies were always in-depth, well-thought-out, and pretty much patently ridiculous, but they were always enjoyable. Mitch hoped that she might log on and be there to talk to him next. He didn't want to discuss his lost soul of a dead wife anymore tonight.

But the prompt strip remained blue and blank, and Mitch recalled that the Director of Technical Operations had been monitoring him. "You still there, Boss Man?"

A window opened on the screen and Mitch saw Greg Castro's lumberjack's grin. "Meet me for a beer, Mitch. You've earned your pay for the night."

The actor assumed Morris Baker's underling obeisance. "But you're not paying me, Mr. Castro, sir."

"Maybe I should start. Meet me at that little dive around the corner from the office."

"I don't really want to go out, Greg–"

"Ah, yes. Your famous face and TMZ and all. I forgot. Maybe you should give up Hollywood and come to work for me full time."

"Will I get instructor pay?"

Greg chuckled. "Anything you want. I'll make you Baker's supervisor. He'll love that."

"I'll notify my agent." Mitch paused. "Don't think I'm blowing you off, Greg. I'd love to have a beer with you. It's just–"

"I know. The swarms of paparazzi. Why don't you come over to my place? I'll call you an Uber."

"All right."

"Wear your hoodie-shades disguise. I wouldn't want you to get chased down like Princess Di."

****

Greg made no apologies to the famous actor for his small, bachelor-messy apartment. He'd cleaned up the atomized chips and the turned-over beer, had he not? Despite his fame, Mitch was his friend, a down-to-earth, regular guy. He wasn't the type to judge somebody based on their digs. Greg supposed that he'd probably had a similar place before he'd made it big, before he'd married that druggie redhead, before they'd bought the hacienda in the hills. Greg knew exactly where Mitch Barlo lived, because he'd looked it up. The currency of the realm wasn't the most valuable currency in Greg's world-view. Information could be worth far more than mere money.

Mitch didn't notice anything out of the ordinary about Greg's place on a cleanliness scale – it reminded him of the tiny pad he'd shared with two other aspiring actors in college. But while the thespians' living room had sported a large painted-on-velvet portrait of a sultry Latina wearing nothing but a sombrero and a come-hither smile, the Director of Technical Operations had a framed schematic of . . . something. Videocassettes and CDs had littered almost every flat surface in pre-fame Mitch's apartment. In Greg's, it was TTAMS Ops Procedurals and thick, closely printed hardware and software manuals.

Mitch was put in mind of the episode of *Star Trek*, where, in some cantina on some space station, the Klingons had tried to start a fight with the red shirts on shore leave from the *Enterprise*. First, they tried insulting her stellar captain, but these jibes passed Chief Engineer Scott right on by. When the aliens stooped to calling his beloved ship a garbage scow, however, Scotty had thrown the first punch.

As punishment, Kirk reluctantly confined his brawling officer to quarters. Scotty smiled. *"Yes, sir. Thank you, sir! That'll give me a chance to catch up on my technical journals!"*

Greg offered Mitch a seat at the kitchen table. With a bottle opener that said *Death Star Tech Support*, he popped the cap on a Heineken and handed it to the actor.

Greg sat in the chair opposite, smiling. *"You're my boy, Blue!"*

Mitch smiled back uncertainly. He waited for an explanation as to what he had done to deserve the praise. When Greg only grinned

234

silently at him, at last Mitch said, "This has something to do with the *special subscriber.*"

"Damn straight, Skippy, it does." Greg giggled, and Mitch's eyebrows went up in surprise. Normally no-nonsense, all-business Greg Castro was positively tickled to death about something. "You'll never guess who she was."

"My biggest fan," Mitch suggested.

Now Greg looked surprised. "Not that I've ever heard. But I knew she'd want to talk to you, the minute spokescat Morris dragged you into the office. *Fate, it seems, is not without a sense of irony.*"

Mitch wondered if the Director of Technical Operations had already had a few too many Heinekens. He wasn't making any sense. "Who—"

"Not *your* biggest fan, Movie Star. *Edison Forbes's biggest fan.*"

"That would certainly explain the off-the-wall question about if I'd done any other Canadian films besides *Erskine.*"

"Indeed, indeed." Greg giggled and sipped his beer. Before Mitch could again attempt to ask who this mystery subscriber was, he began his story. "Once upon a time, there was this girl. In college. She was beautiful. *Brilliant.* We were friends, but because of her incredibly poor taste in men – pretty boy business majors, snowback Foley guys – that's all we ever were. Until now. And I owe it all to you." Greg clinked the neck of Mitch's beer with his own.

"I'm not following you, Greg."

"Allow me to *show you how deep the rabbit hole goes, Neo.* Because she was beautiful, because she was brilliant, because I wanted to get to know her better, I got this girl a job with me at Fox. She was single when she started working there, saints be praised, but still she didn't notice me. I was in the Friend Zone.

"But she's a movie buff, as I am myself, so we talked. She told me all about the best actor in the world. The *prettiest man she'd ever seen. Never seen eyes so blue.*"

"Not—"

"No. Not you. She raved about this guy. She was obsessed with him. She had pictures of him on her laptop, on her phone. I, on the other hand, had never heard of him. So I did a little research." Greg's grin widened. His brown eyes sparkled darkly. *"For if knowledge is power, then a god . . . am . . . I!"*

That's certainly over the top, Mitch thought.

"I Wikipedia-d the guy, Googled him. I read reviews of his films on Rotten Tomatoes. I even downloaded some forgettable barking dog of a cop drama from Pirate Bay, and sat through it, all because the girl of my dreams was besotted with Edison Forbes."

"How had she ever even seen—"

"Who knows?" Greg sipped his beer again. "Then, when you walked into the office, all aglow with the glitter of Tinseltown, I remembered a cast list I had read on IMDb, once upon a time. I remembered that you had starred with Edison Forbes in some Great White North epic called *Two's Company—*"

"Two's a Crowd."

"What, as they say, ever. The important thing was, you had been in a movie with Eddie Forbes. And here you were, on my doorstep, *under my battlements,* asking about the system. Wanting to try your hand at it.

"Why the hell not? I thought. I'd let you poke around awhile, and eventually, if you didn't get bored and split right away, I'd introduce you to her. You could tell her all she wanted to know about her favorite Canuck actor, and then she would—"

"He was a really nice guy. We had a lot of fun on that shoot."

"More's the pity," Greg replied with mock gravity. Then he grinned again. "You'd tell her all she wanted to know, and then she'd be so grateful to me for introducing you, she'd agree to go out with me. Lunch, maybe. Or even dinner."

"And then one thing would lead to another . . ."

Greg frowned. "She's not like that, Mitch. She's above all that. She's brilliant."

Chastised, Mitch said, "Sorry, man."

Greg's smile returned. "But it's working out even better than I'd planned. Out of the blue, she decided she wanted to talk to—"

"How did you know who she'd picked to talk to?"

Greg grinned like a shark, showing all his teeth. *"It's classified. I could tell you, but then I'd have to kill you.* She didn't actually want to talk to you. She wanted to talk to Shamus."

"Your woman wanted to talk *to Baker?*"

"Seriously. Couldn't be havin' that. So with a little digital prestidigitation, I sent her to you instead. And the next time she logs on to chat with you—"

"If there is a next time."

"Oh, I'm sure there will be. She didn't get a chance to ask you about Eddie."

"How do you know she's gonna do that?"

"You're a TTAMS operator, Mitch. A good one. If she doesn't ask you on your own, you're gonna lead her to it."

"I dunno, Greg. That's way off-script. What if she wants to talk about *my* movies?" Mitch remembered the *special subscriber's* statements about Janna. "Or what if she wants to talk about something else?"

"*Something else* can be Edison Forbes. Lead her to it, Mitch. Then, after you tell her all she wants to know . . . The next day, I'll introduce you to her. Let her in on the gag. You guys can talk about Eddie some more, than she'll wanna thank me. I'll say, *It's no problem at all, how would you like to have lunch . . .*"

Mitch thought over Greg's rambling narrative. "Who is this chick?"

Greg was lost in his master plan. "She's gotta love it. Her Number 3 employee got a real actor to work at TTAMS! Even if it is only temporarily." He realized that Mitch had asked him again who the subscriber was. "Oh, I guess that's important, huh? You were talking to Valerie Whitly, Mitch. My boss."

The love of your life, apparently.

Greg waited a heartbeat, and when the actor didn't respond, he said, "What d'ya say, Mitch? It would be just another session to you, but you'd be setting me up for all that gratitude. Who knows where that might lead? You'd be doing me a solid."

Mitch had seen the light of fan-love enough times in his career. He'd seen it shining out from the sea of faces when he walked up the red carpet at premieres; when giggling girls and blushing women scared up enough nerve to approach him on the street and ask for his autograph. He'd seen it in the subscribers who were paying $9.95 a month to talk to their favorite movie star.

It wasn't real love. The fans didn't know him, and he thought that most of them didn't want to know him. He wasn't just another person to them, with his own share of opinions and problems. He was a happy-go-lucky, womanizing cowboy, or a good-looking gambler in a tuxedo. He was just what they wanted him to be: a fantasy.

Similarly, Mitch didn't think that Greg knew Valerie Whitly. But he knew enough to believe that he was in love with her, just like his own fans believed they were in love with Shamus or the Tarot-reading gambler. The same light Mitch had seen a million times was in the tech's eyes. Greg Castro had it bad for his boss. He was her biggest fan.

Hollywood's job in general and Mitch's in particular was to provide the movie-going public with characters that they could dream about. And working at TTAMS, he gave them the added opportunity to actually speak to him, even if they believed it wasn't any more real than the movies themselves.

Telling Valerie Whitly what Greg thought she wanted to hear was the least he could do for the guy who had given him this diversion from his own sad life.

"All right, Greg. Whatever you want me to say."

****

Valerie considered the unscheduled, after-hours meeting with Mortie Fellows to be a bust. He was drunk and wasted most of her obscenely valuable time giggling and exchanging sly grins with an equally drunk Joyce. Their plans for the rest of the evening were a foregone conclusion, Valerie reckoned, so the filmmaker's mind wasn't really on the two-minute drill of pitching his idea for the documentary about TTAMS. For Joyce's sake, Valerie hoped that the drill that he *was* contemplating would last more than two minutes.

A biopic of the women behind the world's hottest infotainment service might materialize due to Joyce's instantaneous *friendship* with the director, but Valerie sincerely doubted it. Mortie was making rather a fool of himself, fawning over Joyce. He was intoxicated by both drink and the dark-eyed loveliness of her friend, and Valerie thought that he would be embarrassed by his schoolboy silliness once he sobered up and again assumed his serious filmmaker persona. He might wish to forget that he'd ever been to The Conga Room, that he'd practically slobbered all over Joyce Vinson in the conference room at TTAMS. *Oh no, it wasn't the airplanes. It was beauty killed the beast.*

Amid promises to have his assistant mock up a basic outline for her, the director and his prize finally toddled out the way they had come in, back to the alternately bright and black streets of LA, out for a good time or worse.

Valerie was glad to see them go, because she had other fish to fry. If her fake Mitch Barlo was an onsite employee, he should still be on the clock. She didn't really want to talk to a movie star any more tonight, but she was curious to get a glimpse of what the talented operator looked like. She again padded up the steel steps to her office and logged back into her system.

Welcome back, Denise! TTAMS greeted her. *Would you like to reconnect with Mitch Barlo (MB426312)? (y/n?)*

Valerie ignored the system's come-on. She typed a command that opened an override window and initiated a trace on the employee working under this particular numerical alias.

Y:\ system> Operator offline
Y:\ system> Last workstation?

Y:\ system> Console 10T OpsPrepCent

Valerie frowned in annoyance. Here she was confronted with yet another bug, and its glaring presence put her in mind of an Aesop's Fable that Aunt Elise had once upon a time related. *The Stag in the Barn.*

"What's a stag, Aunt Elise?"

"A stag's a deer, Valley. You know, with the big antlers?" The child nodded and Sonic Daydream's road manager spun the cautionary tale. "Hunters are chasing the stag, and he runs into the barn and asks the cows to hide him. So the cows do their best, covering him up with straw until just the tips of his antlers are sticking out. The lazy farmhands peek in, but they don't see the stag, because they are thinking about their own lives. This one wants to see his girlfriend. That one wants to get home to supper with his wife. They are just employees, after all, so a quick once-over is enough for them.

"The stag starts to feel safe. But one of the cows tells him, *'You must leave before the master comes back. This is his barn, and he overlooks nothing.'*"

According to Aunt Elise, the moral of the story was, *If you want something done right, do it yourself,* and Valerie saw the truth in it now. Because she had left her baby to underlings, TTAMS had become as buggy as a Roach Motel.

First there were the stops and starts, the program sending her off to talk not to Shamus, as she had chosen, but to a modern-day Mitch Barlo impersonator. Now the system was telling her that the operator had been in the Operator Preparation Center when he had last been online, when he'd been talking to her. That just couldn't be. The booths in the OpsPrepCent were not configured for live sessions.

Valerie sent another command: *Locate 000003.*

Y:\ system> 000003 offline. Remote login 21:42, logoff 22:02.

Greg wasn't onsite this evening, but he had still taken seventeen minutes out of his Friday night to check on the system. Valerie smiled. While she'd thought about giving Greg an earful about the glitches she'd encountered, now that she saw that he was undoubtedly looking into them, she changed her mind.

She wouldn't want the Director of Technical Operations to think that she was questioning his work, checking up on him. And surely that's what he'd think, if she told him that she was logging on to the system, and now had complaints about it. She'd never done so before. Why would Valerie Whitly suddenly decide to talk to a movie star if it wasn't to check out the efficiency of Greg's interface?

Valerie would definitely sic Joyce on Licensing and Research, however, but that wasn't Greg's department. He was the one ultimately responsible for a seamless subscriber experience, and he was also answerable for the subroutine that pinpointed the locations of the operators. Valerie's session had been unacceptably lumpy and the trace was just wrong, defaulting to the Prep Center, from which it was not possible for an operator to link to an actual subscriber. Greg would definitely have to solve these problems eventually.

But Valerie considered that maybe her bad start was a one off. She would talk to MB426312 again, and see how that session went before bitching at Greg. He'd still have to chase down the glitch in the locator program, but Valerie figured that could wait, too. She'd connect with the Mitch Barlo operator again, evaluate the session. Then she'd be fully prepared to discuss error elimination with Greg.

****

The following Friday night found Valerie once more behind her desk, Joyce again out on the town. The CEO was solo, however, as both she and Mortie Fellows had thought better of continuing their relationship, business or otherwise.

It had been a busy week for Joyce, kicking ass and taking names in Licensing and Research. She'd had a few words with the staff of Development, too, and by Thursday, *Stutter and Scream* had been added to Mitch Barlo's filmography; *Two's a Crowd* could be found on its Canadian star's list, as well as its American co-star's, and a subscriber could talk to Mitch or Eddie's characters as they had appeared in the film. Valerie still hadn't gotten around to watching the comedy, however. She was *saving it*.

Welcome back, Denise! Would you like to reconnect with Mitch Barlo (MB426312)? (y/n?)

Valerie typed *y,* and in the split-second before the operator appeared, she clicked the mike icon so that he could hear her. She left the webcam off.

"Hi, Denise! How are you?"

Valerie was surprised, touched almost, by the genuine welcome is his voice, in his smile. Again she patted herself on the back at the lifelike *vividness* of the system she had developed. Also, she reminded herself to track this guy down and praise his acting abilities.

"Oh, I'm about the same, Mitch."

His smile didn't dim. It was his job to cheer her up. "Busy?"

Valerie nodded, then realizing that he couldn't see her, she said, "Yes. Always busy. *And when at last the work is done, don't sit down it's time to dig another one.*"

"Balanced on the biggest wave, you race towards an early grave."

The simulation's smile faltered a little bit, and Valerie thought, *All you touch and all you see, is all your life will ever be,* and that brought back another thought about her Aunt Elise – the voicemail she'd supposedly left for Calvin before she'd taken that irrevocable step to oblivion.

The operator's expression was blank now, and Valerie remembered her first session with MB426312. She recalled how she had been moved to believe that she had hurt his feelings by intimating that Janna Langly had taken her own life. She wondered if perhaps he was also reliving their off-script conversation.

Valerie reminded herself that it was all just a simulation. It wasn't really Mitch Barlo at the other end of the connection. This wasn't the man that had called 9-1-1 and sadly said, "Could you please send an ambulance? My wife has overdosed."

But the ability to suspend disbelief was in Valerie's DNA. For her entire life, the skills of imaginative directors and fine actors had permitted her to empathize with emotions unknown to her personally, as well as to relive joys and solemnities she had experienced in her own life. So it was with TTAMS, the very reason she had concocted the revolutionary service. A TTAMS session was like starring in your own little movie with your very favorite actor.

So it was effortless for Valerie to pretend that she was speaking to the bereft husband of poor Janna. She allowed the feelings of shame at her former rudeness to return.

"You know, Mitch, I wanted to apologize for those things I said the last time we talked. About Janna."

The same sadness colored the excellent simulation of the actor's voice. "It's okay, Denise. Everyone thinks they know–"

"But they don't, do they? I know Janna didn't kill herself. An accidental death is bad enough, isn't it? She was so young, so beautiful . . . Your grief must've been absolute. It still must be. But when it really is suicide . . . It's so much worse. There's the grief, the loss . . . But then there's the dumb wonderment."

The alarm from the keeper had gone off on Greg's laptop moments after he had again settled in on his couch. The TV was dark this time, however; there were no chips or beer to be spilled. He was researching recent advances in voice recognition software with an eye toward incorporating them into instructor training. When the beep sounded and the red ball appeared on his screen, he had merely to click it to begin monitoring Mitch's second session with Valerie.

Greg couldn't believe what his boss was saying. *So it's all true!*

241

Being first and foremost a tech, information was Greg's muse. He was in love with his boss, his old college pal, and wanting to know every detail that he could possibly learn about her, he had long ago Googled her name. A search for *Valerie Whitly* had unfortunately turned up nothing he hadn't already known. The world's most brilliant programmer (in Greg's estimation) had not distinguished herself online before he'd met her.

But since he had wanted to know *everything*, Greg had also Googled her famous father. There were hundreds and hundreds of entries for Dennis Whitly: a lengthy Wikipedia page; old *Rolling Stone* interviews, *Guitar Player* articles, fan sites; YouTube videos of Sonic Daydream's performances, and fan covers of their songs; guitar tabs. About three pages in, Greg had found the listing for Calvin Bascomb's memoir of his days with the *world's premier rock band.* Greg was not much of a reader-for-pleasure, and Borders was long gone. He'd wound up purchasing a used copy of *Sonic Nightmare* from Alibris.com.

Greg had been utterly shocked by the drummer's tell-all. He'd met Valerie's parents once, right after the service had launched. They'd come in for a tour, and the three of them had seemed to be a happy, loving family. But Greg knew better, because he'd done his research. He was amazed at how well the Whitlys disguised their awful family secrets behind smiles and hugs and laughter. He was appalled that Valerie and her mother even permitted the former rock star in their lives after the carnage he had caused.

Besides her brilliance and her busyness, Greg speculated that Dennis Whitly's sin was perhaps another reason why Valerie didn't date. If her own father was a cheating, suicide-inducing bastard, what hope could she think she had of finding a good man for herself?

Her aunt's suicide and the circumstances that surrounded it could have been nothing less than the worst trauma of Valerie's life. Greg felt for her about it; he longed to offer her comfort. But their friendship was not of that intimate caliber, and he was amazed that she would now discuss it with what she believed was an anonymous employee.

"You lost someone to suicide," Mitch stated softly.

Valerie nodded. Again realizing that the operator couldn't see her, she said, "Yes. It was my aunt."

"How old were you?"

"I was eight when she died. I believed it was an accident at the time. Her car went over the side on Mulholland Parkway. My mother was in the car with her. She was terribly injured, bedridden for a long time. Then she was in a wheelchair. She uses a cane to this day. The fact that it wasn't an accident at all, that my aunt had intended to kill

242

herself and my mother, didn't come to light until I was almost seventeen."

That's right, Greg thought. *Not just suicide, but murder-suicide. The murder part just wasn't accomplished. Careful,* Denise, *or you'll give yourself away. You don't know that your anonymous employee hasn't read* Sonic Nightmare, *just like I have.*

"So you suffered two shocks," Mitch Barlo said.

This must be the new and improved talking cure part, Valerie thought. If this operator wasn't a man, she reckoned that he might've been the one that had commiserated so winningly with Marianne Jackson. The standard TTAMS's script was forgotten. No talk about characters and settings and what-the-shoot-was-really-like tonight.

But Valerie had to admit that the guy was good. His statements seemed to come from the heart, and he was right. He'd pointed something out that Valerie had never thought about in the past. Finding out that Aunt Elise had killed herself had been like losing her all over again. Valerie had indeed suffered two shocks. Thinking about it now was almost like a third shock.

"Yes," she told the simulation of Mitch Barlo. Her voice ached with sorrow.

Mitch longed to comfort the grieving young woman. In her, he keenly felt the reflection of his own sadness. "It was kind of like that with Janna," he said slowly. "I was so relieved when she made up her mind to go to rehab. That relief, the incredible hope I felt, was so uplifting. She was gonna be all right. She would go out to the desert, and when she came home, things would be good all the time."

Those hope-filled moments returned vividly to Mitch. "Janna would be happy, not just when she was in the middle of shooting, or when she had self-medicated with a handful of pills. The doctors were gonna cure her – she wasn't going to hate herself anymore. They were going to make her see the one thing that I never could make her see, that she was a beautiful, talented person, not only on the outside, but on the inside as well. They were going to magically banish the hateful demon in her head that was always there, telling her that she was ugly and worthless."

The simulated Mitch Barlo paused, and Valerie was again amazed that he seemed to be actually remembering the hope he'd mentioned, the anticipation of a new and happy life with the wife he'd loved. Then his gaze changed, saddened, hardened. The grim realities of what had followed seemed to manifest themselves, to become readable in his expression.

Valerie was astonished. The motion capture system she had created flawlessly mimicked the manner in which such a play of emotions would appear on Mitch Barlo's famous face. She had to give the operator credit, too. He had to be one of the aspiring actors in the stable. No tech, even with the help of the software, could make her believe that he was truly feeling the sadness that this guy emoted.

The operator suddenly laughed harshly, and Valerie jumped. He looked down, shook his head. "My first shock came after Janna had been back from rehab for about a month.

"I was supposed to be gone on a location shoot all day, at the Santa Monica Pier." Mitch again felt the cool beach breeze, saw the sun glinting on the water. "It was for *Fisherman's Wharf* – it was supposed to be a kind of *Baywatch* knockoff, only darker, grimmer. I thought that they had given it the dumbest name possible for a dramatic series."

The operator grinned humorlessly; it was a not pleasant expression. Age and hard knocks had refined away some of the boyish sexiness Mitch had possessed in *Shamus Alive* and *Two's a Crowd,* and the geniuses that Valerie had on staff in Development had captured the nuances of the features of the older, sadder-but-wiser Mitch Barlo so perfectly that she considered giving the whole department a raise, based solely on this one simulation.

Valerie thought that he should always smile, however. Even with a few years on him, he was still too pretty to look so despondent. She wished that she could think up something to say that would alleviate his dark mood.

The simulation sighed. *'Fisherman's Wharf* never made it past the pilot. The whole thing was plagued with difficulties from day one. Infighting between the director and producer. Stupid technical mistakes. There was some sound problem on the location shoot that day."

Valerie thought fleetingly of Liam Cote, the Foley guy, who had introduced her to Eddie. She hadn't seen him again since they'd left Canada . . .

"So, we were released in the morning, when I should have been on location all day," the fake Mitch Barlo continued. "I had been home with Janna more or less 24/7 since she'd come back from rehab. She'd apparently been waiting for me to be gone, so she could . . ."

The operator glanced down, again shook his head. When he again met the electronic eye of his console's webcam, Valerie could see the painful resignation. *This guy is good!*

"I found her passed out in the bedroom, smiling in her sleep. She hadn't even bothered to hide the pill bottles, or maybe the effects had

244

kicked in before she'd had the chance. There were no labels on them now – filling multiple prescriptions from different doctors all over town was something that people with a drug problem did. But Janna was cured of all that, or at least that's what she wanted me to think.

"She'd gotten these pills the old fashioned way. A quick phone call to someone she knew – I never did find out who it was, but I suspected it was her make-up artist from *Random House* – and Janna was set. I was gonna be gone all day. There was plenty of time to savor the high again, take a little nap – and then be bright-eyed and bushy-tailed, as if she was truly cured, by the time I got home from the shoot.

"I say that the bottles were unlabeled, except for one – the Paxil that they had prescribed for her at Betty Ford. That was the one that was supposed to wipe out the need for all the others." The operator barked a short, harsh laugh.

"But I recognized the contents of the other two bottles, labels or not, because I'd seen them enough times. There were the Vicodins – they made Janna feel calm and in control, she'd always told me, happy and talky. But despite the fact that it was a narcotic, a pain-killer, sometimes it made her a little too talky. Agitated. So there were the tiny, five-sided Ativans, to help take the edge off. In combination, these two had taken her off to dreamland.

"There weren't any muscle relaxers this time – they put a smooth, drowsy perspective on everything, according to Janna. They didn't call them *Soma* for nothing. Nor was there any coke, which pepped her up, helped to disguise the effects of the others when she was filming.

"She didn't need either of those again, at least not yet. She'd just got back from rehab, after all. She was clean. Just the narcotics and the anti-anxiety meds would do the trick."

It was just as Valerie had always suspected: Hollywood types *knew* about drugs, especially the prescription kind. Intrigued, she forgot to remind herself that the person she was talking to was not a Hollywood type at all, but one of her employees.

Mitch remembered the sea-foam green of the bedsheets, how they had complemented Janna's red hair. He remembered the ugliness of the somewhat greasy-looking, label-less prescription bottles.

"The let-down of seeing those pills was devastating for me, Denise, almost more so then seeing Janna passed out on the bed. They were the concrete evidence – everything I'd seen before, everything I'd believed I'd never have to see again . . . The hopelessness was like a physical blow. The realization . . . It was never gonna go away, never gonna stop. The doctors hadn't cured Janna. She was incurable, broken.

245

"I thought about flushing the pills, but what good would that do? She'd only get more. I went downstairs and tried to look over the script for *Fisherman's Wharf* until she woke up.

"She knew that I knew the moment we made eye contact. Maybe she wanted me to catch her – that's why she'd left the bottles out – but probably not. She was awake now, and I wasn't expected back for another hour or so. She would've had plenty of time to hide her relapse.

"But one look at my face, and she knew that I had seen the pills. Janna cried. I cried with her. She told me that it would just be this one time, that she really didn't need it anymore. She dumped the drugs and I wanted to believe her, Denise, I really did." He remembered the scene, how the whiteness of the tiles in their black and white bathroom had been reflected in Janna's pale skin as she spilled the drugs into the toilet.

"But something had just gone out of me. The hope that it could really be over . . . It hurt too much to harbor that hope anymore, because now there was a new element to the whole situation. I caught a glint of deception in Janna's eye as she poured the pills out. Was she lying to herself, or was she just lying to me? I was pretty sure she had some more, hidden somewhere. If not, they were only a phone call away.

"I realized that the pills had become shameful to Janna now. Rehab hadn't cured her in the least, but somehow it had instilled shame. She had admitted that she had a problem, she had faced it, and unable to overcome it, now she had to hide it.

"The fact that she enhanced her moods with prescription drugs had never been a secret to those closest to her. It was just part of who she was – a crutch, surely, but an almost proudly utilized one. Everyone she knew was on one kind of prescription or another, Prozac or Xanax or Darvon or Percocet. It's a stressful business. It wasn't like Janna or anyone she knew had a problem with it.

"But once she realized that she did have a problem, once the whole world knew that she'd gone to rehab . . . To Janna, her fall back into the company of her little helpers became just another symbol of her overall failures.

"The doctors at Betty Ford had taken Janna's crutch away, convinced her for a time that she didn't need it. But Janna couldn't be fixed by a couple weeks in the desert. She couldn't function without her crutch any more than any other cripple could."

Valerie thought again of Sophia and her cane . . .

"I told her that I understood, even though I didn't, Denise. I never understood. Janna was a good person. She had so much talent. She hadn't had a bad childhood – she never told me about anything that would explain why she hated herself so much. There must've something . . ." The operator shook his head, and again Valerie was amazed at the hurt wonder on his face. "But I never knew what it was.

"And I could never understand her addiction, either. I knew it was all tied in together with her self-loathing, but I could never understand why she couldn't just stop." Again there was that disbelieving sadness, like a wounded little boy. It seemed so real.

"She had expressed the desire to stop. The doctors had helped her for a little while . . . I believed that she truly wanted to stop. But she couldn't.

"She dumped out her pills and told me that she would really quit, this time for good. I wanted to believe her, Denise. I wanted to, so badly. But a week later, I found another bottle, hidden behind the silverware tray in a kitchen drawer, where the maid could've found them.

"I confronted Janna, as gently as I could. I told her that I knew these things happened. I said she could talk to the doctors again . . . She cried, said the doctors hadn't helped. They didn't understand. I didn't understand. She became angry, spiteful, resentful. Who was I to judge her?

"I'd had an Oscar nomination. I was already onboard to star in Cronenberg's next picture. And what did she have? The lead in some fluff comedy that would be forgotten almost before it was released?

"'You have me,' I told her.

"But it wasn't enough, Denise. It had never been enough. Not me or her career. Nothing had ever been enough.

"I don't have to tell you what the next big shock was. Thanks to TMZ and their connections, the whole world's heard the call. I'd gone out – a dinner meeting with my agent – and when I got home . . .

"There were still plenty of pills in the bottle. It wasn't suicide, Denise. Janna had started looking forward to working again, had stopped referring to *Angel's Delight* as below her. If she'd wanted to kill herself, she'd've taken the whole bottle."

The operator paused, raked his hand across his face, then laughed self-consciously. Mitch didn't know where this incredible flood of words had come from, why he had loosed them onto Valerie Whitly, of all people. But for some unknown reason, when she'd talked about her aunt's death, he'd felt a kinship with her. Here was another person devastated by the actions of someone else, actions that she, too, had been powerless to prevent. It was just as Baker had told him: talking to an unseen, anonymous, disembodied voice over a computer interface was apt to make a person say anything. To pour out their overflowing well of grief, apparently.

But it wasn't exactly TTAMS material. "I guess this really isn't the kind of thing I should be talking about."

"It's okay, Mitch."

Valerie was caught up in his pain and loss. She felt her own again, acutely, and wanted him to know that there was someone in the world that understood.

"When my aunt died . . . I've often admired religious people – their faith allows them to truly believe that those they love have gone to a better place. It must be an enormous comfort to really believe that.

"But after the accident . . . I was just a little kid. My mom was suffering herself, physically, emotionally. She couldn't comfort me . . . She never could. Dad was quiet . . . Distracted. He tried to keep me busy, with school and play and helping Nurse take care of Mom . . . But no one ever talked to me about the loss of my aunt. She had been my best friend, Mitch. *I missed her so much!*"

A sob escaped from Valerie. Mitch's expression shared her pain.

Greg Castro, monitoring, frowned. He felt for Valerie, surely he did, but this wasn't the kind of thing to be discussing with a TTAMS operator. Even if it was the real Mitch Barlo, even if he had poignantly expressed his own sorrow –

Valerie sighed. "Life went on. We moved back to Riverside. Mom got better. Everything got back to normal. I grew up. I'd never expressed to anyone how my aunt's death had affected me. I didn't really know that it *had* affected me. But by listening to you talk about Janna, I realize . . . It was always there, like an unhealed wound in the back of my mind.

"I thought about her less and less as the years went by, but every now and then, there would be some trigger . . . I'd hear one of Dad's . . ."

Even in reliving her grief, some part of Valerie's mind warned her against divulging too many details. She checked herself and continued. "I'd hear a song on the radio, one of her favorites, and for a time I would be inconsolable. All the grief would come back, fresh, like it had just happened. I would cry, alone in my room . . . Then something would happen, a phone call or an email. Life would distract me, and I would be all right again. Until the next time."

"How did you feel when you found out that it wasn't an accident?"

248

Valerie had never experienced any type of psychological counseling, but she'd seen enough movies. A blip in her mind told her that the operator's question sounded just like Billy Crystal's Dr. Ben Sobel interviewing Robert DeNiro's gangster in *Analyze This,* or a line Richard Dreyfus's smarmy shrink might've asked Bill Murray's nutcase in *What About Bob?*

How did that make you feel?

But the blip wasn't enough to destroy the commiseration she felt with the fake Mitch Barlo on her screen. It seemed so real, his unburdening of his feelings of guilt and pain at his inability to save Janna. It enabled Valerie to speak of her own emotions, for the very first time. The blip said, *TTAMS! Better than therapy!* And then it was gone.

"I was crushed, Mitch. I couldn't believe it. The way I found out . . ."

"Careful, *Denise,*" Greg said aloud in his empty living room.

"I cross-examined my parents. I knew it would be painful for them, too, but after what I'd . . . *heard* . . . I had to ask them."

Is any of this true?

"Someone else told you?" the Mitch Barlo simulation asked in shocked disbelief. "A stranger?"

"He was a . . . family . . . *friend.* Not much of a friend, really–"

"No," the operator agreed. "To tell a teenage girl that someone she'd loved as a child . . . Why did he feel he had to tell you that it wasn't an accident?"

To make money, Greg thought.

Valerie unknowingly echoed the hidden tech's belief: *Uncle Calvin hung out all our dirty laundry for the world to see* to make a buck. *He betrayed Dad, and Aunt Elise, too, really, by selling their sad story to the highest bidder. For* profit, *as if all the wretched details of Elise's delusion and her irretrievable resolution to it had simply been a sensational screenplay that he'd made up.*

Valerie shrugged, then again realized that the operator couldn't see her. "I don't know why he told me." *Why he told everyone.* But she did know why. For the basest of reasons possible. *For money.* "I never got to discuss it with him."

"What did your parents say?"

"They were hurt that I would bring it all up again, just like I'd known they would be. I felt bad about that, but I had to know the truth."

"You can't handle the truth!" Greg said aloud.

"My dad said the theory that she'd killed herself was all bullshit. It was an accident. There was no reason why my aunt would've wanted to commit suicide. He had missed the damning accusation . . ." Valerie again checked herself, continued quickly. "It turned out that my mom had known all along that it was suicide. She'd been in the car, and my aunt had told her . . ." Valerie let that thought die, also. "My aunt told Mom why she felt like she couldn't go on, and before Mom could make a move to stop her, she drove the car off the road.

"Dad had a hard time coming to grips with the truth, too."

Because it was all his fault, Greg thought.

"Your mom never told him that it wasn't an accident?"

"No. She had her own reasons for keeping it to herself. But once it was out in the open . . . They were forced to talk about it."

I bet that was a doozy of a discussion, Greg said to himself. *I would've liked to have been a fly on the wall for that one.*

"And in the end, their marriage was better because of it. Talking about painful things . . . There's a healing to it. Their story is not really like ours, Mitch, our own personal pain is different – in their case, there were . . . misunderstandings that were finally resolved.

"But from talking to you tonight . . . I realize that even when you know the truth about some painful thing, it's not good to keep it inside. It helps to talk about it. Terrible things happen, and the only way to heal yourself is to let them go, to talk about them with another person. Someone who understands."

Greg opened a text box on Mitch's screen and typed, *Congratulations, Dr. Freud.*

Mitch Barlo ignored the snarky comment. He thought about what Valerie had said; he took stock of his emotions. Like her, he had never spoken to anyone about Janna's death.

The piece in *Rolling Stone* had been business, set up by the studio. It had been publicity, a description of events to satisfy Janna's fans and his own. He had flown to New York City and recited the story to the reporter, as calm as he had been when he'd called the paramedics. He'd posed, appropriately solemn, for the photographer.

But Mitch had never once allowed himself to feel the loss and the hopelessness of Janna's overdose the way he had tonight, talking to Valerie Whitly on TTAMS. He had begun, and everything had just tumbled out, unrelentingly, until it was at last, finally said. All the agony and heartache and guilt had come out with the words, and Mitch was amazed to discover that now those myriad sadnesses were more or less gone, like dead leaves washed into a storm drain by an unexpected spring downpour. He was astonished at how *well* he felt.

Valerie was right. Their conversation had opened a door for him, had allowed the healing process to finally begin. He realized that he felt lighter already. Eventually, he would be able to let it all go. He would never forget Janna and her doomed self-loathing, any more than Valerie would forget her aunt. But after this conversation, neither Mitch nor Valerie would be held in thrall to the sad women's memories anymore. They had been at fault for none of it. Both could now get on with their lives.

It was quite the revelation for Mitch Barlo, and he smiled. "You know, you're absolutely right, Denise. I'm so glad that we've shared these things. I feel . . . better. For the first time in months. I want to thank you."

"I feel better, too, Mitch. I guess it's true what they say, that talking things out helps. We've proved that."

Then fell an awkward silence. Valerie was suddenly reminded of who she was, to whom she was speaking. This wasn't psychoanalysis; it was Talk to a Movie Star. It was Rent a Famous Boyfriend.

Real progress had definitely been achieved: just like the simulation had said, Valerie felt better. But she supposed it was the same as any other talking cure. She had stated her thoughts aloud; she had listened to herself, and come to the right conclusions.

Elise was gone. She'd lived a tragic life and died a tragic death. But the crippling sadness that Valerie had experienced periodically could serve no purpose; it helped neither herself nor her aunt. It was best to let it go.

Before the silence could lengthen, Greg took the initiative. He typed, *Hugs, hugs. Kisses, kisses. Tears of joy. You've shared your pain. Everyone's cured. Talk to her about Eddie Forbes, now, Movie Star. Remember your buddy Greg. Help a brutha out.*

Valerie watched the operator glance at his TTAMS prompt. She knew that his timer had rundown. Time to get her talking again. Time to change the subject. Abruptly, he did so.

"When we chatted the last time, you asked me if I'd done any Canadian films, Denise. You mentioned that you'd heard of Edison Forbes?"

Valerie grinned. "Didn't you say you were in a movie with him?"

"Yes. It was called *Two's A Crowd*. It was a lot of fun to make."

Valerie knew that the operator hadn't conveniently recalled their earlier conversation because he was interested in what had been said, or even because he was clever. Maybe he remembered what she'd said about Janna's death — that was way off-the-wall for a subscriber to talk about. But as far as whatever had been said about movies — each TTAMS operator talked to scores, perhaps hundreds of subscribers. It

251

was not possible to keep all those similar conversations straight, regardless of the interest and cleverness of the operator.

He had simply hit *Previous,* and a list of keywords from their last session had appeared in his prompt bar. Valerie knew that in addition to *Janna* and *suicide,* the list no doubt contained the titles of the movies that had been mentioned, as well as *Canadian films* and *Edison Forbes.*

If the keywords alone didn't jog his memory, the operator could click on them and a box would open showing the dialogue that had taken place on the subject. When it worked correctly, TTAMS made the subscriber feel as though she was talking to a movie star that she knew personally, a famous friend who effortlessly recalled all the details of the little chat they had last shared together. All those details were actually remembered, catalogued, cross-referenced and analyzed by the computer, but just like Greg Castro told aspiring operators – to the subscriber, it was magic.

Valerie would tell anyone about her appreciation for Eddie and his films, even when she knew it was just a simulation of his co-star, even when she knew that any information he seemed to give back to her was in fact read off a prompt.

Valerie reminded herself to congratulate Joyce on all this – last week the operator wouldn't have been able to say much beyond the IMDb synopsis of *Two's a Crowd* – but now he could pretend that he actually knew whatever tidbits Licensing and Research had uncovered about the little comedy.

Valerie said, "I'd love to hear all about *Two's a Crowd.* Mitch. About how much fun you had with Eddie. You might say I'm his biggest fan."

Greg sat up straighter on his couch. *Come on, Mitch, my friend. Tell her whatever she wants to hear. Tell her that she's been right all along, that Eddie's just the kinda guy she's always dreamed he was. And even though he's unfortunately unavailable at the moment, she'll still be grateful to me for getting to hear all about him, right from the horse's mouth . . .*

"I actually got to meet him once," Valerie said.

Greg's own mouth dropped open. He blinked in wonderment at this never-dreamt-of news.

He considered that he knew more about Valerie than anybody on earth except for Joyce, but this statement came as an utter surprise to him. He knew that the boss remained sprung on the Canadian nobody – she still had stills from his movies on her laptop and probably on her phone, too – but when had she ever actually *met* him? And if she'd met him, what else had they done? Why had he never heard about it?

The green bile of jealousy roiled in Greg's stomach, but he quickly tamped it down. He rationalized that Valerie thought she was talking to a fake Mitch Barlo – it was TTAMS. It was a fantasy. She'd never met Edison Forbes, nor had she done anything else with him. She was making it up. She was pretending.

Greg typed, *Ask her when she met him.*

In the back of his mind, Greg hoped that Valerie would flesh this fantasy out a little bit. She'd already overshared way too many true facts about her twisted family, so Greg thought that maybe now she might give a few salacious details about her imagined night in Montreal or Manitoba or wherever with Edison Forbes. That would be enjoyable. Greg could pretend, too. He would pretend Valerie was talking about him.

Greg thought of a relevant dirty joke. It's shift change at the hospital and the day nurse tells the night nurse, "Be careful of that guy in Bed Three. I was giving him his sponge bath . . ." She giggled. "He's got *swan* tattooed on his penis. He decided that he was feeling much better and tried to get all grabby with me."

The night nurse thanked her colleague for the warning.

When the shift changed in the morning, the day nurse asked the night nurse if she'd had any trouble with the guy in Bed Three. "Oh, he's okay. And it's not *swan.*" Now the night nurse giggled. "It's *Saskatchewan.*"

Greg grinned at his own humor. He figured Mitch would get a laugh out of that one, and he knew Baker would. He waited for the actor to follow his command.

Ever accommodating, Mitch said, "You met Eddie? You've been to Canada?"

That's all news to me, Greg thought.

"When was this?"

"It was right before I quit . . . where I used to work. I hadn't worked there very long, so I didn't want to let people know that I could afford to be jetting off to Canada when I was still on new-employee probation, so I kept my mouth shut about it. It was very hard to do. I was *so* excited."

It all dropped into place for Greg. The snowback Foley guy, his and Valerie's absence for the long weekend. Greg frowned. The sound guy had come back to Fox all sad and quiet, and Valerie hadn't come back at all. At the time, Greg had thought it was because they'd experienced some kind of bad break up, but if Valerie had been in Canada at that particular time, then it was because –

"I went up there to see him playing Paul Verrall in *Born Yesterday.* We had a nice little chat before the show. I still talk to him all the time."

"On TTAMS?" Mitch asked.

"No." Valerie giggled. "You're the only actor I've talked to on TTAMS, Mitch. Eddie and I talk on a more . . . personal level."

Confused, Mitch's face went blank. "But that's not possible, Denise. Edison Forbes is—"

Greg killed the session, cut Mitch off in mid-sentence. His screen went blue.

"What the fuck, Greg?" Mitch exclaimed.

The tech opened a window on Mitch's screen. They blinked stupidly at each other. At last, Greg said, "You can't tell her that, Mitch."

"She has to know already, Greg. She's his biggest fan, right?"

Greg shook his head. He had to think. He knew Valerie was obsessed with the Canadian nobody, that she considered herself to be Eddie's Number One Fan, but he never would've guessed that she *actually talked to him.*

"Maybe she doesn't know."

"That's ridiculous, Greg. It's crazy. And if Valerie Whitly's talking to Eddie Forbes, then she's—"

"You can't tell her that either."

****

Valerie blinked at the screen, at the message telling her that the star was unavailable. The operator had cut her off.

Valerie swallowed hard. She realized that she'd said too much. She was always reminding Joyce not to tell anyone that she spoke to Eddie, and here she was, spilling it herself, *telling all her bidness,* as Aunt Elise used to say. To a simulation of Mitch Barlo. To a TTAMS operator. To an employee.

Logic tried to soothe her. The operator didn't know who she was – to him, she was just Denise from Riverside.

But Valerie had already told him so much other info about herself, just tonight. The details of Elise's suicide, that she'd been just a child at the time, the fact that her mom was also in the car, that it had occurred on Mulholland Parkway.

It was a known fact on the floor that the boss was an Edison Forbes fan. What had Joyce said? *Anybody that walks by your desk has seen all the pictures . . .* Operators didn't climb the steel steps to her office, but

Marvin and any other number of underlings did. They had each seen *all the pictures,* and any one of them could've made mention to anyone on the floor of the boss's curious fascination with an obscure Canadian actor.

What if Valerie's clever operator put two and two together? What if he had axed their session because he had added up all the clues and figured out who Denise from Riverside actually was? The lynchpin would be her middle name, and that was the easiest detail of all to uncover.

What if he started blabbing it on the floor, letting everyone know that the boss was discussing deeply personal issues with an employee? What if he told everyone that she still talked to Eddie, even though Eddie was not really in the position at the moment to be having conversations with a successful American businesswoman?

Valerie opened a command window and again ran a locator on MB426312. Once more, the bug informed her that his booth was in the Prep Center. *Goddamned errors! I need to find this guy!* She ran a diagnostic on the subroutine and was amazed to find that all was in working order.

Jill! We traced the call! It's coming from inside the house! Do you hear me? It's coming from inside the house! You need to get out! Jill?

Valerie had to locate this operator, had to tell him to keep his mouth shut about what she'd told him. She'd threaten him with termination if she had to. No one could know that she still talked to Edison Forbes.

Valerie strolled down the steps and nonchalantly crossed the floor. She peeped through the door to the Prep Center and was shocked to see a light on above the last booth. There was no bug. The locator program had accurately pinpointed MB426312. Tonight and last week.

Why was he in there? Why had he reconfigured a training module to process live sessions? How had he faked the clearance to do so? Just who was this guy?

Valerie stalked quickly down the narrow hall and let herself into the instructor side of the booth. Even though the chamber was soundproof, she tiptoed up to the console and gingerly sat down.

Valerie switched on the system. She was thankful that the ceiling fluorescent illuminated both sides of the booth, or else the light from the instructor monitor would've alerted the operator that someone else was in the booth, that someone was about to spy on him.

The simulated image window was grayed out on Valerie's monitor for some reason, as was the voice-synthesizer bar; but that was okay, because she was aware of which celebrity was being simulated. Valerie looked at the display of the webcam feed from the trainee side of the console. She gritted her teeth in furious annoyance. *If I'm forced to deal with one more bug, I'm gonna have Joyce fire everybody.*

Here was another glitch, a totally new and different malfunction. The window that was supposed to show the operator was showing the simulation instead.

Valerie stealthily scootched the wheeled chair over until she could peer through the glass.

Her eyes widened in unqualified disbelief. She became rooted to the spot, unable to move, until at last the idea dawned on her that if he just happened to glance to his right, he would be able to see her gawping at him through the glass. Valerie quickly backed away.

At first, she didn't wonder about what the hell was going on, how he came to be there, or even how she had wound up talking to him in the first place. The only thought in Valerie's mind was, *Oh, my Christ! I've been telling all my secrets to the real Mitch Barlo!*

Valerie gulped a few deep breaths to calm herself. She tried to understand what she had seen – what was the real Mitch Barlo doing here, masquerading as an operator?

It was impossible. It was crazy. She peeped through the glass again. It was him.

****

Valerie backed out of the instructor booth. By the end of the hall she had regained her air of carefree insouciance. Just another night at the office for the hardworking boss. The floor was a hive of muted, money-making activity. No operators hung outside of their booths, hoping to catch a glimpse of her gob-smacked expression, now that she had discovered this impossibly unlikely secret. No one knew that an Oscar-nominee was hiding out in the Prep Center. No one knew that she'd been talking to him. Everything was business as usual, SOP. Or so it seemed.

When she again regained her office, Valerie called up the Personnel Records database.

MB426312, the number that had connected her to the real Mitch Barlo again this evening, had been assigned to him by the system. Depending on the actor/character an operator was portraying at any given time, such a number appeared in the corner of his screen, so he could tell the subscriber how to get back to him if she wanted to talk to him in this particular incarnation again. The last operator she had talked to was also the default when the subscriber logged on again.

256

The number functioned in the same manner as a work order number might in a more prosaic profession. If an operator portrayed more than one character, these numbers and how many hours the operator had spent as each character appeared on his timesheet. The system analyzed the time, the trends, the popularity of which operators in which characters, and so on.

MB426312 was certainly popular. The simulation had a following of forty-two repeat subscribers and had talked to several hundred more only once or twice. The number had been in existence for three months, had been online nearly every day.

But there were no employee records connected to it, no name, address and phone, no photo, no social security number, no W2. Not a single paycheck. MB426312 lent his thoughtful conversations to TTAMS subscribers gratis. He was a ghost. He was Mitch Barlo.

****

Valerie blinked in silent wonderment. She had discovered that the curiouser and curiouser rabbit hole of her own system ran deeper and stranger than she could've possibly guessed. The truths she had held to be self-evident were not true in the slightest. She had not indeed been imprudently spilling her guts to a simulacrum of Eddie's co-star from *Two's a Crowd,* but to the actual man himself.

The *why* of his presence in her facility, she reasoned, would have to wait on the *how* and the *who.* Mitch Barlo had not just descended from his Hollywood Hills mansion, wandered unchallenged into TTAMS, plopped down and reconfigured a training booth in the Prep Center, and then proceeded to chat up subscribers. Someone knew he was here. Someone had let him in – *brought him in* – someone had trained him. Someone had taken the added precaution of hiding him, segregating his famous face from the rest of the operators, all of whom would've immediately recognized him.

It was insane. A real actor hiding out at TTAMS, pretending to be himself? It was just nuts.

But that wasn't exactly accurate, though, was it?

It wasn't that Mitch Barlo was pretending to be an operator pretending to be him, reading prompts and replying to subscribers. *He ignores the goddamned prompts!* All the minutia about his movies that hadn't been in the database – he'd known that stuff, because he *was* Mitch Barlo. All the sad words and heart-tugging facial expressions while he talked about Janna's addiction and overdose had seemed so inexplicably real because they were genuine. Talking to the simulation had helped

Valerie to deal with events that had haunted her all her life. But it wasn't a simulation, not one iota of it.

Valerie wondered: *Had their conversation helped Mitch, too?*

But then the more pressing concern pushed all the thoughts of help and healing from her mind. *Why is he here?*

The *why* still waited on the *who*. Someone had let the real Mitch Barlo into TTAMS. Valerie set aside all the therapeutic value of their session for the moment, because it dawned on her that the actor's presence amounted to an incredible data leak, an unimaginable breach in security. For her personally, as well as for TTAMS.

If this famous celebrity decided to blab it all over town that the programmer behind the world's hottest infotainment service was telling all her innermost secrets to a simulation . . . That would be bad publicity indeed. It would make Valerie Whitly look like a nutball, like she was unstable, like her aunt and her grandmother had been. If such a story got out, it would reduce Talk to a Movie Star, in the public's mind, to the equivalent of the confessional booths in *THX1138*.

My time is yours.

The press would say that its founder's actions demonstrated that TTAMS wasn't really what it professed to be. It wasn't happy subscribers having fun talking to their idols about movies. If they were like Valerie Whitly, TTAMS subscribers were confessing their sins, looking for redemption, while a monotone voice periodically said, *Yes, I understand,* and *Could you be more specific?*

Are you now or have you ever been?

Someone had helped Mitch Barlo become a TTAMS operator. The idea that he was an excellent one didn't negate the fact that if he discussed the personal things that Valerie had told him, it would expose her system to ridicule. She obviously had mental health issues, if she was discussing such deeply private matters with an actor; she must have serious bats in the belfry indeed, if she was discussing them with what she believed to be a mere simulation . . .

If this got out, Valerie Whitly would come off as a nutcase. To the public, she would appear to be, as the English term it, *barking mad.*

Valerie recalled Ingrid Bergman's revenge in *Gaslight*. Charles Boyer's deceptions had caused her to doubt her own sanity, and Valerie thought she would deal with whoever had opened the door for Mitch Barlo in a similar manner.

She would lock him in a training booth in the Prep Center, one that wasn't configured for outside access, and when he begged her not to fire him, the boss would at first seem to acquiesce. Valerie would give him hope that he might yet salvage his job, that Joyce and her crack cadre of lawyers wouldn't sue him back to the Stone Age . . .

But then Valerie would paraphrase Paula's words from the legendary movie.

"Do you suggest that I could let you keep working here? *Have you gone mad, my husband? Or is it I who am mad? Yes, of course, that's it! I am mad!*"

With one click, Valerie would delete the employee's payroll records and grin at him.

"Yes, I am mad, as my aunt and grandmother were mad. If I were not mad, I could have helped you. Whatever you had done, I could have pitied and protected you. But because I am mad, I hate you. Because I am mad, I have betrayed you. And because I'm mad, I'm rejoicing in my heart, without a shred of pity, without a shred of regret, watching you go with glory in my heart! Mr. Castro, come! Come, Mr. Castro, *take this man away!*"

Valerie might or might not be mad, but she was certainly pissed. She aimed to get to the bottom of this lunacy at the earliest possible moment. She would let Mitch Barlo finish his shift and sneak out of the building unchallenged, as he had apparently been doing for the last three months. Then, when Greg came in to work in the morning, they would plot out how to catch the interloping actor red-handed.

The Director of Technical Operations wasn't working tonight, and Valerie found his absence significant. Any supervisor on the floor, or any operator for that matter, could've slipped Mitch Barlo in on some other night when Greg had been off, trained him on another similar day. Then on successive similar days, this imposter could've been secreted over there in the Prep Center – it could've been accomplished even on days that Greg was working, right under his nose. It was a situation so insanely unlikely – a ghost employee, famous, working for free – that there was absolutely no reason for Greg to look for such a thing.

Valerie called her Number 3 employee, but he didn't pick up. She tried Joyce, but got her voicemail, also. Getting to the bottom of this inexplicable, impossibly murky well would have to wait until morning.

****

Valerie sat at her desk and drummed her fingers on its polished surface. The Starbucks that Marvin had graciously brought for her was untouched, ignored. A check of the schedule told Valerie that Greg wasn't on until the night shift today, so she decided to see if she could utilize Joyce's considerable studio connections to her benefit, to handle this most inexplicable of situations. She imagined that the training manuals would all have to be rewritten: *What to do in the event of real celebrities sneaking into TTAMS.* And the confidentiality agreement, too: *Employee agrees not to admit real famous people to the TTAMS facility . . .*

Joyce came up to her office promptly when called, but she was in a hurry. Something about a budget meeting.

"Are we running out of money?" Valerie was blithe, but the specter of incipient bad publicity hung in the back of her mind.

Joyce grinned, blinked dollar signs. "Not in the least. But that's just the problem. Every department is clamoring for something, stuff they don't really need. More memory or something in Licensing and Research. You should really sit in on this one, Val. I don't know enough about what they're asking for, and Stevenson knows it."

"Call Greg in."

"Greg said he wasn't gonna come in for a meeting when he was already coming in tonight." Joyce wiggled her eyebrows and grinned. "But he'd come in if you asked him."

Valerie didn't return her partner's grin. Ever since college, Joyce had insisted that Greg Castro had a thing for his fellow code-monkey. Valerie didn't see it, and even if it was true, it wasn't something that Joyce needed to be joking about.

It was just more unprofessionalism, and Valerie wasn't hardly in the mood for it this morning. Greg was the best Ops Director in the business. Valerie valued him for his prowess in their field. If he had a little warm for her, it manifested itself in his hard work and loyalty to TTAMS, and Valerie would recognize him for that. Anything else, well . . . it just wasn't businesslike.

"He said I should just veto everything Stevenson is asking for until the next quarter."

Valerie shrugged. "Then do so."

"I don't know, Val, Stevenson is adamant that we need more space on the—"

"Just go with what Greg says, Jo," Valerie snapped. "I don't know why Stevenson is coming to you instead of him in the first place. What's happened to the chain of command around here?"

Bugs in the interface, imposters on the ops floor. A faulty database, and now infighting over funding, over *money*, the one thing TTAMS had plenty of. Valerie felt like things were falling down around her head.

Joyce picked up on her friend's uncharacteristically sour mood. "What did you want to see me about?"

"How difficult would it be for you to get Mitch Barlo in here?"

It wasn't that she suspected Joyce of instigating this insane breach of security, protocol and . . . and *ethics,* but Valerie had purposely phrased her question in just such a manner that if Joyce was involved somehow, her expression would implicate her.

Joyce's grin was sly, but it was utterly devoid of anything that could be construed as guilt. "What's a'matter, Valley? You getting tired of talking to Eddie? Did you finally get around to watching *Two's Company?*"

"*Two's a Crowd.*"

"Whatever. Did you finally watch it? Does fine young Mitch get the girl in the end? Is that why you had me jump in Research's shit last week? Eddie's not here, so a different, black-haired, blue-eyed white boy's caught your eye?"

Independently, simultaneously, both women thought of Brett Cooke. Joyce hastened to add, "Mitch Barlo doesn't look like he did in *Two's Whatever* any more, Val. Like you say, that movie was a long time ago. He's still fine, though. Did you see the trailer for *The Erskine Dilemma?*"

Mention of the trailer for *The Erskine Dilemma* put Valerie back in mind of her own dilemma. "You haven't told anybody that I talk to Eddie, have you, Jo?"

"No, Val. You know that I'd never—"

"Not anybody? Not Mortie Fellows or anyone here at work?"

"No, Val. Not anybody. That's your own personal business."

Joyce was alarmed at her friend's line of questioning. Eddie's conversations with his Number One Fan were intimately intertwined with TTAMS – it had been Eddie who had given Valerie the idea for the service in the first place, or so she claimed – and Joyce wondered what these repeated queries might mean for the service. God only knew what Eddie was telling her now.

It was worrisome to speculate about, so Joyce deflected the conversation back to Val's original question, answering it with one of her own.

"Do you really want to meet Mitch Barlo?"

"I do."

If I ask why, she's gonna start talking about Eddie again. This has gotta have something to do with that stupid old movie they were both in. Ah, Valley, why do you have to be so strange?

"How difficult would it be for you to get him in here? Request a little meeting? Do you know who his agent is?"

"Not right off hand, but I know people who know people."

261

"Maybe he wouldn't do it," Valerie suggested blankly. "Maybe he's too busy, or–"

"You're a millionaire, Val. You buy and sell these people all day long. You license this guy – you make him money. You can command anyone you want, like some kind of Ottoman Empire potentate." With one hand, Joyce described a turban in the air around her head. She grinned. "Like the Pope. If Mitch Barlo's in town, I'm sure he'll answer a summons from Valerie Whitly."

"Oh, I'm pretty sure he's in town."

Joyce waited for an explanation as to how Valerie knew this, as to why she had, out of a clear blue sky, in the past week or so, developed such an interest in Mitch Barlo and his early, pre-fame movies. The ones that nobody had heard of. *The Canadian one.* Joyce couldn't shake the idea that it had something to do with Edison Forbes.

When Valerie remained silent, Joyce said, "I'll see what I can do. You're gonna be in all day?"

You're not going to all of a sudden drive across town to Fox and scare up Liam Cote are you? Once upon a time, he knew Eddie, too, dragged us all the way to the Great White North to meet him . . .

"Where else would I be?" Valerie replied.

It was true. Valerie practically lived at the office. Joyce thought that maybe it could be some kind of a good thing that her solitary friend had suddenly gotten it into her mind to be requesting meetings with fine-looking, Oscar-nominated actors. Valerie Whitly, head of the hottest infotainment service in the world, certainly possessed the power necessary to command such audiences, especially in this town.

"If it's at all possible, I'll make it happen."

"I appreciate it, Jo." *When I'm a good dog, they sometimes throw me a bone.*

"Get me an autograph, will ya? Mitch Barlo is fine, and he's single. I wish he'd show up at The Conga Room some night."

What a Philistine you are, my friend, Valerie thought, not unkindly. *But it looks like we might make you into a fan yet.* Despite her worries, Valerie smiled to herself at that thought.

As she left the elevated glass office and headed for her budget meeting, Joyce pushed the appropriate buttons on her phone. Her friend had asked a favor, and it was Joyce's job to take care of her friend. She would see to it that Mitch Barlo made a personal appearance at TTAMS.

****

Christ, Ronny! Will you just calm down?

The undercover TTAMS operator's agent was yammering excitedly to him on the phone. "It was Joyce Vinson herself, Mitch! Damn, she's hot. I'd hoped to talk to her when you did that promo for *Erskine,* but all I got was some full-of-himself assistant. The guy talked to me like I was Max Bialystock, pre-*Springtime,* instead of the biggest–"

"The biggest agent on the West Coast. I know, Ronny." *Yeah, Dad, you told us.*

"And don't you forget it, Mitch, my son. Because I am the biggest agent on the West Coast, I am able to afford for you just these kinds of incredible opportunities."

Mitch smiled. Ronny had turned the situation around, as always, to his advantage. Joyce Vinson was no longer the initiator – it was now Ronny's own acclaim that precipitated this request for a meeting from TTAMS.

Mitch reflected that Ronny Prince, self-proclaimed King of Hollywood, did indeed bear many resemblances to Zero Mostel's Max Bialystock from *The Producers.* He was fat and fast-talking, and just as crooked as a dog's leg. But his conniving bulldog's flair was just the kind of thing one wanted in an agent. The indefatigable Mr. Prince had become rich representing Mitch Barlo. This bothered the actor not in the slightest, seeing how Ronny's representation had made him rich, also.

"Ms Vinson was all mysterious about it. Wouldn't give me any details. She'd only say that Valerie Whitly wants to see you, by yourself, without me, ASAP, chop-chop, like yesterday."

You are a cliché, Ronny. But I love you for it.

"Something about a deal. Maybe it's some kind of an endorsement. I told her you were available at two. You'll be there, right?"

"Actually, I have an appointment to get my shoes shined at two, Ronny."

"Comedy's not really your thing, is it, my son?"

"I'll be there."

"Of course you will. Don't sign anything."

"I wouldn't dream of it."

"Excellent. Call me after. I'm seeing large ducats, Mitch. I'm gonna call Cronenberg and see how much he'll pay for an exclusive endorsement for *Erskine* on TTAMS. We're gonna be rich!"

We're already rich, Ronny, and you're a cliché. "I'd hold off on that call to Canada."

"Wha-at? You know something I don't?"

"Now how could that even be possible, Ronny? I'd just wait until we see they want."

"Okay, Mitch. You're the boss. I'll wait. Call me."

After hanging up with his enthusiastic agent, Mitch pressed the button that dialed Greg Castro. He got the tech's voicemail: *Did you try rebooting?*

Mitch said, "The gig is up, my partner in crime. Joyce Vinson called my agent. Denise wants to see me. Maybe you shouldn't have cut her off when she was talking about Eddie Forbes. But fear not. Your stalker secret's safe with me. What's the worst she can do? Fire me?"

****

Heads turned and voices became hushed when the real Mitch Barlo sauntered into the lobby of TTAMS's Los Angeles headquarters. Even for a Saturday afternoon, the place was packed. Mitch wondered who all these people could possibly be. Subscribers? Industry movers and shakers, like Ronny Prince, angling for *endorsements?*

Before anyone in the crowd could step up and ask Mitch for an autograph, a flawless young woman in an impeccably tailored business suit materialized and said, "Right this way, Mr. Barlo." She wasn't star-struck, or at least she'd been instructed not to be. He was expected.

She slid a card through the reader on a non-descript steel ingress and led the actor down a short hall to the operations floor. Mitch reflected that it was the first time he'd ever entered the facility through the front door. The booths were all manned, as always, but none of the operators peeped out at him. Valerie Whitly had not informed her other employees that a real movie star would be onsite. Not even Baker turned his head when Mitch passed his booth.

As the girl led him to the foot of the steel steps, Mitch glanced to his left and noted that Greg's office was dark, the door closed. *Hope you check your phone soon, my friend. You're in for a helluva surprise.*

When Mitch paused in the open doorway to her office, Valerie Whitly arose from behind her desk, smiled winningly at him. "I'm so glad you could come on such short notice, Mr. Barlo! Please come in. No need to close the door. No one can overhear us up here."

Mitch stepped inside the glass office. He waited for her to offer him a seat, but the founder of TTAMS just stared at him, the bright smile pasted on her face. Mitch had seen that smile throughout his career.

Greg is wrong, he thought, with a little satisfaction. *His lady-love is a fan.* Had she not picked him to speak with, of her own volition, even if it had been in his younger, Shamus incarnation?

Maybe I'm wrong about all this. Maybe she doesn't know I've been here at all. She got cut off from talking to my simulation, so maybe she just got it into her head that she wanted to meet me in person. Such whims are the norm for powerful Hollywood players such as Valerie Whitly. She could obtain a Bengal tiger and chain him to the catwalk outside her office if she so chose, Mitch mused. *Surely, she feels that summoning one actor is completely within her rights.*

Despite her fan-blank smile, Mitch found Valerie Whitly to be lovely. In person, there was an airy, almost delicate quality about her that hadn't shown through in the photograph that had accompanied the piece he'd read on Variety.com. From looking at her, one would never guess about the trials of death and sadness she had endured. Mitch congratulated himself. Perhaps their little talk had helped her to let go of some of her sorrows. It had certainly helped him to do so.

At last his summoner spoke. "Wow. It's really you! Before we begin . . . I hope I'm not being too silly . . ." Valerie giggled adorably. "But do you think I could . . . Could I have an autograph?"

Mitch allowed his own ego to seize him. He flashed that famous killer smile, glanced away with all the false humility he had. *She doesn't know I've been here. This is just a meet and greet.*

"Sure, Ms Whitly. It would be my pleasure . . ." He reached into the breast pocket of his jacket for a pen. *To Valerie Whitly, my biggest fan,* Mitch would write. *Thanks for all your support . . .*

But when he looked again at the owner of TTAMS, she wasn't gazing adoringly at him anymore. She had reseated herself and was looking at the screen of the laptop on her desk. She hit a key, then another one. Only then did she seem to recall that he was there.

The star-struck fan was gone. She noted the pen in his hand and an expression of embarrassment crossed her features. *Embarrassment for him.*

"Oh. You thought that I really wanted . . . I'm sorry, Mr. Barlo. I was just kidding. My dad was a rock star. I don't do autographs."

Valerie steepled her hands upon the polished surface of her desk. She looked at him expectantly, but still didn't offer him a chair. Mitch thought of Major Toht, the fearsome Nazi interrogator from *Raiders of the Lost Ark.* Valerie's smile had taken on just the same kind of predatory gleam. *Now . . . What shall we talk about?*

The change in Ms Whitly, from shyly smiling fake fan into hard-nosed executive was absolute, accomplished instantaneously, like the oft-mentioned light switch flipped, but Mitch thought, *Yeah, you don't do autographs. Unless they're from Eddie Forbes.*

"What can I do for you, Ms Whitly?" Mitch kept his face neutral. He put the pen back into his pocket and remained standing.

"Two things, Mitch. I can call you Mitch?"

Yes. Certainly, Tammy. The actor felt a moment of unreality. "Of course."

"First of all, I want to know how you got in here."

"A very polite young woman brought me in from the lobby and pointed me toward your office. I must say, you've got quite the operation here. I'm impressed."

"So impressed that you decided you wanted to work for me. I'm asking you who it was that accommodated you."

All right, Denise, let's play. Mitch flopped down into the leather chair in front of Valerie's desk. He didn't particularly care for her tone.

"I think your service is brilliant. It intrigued me. I wanted to know what it was like to play an actor playing me. I find it enjoyable, talking to my fans." Again he flashed his famous smile. "What do you want to do, Ms Whitly? Fire me? Sue me?"

"Please, Mitch, call me Valerie." *We're already on a first name basis as it is. You just don't know it.*

The possibility that she had somehow been directed to talk to the one real celebrity on TTAMS had not crossed Valerie's mind. She had chosen Shamus, had she not? Her incredibly buggy system had then just arbitrarily connected her to MB426312, the modern Mitch Barlo.

The fact that it was really him was immaterial, the luck of the draw. He was a popular operator, or perhaps he'd been the only one on the ops floor portraying modern Mitch that night. Valerie had convinced herself that there was absolutely no way he knew he'd been talking to her, despite her confessions, despite the fact that he had abruptly ended the session when she'd started talking about Eddie. He probably hadn't even done that; it had undoubtedly been just another bug, like the one that had cut her off from talking to Shamus.

Mitch Barlo didn't know that she was Denise from Riverside. Valerie could tell by the look on his face.

"I want to know who it was that let you in here. Did they even make you sign a confidentiality agreement?"

"Yes."

This admission caused Valerie to relax a little bit. "So you know you can't discuss anything that subscribers tell you—"

"I wouldn't do that anyway, Ms Whitly. Like I said, I like talking to my fans. I'd never betray their trust."

And I'm a Chinese jet pilot, Valerie said to herself. *I know what town I'm in, Mr. Barlo, even if you seem to have forgotten. Trust is just another commodity around here, for sale to the highest bidder.*

"I'd still like to know who it was that let you in. Trained you. Gave you access to the system."

Mitch remained silent. No. He didn't care for her tone in the least.

He continued to stare steadily at her, and after another heartbeat, Valerie offered the actor a boss's indulgent, annoyed smile. "Perhaps you misunderstand my motivations, Mitch."

You have a problem with authority, Mr. Anderson. You believe you are special, that somehow the rules do not apply to you. Obviously, you are mistaken.

"You think that I want to punish this person. Seal up this security breach with a pink slip. That's not the case at all. I'd like to congratulate your mentor. Give him a raise. It's quite an achievement to have a real personality onboard at TTAMS. But if you won't tell me who it was, I can't give him his due." Her smile tightened with hostility.

Ve haff vays of making you talk. This wasn't a meeting. It was an interrogation, and a rather heavy-handed one at that. A trace of Ronny Prince's hubris colored Mitch's mind. *I don't care how much money you have, or how powerful you think you are.*

There's a sign on the front that says, "Lou's Tavern." I'm fucking Lou. Who the fuck are you?

I'm Mitch Barlo, Ms I-Don't-Do-Autographs, and if you want any information from me, even if it is about your own place of business, you'd best start being a little more polite.

Valerie glanced at her laptop again, hit another key. She was too busy to play games with an actor. "Okay. I appreciate your loyalty, Mitch. My Director of Technical Operations is the best in the business. He'll figure it out.

"The other thing – I'd like to offer you the operator position you've already been filling. Put you on the payroll. I looked at your stats. You have quite a little following, especially for someone who doesn't work a full shift."

When Mitch's eyebrow raised a bit at this remark, Valerie hastened to add, "Don't get me wrong – I saw that you've been here damn near every night. Things must be a little slow for you in the biz these days, eh? You're actually due some OT for your daily attendance. It's just that the individual shifts were a little short." Valerie waved her hand dismissively "Oh, never mind. *I'm a doctor, Jim–*"

"Not a Payroll Clerk."

But Mitch didn't smile. Valerie Whitly, soon to be on the list of the wealthiest people in the country (if she wasn't there already) was allowing her newfound status as *nouveau riche* to go to her head.

I hope you're saving all that money, honey, because you're gonna have to buy your friends in the future. Your people skills are sorely lacking.

Mitch was astonished that the woman sitting before him, this . . . *this tech,* was so puffed up with her own importance that she could actually condescend to offer him a job, as if he was – how had Greg Castro put it? – as if he was *a Performing Arts refugee.*

Mitch couldn't believe that this was the same woman that he had talked to online. No wonder she wouldn't show her face there. The cloak of anonymity that the interface had provided undoubtedly made it easier for her to forget their emotional, tear-fraught conversation. Valerie Whitly knew that they had each exposed stark vulnerabilities, that they had both come out of it as healthier individuals.

But Mitch realized that Valerie didn't know that he knew that she was Denise from Riverside. She had found him out somehow, but she was unaware that he had known all along that he was sharing sad secrets with the boss of TTAMS herself. It was just as Baker had told him from the beginning. People would say damn near anything when they felt securely hidden behind an anonymous interface.

Denise from Riverside was a sad, hurt little girl, but she surely wasn't going to show it to the real Mitch Barlo now, as she had when she thought he was just a simulation, an employee that could never expose the real person behind the screen.

The real person behind the screen was Valerie Whitly, obscenely successful entrepreneur, coldly calculating, powerful businesswoman. Mitch didn't like her very much.

"We'd still keep it all on the down low, of course," Valerie continued. "It'll be our little secret, just yours and mine, and whoever it was that let you in here. We couldn't have it getting all over town that you were–"

"That's okay, Ms Whitly. I pay enough taxes." The attitude displayed by the real Valerie Whitly offended the real Mitch Barlo. She acted as if the closeness she knew they'd shared had not occurred. She was treating him like a dismissed whore.

"If there's nothing else . . ." Mitch stood.

Valerie blinked in surprise at his obvious pique, and just like that, her haughty boss's façade vanished as quickly as it had appeared. The face that she presented to him wasn't of an adoring fan this time – that ship had sailed. Now she had become just a regular, earnest person who's realized her own misstep: she had offended him, quite unintentionally. She saw that her meeting had gone awry, that her aims were going to fall short.

"I'd really like you to stay on, Mitch. Your numbers are amazing . . ."

No, that isn't the way to go. He's Mitch Barlo. He doesn't need a job. He just likes talking to his fans. He's not going to tell anyone what he's talked about with them or with me . . .

Valerie tried again. She said softly, "You will stay on, won't you? At least until your next picture starts? I'm so pleased that you're enjoying yourself."

Mitch heard Denise's voice, kind and thoughtful. The change in Valerie Whitly was again startling. Once more, he saw the burdened, damaged, lonely young woman that talked to Edison Forbes. She was happy that he liked being a part of her service.

Mitch reconsidered. Maybe this gentle spirit was the real Valerie after all. Mitch could tell from the look now present in her bright blue eyes that this Valerie not only remembered but valued the profound heart-to-heart that they'd shared.

He speculated that perhaps the steely gruffness that she had initially displayed was the same reaction as any mother might show when she felt her baby was in danger. He was an interloper, after all, an unauthorized stranger on her operations floor. The coldness she had delivered to him was just a reaction to feeling powerless and stupid once she'd uncovered that there was an unauthorized person in her building. She had just been protecting her livelihood in a town where one's reputation could be severely damaged by an idle word.

People in show business told themselves that they liked to see their peers succeed, but they also took a secret glee when these same people stumbled. The Germans even had a word for it: *schadenfreude. Pleasure derived from another person's misfortune.*

Mitch offered the founder of TTAMS a mild, grateful smile. "Sure, Valerie. It would be my pleasure. I really enjoy talking to people." Mitch decided that he would play into her fantasy of anonymity. "Look me up, sometime. We'll talk about the movies. My number is—"

"I know what your number is, Mitch." She gestured at the screen, but her voice was still soft, still Denise's voice.

Then she smiled brightly once more, an executive again, but a more respectful one now. Their meeting had been a success. Their continued association would be beneficial to both.

"I'll certainly look you up, though, if I get a minute." Valerie arose and unreservedly shook his hand. "Welcome aboard!"

****

The limo that had carried Mitch Barlo, instantly recognizable, Oscar-nominated, internationally acclaimed star of stage and screen, idled at the curb in the no-parking zone in front of TTAMS's headquarters, waiting for him. Some of the fans that had spotted him in the lobby had gathered patiently beside the black car. Mitch smiled, shook hands, posed for selfies with them, signed autographs. His celebrity duties discharged, he told the driver to take him to Greg Castro's apartment.

On the way there, Greg finally answered the phone. "Well? Do I still have a job?"

"You do. It's too much to tell you on the phone. I'll be there in ten minutes."

Mitch released the limo driver. He would find his own way home.

****

Greg paced the short length of his living room, nervous, disbelieving. "She asked you to stay?"

Mitch nodded. "After I turned down her offer for a paying position."

"And she didn't ask you again who let you in?"

"Nope. You're supposed to figure all that out."

"If she asks me, I'm gonna have to throw Baker under the bus."

Mitch laughed. "You can't do that, Greg. You're in on it, too. It would make you look stupid. If you don't cop to knowing what was going on, it'll look as if Morris had gotten one over on you."

"But I can't tell her that I knew about it, Mitch." Greg chewed a fingernail in dismay. "She trusts me. She doesn't even suspect me."

"I don't think she's even gonna bring it up, Greg. She said it would be *our little secret.* Just hers and mine."

"But why does she want you to stay?" Greg switched fingers, continued to gnaw. "I don't get it. I thought she'd dig it, a real celebrity at TTAMS. But I guess I was wrong. Maybe if I would've gotten to introduce you first . . . Did she say how she found out you were there?"

270

Mitch shook his head.

"Why didn't she fire you?"

"Because I don't work there."

"You know what I mean. You just slipped in unnoticed. You're a security breach. For all she knows, it could be, what d'ya call it? *Industrial espionage.* You could be selling all our proprietary software secrets to Mark Zuckerberg."

"I don't know anything about computers, Greg."

"You could be taught. It wouldn't take much. A thumb drive, a few simple commands. Valerie knows all that. That's why she's so pissed. I just don't understand why she didn't have security escort you to the door."

Then realization dawned on Greg and he smiled from ear to ear. "Of course! I don't know why I didn't see it!" He paused, considered his famous friend. "Why do *you* think she wants you to stay?"

Mitch shrugged. "She likes me. We had a nice little talk—"

"Valerie Whitly doesn't care about you, Movie Star! It's not you at all, but *what you know*. Damn, I'm good!" Greg clapped his hands in self-satisfied delight. "I was right all along. She still wants to talk to you about Eddie Forbes!"

"Oh, Christ, Greg. Not that again. Eddie's—"

"No, Mitch. Forget about all that. Tell her whatever she wants to hear. You're a TTAMS operator. That's what you do. You tell 'em what they want to hear. And eventually, when the time's right, I'll sneak up on the idea that it was me that brought you onboard. She'll be grateful—"

"I dunno, Greg. It just doesn't seem—"

"What? If your subscriber wants to talk about Eddie Forbes, then that's what you talk about. It's their fantasy. Why should it be any different, just because you know who you're talking to?"

****

Another week passed, and it was business as usual at TTAMS. On Wednesday, Valerie chaired a meeting between Greg and Joyce and Mark Stevenson from Licensing and Research. Joyce was right – Stevenson was resolute about the need to expand and update TTAMS's already vast array of servers. He even intimated, ever so subtly, that the database omissions that the boss had recently discovered regarding a few obscure films and characters were the result of this pressing need for additional memory.

"If certain files are rarely accessed, the system sees them as extraneous and dumps them, so as to free up space to add data to more frequently accessed subjects. I don't need to tell *you*, Valerie–" Stevenson ignored the Director of Technical Operations, his immediate supervisor, "– that storage is finite. Unless we acquire more space, we're not going to be able to offer every single movie ever produced in the English language."

Greg grinned. "You people in Licensing have the worst communications I've ever seen, Stevenson. Haven't you heard? Oliver and Ellis have already submitted a proposal for expansion into foreign films. Soon our Japanese friends could be discussing the finer points of *The Seven Samurai* with Kurosawa, or we could have Frenchmen talking to Amelie, or Italians chatting up the projectionist from *Cinema Paradiso.*"

Stevenson frowned coldly at his boss. "Not without more servers, we won't." He looked to Valerie for validation.

The founder of TTAMS sighed theatrically. *"At this moment, for example, I'm quite convinced I'm never going to see you again. I'm so bored, you see. It's beyond my control."*

Stevenson blanched and Joyce rolled her eyes.

Greg grinned and supplied the next line. *"What do you mean?"*

"Well, after all, it's been four months. So what I said – it's beyond my control!"

Valerie shared a smile of pure delight with her Number 3 employee, the smile of the consummate fan. Greg never blinked stupidly at her cinematic references. Sometimes Valerie forgot that he was also a movie buff, that he could also recite scenes from *Dangerous Liaisons* as effortlessly as John Malkovich. Sometimes she forgot that the Ops Director was almost as fluent in trivia and quotations as Brett had been.

Joyce wasn't versed in the movies, but she had witnessed enough of these kinds of scenes, between Valerie and Greg, and Valerie and Brett, and even once or twice between Valerie and her mom, when her parents would visit. With her dad, Val would sometimes banter song lyrics. Joyce sighed. It was just another day of curiousness at TTAMS.

Stevenson, on the other hand, had not a clue as to what was going on. He was a tech, a cataloguer of information. His job was to compile an exhaustive list of films, *every single movie ever produced in the English language,* if he was to please Valerie. But that didn't make him a fan. Joyce thought that he would be just as happy, though not as well paid, working for Chrysler, toting up the minutia of auto parts.

Not realizing that this was all from a movie, Stevenson now feared for his job. He believed that he had overstepped some unseen boundary. *It's beyond my control!* Ms Whitly was throwing him to the Ops Director, a man with whom he'd just openly clashed.

Joyce pitied Stevenson. The situation was not even remotely how he saw it. His job wasn't in jeopardy. Valerie was just being her odd, non sequitur, movie-quoting self.

Time was money, however, and the boss was wasting it, so Joyce spoke up.

"I'm a lawyer, not a technician, but it seems to me that Mark has a valid concern. If we're going to expand into foreign markets, we'll definitely need to upgrade, eventually."

"We need to upgrade now," Stevenson insisted. Ms Whitly might fire him for his impertinence, his jumping the chain of command, but it wasn't going to make him change his mind. TTAMS needed more servers. Smug Greg Castro could kiss his ass.

Valerie smiled at Joyce. *"So shall it be written—"*

"So shall it be done." Greg signed off on Stevenson's request with a flourish and slid the paperwork across the slick conference table to him.

Stevenson was speechless. Not for the first time, he thought that the triumvirate that ran TTAMS was the oddest collection of bosses ever assembled. Greg Castro knew he was right – one look at the numbers, and even a first year ITT Tech student would've seen that TTAMS needed more servers – but the Ops Director had decided to fight him on it, just because he could. Joyce Vinson wouldn't know a motherboard from her own mother, even if it sang a lullaby to her, but she instinctively knew where TTAMS's budget was best spent. Stevenson had believed all along that she would give him the necessarily funding. That's why he'd dared to go over Castro's head and talk to her.

But the big boss always had the finally say, and to Stevenson, Valerie Whitly was the strangest of the three of them. She was the mind behind TTAMS – that made her odd enough in Stevenson's estimation. She had single-handedly created a fantasy world for movie fans, a wonderland where they could say anything they had ever dreamed of saying to the men and women that so fascinated them. Mark Stevenson had never had this fascination himself, and had always been uncomfortable with people who got all hushed and awestruck when they talked about movie stars. Actors were just pretty people to him; he could never fathom the millions of dollars and the downright worship that so many paid to them.

Valerie Whitly had her finger on the collective pulse of the fans, her hand in their wallets. But Stevenson still believed that she was as nutty as a shithouse rat, and the incomprehensible exchange he had just witnessed between her and her contrary watchdog of an Ops Director had further reinforced his opinion. He'd been in enough meetings with her – one never knew what kind of weird, rambling bullshit was going to come out of her mouth, just like this time.

Still, Stevenson couldn't deny her genius, even if he wasn't a movie fan himself. Maybe all geniuses were nuts. Either way, the boss's mental health was no longer a concern to him. He'd secured the funds he needed to assure the continued smooth operation of his department, and of TTAMS as a whole. That was all that mattered.

****

After the meeting, Valerie played subscriber and talked to a few more movie stars. She uncovered no more bugs in the interface, agreed with her own initial assessment that her lumpy first session was a one off. Although these additional interactions didn't seem quite as real as her sessions with Mitch Barlo – it really was Mitch Barlo that had talked to her, after all – she still found her motion capture technology to be stunningly lifelike, and the voice simulations to be dead on. Valerie loved her baby again. She was proud of TTAMS.

Valerie enjoyed movies for the way they made her feel. She had never been too big on the mechanics that went into creating the moods: the lighting or the camera angles, the composition of the shots. But because her father was a musician, she was somewhat attuned to the music that helped to set the tones in certain scenes. One song could denote an entire era: Buffalo Springfield's *For What It's Worth* clued the viewer that the tale would be set in the more troubled part of the 1960s. *Do Ya Think I'm Sexy?* or *Stayin' Alive* signaled the disco days of the late 70s. But sound effects themselves bored Valerie. On the plane to Canada, when Liam Cote regaled Joyce with the intricacies of the Foley art, Valerie had drifted right off to sleep.

She did get into one uncharacteristically technical discussion with Orson Welles on TTAMS, however, regarding the famously continuous shot in *Citizen Kane*, wherein the banker has come to whisk the young Charles Kane away to a better life.

Valerie had read numerous articles about the elements of deep focus and placement of the characters in the frame. What better way to get clarification on what she'd learned, than to speak to the director himself? Even though she knew that it was simply an operator

274

mouthing the opinions of various film critics and cinematography students through the years, compiled by the system and fed to him via prompts, it seemed so much more real and interesting when Valerie heard them in the legendary auteur's unmistakable voice.

But mostly, TTAMS's founder used her system precisely as it had been intended to be used. Valerie spent a few minutes talking to Marilyn Monroe about the ukulele scene on the train from *Some Like It Hot,* and of course, she asked about the famous subway grate scene from *The Seven Year Itch.* She checked in to see what Chris Hemsworth was looking like these days, and had a few words with poor, doomed Paul Walker. She asked Rachel McAdams what Ryan Gosling was really like, then switched over to see if Eva Mendes agreed. Valerie chatted with a cross-section of Hollywood's biggest and brightest. She even enjoyed a short session with an adorable, long-haired cowboy named Shamus.

But all the hours in the week seemed to get away from her somehow, so she didn't get the chance to connect with MB426312 again. Valerie decided that she would've felt silly discussing movie trivia and characterization with the real Mitch Barlo, anyway. They had shared so many actual feelings and emotions that she felt that a TTAMS-style conversation with him would've been just that: trivial. Just meaningless small talk.

Valerie felt that she and Mitch could actually become friends IRL. She just hadn't found the time to talk to him during the past week. The closest she'd come was slipping into the instructor side of his booth in the Prep Center a few times, knocking on the window and waving at him. Mitch had smiled, but then had gotten right back to his conversation with Maisie from Poughkeepsie or Betty from Philly. Valerie's phone always buzzed anyway: Joyce texting her about some production decision, or eager Japanese investors calling her away to a teleconference.

Valerie would have to consciously make time to talk to Mitch Barlo. As soon as possible, whenever she could squeeze it in. She discovered that she was looking forward to it.

****

Friday night arrived, as it always does, and Valerie was at her desk once more. She hadn't gotten the chance to talk to Mitch as she'd planned; things just kept coming up. But whenever there was a moment of calm, Valerie had discovered the good-looking actor in her mind. She ruminated on how much she had grown, just based on one

275

conversation with him. What good friends they might become, if she could only get a spare minute . . .

Besides his healing influence, Valerie recognized that there were other qualities about Mitch that kept bringing him to the center of her thoughts. He was single, as Joyce had not failed to observe, and he was attractive. He was just Valerie's type, dark-haired and blue-eyed and pretty. Confident. Valerie grinned to herself. Who knew where pursuing a friendship with him might lead?

Valerie decided against letting Mitch know that she had been Denise from Riverside.

When they had met in person, she had been up on her high horse. She had somewhat forcefully cross-examined him, and Mitch had not responded well to that tactic at all. He had flat-out refused to tell her anything. So how would it look if he found out that she had been masquerading as someone she was not, in almost the same manner as he had?

Sure, his lie was minimal: he was indeed Mitch Barlo, precisely who he claimed to be on TTAMS, but none of the subscribers knew that. They were under the impression that it was all a game, just as Valerie herself had been, that they were sharing their secrets with a simulation. Valerie had overshared, that was true, because the *realness* of the simulation had led her to it. How many other subscribers might have overshared, too, caught up in the TTAMS magic, never dreaming that it was really him?

When Valerie had talked to Mitch online, she had been carried away by his sadness, his own confessions – but she'd told herself then that she'd responded so fully because she'd believed that it was *only a simulation*. She had allowed herself to be carried away with the fantasy that a movie star was telling his troubles to her, and she had responded in kind. In the process, she had relieved herself of a lifelong burden.

But it wouldn't have occurred that way in real life. If she had met Mitch Barlo at The Conga Room (as Joyce wished for) or had been introduced to him at an industry party, or had spied his famous face on the street, their conversation would've consisted entirely of the customary pleasantries. There would have been no heart-to-heart confessions, and it would've also been the same, even on TTAMS: if Valerie had imagined for one moment that she was indeed speaking to the real Mitch Barlo, she would've kept her mouth shut.

But once she discovered that she had indeed confessed to the real him, she felt differently. She believed that she could confide in Mitch IRL, because during the brief meeting in her office, he had made her believe that she could trust him. So she had let slide the whole idea of ferreting out how he'd gotten in here and who had trained him. She had decided to let sleeping dogs lie, had mentioned his presence to no one. Mitch had admitted that he liked talking to his fans, and Valerie saw that as admirable.

She knew that if she let the cat out of the bag, everything would be ruined for him. There would be stares and giggles when he came in to work, maybe even requests for autographs from his amazed fellow operators.

Valerie knew a little about fame. Denny Whitly could never get a job at Guitar Center, and no one could know that a world renowned actor was killing time, talking to his fans on TTAMS. Eventually, a TMZ camera crew would be waiting for him outside in the alley some night, and the gig would be up. It would fall out as more incredible free publicity for the service, but for Mitch himself, maybe not so much. It was rather an odd pastime for someone as famous as he was, after all.

Valerie believed that keeping his secret showed Mitch that he could trust her, too, that she was as good as her word. So if she wanted to expand their friendship beyond this simple business arrangement, Valerie figured that it would be starting off on the wrong foot to reveal that she had also deceived him by pretending to be Denise from Riverside. That was a little secret best kept to herself.

****

Valerie had gotten it into her mind that she was genuinely fond of Mitch Barlo, and she had gotten the impression that he liked her too – at least he liked Denise from Riverside. She wasn't too sure how he regarded Valerie from LA. In their single face to face interaction, she had come off as a rather impatient shrew. He had been prepared to tell her where she could stick TTAMS, but he had then relented when she asked him to stay on. She had shown him that she no longer saw him as a threat. Once he'd made it clear that he was simply enjoying himself, talking to his fans, the boss had let him know that that was okay with her.

Valerie realized that the movie star was not even aware that a kind of friendship between them already existed, because he didn't know that they had shared their sorrows on TTAMS.

Valerie was feeling in a playful mood on this Friday night. She decided to disabuse Mitch of his impression of her as a hard-nosed bitch. Valerie had treated him as a somewhat disgraced employee; now she would show him what she could treat him as an equal.

277

The inescapable fact of his fame didn't even enter her thoughts. Fame meant nothing to Valerie. Had she not gotten her dreams and fantasies of Eddie under control, before she met him? Hadn't she simply shook his hand, chatted with him, just like he was a regular Joe? Weren't they still friends?

So on Friday night, Valerie decided to take the bull by the horns. Her single IRL meeting with good-looking Mitch Barlo had reminded her that she knew how to approach pretty men, be they Oscar-nominees, famous Canadians, or gorgeous business majors. Feeling ever so clever, she found a pad of Post-It Notes in her desk and scribbled a message. Then she arose, gathered up her phone and her purse and her car keys, and shut off the lights in her office. The founder of the world's hottest infotainment service had been at work long enough for this week.

Valerie crossed the busy floor. She paused at the hallway that led behind the instructor booths of the OpsPrepCent, and after glancing this way and that to make sure she wasn't observed, she skipped down the hall and let herself into the last booth.

Even though she couldn't hear him through the soundproof glass, Valerie could tell that Mitch was hard at work, talking to a subscriber. She knocked on the glass and smiled at him; he acknowledged her presence with an almost imperceptible nod. She stuck the Post-It on her side of the glass, waved goodbye, and left the booth.

Valerie was in the mood for some alone-time, for a nice hot bath and her soft old pajamas and a big bowl of ice cream. The work week was over (because she had decided that it was), and for a change, she wanted to relax. She thought she would at last watch *Two's a Crowd*. She would think about what Mitch's reaction to her note might be.

What that could bring, coupled with the anticipation of at last watching the movie she had saved for so long, brought a smile to Valerie's face, brought an additional spring to her step. She whistled to herself as she stepped into the empty elevator that would take her down to the parking garage.

Mitch would be curious about the sticky note that she'd left for him, but Valerie knew that he wouldn't be able to retrieve it until he was finished with his session. She was confident that he would read nothing more into it than the companionable mischievousness that she had intended, and if he did, well . . . that might be all right, too.

****

278

Mitch listened patiently to Jackie from Torrance. The plot of *The Erskine Dilemma* as outlined in the trailer was foggy to her, and she was trying to wheedle more details about it from him.

"If I tell you, then I'll have to tell everybody, Jackie." Mitch Barlo smiled, and like Valerie before her, Jackie was amazed at how *real* he seemed. "If everybody knows everything about it, then nobody'll want to go see it."

"Oh, I'll go see it, Mitch!" Jackie promised. "I sat through *Two of Swords* three times! You just looked so *scrumptious* in that tux!"

Mitch supplied the proper *ah, shucks* grin. "Thanks, Jackie. That film was a lot of fun to make."

It really hadn't been. The location shoot in Vegas had been hot and tedious; Mitch had positively baked in that tux that everybody liked so much. But TTAMS had analyzed hundreds of subscriber comments on *Two of Swords* and had come to the conclusion that his fans wanted to believe that running around on the roofs of casinos in the desert sun had been fun, and it had prompted him to tell Jackie from Torrance just that.

Jackie was telling him that her grandmother was of gypsy stock –

"That must be where you get all that lovely black hair," Mitch commented, completely off-script.

Jackie blushed to the roots of it and stammered out a thanks. Mitch used her moment of thrilled discomfiture to glance again at the note Valerie had stuck up on the glass. Jackie regained her composure, and while she was telling him how her grandma the gypsy used to read her future in the Tarot, just as he had predicted winning poker hands in *Two of Swords*, Mitch had a second to wonder what could possibly be written on the little pink square.

The fact that it was pink made him wonder if Valerie was giving him the boot – literally *sealing up this security breach with a pink slip*, as she had so shrewdly put it in their terse mano-a-mano meeting. But Mitch didn't think so. Valerie hadn't talked to him again since she had so graciously given him the run of the place, but she had dropped by the instructor side of his booth a few times, smiled, waved; something that Denise from Riverside would do.

This time she had taken it a step further and left him a note – she was showing him the schoolgirl part of her, the part that he had sensed whilst he'd listened to her online. Mitch liked that. He couldn't imagine what her note might contain, but he discovered that he was extremely curious to find out. Whatever it might say, he was sure it wasn't showing him the door.

Valerie had not mentioned Mitch's presence to Greg, and the Director of Technical Operations continued to be amazed about that. Mitch was amused that the Ops Director now lived under a cloud of not just a little fear, waiting for the other shoe to drop. He told Mitch that apparently the status quo would remain unruffled, at least until after Valerie made the time to query him about Edison Forbes. After that, what would happen was anybody's guess.

When Valerie inevitably brought up the actor's presence, Greg knew that his response would depend entirely upon her mood. He told Mitch that he still hoped that she would be pleased about it somehow. He still hoped that he would be able to take credit and parlay things into a heightened friendship with the boss.

But Mitch believed Valerie would be true to her word, that she wouldn't say anything to Greg or Joyce or anyone else until long after he was gone. Maybe not even then. It would all remain their little secret.

Valerie had to know that his working here couldn't last forever. Mitch Barlo was a movie star, not a TTAMS operator. Neither he nor Ronny Prince had seen a script worth reading recently – "If I open it and your character is on the first page, and if I check and he's on the last page, then we might consider it." But despite the bad publicity of Janna's death, Mitch Barlo was still a hot property in Hollywood. He was still on top of the A-list. As soon as *Erskine* was out, another good script was bound to come along. Sooner rather than later.

No, Mitch didn't think that Valerie was firing him, although doing it via a Post-It would no doubt be how the steely executive part of her would've accomplished it. He wasn't on the payroll, so nothing more formal than a sticky saying, "Get out," would be necessary.

Mitch's full attention was drawn back to his screen when Jackie abruptly stopped talking. A man's voice, muffled, had called her name from somewhere within her apartment there in Torrance.

"That's Jason, Mitch. My husband. He wants me to watch television with him." Jackie glanced down, veiling her eyes shyly, almost guiltily. Mitch wasn't sure if it was because she didn't want to cut him off, or if she didn't want him to know she was married. "He sat through all three showings of *Two of Swords* with me."

So the least you can do is stop talking to a simulation when he calls you, and go watch television with him.

Mitch smiled. "I understand, Jackie. Look me up again sometime. I'd like to hear more about your grandmother's fortunetelling secrets." He thought of Valerie's note, still tantalizingly out of reach. *If anyone could use a peek at what the future's gonna bring, it's me.*

280

Jackie giggled, smiled winningly. "I'll be sure to do that, Mitch." Jason's voice called her again, closer this time, and Jackie quickly said goodbye and logged off.

Mitch's screen went blue, and he hit the *Pause* key, so TTAMS wouldn't immediately send him another subscriber. He stood, slid the glass aside, and retrieved Valerie's note. He took a deep breath, exhaled, and turned it over.

Some night when you're not working, if you're not too busy . . . For a good time, call Valerie. ☺

Her number was scrawled underneath.

Mitch sat back down, nonplussed.

The boss was flirting with him, and Mitch discovered that he was uncharacteristically stoked about that. "I'll be a son of a bitch," he said aloud.

He debated whether or not to call Greg and tell him about this unforeseen development. Tell the tech that the time had come, as the walrus was rumored to have said.

"Time to say your piece, my friend, stake your claim. Your lady-love has decided she's tired of being single."

Mitch grinned to himself. *How childish the interactions between men and women really are, once you get down to it.* Despite all the technological miracles afforded to Greg by his own genius with electronics, the tech couldn't express his feelings for Valerie any more than Charlie Brown could approach the little red-haired girl.

We're all really children when it comes to desire. Once you set aside all the poetry of romance, the caviar and champagne and candlelit dinners – once you set aside sex – what it all came down to was grade school: *Do you like me? Circle yes or no.*

Mitch carefully folded Valerie's adorable come-on and put it into his wallet behind his SAG card. He sighed. He did like Valerie. He would circle *yes*, he would call her right this minute and explore further this concept of *a good time* . . . if it wasn't for the tech and his affection for her.

Greg had known her for years, after all. She was the *woman of his dreams*, and all that. It wouldn't be fair for Mitch to just swoop in on Greg's lady-love, not after all the kindness the tech had shown him.

Mitch would like to tell Greg that he was about to miss his chance. He'd like to say, "There's a time limit on these things, my friend. You know that. If it's not me, it'll be someone else. You should make sure it's you."

But Greg would be offended, embarrassed. "Thanks for the advice, Mitch, but who are you to be telling me anything about relationships? You couldn't even keep your own high-strung wife above ground, now could you?

"You get paid for your pretty face. You're an actor. You're a damn good TTAMS operator. Be that. But don't let it go to your head. Don't let it make you think you can start talking to me like I'm a subscriber."

Greg might not say all that, but he'd think it. If Mitch dared to suggest that it was time for the Ops Director to step up, it would be detrimental to their easy-going friendship. Mitch didn't want that. Greg and Baker were the only non-showbiz friends he had, and he valued them.

So the actor decided it would be best to keep his mouth shut, to just let the whole thing ride. He pushed the *Pause* button again and waited for the next fan.

****

The elevator door opened and Valerie walked the few steps to her car. She reveled in her good mood. She sang out loud, *"Kitties and cats wanna do their thang–"*

"Been thinkin' 'bout lovin' since the school bell rang."

Out of the corner of her eye, Valerie caught movement. A man had pushed himself off of the pillar against which he had been leaning and was approaching. Valerie's hand froze on the door handle to her car, and fear coursed through her.

The top floor of the parking structure was private, reserved for TTAMS's management. Joyce's Porsche would've been there beside Valerie's S550, had she ever been onsite on a Friday night. There was Greg's Lexus a few spaces down. There was a guard in a booth, just around the corner.

Valerie wasn't afraid that she was about to be mugged, that no one would be able to hear her scream. She knew that the man that was walking up to her wasn't some junkie that had managed to slink in off the street. Someone had let this guy in to this level of the structure, just like someone had let Mitch Barlo onto the ops floor. Someone had given him the access code to the stairwell so that he could descend from the lobby.

Still Valerie felt fear. She recognized his voice.

Brett Cooke sauntered up and leaned against the Mercedes.

****

Within a month of his graduation from UCLA, Brett had landed an Assistant Payroll Accounting Manager job with a tech firm in Monterey. He'd said in the interview that he didn't know anything about computers, but he could add up the forty hours in a standard work-week. Brooke, the Senior Payroll Accounting Manager, had been charmed and had hired him immediately.

She was in her early forties and was too much of a professional to be overly charmed by a good-looking college kid, however – Brett's request for dinner and a movie had gotten him nowhere. But he liked the job well enough, and found that he was good at it. And there were plenty of non-management types on staff that didn't ascribe to Brooke's *don't play in your plate* work ethic. As in college, Brett Cooke had never wanted for a date.

It had been one of these girls, in fact, that had put Brett in mind of his odd college sweetheart again. He and Patty from Software Development, a statuesque redhead, had been lounging in bed on a Saturday morning, each perusing their own laptop, as is the par-for-the-course, post-coital practice in the modern world.

"You went to UCLA, right?" Patty asked.

"Yay, Bruins," Brett replied, not looking up. He was watching a quite entertaining video of animals, wild and domestic, bouncing on trampolines, to the accompaniment of House of Pain's *Jump Around.*

"Did you ever know Valerie Whitly?"

Brett looked up now, the hilarious goats and dogs forgotten. He blinked in surprise. Not a single original phrase came to his mind, so, non sequitur, he said, *"Excuse me, are you saying meow?"*

"What?"

"Never mind. What did you–"

"I said, did you ever know a girl named Valerie Whitly?" Patty turned her laptop around and showed Brett the article on Variety.com. *Now You Too Can Talk To a Movie Star.*

"Well, I'll be damned!"

You may indeed, if you get lucky, Valerie would've replied, à la Doc Holliday in *Tombstone.* But Patty just repeated, "Did you know her?"

"In passing," Brett replied. No need to bring up old girlfriends with present . . . whatever Patty was. *Not my girlfriend,* he thought. *Not like Valerie was.*

Patty wondered if that was how Brett thought of their after-work relationship – did he tell their co-workers that, yeah, he knew her, but it was *just in passing?* Even though they spent a few weekends a month in bed together? Patty didn't know whether she was hurt or relieved about that.

Brett took the laptop from her and read the article. "I knew Joyce Vinson, too. To say hi."

"Well, apparently, she's brilliant."

"Joyce?"

"No. Valerie Whitly. There was a piece about her system in *The Journal of Information Technology,* and one in *Cutter IT.* Now she's on Variety.com."

"She always was a movie fan," Brett said absently.

Patty squinted at him suspiciously, absorbed with reading about his college chum. He liked the movies; he always made a big deal out of making popcorn and choosing something special on a Friday night. It was the main reason that they didn't spend *every* weekend in bed together. He was cute and he was good, when a girl could pry his interest away from Netflix. Patty liked to go out, she liked to dance, to see and be seen. Watching movies, even with cute Brett, was not really a big thrill for her.

This Valerie Whitly was obviously a movie fan – she was making millions off of her fellow fans with her fascinating new service – so Patty knew that if she and Brett had been friends in college, they had no doubt shared the whole fan thing, and whatever else she had been of a mind to share with him. Patty knew that Brett was not being entirely forthcoming about how well he'd known the programmer.

"What a coincidence that you knew her. Just in passing of course."

"*I don't subscribe to coincidence, Corporal. I believe that, no matter how random some things might appear, there's still a plan.*" When the redhead just looked blankly at him, Brett said, "Come on, Patty. You didn't see *The A-Team? I love it when a plan comes together?* Bradley Cooper?"

Patty shook her head. She wasn't a movie fan, not in the slightest, not even of Bradley Cooper. Brett realized that this was probably the first time she'd ever read Variety.com; the story about Talk To a Movie Star had simply come up on her newsfeed for trending technology. She hadn't clicked on it because she was looking for news about the biz.

Patty took her laptop back and moved on to the next article.

But Brett didn't return to the funny animal antics on his own computer. He gazed at the paused video, not seeing it, recalling instead his former girlfriend, how she'd dumped him out of the blue because he hadn't deleted the dating apps on his phone. Her rationale had seemed insane, unreasonable. One minute, Valerie had been so completely in love with him, and then, to give it all up for such a stupid reason in the next heartbeat . . . It was just nuts. Brett surely would've uninstalled the apps if she'd just asked.

284

At the time, he'd figured that the sudden ending was probably all for the best. Breaking up with him over such an innocent thing had seemed a completely crazy thing to do, but Joyce had said Val was under a lot of pressure, looking forward to starting a career at 20th Century Fox. Brett really hadn't had time to miss her, anyway, because he'd moved to Monterey. It probably never would've worked at the time.

But now . . .

"Have you heard this one?" Brett asked himself, as much as he asked Patty. *"Do you ever do this, you think back on all the times you've had with someone and you just replay it in your head over and over again and you look for those first signs of trouble?"*

Patty shook her head, clicked on a link. "Nope. What's that from?"

But Brett didn't answer her, nor did she notice. Patty was more interested in the latest in tech than whatever stupid movie he was quoting, and Brett was lost in nostalgic memories of college and Valerie Whitly.

This service she'd started — well, that was certainly right up her alley. Brett had never known anyone with as depthless a store of movie quotes and trivia. It had always been fun to banter the lines, famous and obscure, with her. Brett had initially suspected that his ability to keep up, quoting the ones no one had ever heard of as easily as *Here's looking at you, kid* — at first he had been convinced that this odd little talent had been the sole basis of Valerie's affection for him.

After a while, her fondness had seemed to grow into love and devotion, but then she'd abruptly ended it. Over the phone, no less. Brett had gone back to his original supposition — Valerie had enjoyed their little game, but now that her life was taking off, she was done. He'd tried a few more phone calls, but she hadn't responded, so he'd let her go. There were, as the saying goes, plenty of other fish in the sea, and Brett Cooke was not the type to keep casting his hook for one that had gotten away.

He'd dated plenty of girls since graduation, but looking back, Brett realized that not a single one of them had been even remotely like Valerie. *I, myself, am strange and unusual.* Like Patty, all the women he'd been involved with had been unimaginative, focused narrowly on their careers. Brett Cooke had meant nothing to any of them but a weekend's diversion from their ambitions.

From the piece on Variety.com, it was clear that Valerie, too, had concentrated on her career. Through her own creative genius, she had become an obscene success by bringing the thing she loved best to all the other legions of fans just like herself. Brett thought the service sounded like the most innovative, ingenious thing ever invented.

But he didn't think that he wanted to sign up and talk to a movie star.

As he sat there in bed beside Patty from Software Development, Brett knew exactly what it was that he wanted to do. He wanted to talk to Valerie again.

****

A new sense of purpose seized him. On Monday, he told his supervisor that his mother had had an accident. He had to return home immediately. When Brooke expressed concern, he said it was nothing life-threatening – just a little slip in the garden, resulting in a broken ankle. He would be gone at least until the following week.

"Take as much time as you need," Brooke replied, and gave him the rest of the day off with pay. Even though she wouldn't go out with him – she was his boss, and that kind of thing was frowned upon – it didn't mean that she hadn't noticed how cute he was.

Brett drove home and surprised his mom, who had not slipped in the garden at all. The next morning, he called the LA offices of Talk To a Movie Star. He got a pleasant computerized voice that told him politely that if he would like to talk to Joyce Vinson, he should press 6885.

"Joyce Vinson's office." A man's voice, real, not electronic.

"If it's at all possible, I'd like to talk to Ms. Vinson. My name's Brett Cooke. We went to college–"

"Do you have an appointment, Mr. Cooke?"

"You're telling me that I need an appointment for just a phone call with Ms Vinson?"

"She's a very busy woman, Mr. Cooke."

"I know, but I'm an old friend. I'm sure she'll want to speak to me."

The man on the other end of the line wasn't impressed. "I can make you an appointment."

Brett asked, "What's your name?"

"My name's Marvin, Mr. Cooke. I'm Ms Vinson's assistant. She's very busy, and if you don't have an appointment . . ." Marvin sighed heavily. "I'm sorry, but I can't just be patching through everyone that gets it into their head that they want to talk to the CEO of TTAMS. Even if they are old friends." *She'd fire me if I did.* "Now, if you'd like to leave a message, you have my assurance that she'll get it."

"Watch a lot of movies, do ya, Marvin? What with working at Talk To a Movie Star and all?"

Marvin sincerely didn't have time for this, but he couldn't just hang up on the guy. "I'd consider myself a fan, yes."

"Ever see *Escape From New York?*"

"Of course, Mr. Cooke. I'm from New York."

"Then you're a long way from home, my friend." Brett giggled. "You remember the part – Brain wants to see the president, but the Duke's henchman doesn't want to let him in?"

"Yes." Joyce's assistant looked at his watch, wondering how he could politely get rid of Ms Vinson's persistent college buddy. Marvin had graduated from UCLA Law, just like the CEO had, and sometimes he asked himself how it was that he had wound up spending several hours of the work day answering her phone, playing secretary. *For the money, that's how.*

"But the henchman *does* let him in," talky Mr. Cooke was saying. "Do you remember why, Marvin?" When he didn't respond immediately, Brett continued. "The henchman lets Brain in because if he didn't, and the Duke had wanted him to be let in, then he knew that the Duke would be mighty angry. And making the Duke angry was not the thing to do."

"Are you threatening me, Mr. Cooke?"

"Not in the slightest, Marvin. I'm just reminding you of something we both already know. Now your boss certainly doesn't look like Isaac Hayes – she's just the cutest little brown-eyed thing I ever did see."

She's no Valerie Whitly, Marvin thought.

"But Joyce's certainly got a temper like the Duke of New York. Wouldn't you agree, Marvin? And if she finds out that you gave *me* the runaround . . . I think you might just find yourself on the slow train back home. *No sleep 'til Brooklyn."* Brett paused. "Of course, if she's really in a meeting or something, I'd be happy to get her voicemail."

Just like the Duke of New York's henchman, Marvin weighed the odds. This guy certainly seemed to know the boss's temperament. Maybe he was an old boyfriend or something. Maybe she wouldn't mind the interruption. Marvin wouldn't just send him through unannounced, however. That would just be suicide. This guy might know Joyce, but she still might not want to be bothered with him.

He told Brett to hold and buzzed her office. "This better be good," Joyce said. It was what she always said.

"I have a Mr. Cooke on the line for you."

"Who?" Irritably.

Oh shit. But Marvin was in it now. There was no turning back. "A Mr. Brett Cooke. He says he went to college with—"

"Oh, my God! Brett!" Joyce's squeal expressed more girlish enthusiasm than Marvin would've believed she possessed. Even when she'd been a girl. "What the hell are you waiting for, Marvin? Send him through!"

****

Busy executive or not, the CEO dropped everything and made time to have lunch with her old college friend. He would've been surprised had it been any other way. Joyce still loved him, even if Valerie did not. Brett aimed to see about changing that, too.

He found Joyce to be smugly happy with her success, even more beautiful and polished than she'd been in college. She'd given him the bad news that Valerie was unable to join them for lunch with blithe unconcern, citing the owner's many pressing responsibilities. She'd ended on an upbeat, "Some other time, I'm sure."

Joyce took Brett on a tour of the TTAMS facility, pointing out Valerie's glass-walled office at the top of the stairs. "Our hometown girl's made good," she said proudly.

"Maybe I should just run up there and say hi."

Brett put one foot on the bottom riser, but Joyce quickly stopped him, placing her hand firmly on his arm. She shook her head. "Val doesn't want to see you, Brett. Not yet. You know how she is. Give her some time. She just found out that you're back—"

"I'm not back, Jo. I'm just here for a week."

"Maybe next time, then."

Joyce was counting on the brevity of Brett's visit. She knew that she could keep him away from Valerie, put him off for a few days by citing her busyness. Eventually he'd have to return to Monterey. He'd give up.

But then again, maybe he wouldn't.

Joyce sensed a new maturity about her old college friend. He was still just as fine as he wanted to be – heads had turned when he'd walked through the lobby and enthusiastically hugged her – but he seemed more focused than he'd been in school. Driven. Brett Cooke wanted something.

By the time they'd finished their second lunch together, Joyce knew what it was. This wasn't just a run of the mill visit home for Brett. He'd come back specifically to see his ex-girlfriend.

****

Brett's holiday stretched from a week to two. He bought a new suit – because he hadn't packed one – and on a whim, he interviewed for a Payroll Accounting Manager position at Bancorp on Wilshire Boulevard. He was not at all surprised when they offered him the position. He didn't know anything more about banking than he did about computers, but he could still count to forty. The Personnel Manager was a woman, and he was still charming.

There were trade-offs. This job paid less than the one he held at the tech company, but he would be the accounting manager, not an assistant. The Wilshire branch didn't have a lot of room for advancement, but on the other hand, his life had been going nowhere in Monterey, and he'd been looking for a job when he'd found that one and this one, so Brett figured that he could always look somewhere else if he felt the need to move up.

The main draw of the new job was the idea of being back home. Driving around in the heat and the traffic, Brett realized that there had been something absent from his life in Monterey. He saw that he'd missed LA; he'd missed his mom and the house in which he'd grown up. He'd missed Joyce. But most of all, Brett knew that he'd missed Valerie.

He accepted the position at Bancorp. He left his car parked in his mother's driveway and flew back to Monterey. He didn't give two weeks' notice because he knew Brooke wouldn't give him a bad reference. He packed his belongings into a U-Haul truck, told Patty it had been fun, that maybe he'd see her around sometime, if he ever came back up the coast.

Brett had a new job waiting for him. That was all he'd needed to induce him to leave home after graduation, and it was all he needed to make him come back. That, and his desire to look up his ex-girlfriend.

Their relationship had ended so ridiculously, so abruptly, over nothing. There hadn't even been an argument, no tears. Just, "I don't want to see you anymore." Nothing had been said that couldn't be unsaid. Nothing had been said at all. It should be easy . . .

Brett reasoned that he and Valerie had both grown and matured. Surely, nowadays she would laugh at the unfounded idea that he'd been cheating on her in college, just because he'd been texting a few girls.

Adult women didn't worry about such adolescent things. Adult men didn't bother with them: all those apps were long gone from his phone.

If Brett could just talk to her, he was confident that they would be able to take up just where they'd left off.

****

Brett had carefully watched Joyce press the buttons on the door to the stairwell. He found that her code was the same as her phone extension, so it was easy for him to remember. If his old pal wasn't going to get him in to see Valerie, then he would just use a little subterfuge.

Brett had waited in the parking garage for a long time. He'd amused himself with games and videos on his phone until the battery had died. But it was all worth it. Valerie was just as lovely as he remembered.

She was shocked to see him. Dumbstruck. He smiled. *"Hello? Is there anybody in there? Do you remember me? I'm the one from the registry office."*

Pink's lyrics from *The Wall* played immediately in Valerie's head. *Tell me, is something eluding you, Sunshine? Is this not what you expected to see?*

She certainly had not expected to see Brett. She'd never wanted to see Brett again. *Goddamned Joyce!* No one else could've let him in here.

Valerie felt a gush of warmth throughout her being. Brett looked exactly the same, just as alluring as ever – sure, young Mitch Barlo as Shamus was cute – he had reminded her of Brett. But this actually *was* Brett, and seeing him took Valerie's breath away. Memories of the passions they'd shared caused her nerve endings to ache; memories of the love she'd had for him spoke to Valerie, encouraged her to take him into her arms, to crush him to her, to kiss him.

But she didn't do it, because the warmth changed, turned icy, from all good to all bad. It was like the scene in *Indiana Jones and the Last Crusade,* when Donovan at last drinks from what he believes is the Holy Grail. He closes his eyes, smiles for a second. Then there is a change. He opens his eyes.

Just like Donovan, Valerie heard the ominous music signaling that something was amiss. The fire of passion suddenly turned into the sting of betrayal, breathless desire to the breathlessness of a panic attack. Valerie didn't gasp in pain, like Donovan did; her face didn't morph into a Christopher Lloyd-looking skull. Her body didn't crumble to dust. But her initial thrilled reaction to seeing Brett curdled, nonetheless. With that reaction, she had *chosen poorly.*

Valerie's soul had been immersed in a hot lagoon of carnal memory for a split second upon seeing Brett, but now the bottom dropped out, bringing on the boiling, swirling maelstrom of an emotional whirlpool: hope dragged down by fear, love and longing soured by betrayal and resentment. Valerie was suddenly drowning in it.

Insanely, she thought of *The Odyssey* – the only book she'd enjoyed reading in high school, because she couldn't find a decent movie version of it. The goddess Athena would frequently amplify the beauty or strength of Odysseus or Telemachus or Penelope in order to inspire those around them – and so it seemed with Brett, as if some god had touched him. He couldn't possibly look this good, but he did.

He was dressed casually, in black jeans and a faded blue flannel shirt. But the plain overhead lights seemed to mystically reflect the blue back into his eyes until they glowed. His black hair was longer, curly around the ears, the way it had been in college, before he'd cut it to a more businesslike length for graduation and entry into the workaday world. His smile was as flawless as ever.

As if reading Valerie's mind, Brett said softly, *"You found me beautiful once . . . "* His words, a quote from *Army of Darkness,* cut her to the bone.

But she composed herself, ignored his stunning splendor. Coldly, she supplied Ash's next line. *"Honey, you got real ugly."*

Brett's smile faltered for a split-second, but then bloomed anew. He'd thought of another movie. *"You know I love ya, baby. I wouldn't leave ya. It wasn't my fault!"*

Brett's John Belushi impression was dead-on. The unforgettable scene from *The Blues Brothers* materialized in Valerie's mind, and despite the agony of seeing him again, Carrie Fisher's affronted amazement seized her. *"You miserable slug! You think you can talk your way out of this? You betrayed me."*

"No, I didn't. Honest . . . I ran out of gas. I . . . I had a flat tire. I didn't have enough money for cab fare. My tux didn't come back from the cleaners. An old friend came in from out of town. Someone stole my car. There was an earthquake. A terrible flood. Locusts! It wasn't my fault, I swear to God!"

Brett wiggled his eyebrows, and seeing as he was so much better looking than Belushi, it almost worked. Just like Carrie Fisher, Valerie almost relented; she almost forgave him. She actually thought, *Oh, Brett . . . Brett, honey . . .*

But then another line from *Army of Darkness* occurred to her: *It's a trick. Get an axe.*

Valerie opened the door and slid into her luxurious car. She put the key into the ignition, started the powerful beast, lowered the window. She said to Brett, *"Fuck you, fuck you, fuck you; you're cool; and fuck you. I'm out!"*

Brett was not daunted. He reached back in time, back to when films were still in black and white. He quoted *The Apartment. "Do you realize what you're doing? Not to me, but to yourself? Normally, it takes years to work your way up to the twenty-seventh floor. But it only takes thirty seconds to be out on the street again. You dig?"*

Valerie grinned humorlessly. *"I don't know what to do about the depression and the inflation and the Russians and the crime in the street,* Brett. *All I know is that first you've got to get mad."*

"Christ, Val. It's been a long time. I didn't do anything wrong. You can't still be—"

"But I am. *I'm as mad as hell, and I'm not gonna take this anymore."*

"I miss you, Val. That's why I moved back to LA, because I thought we could . . . Why won't you just let me talk to you for a minute?" Valerie's face remained set, and Brett realized that real words, his own words, weren't working either. He was losing.

He switched from the movies to the world of music. *"I'll give you candy, give you diamonds, give you pills, give you anything you want, hundred dollar bills, I'll even let you watch the shows you want to see . . ."*

Valerie's eyebrows went up. The next line was *Just marry me, marry me, marry me.* Brett had decided that he wanted to talk, surely, but he wasn't going to go that far. Valerie told him, *"You're a bum! And that's all you'll ever be, a bum!"*

That one threw Brett. There were many movies wherein characters were called bums. But then he had it. Valerie was referencing *Stripes,* one of the last movies they'd watched together.

"Well, that hurts, ma'am. And I don't think—"

Valerie cut him off, made the line hers. *"I don't think I want to take your abuse. And I know I don't want to take you and your luggage to the airport. How about that, huh?"* Valerie put the car in reverse.

"I'm gonna say my piece, Val. If you won't listen to me now . . ." Brett grinned. *"Did you say 'over?' Nothing is over until we decide it is! Was it over when the Germans bombed Pearl Harbor? Hell no!"*

He couldn't expect her to just throw herself into his arms, now could he? It had been a long time. He'd surprised her. He'd let her think about it. He'd said enough for tonight.

Frankly, my dear, I don't give a damn, came to Valerie's mind, but that one was just too much of a cliché. Sometimes words, even the immortal words of the movies, were unnecessary. Sometimes a gesture was enough, and this was one of those times. Valerie closed the window and backed out of the parking space.

"That went well," Brett said to her taillights.

It was the strangest conversation he'd ever had, with Valerie or anyone else. Even his mother would've broken out of movie quotes and interjected some of her own feelings, had the situation been similar. If her son had displeased her in some way, if it was the first time she'd seen him in all these years . . . Geri Cooke would've let some of herself show.

But not Valerie. The movies had always spoken with the utmost eloquence *to* her, so she invariably let them speak *for* her. That was a part of her unique charm.

Brett left the TTAMS facility. He was not too disappointed. Tomorrow was, after all, another day.

****

Almost too late, Valerie stopped the car. Blinded by tears, she hadn't seen the homeless woman, pushing her shopping cart full of cans across the driveway in front of the garage. It wasn't a baby carriage, like in *Speed*, and unlike Sandra Bullock, Valerie hadn't hit it or her. The impeccably responsive Pre-Safe had sounded and Valerie had stomped on the brakes. The Mercedes had saved the homeless pedestrian as well as the wealthy driver.

Now there would've been some bad publicity. *Owner of TTAMS involved in hit-and-run with vagrant . . .*

Valerie thought she might've run, too, even if she had hit the old woman. She couldn't interact with authority at the minute, with any strangers. She was a mess, a basket case. The only thought in her mind was to flee, to escape, to get away from Brett and all the memories that had returned with him.

Valerie gripped the steering wheel ruthlessly, until all the color drained from her hands. *I have to calm down.* She had to run, it was true, but she couldn't be killing anyone in the process. The bag lady moved on and she slid the big car forward sedately into the street.

Valerie and Joyce still lived in the guesthouse of former District Attorney Vinson's Beverly Hills mansion. Though young and wealthy, neither wanted to live without the other, and Joyce's parents were happy to have them.

By the time she neared home, Valerie was speeding again. She slewed the Benz into the driveway like William Holden running from the repo men in *Sunset Boulevard*, and then threw the car into park before it was fully stopped, eliciting a jarring jerk from the transmission. The need to run, to escape, overtook Valerie again, and she fled inside. Now she was home. There was no place else to run. Surely, Brett wouldn't follow her here . . .

Mercifully, the guesthouse was dark. Joyce wasn't there. But she wasn't out on the town with Brett this time, now was she? She'd told him where to find his ex-girlfriend, then had gone on to The Conga Room by herself.

Valerie left all the lights off and locked herself inside her bedroom. She was having a full-blown panic attack now, her breath dragging in and out in ragged, hyperventilating gasps. Valerie was sure that she would pass out if she didn't get control of her breathing, so she willed herself to slow it. At last it came almost normally, broken only by small pants.

Brett had looked so beautiful, and the emotions tore at Valerie's heart, her mind, her soul – the pain, the desire, the yearning, the dread, all overarched by a nagging indecision. She had to talk to somebody about Brett's sudden reappearance, about how it was making her feel. She felt as if she would lose her mind if she didn't.

She knew it had to have been Joyce that let him into the garage. Joyce, who had kept Brett away from her for so long, had at last succumbed to his wheedling. A stain of betrayal colored Valerie's mind at her friend's actions, but then she thought, *Maybe Joyce is right. Maybe I should let Brett come back.* The uncontrollable stirring of desire that she had felt when she saw him standing there . . . *Ah, Brett, honey . . .*

But Valerie had controlled it then and she would control it now. She didn't want to see Brett. *I never want to see Brett again!* Joyce was being uncharacteristically emotional, sentimental, allowing him to sneak up on her like that. Joyce was wrong. There could be no reconciliation, no happily-ever-after. Brett had betrayed her.

But he'd just wanted to talk, and what was the harm in that? He'd looked so good . . .

No . . .

Valerie had to talk to Joyce, even though she had been the one that had let Brett back in. Joyce would help her, Joyce would listen. She would know what to do, she would handle it.

Joyce didn't answer her phone.

Valerie's anxiety ratcheted up a notch. She had to talk to someone, and immediately, before she lost her breath again, before she lost her mind.

Eddie . . .

But Valerie had seldom talked to Eddie about Brett. It had been Eddie and her obsession with him that had allowed her to forget about

294

Brett in the first place. *Sonny's Diner,* his movies; going to Canada and meeting him, all their conversations since . . .

Whenever Valerie saw Eddie's picture, whenever she talked to him, it drove all thoughts of Brett from her mind. He knew about Brett, of course, but she didn't want him to see her all upset about him now. She couldn't talk to Eddie about Brett.

But Valerie had to talk to someone. She had to free these awful, conflicting emotions. She had to hear what someone else thought about what she ought to do, someone calmer. Someone kind.

But who? Valerie had never been able to talk much to her mother about anything, and distraught romantic drama would just embarrass her dad. Her parents had never even heard about the pain and betrayal Valerie had suffered at the hands of Brett Cooke. All Denny and Sophia knew was that things hadn't lasted between their daughter and the nice young man that they had met, only the one time, on graduation day.

For Valerie to bring Brett up now, in her present state, would only confuse her parents, make them worry. To call them out of the blue, crying and distraught over the sudden reappearance of some old boyfriend . . . They would think she was crazy, unhinged, unstable, just like Aunt Elise had been.

Beautiful, tough, fun Elise. She would've understood.

But she hadn't been so tough in the end, had she? Still, Valerie knew that her aunt would've understood.

Valerie hurt. She was distressed, damn near hysterical. She had spackled over Brett's betrayal with her obsession with Eddie, with TTAMS and work. She had buried her feelings for her gorgeous ex-boyfriend so deeply that his inexplicable, surprise reappearance had caused them to erupt into her mind with all the force, all the confusion and destruction of Vesuvius.

But for the first time in her life, the memory of her Aunt Elise didn't add to Valerie's woes. She recalled her mother's sister only with fondness now, as a caring and loving free-spirit, the light of her childhood. Her tragic end . . . The agony once associated with that memory no longer afflicted Valerie, because she had let it all go.

Valerie had been freed, because she had commiserated with the sorrows of another wounded soul. She had shared her own terrible childhood memories with . . .

Mitch Barlo.

Valerie grabbed her laptop off the desk, and scooted with it onto her bed, her back pressed into the corner where the two walls of her bedroom met. She had been in just this spot, remote in hand, cobbling together sad movie clips and contemplating suicide, when Joyce had found her, after she had discovered Brett's betrayal.

Valerie felt the same hopeless, empty confusion now, but within the bleak hollowness, she now sensed the tiny, hard, bright gleam of hope. Mitch would help her. She could talk to Mitch, and his sympathetic, thoughtful responses would help her to sort through the devastating tangle of fear and doubt, love and longing that gripped her. Mitch would listen, help Valerie to unravel the confusion, stymie the pain. Mitch would help her to get a leash on her out-of-control emotions; he would help her to decide what to do about Brett and his sudden reappearance . . .

Welcome back, Denise! Would you like to reconnect with Mitch Barlo (MB426312)? (y/n?)

Valerie prayed that the actor was still online. He never came in at shift change, but he always worked until the next shift started. She had left him chatting happily away with Maisie from Poughkeepsie or Betty from Philly. He had to still be there.

Valerie looked at the time in the corner of the screen. Barely forty-five minutes had gone by since she had stuck the pink Post-It onto the glass in the instructor booth. She felt as if a lifetime had passed since then, a lifetime of despair and indecision.

Valerie had been feeling frisky only a short three-quarters of an hour ago, anticipating a friendship with good-looking Mitch Barlo, what could be a new and fun adventure. Now all those playful feelings had fled. She *needed* Mitch now. He would help her.

At the bottom of the TTAMS welcome screen were the customary links, common to all internet companies. Beside *Contact Us* and *Help Center* and *Investor Relations*, at the end of the list after *Jobs at TTAMS* and *For Employees*, Valerie clicked on the link that said *Maintenance.*

A simple box appeared, and Valerie typed *000001; execute,* then entered her password.

The user-friendly, multi-colored facade of Windows disappeared from Valerie's laptop. The screen went black and she was transported to a place that only code-monkeys understood: TTAMS's programming interface.

TTAMS [Version 3.6.5]
© Copyright 2015 TTAMS, Inc.

Y:\ system> Welcome, Valerie . . .
Valerie typed *Locate MB426312*
Y:\system> OpsPrepCent10T
Valerie typed *MB426312, session override* and hit *Enter* again.

A window opened and showed her Mitch's face; he blinked in surprise. His subscriber was sent a blue screen and *We're sorry, but the star you've chosen is unavailable at the moment. Please try again shortly.* But try as she might, the subscriber wouldn't get MB426312 again. She'd just have to pick someone else to chat with tonight. TTAMS's owner needed to talk to this particular incarnation of Mitch Barlo at the moment.

"Hi, Valerie," he said with a smile. "What can I do for you?"

She doesn't waste any time. First a note and now a face-to-face. Mitch wondered how he was going to figure out a way, Cyrano-like, to talk up his buddy Greg to her.

Valerie sighed. The fear that Mitch might've been offline vanished. Just knowing that he was there, that she'd found him, made her feel calmer already. "I need to talk to you, Mitch. I've had . . . I've had a terrible shock."

Concern marred the famous brow. "Are you all right?"

"No. I'm not all right at all."

"What happened?"

"My ex-boyfriend showed up. Joyce had to have let him in, just like you–"

"Joyce didn't let me in, Valerie. I've never even met Joyce."

Valerie shook her head. "No, not like that. Not on the ops floor. He was in the parking garage, waiting for me. It's a secure facility. Joyce had to have given him the code, so he could come down from the lobby. She never would've let him on the ops floor, so he didn't take the elevator . . ."

Mitch waited. Valerie's eyes were red from crying. She seemed distracted, afraid. It was clear that something bad had happened to her. When she didn't go on, Mitch prompted gently, "Did this guy hurt you?"

Valerie barked a single note of harsh laughter. A tear ran down her face. "Yes."

Now Mitch was more than just concerned. "Are you all right, Valerie? Do you want me to call the cops? Where are you?"

"The cops?" Valerie was confused. Then she laughed without humor. "Oh, no, Mitch. It's nothing like that. I'm sorry. When you asked, did he hurt me . . . He didn't assault me or anything like that."

Mitch relaxed a little bit. Valerie Whitly hadn't been raped on the parking garage concrete by some ex from her past. But she was still distraught. Mitch asked her again where she was.

"I'm at home. I had to get out of there, Mitch. I had to get away from him. Joyce isn't here. I had to talk to somebody . . ."

"Tell me what happened, Valerie. Who is this guy? What did he say to you?"

Valerie exhaled a long shuddery breath. "His name is Brett Cooke. We dated in college. I was in love with him . . ." Another tear traced the first down Valerie's face, then more silently followed. "He betrayed me. I thought that he loved me . . . But I found out that he'd never stopped talking to other women, texting them."

It suddenly seemed ridiculous to Valerie, trivial, to be saying all this to a man. Joyce had understood, but Mitch just looked at her blankly. But it was immaterial what Brett had done. All that mattered was the pain it had caused.

"It hurt so bad!" Valerie sobbed. "And seeing him tonight . . . I felt it all again, the same kind of dumb surprise, like when I read those texts." The tears flowed freely now.

Just what this guy had done to destroy Valerie so utterly was unclear to Mitch. Something about texts?

"He was cheating on you?" Mitch asked uncertainly. "You caught him talking to her? Texting her?"

"It wasn't just one girl. It was hundreds of girls."

"Really?" Mitch was immediately sorry he'd said that, but his curiosity had gotten the better of him.

"He had all these dating apps on his phone. He talked to all these girls . . . He said they were just friends, that he didn't do anything with them . . ." Valerie sobbed. "It hurts so much to see him again, Mitch!"

So maybe this guy hadn't been cheating on her. Maybe he had been, or maybe she had just imagined it, *assumed* that he was. Regardless, seeing him again had shaken Valerie.

"I told him I didn't want to see him again. I told him to go to Vegas without me."

"You're going to Vegas?"

"Not now, Mitch. I found out that Brett was still texting girls the day we graduated from college. We were supposed to go to Vegas that afternoon. I took off, I told him that he had plenty of other girls to go to Vegas with him. I told him I didn't want to see him anymore. He tried to call back—"

"You broke up with him over the phone?"

Valerie pursed her lips, her sadness momentarily forgotten. "You sound just like Joyce, Mitch. Yes, I broke up with him over the phone. No, I didn't let him explain." The tears welled up again. "I didn't want to see him again!" The tears fell. Then Valerie suddenly, softly confessed, "I almost killed myself because of Brett, Mitch."

"Ah, Valerie, honey. I doesn't sound like such a big—"

"Now he's back!" she shrieked. "Now he wants to talk to me. I don't want to feel like this again, Mitch! This is how I felt when Elise died, and then again when I found out it was suicide."

Valerie calmed down a little, her voice lowered; but she didn't realize that she had just outed herself as Denise from Riverside to her confessor.

"When I read all those texts on his phone, I wanted to kill myself. It hurt so much. I almost did it, but Joyce . . . I remembered that I still had Joyce." Valerie paused, swiped at the tears on her face. When she spoke again, the hysterical upset was back. "I don't want to feel like this anymore, Mitch! It's the same way I felt in Canada, after Eddie . . ."

Valerie blinked. Her mouth was open, but no words came out. A faraway look shrouded her round, tear-bright eyes. She repeated, "After Eddie . . ." and Mitch waited for her to say it.

But Valerie caught herself. "Never mind about that." *Christ, I almost did it again. I have to stop talking about Eddie!*

Valerie put her hands over her face. The sobs wracked her. "I don't know what I'm gonna do, Mitch!"

The actor was dumbstruck by Valerie's helpless weeping. He struggled to find words to comfort her, and while he searched his mind for them, Mitch suddenly remembered that Greg Castro had a keeper on his boss's TTAMS profile, that he was no doubt monitoring their session right now.

Mitch had never been comfortable with the tech's secret presence during his talks with Valerie, even though it had seemed harmless at first. Greg just wanted Valerie to be grateful for hooking her in to someone who could tell her what she wanted to know about Eddie Forbes. Greg wanted to hear her ask the question. That was innocent enough.

But after Valerie had dropped the bombshell about having met Eddie, about still talking to him . . . And tonight, as she'd exposed all her naked, confused vulnerability . . . Mitch didn't think it was right that Greg should be learning about quite so many of his boss's secrets.

Valerie had come to Mitch with her problems, not her Ops Director. She trusted him. She would be crushed if she knew that Mitch had allowed a third party to listen in, that it had been one of her employees, no less.

Valerie continued to cry piteously. Mitch didn't know enough about how the system worked to cut off Greg's surreptitious surveillance. He thought he could perhaps hit the mute button so Valerie couldn't hear him tell Greg to log off; but then maybe Greg wouldn't be able to hear him, either.

Mitch wanted to comfort Valerie, but he also wanted to make sure that Greg Castro wasn't a party to any more of her sorrows. At last he came up with the solution. It was true that he didn't know how to cut Greg off and still keep the connection to Valerie, but there was more than one way to deafen the tech's ear to their conversation.

Mitch hit the *Pause* key – it would freeze his image on Valerie's screen, if she should stop crying, take her hands away from her face, and look at him again. He quickly took the pink Post-It Note out his wallet. He unpaused the screen, picked up his phone, and sent Valerie a text.

He heard a muffled beep through his monitor. Mitch was counting on the idea that, even in the throes of grief, Valerie was a modern girl. She would be powerless not to respond to the little rectangular tyrant and find out who was communicating with her, because the habit of doing so was ingrained. Answering one's cellphone, come hell, high water, or heartache, had become almost instinctual to 21st century man.

Valerie took her hands from her face. She sniffled, set her laptop aside, so she could reach somewhere off camera for her beckoning phone.

Mitch's text read, *I'm sorry, Valerie. All of a sudden, my sound went off. I can't hear you.*

Valerie retrieved her laptop, increased the gain on the mike. "Can you hear me now?"

Mitch could hear her perfectly, but he shook his head. Voicelessly, he mouthed, "Can you hear me?"

"No." Valerie shook her head. "Goddamned bugs."

Before she could switch over to text-only – Mitch knew that Greg could still read what she typed – he sent another message to Valerie's phone.

I'm sorry the system is acting up. I really want to talk to you about all this.

Just log off and call me. Valerie waved goodbye, and logged off herself.

Mitch's screen went blue. He said, "Sorry, Boss." He hit the *Pause* key before TTAMS could sent him another subscriber, then he logged out entirely. He felt like some kind of suspicious Luddite, but to be completely sure that Greg Castro could no longer hear him, Mitch stepped out of the booth to call Valerie.

"Thanks for listening, Mitch." Valerie paused, exhaled another long sigh. For a second, he thought she had herself under control, but then he could hear the tears again when she repeated, "I just don't know what I'm gonna do!"

"Look, Valerie. I don't want to talk to you on the phone." *It's almost as uncomfortable as over a bugged TTAMS link.* "I feel bad about you being there all alone. You shouldn't be alone. Will you come up to my house?"

"I'm not in any shape to drive, Mitch. I almost hit a bag lady coming out of the parking garage." Valerie tried to laugh, but Mitch could still hear the tears. "I'm a mess."

Mitch smiled. "You don't have to drive, Valerie. Text me your address. I'll send a limo."

****

Mitch put on his shades and flipped the hood up on his sweatshirt. As he slid down the hall and out the back door, he noted with relief that Greg's office was dark. Mitch was sure he'd get an earful for apparently bailing on a tearful Valerie Whitly, but he was glad it wasn't going to be tonight. Mitch wasn't sure exactly what he'd say to his friend about his newfound reservations on the whole stalking-the-boss issue, and he had other things on his mind at the moment. Mitch would, as Ronny Prince often put it, *burn that bridge* when he came to it.

Mitch paused in the secret darkness of the alley behind TTAMS's headquarters and called the limousine service. He ordered one for himself and had one sent to Valerie's house in Beverly Hills, as if he was calling a Yellow Cab.

Ronny Prince deemed himself the King of Hollywood, and when he started representing Mitch Barlo, he'd taken the young actor aside and taught him the precepts of what he called *How Not to Fuck Up in This Town 101.*

"First of all, don't screw the help. That includes all of them. Script girls, fans; strippers, waitresses. When they figure out that they're not gonna be Mrs. Mitch Barlo, they decide to talk, and they don't ever say anything nice. You don't have to slum it, my son. There are plenty of models and actresses that would give their front seat in hell for a little piece of you. And they're professionals, most of them. They know how to keep their pretty little mouths shut."

Mitch had taken Ronny's dating advice, taken it too far. No script girls or strippers for the Oscar-nominee. Just one pill-popping actress.

"Secondly, like the song says, *nobody walks in LA,* Mitch. Neither do you drive. Too many fans, too many photographers deciding they want to follow you. Too many cops wanting to pull you over, thinking they'll make a name for themselves if you're drunk. *Hey, what might we find if we search Mitch Barlo's car?* And no cabs, either. Cabdrivers talk more than whores.

"If you want to go anywhere in this town, my son, be it Schwab's or the Cinerama Dome, do yourself a favor and call a limo."

"They tore Schwab's down, Ronny."

"It's just an expression–"

"A nod to the Hollywood of yesteryear, right? When men were men–"

"And stars took limousines. And you're my smart boy, aren't you, Mitch? You know Uncle Ronny knows wherein he speaks. Think how much better off Lindsay would've been, and Kiefer and Paris, and Shia and Mel, and *Christ,* the list goes on and on! How much better off would they all have been, my son, how unsullied and more successful their careers, if they would've just called a fucking limo?"

"You're the boss, Ronny."

"No, you're the boss, Mitch. *I've got the brains, you've got the looks . . . Let's make lots of money . . .*"

Mitch didn't recognize the song, as he'd only been about four years old when it was released. Ronny went up to the DJ booth, and Mitch watched him hand the kid a twenty to play his request. Mitch would forever afterward remember the Pet Shop Boys' tune, because it summed up Ronny Prince's philosophy, and in their long, profitable association, Ronny had never steered his famous client wrong. He was the biggest agent on the West Coast, after all.

With the exception of the Uber Greg had called for him once, Mitch Barlo took a limo everywhere he went.

****

But if the movie star in Mitch expected Valerie to be impressed, he was mistaken. Dennis Whitly was a rock *legend;* his daughter had rode in more than a few long, black, tinted-glassed Cadillacs. She knew that it was unnecessary to tip the driver, or even speak to him. She alit from the car and climbed the slate steps to the big house without a backward glance.

The only thought in Valerie's mind was relief. Mitch would help her. They would talk and he would help her to banish all the feelings of painful confusion engendered by Brett's return.

Mitch felt a flood of warm fondness for Valerie, for Denise from Riverside, as she hurried up to meet him. Even tear-stained and disheveled, she was lovely. He sensed that she was comforted a little,

302

just by seeing him. A calmness settled in her frantic eyes, and Mitch felt needed. Useful. These were things he hadn't felt in a long time.

It was as if the two of them were dear old friends, long separated, glad to see each other. Mitch was relieved that she was all right; Valerie was just grateful that he was there. Like Ashley and Melanie's reunion scene in *Gone With the Wind,* they smiled, they embraced. Mitch kissed her lightly on the cheek.

"I'm so glad you could come," he said simply.

"I'm so glad you invited me," Valerie replied.

Mitch put his arm around her shoulders. Valerie put hers around his waist, and they entered the house.

****

When the keeper alerted Greg Castro that Valerie had again logged on to TTAMS, he was at the little dive bar around the corner from the office with Morris Baker.

Greg looked at his phone. He quickly thought up excuses to dump the operator, so he could listen to Valerie's third session with the real Mitch Barlo. She knew it was not a simulation now – had she not somehow discovered that he was precisely who he was claiming to be? She might even turn on her webcam. Greg wanted to hear the culmination of all his plans – he wanted to hear her ask Mitch about Eddie Forbes. Greg wanted to hear the actor's response. He wanted to gauge if the time would now be right to take credit for Mitch's presence at TTAMS, or if it would be best to just let it ride.

But Valerie only played Denise from Riverside for a moment. She typed neither *y* nor *n* to the prompt that asked her if she wanted to again connect with MB426312.

Denise from Riverside and her TTAMS profile disappeared back into the realm of random ones and zeros when Valerie entered the system's programming interface. After she clicked on *Maintenance* in the lower right-hand corner of the screen, after the box opened and she typed *000001; execute* and entered her system password, Greg's loyal watchdog shut down, abandoned its eternal vigilance. It was designed to alert him only when the boss logged in as a subscriber.

Quite without knowing that she had done so, Valerie had thrown off her clever employee's unseen shadow twice. The first time had been when she'd ignored TTAMS's offer to talk to Mitch and had instead opened a window to search for MB426312's location. Greg's keeper had abandoned him in the face of Valerie's override: that was the

303

reason he hadn't been able to figure out how she'd eventually discovered the actor in the OpsPrepCent.

And it was the same this evening. By the time she typed *MB426312; session override,* Greg's electronic bloodhound had already lost the scent. It had gone back to sleep as soon as she opened the *Maintenance* portal.

Greg put his phone back into his pocket. He had faith in his keeper – if Valerie logged on again to talk to Mitch, it would alert him. She'd probably gotten a phone call, been interrupted somehow, before she'd been able to connect. If she decided to look the actor up again tonight, Greg's phone would beep again. He'd figure out how to ditch Baker then.

"We've got to get our stories straight," Greg told the operator.

"Synchronize our watches, as they say in the spy game."

Since they were in the tangled web of Mitch Barlo's unauthorized presence at TTAMS together, Greg had more or less abandoned his haughty supervisorial stance toward Morris Baker. He sipped his beer, frowned. He didn't care for Baker's reference to spying, however.

There was no way that the operator could know that his supervisor had monitored the boss's sessions with Mitch. Baker had no reason to suspect such a thing, so he surely hadn't looked for it, and he'd been on the clock, talking to his own subscribers, whilst Mitch and Valerie had had their brief sessions. Greg knew this because he had checked.

Baker's remark about spying had just been a coincidence. He knew that Valerie had outed the imposter, and had inexplicably allowed him to stay on, but that was all he knew. Baker had not a clue as to how deep the rabbit hole actually went, because Greg had not gone so far as to confess his love for the boss to his underling, either. He'd only told Baker that he'd believed that having a real celebrity onsite would've pleased Valerie. Now he wasn't so sure, and he was asking Baker's opinions about how they should proceed.

"Maybe you should take the initiative, Mr. – Greg." Baker smiled. "You could say, 'Uh, Ms Whitly, I've been meaning to tell you, one of our operators is friends with Mitch Barlo.'

"Don't tell her my name," Baker added quickly, in alarm. "Tell her that Mitch expressed an interest, so we let him in. Tell her that he's good, that he's doing it for free, that he's making *her* money."

"She already knows all that."

Baker shrugged. "Then she must be okay with it, or she would've kicked him to the curb by now."

She still wants to ask him about Eddie.

Baker tried again. "Go with the busyness angle. You wanted to tell her, but just haven't gotten the chance. Act like you knew all along that she'd be onboard with it." Baker peeped over his beer at the Ops Director. "The longer you let it go, the more it looks like you *are* hiding it."

Greg weighed the operator's words, then he smiled. "I think you might be right, Baker. You've hit on the best angle. Of course I knew she'd be down with it – she's always trusted my decisions before. Surely, I'd think she would on this. Like you say, our boy's making her money. It's all good." Greg did his best Strother Martin impression. *"What we've got here is . . . failure to communicate."*

Baker grinned. Even the barely twenty-something operator had seen *Cool Hand Luke.*

"It's just like you said," Greg continued. "Busy, busy, busy! What with Joyce jumping on Licensing, and Stevenson whining about more servers . . . Something as trivial as some actor working for free . . . Why, it just slipped my mind."

The Director of Technical Operations grinned. He slapped the chubby operator on the back. "I don't care what anybody says about you, Baker. You're all right. Let me buy you another beer."

****

Mitch asked Valerie if she wanted a drink, and she nodded gratefully. "You read my mind."

Valerie sat on the end of the couch. It was white, as was the other couch, across an intricate glass and wrought iron coffee table from it. Except for the dark, impossibly polished wooden floor, the whole room was white: the walls, the bumpy rug under the coffee table. The bricks of the middle-of-the room fireplace. Valerie felt as if she was in an igloo; she shivered. The room felt as cold as it looked.

The only splash of color was a huge, Warhol-style portrait of Janna Langly, above the mantel-less fireplace. Valerie looked solemnly at it. *All your troubles are over, Janna, whereas mine are just beginning . . .*

"It's like a set, isn't it?" With a kind of chagrined amazement, Mitch gestured with his drink at the picture, at the white room. He threw a white pillow from one couch to the other. "Like something out of *Miami Vice.*"

Valerie nodded, accepted a glass from him. *Like a movie star's house is supposed to look.*

Mitch shook his head. "Janna . . . the decorator's coming next week. Janna's gone, and this isn't me."

305

"It's . . . it's lovely. But I'm glad you can move on now."

Valerie blinked in embarrassment. Just that easily, she had exposed her secret: it had been she, and not an anonymous, voice-only subscriber, with whom Mitch had shared his pain. He would realize that she had deceived him. She gulped her drink, then abruptly arose from the couch and went to the glass wall that showcased the fabulous view. She heard Joe Friday's voice in her head. *This is the city: Los Angeles, California.*

Mitch came up beside her and opened the door to the patio, and they stepped out onto it. Between them and the lights below, there stretched an infinity pool, narrow but deep. Lit subtly from beneath, its surface was as motionless as the smoothest glass. Mitch indicated a Caribbean Blue glider nearby. It rocked gently when Valerie sat down; through-her shirt, the steel felt cool against her back.

Valerie wouldn't meet his eyes. She just stared silently out at the city. At last, Mitch said, "I knew it was you, Valerie, that you were Denise from Riverside." He sat down beside her.

"How?" The announcer from *Dragnet* spoke in Valerie's mind. *Ladies and gentlemen, the story you are about to see is true. The names have been changed to protect the innocent.*

But Mitch only shrugged, remained steadfastly silent.

Joe Friday's voice again: *I work here. I'm a cop.* Valerie displayed a flash of anger. "I'd really like to know how you knew who I was, how you got in in the first place . . ." But then her voice softened, and her momentary executive's pique collapsed. "But I don't really have the energy to think about any of it right now." The tears welled up and fell again.

"When I saw Brett . . ." *Sweet Jesus, he looked so hot!* But then the pain had returned. "I felt like I was suffocating, Mitch. He says he's moved back to LA. He's just gonna keep coming back. I don't know how I'm gonna deal with him . . ."

"It's gonna be all right, Valerie. You don't have to deal with him, if you don't feel up to it." Mitch put his arm around her, touched his forehead to hers. "If you want, I'll say something to him."

Valerie marveled at how completely Mitch seemed like an old friend, someone who could effortlessly make her smile through her tears. "Now there's a scene."

Perhaps he hadn't meant to be funny. Perhaps it had been unintentional, but just how ridiculous would it be if Mitch Barlo, Oscar-nominated star of stage and screen, accosted Brett on Valerie's behalf, like some protective big brother? As if it were some sordid domestic scene from a bad movie about bitches and bros?

EXT. A DUSTY TRAILER PARK - A BLAZINGLY HOT
SUMMER DAY.

MITCH is wearing boots, greasy pants, a
sleeveless vest with biker patches. He knocks
on a trailer door.

BRETT comes to the door. He looks quite seedy,
wearing a wife-beater and smoking a cigarette.

                    BRETT
           Yes? What do you want?

                    MITCH
      I need you to do me a favor, sonny. I need
   you to stay away from my friend Valley, or I'm
                going to have to -

                    BRETT
                  (laughs)
        Who the fuck are you, Dad? Not anybody to
      be telling me what to do, I don't think.

                    MITCH
            (smiles dangerously)
        I'm trying to be polite here, asshole. But
      if you don't leave Val alone, I'm gonna have
              to kick your college-boy ass.

Mitch didn't play such characters, nor did he appear in movies
with such appallingly tiresome plots. It was funny that he would
volunteer to enact such a scene IRL.

Valerie grinned. *"They'll love it in Pomona."*

Mitch returned her grin in pleased surprise, recognizing the line
from *Sunset Boulevard.* He did his best Norma Desmond impression:
"They'll love it everyplace."

"I don't need you to fight my battles for me, Mitch. I just need
you to help me figure this out. I just need you to . . ." Mitch's face was
still close to hers. She inhaled and was surprised with how good he
smelled. Valerie gazed into his dark blue eyes. "I just need you too . . ."
She kissed Mitch Barlo then.

Mitch hesitated, not really kissing her back. He thought again about how he shouldn't be swooping in on Greg. He thought that romance wasn't really what Valerie wanted, at this vulnerable time . . .

Mitch let her kiss him. He waited for her to realize that she didn't in fact want this kind of comfort. He waited for her to stop, to giggle in adorable embarrassment, to perhaps spring up from the glider and gaze out at the view again, once more unable to meet his eyes.

But Valerie just kept kissing him. She ran her fingers through his hair. Noting that his response was minimal, she spoke to his hesitation. "Forget about Brett for right now, Mitch." She breathed against his mouth. "I've actually been thinking about you and me for a few days now . . ."

Just like Joyce had said, he was fine and he was single. He was right here, and it had been an extremely long time. Valerie didn't wait for a response but kissed him harder, pushed herself against him.

Mitch remembered the note that she had stuck up on the window of his booth at TTAMS – that little cute come-on had been before the old boyfriend had returned. Maybe this action wasn't a result of vulnerability after all. Surely, she was upset about this guy surprising her in the parking garage, but maybe her sudden kisses didn't have anything to do with that. She'd needed to talk to him about it; she'd needed advice and a kind word. He'd given her that. But maybe she'd known exactly what else she wanted, all along.

The high road would still be to turn her down, because of his friend Greg, but Mitch realized he wasn't that much of a saint. Valerie didn't know Greg Castro was even alive, and she wanted Mitch *right now* – she was pushing him over sideways on the glider with the force of her ardor. So with a thought of, *I'm sorry my friend, truly I am, but when you snooze, you lose*, Mitch pulled Valerie the rest of the way on top of him. He kissed her back with the same fervor.

The idea struck Valerie that there was no truer statement than *the cure for a man is another man*. All the pain and confusion she'd felt when she'd seen Brett hadn't blotted out how good he looked – only the remembrance of his betrayal had prevented her from acting on her desire. It was only her self-respect that had curbed her.

But there was absolutely nothing that smacked of weakness in nailing fine-looking Mitch Barlo. Not one thing other than empowerment right here – that's how anybody would see it. Valerie didn't think about empowerment, however. She thought about Brett and how sexy he was, the goddess-given glamour he'd seemed to possess, *Goddamn, he hasn't changed a bit, he looked absolutely good enough to eat . . .*

But Brett was a cheating bastard, and Mitch . . . Mitch was her friend. Mitch was a good man, honest and a little sad, world-weary from Janna and the tragic hand that she'd dealt him. And Mitch was sexy, too. *Fucking-A, Skippy, he is,* and he was right here with his beautiful black hair and his gorgeous blue eyes, just like Brett's, just like Eddie's, *just my type* . . .

The sun'll come out tomorrow, and there'd still be Brett, still looking impossibly appetizing, and Valerie would still have to deal with him. But for tonight there was Mitch, and the thought of the delicious *release* that would come from loving Mitch . . .

Ah, the warmth, *that space-cadet glow,* the glorious *satiety* that was the result of spending the night with a gorgeous, confident, *pretty man!* Valerie had almost forgotten the joy and fun of that! Seeing Brett had reminded her, emotionally, viscerally; and Mitch was here to remind her physically: *sex was invariably the cure for what ailed ya.* At least temporarily, at least until the sun came out tomorrow. For right this moment, it was more than enough for Valerie.

Valerie broke their kiss, pushed herself up until she sat astride him. *Yes, indeedy, Joyce is right, he is fine!* Valerie had never really noticed Mitch during his career, because there had been Brett, and then there had been Eddie, but now, Mitch was right here, and he was ready and willing and was just as irresistible as he wanted to be.

Valerie stood. "Come on, Mitch! Let's take a swim!"

She turned and quickly, deftly removed her clothing. She dove gracefully into the pool, disturbing its glassy surface, sloshing the water over the side that faced the city.

Mitch didn't hesitate now. He didn't think of Greg Castro. His mind was filled with the naked blonde in the pool, a beautiful woman who didn't want him because he was famous, because he had played various and sundry characters that had peopled her fantasies. They had shared their sorrows; they were friends. They trusted each other.

Mitch stood, and while Valerie smiled impatiently, appreciatively, he tore off his clothes. He dove into the pool and took her into his arms.

The night air was cool, but the water in the heated pool was as warm as blood. The lights of the city below twinkled, and Valerie forgot completely about Brett and even Eddie as Mitch pulled her to him and kissed her – *savagely,* she thought, in the parlance of a romance novel.

The whole scene struck Valerie as something out of a remarkably good movie. Making love with an exceptionally desirable and beautiful man – just her type – al fresco, in the warm infinity pool of his

Hollywood Hills mansion – it was just the stuff that dreams are made of. It couldn't have been a better screenplay if she'd written it herself.

****

The following morning, *Eye of the Tiger* blared from Valerie's phone, waking her as well as Mitch.

"Where are you, Val?" Joyce asked, panicked. "Are you all right?"

"I am absolutely awesome, my friend." She smiled and kissed her new good friend. "I had . . . a date."

No sound came out of the phone.

Joyce searched her mind for a man with which Valerie could possibly have had a date, one she had so obviously enjoyed, and came up zeros. Valerie hadn't had a date since Liam Cote, and that had been before they'd launched TTAMS.

Valerie glanced around at Mitch's bedroom while she waited for Joyce to respond. It was stark, like the living room, done in a pale green, all lines and angles and square furnishings. Floor to ceiling glass slid cleverly aside and disappeared into an adjoining wall, leaving a cabana-like opening out onto the balcony, which formed the roof of the patio below, where she and Mitch had gotten so much better acquainted in the infinity pool the night before. Valerie suddenly remembered thumbing through a magazine at a visit to the dentist a few weeks prior, and took the phone away from her ear. She asked Mitch, "Did I see this room in *Architectural Digest?*"

He nodded. "From a few years ago."

Joyce still hadn't spoken, because she was yet trying to figure out who on earth Valerie's date could be. Had her friend suddenly thrown caution to the wind and picked up some stranger? No. That couldn't be it. Valerie was proudly aware of her station in this town nowadays. Since the piece in *Variety,* and even before, she had become mildly famous in her own right. An anonymous pick-up, why . . . it might make TMZ, or at least Valerie would think it might. No, this *date* had to be someone Valerie already knew. It could be none other than . . .

"Did you finally answer Brett's calls?"

"No. I don't want to talk to Brett, Jo." Valerie glanced curiously at her phone, and noticed that there had indeed been two missed calls and a voicemail from *ZZBC*. Since she had last seen Brett, there had been new phones and service upgrades galore, but Valerie's contact list from college had more or less remained the same. She had never wanted to see Brett again, but something in her had refused to delete his number. She had just put Zs in front of his initials, so she could effectively forget he was on the list – but his number was still there. Valerie was sure that Brett had not kept her number for all these years. Joyce must've supplied it to him again.

"Why did you give him the code to the staircase, Jo?"

Was this a line from some movie? "What?"

"Brett was waiting for me last night." Valerie affected her best Tim Curry voice. *"It was part of your plan, was it not? That he and his female should check the layout for you? Well, unfortunately for you, all the plans are to be changed."* Mitch recognized her impersonation and grinned at her. Valerie kissed him again.

"What the hell are you talking about?" Joyce's mind was a wallow of relief and annoyance. She had freaked out this morning to find Val's car in the driveway but no Val. Her friend never went anywhere, and certainly not overnight, and therefore, Joyce was flooded with a giant wave of thankfulness when she'd answered the phone. Wherever she was, Valerie was all right.

Then she'd started talking about dates and codes and Brett waiting for her; about *plans*, in a bad British accent. Valerie was okay, and now she was being irritating. "Where are you, Val? Are you with–"

"No, I'm not with Brett, Jo. I'm with someone much better than Brett." *Or at least someone entirely different than Brett, just as good, but also kind and trustworthy.* "Why would you let him sneak up on me like that?"

"Who?"

"Brett!"

Joyce shook her head. "Start over, Val. You saw Brett?"

"Brett was in the parking garage, waiting for me last night, just like you knew he would be, because you gave him the code to the staircase, so he could sneak up on me."

Goddamned tricky, conniving Brett!

"I didn't give him the code, Val. We went down to the garage a couple of times, when we went out to lunch. He must've just watched me. You know I'd never do that to you. I promised I wouldn't, no matter how many times he asked." Similar to Brett's MO, Joyce's curiosity snuck up on her. "So you saw him? What did he say?"

"I told him I didn't want to see him. I've got other fish to fry."

Joyce heard a man's voice; a low murmur. Valerie giggled. Joyce thought the voice may have sounded familiar, or maybe not. But it wasn't Brett.

"Where are you, Val? Who're you with?"

"It's none of your goddamned business where I am or who I'm with, Jo," Valerie said gaily, without meaning any insult. "I can't tell you right now. It's all *off the record, on the QT, and very hush-hush.* Let's just say I'm on vacation.

"Unless the building's on fire, call Greg. If the building's on fire . . ." She giggled again. "Call the fire department. I'll see you . . . maybe Monday."

"Christ, Val, I'd really like to know where you are . . ." But Valerie had already hit the *End* button.

****

There was a chef in Mitch's stable of servants, along with a maid and a gardener. The man came by a couple times a week to cook for the A-lister, but he invariably wound up leaving the gourmet dishes in stainless steel, covered trays.

He'd spent years clawing his way to the top of LA's cut-throat restaurant scene, so he frequently wondered why he had allowed himself to become nothing more than an unappreciated short-order cook to this moody actor – he didn't even get to show his flair for presentation anymore.

Thanks, Alex, Mitch Barlo always told him. *Just leave it in the fridge.*

It wasn't like this when Janna was alive.

With a sentiment akin to Marvin's, Alex answered his own question. *For the money. That's why I put up with it. For the prestige of being Mitch Barlo's personal chef.*

So Alex was delighted when Valerie Whitly came out to the kitchen and respectfully asked him if she could watch him prepare tonight's dinner. She was of course no Janna Langly, but the chef was still a tiny bit star-struck. He'd recognized her immediately from the piece on Variety.com, told her how much he loved her service. A subscriber's show of appreciation was a first for Valerie, and she smiled humbly.

Quite without reservation, Alex told her of a long, slightly drunken conversation he'd had with a flawless Montgomery Clift, about the tortures of being a closeted homosexual in 1950s. Then he'd talked to a young Roddy McDowell about the break-up between him and Clift, about the British actor's attempted suicide over it.

"You've created a wonderful thing," Alex whispered and gave her a hug. It was just as Valerie had always suspected: subscribers might share tales of such intimate conversations with TTAMS's creator, but they weren't going to go blabbing to the press about them. Joyce had not a thing to worry about.

Alex told her that he was a big fan, but not only of old Hollywood stars. He'd also spent many glorious sessions relating his deep admiration to a devastating simulation of Zachary Quinto.

"He's so cute!" Valerie commiserated.

"Isn't he though!"

"My mom's a big movie fan," Valerie confided. "It's in my blood. I love actors."

There was a heartbeat where Alex's expression said, *And haven't you just gone right ahead and caught yourself one? You go, girl!*

He said aloud, "I dated an actor once. In college. A Shakespearean actor, no less. It was . . . complicated. They can be whomever they choose to be."

They can be whoever you want them to be, Valerie thought.

"He was . . . different," Alex was saying. "Sometimes he was Romeo, loving, poetic. Sometimes he was indecisive – he would become emotionally torn between this and that, like Hamlet. Sometimes he was devious, cruel, like Macbeth." Alex laughed nervously. He realized that perhaps he shouldn't be throwing shade on actors when there was one in the other room. He ended on an upbeat note. "It was like three for the price of one."

"I think all of you men can be like that," Valerie said playfully. She glanced over her shoulder. "Loving, maybe momentarily indecisive." She returned her attention to the chef. "I definitely knew one that was devious and cruel."

"In the end, I found my actor to be mostly that," Alex admitted. "And yet . . . Why is it that those types are the ones that we can't stop thinking about?"

A picture of Brett and his gorgeously sexy smile bloomed in Valerie's mind. Mitch had taken the edge off, beyond a shadow of a doubt, but he hadn't made her forget about Brett entirely, nor had she expected him to. Brett had meant the world to her once, and now he wanted back into her life. She knew that she would still have to deal with him.

"Some people just leave a mark, I guess," Valerie said with a bright smile. Yes, she would have to deal with Brett eventually, but not right now. She was happy, thrilled, in fact, with her actor and his beautiful house, with his five-star personal chef.

"What are you creating tonight, Alex? Is there anything I can do to help?"

****

Mitch was glad that the chef was there, because his presence provided a convenient diversion. The actor stepped out onto his patio and closed the door behind him, and like a loyal employee, he called to let his supervisor know that he wouldn't be coming in this evening. He made some excuse: the studio, his agent, it was gonna keep him busy all weekend.

"It's okay, Mitch. Valerie's not here. She hasn't been here all day. Joyce said she's on vacation. I don't know what the hell that means. Valerie never goes on vacation." Greg sighed. "I don't know where she is."

Mitch felt a pang of regret, but then it evened out and disappeared. Valerie was discreet – hadn't she told her best friend absolutely nothing, said it was all *hush-hush?* Mitch hoped she'd keep things on the down low, at least for a while. But he couldn't be sure if she would because he didn't know her very well.

That fact brought along its own embarrassment. Ronny's long-ago warnings about *screwing the help* rang in his head. But Valerie Whitly wasn't hardly a waitress or a script girl, although it still might have been prudent to get to know her a little better, before plunging – quite literally – into intimacy with her.

Mitch felt a flash of ego: like Hamlet, *his greatness weigh'd, his will was not his own; he could not, as unvalued persons do, carve for himself.* Not unless he was prepared to withstand the publicity, undergo the public scrutiny. Being a celebrity, Mitch was aware that he was not like other people.

On the other hand, because she was a powerful executive in this town, Valerie knew how to *keep her pretty mouth shut.* If nothing else about her, he knew that much. Ronny would no doubt give him an *atta boy* for not bothering to get to know the owner of TTAMS better before going right on ahead and getting to know her quite well. Mitch could hear him already: "Hell, it might lead to *some kind of endorsement."*

"If anybody deserves a vacation, it's Ms Whitly, wouldn't you say?" Mitch told Greg. "Didn't you tell me she's always at the office?"

The Ops Director was glum. "I just wish I knew where she was."

Mitch blanched at the thought that if Valerie logged back onto her system from his house, Greg would probably be able to figure out precisely where she was. The tech was brilliant; his keeper was probably equipped with some kind of GPS.

Then Mitch grinned to himself, savoring his own arrogance again. It was something that he hadn't done in a long time, and he reckoned that he owed that to Valerie, too. It wasn't likely that she would be signing on to talk to a movie star when she had one right here with her.

"Let me know when she comes back to work," he told Greg. *If she decides not to be discreet, after all, I'd like to be prepared if you're gonna want to kick my ass.*

"Sure thing, Mitch. But you don't have to wait for Valerie. Come back whenever. Your numbers are great. I still say you should quit Hollywood and come to work here full time."

"I'll tell my agent," Mitch said again and told Greg goodbye.

Janna's sudden end had been shocking, but other than that, Mitch reflected that his career had been untouched by scandal. Janna's death had been scandal enough, but as the months passed, its association with him had faded. He'd never been thought of as *Janna Langly's husband*. She'd never been in any Oscar-caliber films before they'd appeared together in *A Random House Is Not a Home*. Mitch had been a star long before they'd met and married.

And if Mitch's relationship with Valerie became public knowledge, if it lasted, which he could not predict yet – there would be not one thing scandalous about it. She was few years younger than him, but not glaringly so; they were both single.

The scandal would only exist in Greg Castro's mind. He would be outraged, would quite justifiably feel betrayed. He had confided his secret affection to Mitch, and Mitch had not only ignored it, Greg would feel that the actor had taken advantage of it. It would destroy their friendship, and Mitch was truly sorry about that.

But maybe he and Valerie wouldn't last. It had only been one night and a day. Maybe she would stay the weekend, and then her vast responsibilities would call her back to work on Monday. Maybe they would see each other again. Maybe not. Either way, Mitch hoped that she would continue to keep it all *on the QT*. If luck was with him – and it seemed that luck had returned to Mitch Barlo, if only for a visit – then Greg might never have to know about his little thing with the boss. Greg could go on worshipping her from afar, oblivious.

Mitch went out to the kitchen to see what Alex was whipping up for dinner. He knew he didn't have to worry about the chef's discretion. Alex had seen far worse goings-on at *Chez Barlo* when Janna was alive, and he liked his job, or at least he liked his paycheck. He knew how to keep his mouth shut.

****

But Valerie didn't go back to the office on Monday. She checked in with the CEO, verbally signed off on a few issues, remained silent on where she was and who she was with.

"I'll tell you all about it when I come back, Jo." Valerie giggled. "Maybe. Or maybe . . . Did you ever see *Agatha?*"

Joyce sighed. "No." She waited for the plot summary.

"Agatha Christie's husband had asked her for a divorce; then she disappeared. The world went crazy; eventually she turned up after ten days or so. She'd checked into a hotel under her husband's mistress's name, but she never told anyone what she'd been doing. The movie offered an explanation. Something about revenge. She's saved from her dark plot by an American journalist, played by Dustin Hoffman."

Now Joyce waited for Valerie to explain what relevance some forgotten Dustin Hoffman flick had to her own life. "Maybe this chapter of my story will be like Agatha's. Maybe I'll never tell anyone where I've been." She giggled again.

"Well, that's entirely your prerogative, Val. You're free and twenty-one."

But Joyce remained annoyed at her suddenly wayward, suddenly secretive friend. Sure, the best cure for a man was another man – Brett didn't know where Valerie was either, and was as upset about it as Joyce was. She thought it served him right for the way he'd approached his ex-girlfriend.

Brett had obviously rattled Valerie with his sudden reappearance, but her reaction was just too much. This was just not like her. Joyce's discreet inquiries had come to nothing – but then she only knew computer vendors and people in showbiz, anymore. Valerie wouldn't give computer geeks the time of day, and all of the industry lawyers and agents to whom Joyce had offhandedly said, "Hey, did you see Valerie over the weekend?" had just looked at her blankly. None of them knew the head of TTAMS past meetings and the occasional business party, anyway. None of them had seen her.

Joyce imagined sleaziness. She saw Valerie take a cab to some downtown bar, dark, seedy, anonymous. She saw the bartender set her up – Valerie would assure him that she wasn't driving. Joyce imagined Valerie, sloshed and slurring, whining about Brett to some attentive stranger. Some confident, good-looking hustler – Joyce saw him glance at his buddies and grin, unable to believe his luck. Beautiful, rich Valerie – he'd just take her right on back to his little place, give her a shoulder on which to cry, love her a little bit, for just as long as she wanted him to. Hell, maybe she'd like him enough to pay his rent. She could obviously afford it . . .

316

Joyce shook her head. Maybe it wasn't as bad as all that, but there had to be some reason for Valerie's reticence to divulge where she was, to tell Joyce exactly what stripe of Mr. Wonderful she was with, *and that was all bad.* Joyce hoped that when the owner of TTAMS finally came to her senses and tried to ditch this guy, that it wouldn't be necessary to employ her staff of attorneys to ensure that he stayed gone.

"When do you think you might be back, Val?"

"I'm sure you're holding down the fort, Jo," Valerie replied gaily.

Joyce heard a man's voice in the background, and again she thought that there was something familiar about it. But the voice was muffled. Joyce didn't know who he was.

"Saturday. I'll be in Saturday, at the latest. My friend has just said he has an appointment, and that he'll drop me at the office." Valerie said something that Joyce couldn't hear; the man's voice answered and they both laughed.

Live it up, Val, Joyce thought crossly. *While the rest of us are left sitting around wondering what the hell is going on –*

"I'll see you on Saturday, Jo," Valerie concluded and was gone again.

****

Valerie stayed at Mitch's Hollywood Hills, looks-like-a-movie-star's-house-should-look compound for the entire week. Brett called, texted, left messages; she deleted all without reading or listening to them. *The hell with Brett.* At least for the moment.

On Tuesday, when Valerie knew Joyce was at work, she and Mitch took a cab to Mr. Vinson's guesthouse, giggling like truant schoolkids. Mitch had offered her Janna's things to wear, but she preferred to pick up some of her own. Janna's would've fit: the late actress and Valerie were the same size. Like Valerie herself, Mitch had a type. But there was just something disrespectful to Valerie about wearing his dead wife's clothes. It wasn't like she aimed to take Janna's place in his life. She suggested that Mitch could donate them to Look To the Stars, after which they would be auctioned for charity. He made arrangements to do so for the following week, and felt his burden lighten further.

On Wednesday, they took Valerie's Mercedes to the beach, then accompanied a charter full of studio execs to Catalina Island. Valerie had met several of them before, and none of them looked askance that she was with Mitch Barlo. These were business professionals, after all – some of the companions along for the cruise were neither husbands nor wives of the movers and shakers. These people were not members of the public clamoring for gossip and autographs.

In the evenings, Mitch and Valerie looked at the view, and ate Alex's flawlessly presented meals, and watched movies in the screening room. Valerie finally got to see *Two's a Crowd*, sitting in the dark, holding hands with Eddie's co-star. In the end, neither of the brothers got the girl. She chose someone else.

"What a stupid woman," Valerie observed. "She was offered two incredible choices, and she picked some Canadian nobody."

Mitch grinned, but didn't comment. He'd watched Valerie watch Edison Forbes on the screen, glassy-eyed, enrapt. He had no doubt whatsoever which brother she would've picked. Valerie Whitly was indeed Eddie's biggest fan. *More's the pity*, Greg Castro's voice said in Mitch's mind.

On Thursday, Ronny Prince sent over a script for his client's perusal. The plot: a senior partner at a prestigious law firm dies. To everyone's surprise, he leaves all his assets to a junior partner, cutting his three daughters out of the will. The daughters each make a play for the junior partner; he must decide which of them truly wants him, and which of them is just angling for a share of Daddy's money. In the end, the junior partner chooses the daughter that is willing to share his fortune with her sisters. Everyone lives happily ever after. Fade. To. Black.

I know it's been done, Ronny's accompanying note read. *But see what you think. It's time for you to be a romantic lead again. Oscar-contenders and foreign thrillers be damned. Let's make lots of money . . .*

Hopefully, it's not the last time I'll be the romantic lead, Mitch thought ruefully, suddenly feeling old. *Hopefully, we can do better than this.*

But Valerie was tickled silly to do a read through with the actor. She sat in his lap and made up a different voice for each of the sisters, giving all three a backstory not inherent in the script. The oldest had been educated in Europe – Valerie gave her Greta Garbo's throaty *I vant to be alone* whisper. The middle sister was ditsy, at least in Valerie's estimation. She played her as Ana Faris, à la *The House Bunny*. The youngest sister was a lawyer like Daddy had been, cold, bitchy. Valerie played her like a junior version of Miranda Priestly from *The Devil Wears Prada*.

Hilarity ensued, much more than was in the script, when Valerie got all these characterizations mixed up.

At night, she and Mitch made love, in the infinity pool, in the pale green bedroom that had been featured in *Architectural Digest*, on the white couch in front of the white-brick, middle-of-the-room fireplace. Janna's portrait looked on but did not advise.

Valerie enjoyed Mitch's company. He was kind and funny and loving, and that was nice, but Valerie also observed that he could turn into a Hollywood player in a heartbeat. She witnessed this aspect when he was discussing dollars and cents and tie-ins, premieres and talk-show appearances with his agent on the phone. Mitch wasn't sure if he wanted to do the three sisters rom-com, and there was a certain calculation to his words, his tone, when he spoke to Ronny. This element was completely absent when he spoke to Valerie. She wondered for a second which was the real Mitch Barlo. It was just like Alex the chef had said: actors could be whoever they wanted to be. And good actors, like Mitch . . . *Will the real Slim Shady please stand up?*

Valerie reveled in her fantasy vacation, alone and above the trials of life, nestled in the Hollywood Hills, making love daily with a sexy A-lister. But by Friday afternoon, she discovered to her surprise that she was missing the office. She was missing Joyce. Pictures of Brett kept popping into her mind, sometimes at moments when Mitch would not have been thrilled to know that they were there.

Valerie was unsure about how long she wanted this thing with Mitch to last. She had to be getting back to the office, and . . . what was going to happen then? He was welcome to stay on working at TTAMS, incognito, undercover, for as long as he wanted. Until he made up his mind whether or not he wanted to make that comedy. Of course he was welcome to stay. They were friends. *They were lovers.* But it wasn't as if they could be having lunch together in the cafeteria. That was just silly. He was famous, and she was the boss.

But she liked him very much. He had helped her get over a rough patch, and gloriously. *If you don't know the thing you're dealing, oh, I can tell you, darling, that it's sexual healing . . . Makes me feel so fine, it's such a rush, helps to relieve the mind, and it's good for us . . .*

Except Valerie wasn't sure if there was going to be an *us.* She liked Mitch a lot. In the short span of a week, he had become her good friend; definitely her best male friend. But she would still have to deal with Brett – her previous best male friend – and she really needed to be getting back to work.

And yet . . .

Valerie was seldom indecisive, but she couldn't discuss her feelings *for* Mitch *with* Mitch. Usually, she could discuss this kind of thing with Joyce, but she wasn't ready to tell Joyce about this adventure quite yet. When she found herself in times of trouble, Mother Mary didn't come to Valerie, speaking words of wisdom. If she couldn't talk to Joyce or her new best friend Mitch, there was only one person to whom she could turn.

The sun was setting, dying in all it splendor, sinking behind the LA skyline. Valerie considered its awesomeness, then took out her phone. She paused and smiled at Eddie's picture, as she always did. Just like on her laptop, she had quite a few on her phone, but this was one of her favorites: the second still from *Two's a Crowd*. The picture was cropped; there wasn't enough room on her phone's screen for the Canadian's smoky-eyed American co-star. Just Eddie's smug, no longer curious face.

"So what about this, eh?"

"I thought you'd never ask," Eddie replied.

"And?"

"I think you should give it a go with the Yank, Valley."

"What about Brett?"

"You can't possibly be considering Brett." Valerie had never whined to Eddie about Brett, as she had to Joyce. *To Mitch*. But he knew about the pain Brett had put her through.

But that was all in the past. "It's been a long time, Eddie. He says he just wants to talk."

"What do you think he wants to talk about? The same things he used to talk about, once upon a time, with all those girls?"

"He said he moved back to LA just for me. The least I can do is hear what he has to say . . ."

"That's all up to you. But I say, you should give it a try here. Just look at that view."

"Christ, Eddie! This is all so sudden, so unreal. It's all like some fantasy. Like a movie."

"You like movies."

"But this movie has been done, Eddie. Famous actor is on hand to sweep sobbing girl off her feet? It's the old *sex for solace* gag. On the rebound. The best cure for a man is another man. What did Betty Schaefer say? *It's just a rehash of something that wasn't very good to begin with.*"

"*You'da turned down Gone With the Wind.*"

"*I'm sorry, Mr. Gillis, but I just didn't think it was any good. I found it flat and trite.*"

"*Exactly what kind of material do you recommend? James Joyce? Dostoyevsky?*"

"*So you take Plot 27A, make it glossy, make it slick . . .*"

"Are those really dirty words, Valley? *Sunset Boulevard* aside, do you really want to pass this one up?"

"I don't know, Eddie. It's just all so fantastical. Me and Mitch Barlo, star of stage and screen. Seriously? It's wish-fulfillment, like something out of *Aladdin.*"

"Have some of Column A, try all of Column B . . ."

"It's just all so *much*, Eddie. I like him a lot, but I just can't see . . . And there's still Brett . . ."

Eddie left off of Disney and went back to *Sunset Boulevard. "That's the trouble with you readers, you know all the plots."*

"I gotta go back to work tomorrow, Eddie. I'll figure it out while I'm at the–"

Valerie heard the scrape of a footstep. She hadn't heard the silent glass door open. She turned around to see Mitch standing behind her. She blinked guiltily.

He crossed the short distance and kissed her lightly. Matter-of-factly, he asked, "Who're you talking to?"

Valerie sighed. "I was talking to Eddie." Mitch had to have overheard her say his name. What else had he heard?

Mitch's smile faltered, became pasted on, phony. "That's not possible, Valerie. Eddie's–"

"I know what Eddie is, Mitch," she said evenly. "Nobody knows better than me."

She pushed the button on the side of her phone, and the still of Edison Forbes from *Two's a Crowd* blinked off.

Mitch sat on the Caribbean Blue glider, invited her to sit beside him. Valerie complied, and Mitch put his arm around her. They were silent for perhaps thirty seconds, then Valerie sighed again. "I suppose you'd like to hear about it?"

Mitch nodded speechlessly. Not a single word occurred to the Oscar-nominated thespian, because he was on fairly unfamiliar ground now. Janna had been unstable, self-destructive; he hadn't learned exactly how much until it was too late. She'd kept all the crazy well-hidden until after the honeymoon. Valerie wasn't self-destructive, but she was certainly an odd one . . .

"I met this Foley guy at Fox. Liam. He was from Canada. He said he knew Eddie, had worked on one of his pictures. He said he could introduce us. I, of course, was completely down." Valerie grinned.

"Before we went to Canada, Liam and I became . . ." She looked at the actor's expectant, neutrally attentive face. Mitch Barlo, whom she had just recently *became* with, his own self. No need to use the same word; no need to describe a similar scenario.

Valerie started over. "Before we went to Canada, I guess you could say that Liam was my boyfriend. It had all happened so quickly."

Just like us. She hurried to explain. "He was nice. Kinda cute, with his little Canadian accent. And he was going to introduce me to Eddie . . ."

So why not sleep with him?

This isn't going well. It was not what Mitch wanted to hear at all. *Liam was going to introduce me to Eddie, so why not sleep with him? You've calmed my shattered nerves. You've been so kind to me. So why not sleep with you, too?*

It was definitely not what she wanted to be saying. No one's ego was too amenable to hearing that they had been a gratitude-fuck. *They call that trade,* Elise's voice said in Valerie's head, with an echoing laugh.

Valerie stopped, began a third time. "Maybe I should go back a little bit. Let me describe for you what Edison Forbes had come to mean to me." Valerie smiled brilliantly at him, and a little bit of a return smile crept into Mitch's somewhat patently nonplussed expression. Valerie was assured that he hadn't heard all of her conversation with Eddie. He didn't know that she'd been discussing him. Mitch had just come in at the end, heard her say Eddie's name.

"You how your fans are. But you're the movie star, Mitch, the idol. The adored. You know about your fans, the way they look at you. But I doubt that you've ever stopped to consider what it's like to *be a fan.*

"I remember sitting between Joyce and Liam on the big Air Canada jet, holding hands with both of them. *I was going to get to meet Eddie!* I'd never been so excited about anything in my entire life. *No pleasure, no rapture, no exquisite sin greater . . .* than the idea that I was going to actually meet his Canadian Majesty." Valerie giggled adorably. "The possibilities were simply mind-blowing.

"Liam started to talk to Joyce about sound effects. I switched seats with her, so they could chat. I looked out the window and thought back over the past year of my life. College was over. I had this great job at Fox. Brett . . . ah, the hell with Brett. Brett was a bad memory. I thought about what he had almost driven me to, but I didn't think about it sadly. What Brett had driven me to was the best thing I'd ever seen. If I hadn't broken up with Brett, I might never have discovered Edison Forbes."

Valerie paused; she closed one eye and considered her good friend curiously. "Did you ever catch *Sonny's Diner,* Mitch?"

Cautiously, Mitch shook his head. Not only had he not caught it, he'd never even heard of it.

"Yeah, well, I understand that it was big in Canada." Valerie grinned ruefully. "It was a television show, kind of like the restaurant from *Seinfeld* or *Central Perk* from *Friends* meets all those old those old

Irwin Allen disaster movies. You know? They were always made up of an ensemble cast of famous has-beens.

"I didn't realize this at first, of course; not until about the third time through. I recognized one guy – he was old and fat now, but I'd seen him in something, so I Googled him and found out that he had indeed been the slim, good-looking blondie in *The Barber's Habit.*"

Another one that rang absolutely no bells for Mitch. Just like everyone that knew Valerie, from Joyce to Greg to Brett, to people who had just sat in meetings with her, such as Mark Stevenson – Mitch began to understand that Valerie *knew* about movies. Famous movies, not-so-famous movies. It shouldn't have come as a surprise to him, seeing as she had created TTAMS.

He realized that it was just another indicator that he didn't really know the woman with whom he'd spent the last week; didn't know her very well at all. All he really knew was that she'd suffered traumatic sadness in childhood, had experienced a bad break-up in college. Mitch also knew that now, as an adult, she quite thoroughly enjoyed the horizontal bop.

Outside of the bedroom, however, he was learning, with a growing feeling of disquiet, that she just might be . . . Well, maybe it would be best to just let her finish her explanation.

Valerie noticed Mitch's blank expression. It was the same one she often received when she mentioned obscure movies to non-fans. She explained, "It was a comedy from like 1984. I saw it when I was a kid.

"So I Googled some of the guest stars that appeared on *Sonny's Diner,* and discovered that most of them had had stellar careers in Canadian cinema in the somewhat distant past, but now they were appearing on a TV show in which their problems were solved in forty-three minutes by a former high school teacher turned diner owner and his feisty grandmother. Merriment, pathos, et cetera."

Valerie sighed and eyed Mitch sheepishly. *"Sonny's Diner* wasn't very good, Mitch. At least, not to my refined American tastes. It was formulaic, a vehicle to showcase all these old stars. But I didn't care, and I still don't care. I've seen all three seasons, probably hundreds of times. It's not very good, but Eddie's good in it." She grinned. "I don't suppose you caught his turn as a New Orleans bank robber in *Desperate Caper?"*

"I've never been much of a Canadian cinephile."

"Oh, no, *my brother and only friend.* It's an American film. You may lay it at the feet of Hollywood Pictures. They can't deny it, because their name's on it. Eddie affects the smoothest, darkest southern accent I've ever heard. Ah . . . Eddie's voice, all *honeys* and *darlin's.* Sweet and probably not very good for you, like maple syrup." Another sigh, of appreciation this time.

"I cannot tell a lie, however. *Desperate Caper* is not *the worst* movie I've ever seen, but it is in the top four. And I've seen *a lot* of movies. No one wanted to like it more than me." Another giggle. "I played film editor and reduced it to about twenty-five minutes. I took out all the scenes Eddie wasn't in.

"Don't get me wrong, Mitch. It's not that Eddie's a bad actor. I think he's . . . *a good actor.* He's just been in some dogs. It's not Eddie's acting that I like so much. *It's him.* The way he talks, his voice. His hair, his eyes, his smile. *Prettiest man I ever saw.*"

So Greg told me, Mitch remembered. Again he thought that he wasn't looking forward to dealing with *that,* telling his good friend that he hadn't been in to TTAMS for the last week because he'd been at home, doing the boss, the woman whose gratitude he had been brought onboard to secure for Greg . . .

"Every single time, Mitch," Valerie was saying, *"Every single time* I see Eddie's picture, I think, *Goddamn, he's cute.* I can't explain it – why him? He's obviously not as devastating to the rest of the world as he is to me, or he would've been a bigger star. I wait for it to go away, but it never does. He's simply the best looking man I've ever seen. There's something about his expression that just does it for me. He is the sum total of what a man should look like, to me. And it all started with *Sonny's Diner."* Valerie's smile took on a shade of embarrassment.

"It's okay, Val. You're a fan. There's nothing wrong with that."

"But *I'm not,* Mitch," she said emphatically. "Not really. Not like your fans. Your fans – my mom is a movie fan, but not really a fan of *movie stars.* She loves the characters and the stories more than the actors. But I think that *your* fans and the fans of all the great actors – they love *you* for the characters you played. They love Brad because they remember how hot he was in *Thelma and Louise,* or they think he's Tyler Durden. They love Bruce because they think he's John McClane. They love your sexiness as Shamus and the gambler . . ." Valerie squeezed him.

"My dad was a singer. His music moved his fans, so they invariably wanted him to move them, too." Valerie winked. "The groupies allowed themselves to fall in love with Dennis Whitly, the singer, the poet, the *tomcat.* They didn't want to see him as Dennis Whitly, doting father, loyal husband – what he always was to me.

"Eddie hasn't played any really great characters. I never particularly liked any of them. Don't get me wrong, he made me believe he was them, like a good actor does. But Sonny was a little bit too much of a goody-two-shoes for me. The New Orleans bank robber was just stupid – the whole movie was stupid. And Chris, in *Two's A Crowd?* He should've just punched you in the mouth and run off with the girl." Valerie grinned. "I did like him in *Undercover Homicide,* though. He was a heartless son-of-a bitch in that one, but sexy as hell.

"I never cared about the parts Eddie played, except that he looked good playing every single one of them. He wasn't so much an actor to me – it's not like he's very famous here. He was more like some incredibly attractive guy that had smiled at me on the street once. He was like the Mona Lisa – what exactly is she smiling about? What *kind of a person* was she? That's why I say I'm not really a fan, like most."

Mitch thought, *That's just what junkies say. I'm different, I'm not like other junkies . . .*

"I became . . . Joyce says I became *obsessed.* I watched his movies, I collected his pictures. I downloaded every clip he ever did, promos, little interviews on the snowy red carpet." Valerie grinned again. "I looked up every available article, trying to read between the lines to catch a glimpse of the person. The actor, the characters that he'd played . . . to me, they were *meh.*

"But the question was always in my mind – *what's Edison Forbes really like?"*

Greg truly does know her, at least on this. Again Mitch felt a little stab of guilt. But things were what they were. Valerie had picked him, and if it wasn't him, it might've been someone else. But it probably wouldn't have been Greg Castro, always too shy or nervous to speak up.

"It all drove me deliciously crazy, Mitch. In looks, he was the sum total of all my fantasies. The perfect man. But was he a goody-two-shoes, like Sonny? Was he a bastard like the dirty cop in *Undercover Homicide?* I read that he was linked with a couple of models, but they never lasted. Was that because he was an unrepentant womanizer, or because he was just picky in his relationships? Or was he something else entirely?

"And then, thanks to a short Canuck Foley guy, I was going to meet him. I had to get a hold of myself. I had to be cool. I know how Dad looks at his fans – he appreciates their admiration and all – but the fact that they think that they love him so utterly, without even knowing him – fans are different to Dad. They're just a little bit . . . *off.* The idea that someone is obsessed with you . . . Fans buy the records, pay the bills . . . But you're not going to invite them out to dinner."

Mitch was amazed at Valerie's perfect grasp of this interpersonal price of fame.

325

"I've met a lot of famous people since I launched TTAMS, Mitch. But I'm ambivalent to the fact that they're the idols of millions, because I saw how the groupies worshipped my dad. It's just silly. Actors, musicians. They're all just people. Some are a little sexier than others . . ." Valerie tickled him. "But you're all just people to me."

My dad was a rock star, Mr. Barlo. I don't do autographs.

Unless they're from Edison Forbes.

"But all of a sudden, I was about to meet the most attractive man I'd ever seen. I was in love with him, based on nothing but his looks. I wasn't a big fan of his work, but I was a rabid fan of *him*. Inside, I was no different than all those girls, screaming hysterically when my dad walked onstage.

"So I had to be cool. Eddie couldn't know the effect he had on me. I didn't want him to see me as a fan. I wanted him to see me as a person, just a friend of the Foley guy. Someone that he might like to get to know – but not as someone who was obsessively curious to get to know *him*. Not as someone who had pictures of him on her phone, on her computer, someone who laid awake at night wondering what he was really like, what kind of a person he was.

"At last the moment arrived. Liam parked our rental car behind the theater in a space marked *Reserved*. It was snowing lightly. It had been snowing for a while. The parking lot hadn't been scraped or plowed, or whatever they call it. It was completely white, except for our tire tracks."

Valerie smile faded. She frowned. "Canada was a revelation for me, Mitch. You're from Michigan, right?"

So she has read my bio. He nodded.

"So you know all about the cold and the snow. But it was a first for me, and Joyce, too. I'm from Riverside, California, USA. It doesn't fucking snow in Riverside." Mitch flinched at the profanity, and the fact that Valerie's voice had taken on a flat, almost harsh tone. "Liam had taken us shopping before we left, but the purpose of the coats and hats and gloves and boots hadn't really sunk in to me until we got off the plane. I'd never even *seen* snow, except in the distance, on Mt. Baldy. We'd taken off from LAX, and it was probably sixty-five degrees. We landed on Ice Planet Hoth. I expected to see a Mountie ride by on a tauntaun at any moment."

Mitch grinned, but Valerie did not.

"The air was absolutely freezing. It knifed through me . . . I thought about Eddie again, and to a lesser extent Liam – what kind of a personality did this bitter cold produce?"

Mitch attempted to explain. "You're just used to it when you grow up in it."

Valerie shook her head, uncomprehending. "Liam held our hands and helped us pick our way across the parking lot. The snow wasn't that deep, only a couple of inches, but Joyce slipped, almost went down. She said a few four letter words about the climate, what she always refers to as *Anglo-Saxon terms of dismay.*" Still Valerie didn't smile.

"There was a little concrete porch behind the theater. Five or six steep steps up to the stage door. Liam told us to be careful, to hold on to the handrail, because the steps were icy . . . Dangerous . . ." Valerie's eyes took on a sad, faraway look, recalling the frosty Canadian scene, so alien and other-worldly to her. Mitch felt for her sadness. He was sure that despite all her riches, the owner of TTAMS would probably never visit Canada again, or anywhere else where it snowed.

"We crept up the icy steps. Joyce almost fell again, but Liam caught her. The porch was cleared, with just a couple of piles of snow in the corners. Not like the steps . . ."

Valerie paused. Then she blinked, and the haunted expression was gone.

"Liam knocked on the stage door, smiled and waved at the peephole. The door opened immediately, and then a stagehand was shaking hands with him, thumping him on the back. Joyce looked at me – apparently Eddie wasn't the only person that Liam knew here. He and this guy were buddies. It was like Old Home Week.

"Liam briefly introduced us, then without further ado, he led us down the little hall to the green room, or whatever you call it in the theatre."

"It's the same," Mitch said.

"And then . . . There he was. He was already in costume, wearing a little natty brown suit, as befitted his newspaperman character. His beautiful black hair was cut short for the part." Valerie's eyes glowed in the remembrance. "I hung back in the doorway with Joyce while he greeted Liam, giving him a big ol' Canadian hug, thumping him on the back, just like the stagehand had done. Joyce looked at me again – apparently Liam was best buds with Eddie, too.

"Then Liam turned and introduced Joyce. She's never been a movie fan, Mitch, no matter how much I've tried to make her one. Although she does think you're *fine.*" Valerie squeezed him again. "If I had to say that she was anyone's fan, it would be yours. But she's never been at all impressed with Eddie. She just shook his hand and said it was nice to meet him.

"Then she turned to watch my reaction. She was waiting to see if I might just faint dead away. Liam said, 'Eddie, this is my friend, Valerie. She's a big fan of your work. Valerie, this is Edison Forbes.'

"He smiled at me, and I thought that I might indeed stop breathing. But then I reminded myself to be cool. He was just a person, maybe a shade shorter than I'd expected, a tiny bit older-looking."

Mitch grinned. *"Look here, Marilyn, America's schweetheart."* It was the line that Clark Gable, sans his false teeth, had allegedly said to Monroe while on the set of *The Misfits*.

Valerie knew the story; she smiled. "He shook my hand and said, 'How nice of you to come such a long way. It's always a pleasure to meet someone, especially from the States, who enjoys my films.' I was surprised by his accent, but thought I shouldn't've been surprised."

"His accent?"

Valerie grinned. "You never noticed?"

Mitch shook his head.

"Oh, yeah. They just *don't talk like us*. Something about the short vowels. I can't imitate it, but I can pick it out. Watch as many Canadian movies as I have, and you'll be able to pick it out, too. Joyce jokes that they're all sneaking down here, undetected, appearing in our flicks."

Mitch was astounded, as her best friend had been: Valerie could differentiate between American actors and Canadian ones by the way they said their short vowels. He'd done two Canadian films, and except for a Newfie grip, who'd frequently asked him, *Whadda y'at?* and told him *I dies at ya, b'y* (boy) when he thought Mitch was funny, all with a not-quite-Irish, not-quite-English, certainly-not-American fast-talking strangeness, Mitch had never noticed that most Canadians spoke any differently than he did. He'd never even heard any of them say *Eh?*

"But he was still perfect to me," Valerie was saying. "Maybe even more than before, because now he was right there, talking to me. He was real. I could smell his cologne, see the little twinkle in his eye, directed at *me*. It was so awesome because it was like I *knew* Eddie, Mitch, before I'd ever met him. I'd watched damn near everything he'd ever been in. I knew his little mannerisms, the way he'd tilt his head when he listened. I knew his smile, his voice — even though he was a little bit more . . . Canadian in person, than he was on the screen." She smiled fondly. "It was like we were already friends, and it seemed like he held onto my hand forever. He said, 'After our little play, I hope you'll all come back to my suite. We'll talk about the movies.'

"Liam said, 'Where are you staying?' and Eddie let go of my hand. I hated Liam then, Mitch. For interrupting. Couldn't he see that Eddie was talking *to me?*" Valerie grinned.

328

"Eddie said, 'At the Royal York.'"

Of course, Mitch thought. The famed Fairmont Royal York, Toronto's jewel, the tallest building in the commonwealth. They even had a ghost: the eighth floor was supposedly haunted by an elderly man in a red smoking-jacket. The room service was flawless. Mitch had stayed there himself while filming *Erskine*. No other lodging would have sufficed for big-in-Canada Edison Forbes.

"Eddie turned back to me and said, 'Tell me, Valerie, which of my movies is your favorite?'"

Mitch felt a jolt of unreality. He was suddenly transported back to his booth at TTAMS, being prompted by the system to ask subscribers exactly the same question.

"I told him that *Undercover Homicide* was my favorite. He winked at Liam. 'That's his favorite, too.'

"Liam said, 'It was definitely one of my favorite paychecks.'

"Eddie asked me, 'You didn't care for *Desperate Caper?*' He grinned, and again I felt weak. I caught Joyce rolling her eyes. I said, 'I loved your Southern accent in that one.'

"Eddie laughed, and it was like something out of a rom-com, Mitch, like a cliché. My heart skipped a beat. Everything about him seemed *so familiar* to me. He said, 'You're much too kind, Valerie. *Desperate Caper* is one I'd desperately like to forget.'

Mitch felt that way about *Shamus Alive* sometimes. He definitely felt that way about *Stutter and Scream*.

"Someone knocked on the door, said, 'Five minutes, Eddie,' and I thought they should've said *Mr. Forbes*. He was famous, after all, despite one American-made, Hollywood Pictures' flop. He took my hand again, and said, 'I'll see you after the show?'

"*As much of me as you'd like*, I thought." Valerie giggled. "I told him I wouldn't miss it for the world."

A little bit of the fan peeped out there. Mitch smiled to himself.

"Eddie told Joyce it was great to meet her, and he slapped Liam on the back again. Liam told him to break a leg. Eddie smiled at me once more, and we left the green room. We went out to the theatre and found our seats, second row center, just like Liam had promised.

"The play was great. Eddie was great. There was an intermission — the three of us went out and mingled with the crowd in the lobby, because I wanted to listen to the Canadian accents. Perhaps overhear someone speaking French. I was on vacation, was I not?

"The intermission wasn't supposed to be very long, maybe fifteen minutes . . ." Valerie's voice faded, and her eyes became faraway, unfocused. She looked out at the lights of LA, but Mitch knew she wasn't seeing them.

Valerie sighed. "But the time stretched to a half-hour. The murmurs of the people in the lobby took on a questioning tone. Some went back to their seats. Some of us stayed in the lobby. After forty-five minutes, Liam said he'd just sneak backstage and see what was up. The moment he disappeared into the crowd, the houselights dimmed. As we made our way back to our seats, a voice came over the PA. 'We apologize for the delay, ladies and gentlemen. For the second half of our performance, the part of Paul Verrall will be played by Dean Knutson.'

"'Who?' Joyce whispered.

"I told her that he was probably the understudy."

The show must go on, Mitch thought.

Valerie sighed again. "The curtain went up. The rest of the play seemed rushed, as if the cast was just trying to get it over with. The audience applauded uncertainly; there was no curtain call. Liam didn't come back. When the houselights came up, there were only hushed, wondering murmurs as the crowd got up to leave.

"I felt my phone vibrate. It was a text from Liam, telling us to meet him out front. The car was double-parked; Liam was yelling at someone who was not vey politely telling him to move it."

Insanely, Mitch thought, *Is this not a reasonable place to park?*

"We got into the car, and amid honks and obscene gestures, Liam pulled out. It was snowing heavily now, and the traffic was a mess, so we were silent, letting Liam negotiate it. I noticed that he was as white as the snow – I wondered what was going on. I thought that maybe it was planned that the understudy would take Eddie's part for the second half. He and Liam had probably been sitting around backstage, reminiscing. It was all strange, but it was Canada, Eddie was famous. Maybe it was par for the course for him to blow off the second act. I didn't know.

"Liam didn't speak while he parked the car, or while we went up to the lobby of our hotel. Joyce looked at him curiously, and I thought I saw his eyes widen a little when he looked back at her. He sat down on a couch in the lobby and put his head in his hands. I couldn't imagine what was wrong, but the play was over – I was going to get to see Eddie again! We were going to his suite at some fancy hotel, and I was going to get to talk to him to my heart's content! He would tell me what had happened with the rest of the play.

330

"Liam was just being . . . I didn't know what Liam was being, but he was wasting our time. Eddie was waiting for us. I said, 'I'm gonna go upstairs and change.'

"Not taking his head from his hands, Liam at last spoke. His voice was a croaky whisper. 'You do that, Val. I'll be . . . I'll be there in a minute.'

"I thought that maybe he was just overreacting to the fact that Eddie had abandoned the second half of the play, the play we had come all the way from California to see him in. I thought that Liam was just being silly – I didn't care about the play. I was going to get to see Eddie again, when he wasn't rushed, when there wasn't some stagehand knocking on the door telling him, *Five minutes, Mr. Forbes*. It was gonna be fantastic.

"I looked at Joyce. She studied Liam for another second, then said, 'You go on, Val. I'll be right there.'

"I thought she was just being silly, too. When had Joyce become a theatre critic? Didn't they realize that I didn't care about the play?

"I went up to our room, and was in the middle of changing into something more comfortable, something *warmer*, when Liam knocked on the door. I told him to come in. But it wasn't Liam. It was Joyce."

Now the words poured forth from Valerie. Mitch was reminded of his own confession to her on TTAMS, about Janna. Her words were like a waterfall, spilling, free-falling. He wondered if she had ever told this story to another living soul.

"Her face was white; her eye make-up was all smudged. I told her to hurry up and fix her face, Eddie was waiting for us. I flitted around the room. She stood in the open doorway and just stared at me. I told her to come in and shut the door, she was letting in the cold. She closed the door and still just stared at me.

"Finally, I said, 'What is *wrong* with you people? It was just a play! I don't care about the stupid play! Come on, Jo, change your clothes, Eddie's waiting for me!'

"She told me to sit down. I told her we didn't have time. A tear ran down her face. I stopped then. Joyce never cries, Mitch. She's *one tough cookie*.

"I sat on the bed, and she sat next to me, took my hands. The tears were running down her face now. I forgot about the play, I forgot about Eddie. I thought that something must've happened back home, some terrible thing. She must've got a call when she was downstairs with Liam . . . Maybe her mom or dad . . .

"It even started out that way. Joyce said, 'There's been an accident, Val.' At this tired, worn-out cliché, all the choking sorrow came back –

331

I suddenly couldn't breathe – just like when Daddy told me about Mom and Aunt Elise. Somebody was hurt – was it my family or hers? If it was my family, surely, they would've called me? Maybe something had happened to Brett . . .

"'Eddie's dead, Val,' Joyce said softly. She sobbed, and I was dumbstruck at her incredible theatrics.

"'It's just a play, Jo!' I said. 'He's had bad reviews before! Hell, *Desperate Caper* got a Tomatometer rating of –'

"Joyce squeezed my hands. 'Listen to me, Val. There was some kind of an accident. He went outside, at intermission. Probably to have a quick smoke, Liam said.'

"I knew he smoked Camels, Mitch. I had read it in some interview.

"'He slipped,' Joyce said. 'Or maybe somebody mugged him. Liam says they don't know for sure yet. He hit his head. A stagehand found him at the bottom of the stairs, but it was too late. Eddie's dead, Val.'

"It was like the climactic scene from every tragedy ever filmed. I even said the expected response, Mitch. I said, 'This isn't funny, Jo.'

"She sobbed again and hugged me. 'I'm so sorry, Valley! Liam went back to the theatre . . . Eddie doesn't have any family here . . . he's gonna go to the –'

"I put my hands over my ears, accidently knocking Joyce backwards on the bed. I couldn't bear to hear her say *morgue*. All the horrible, suffocating feelings came back. I was paralyzed; I couldn't breathe. I felt like I was gonna die."

Mitch realized that he had never felt that all-at-once, devastating inundation of pain and grief. When he had found Janna, cold and unresponsive, he'd just felt one brief shock of agony. He had gasped, then it had passed, when the door of inevitability had closed softly in his mind, trapping all the guilt and sorrow inside his head. He had known this was how it was going to end when he'd found her sleeping peacefully beside her pills that day, post rehab, when she wasn't expecting him to find her. It could've ended no other way.

And this woman sitting beside him now had helped him through the aftermath of that. Mitch took her hand and squeezed it.

"Joyce got up. She told me to try to catch my breath, that she had to get something from her room. She told me not to go anywhere – where was I going to go? I was in a strange town, a strange country. It was snowing. Eddie was dead, lying in a cold *morgue* somewhere, with nobody with him but *the Foley guy* . . .

"Joyce was only gone for a minute. I hadn't gone anywhere. I heard the water running in the bathroom, then she came back out with a glass of water and three pills.

"'I want you to take these,' she told me. 'They'll make you sleep. I'll get us a flight home in the morning.'

"I heard Joey Ramone singing in my head, Mitch. *Just get me to the airport, put me on a plane. Hurry, hurry, hurry, before I go insane. I can't control my fingers, I can't control my brain. Oh, no, oh, oh, oh, oh* . . . I took the pills from her and swallowed them. Joyce always knows what to do. The most perfect man I'd ever seen, that I'd finally *got to meet*, was dead. No one needed to be sedated more than me.

"I only saw Liam once more. He came to get his luggage from our hotel room the next morning, as we were checking out. We cried together. It turned out that he was more than just the Foley guy on one of Eddie's movies. They were childhood friends. He was going to stay on in Canada until after the funeral."

Valerie took a deep, shuddery breath. "Needless to say, Eddie's death was another monumental tragedy in my life. At the airport, on the plane, Joyce watched me like a mother hen. She was worried that I might freak out again, might suddenly turn suicidal on her. This was surely a bigger shock to me than breaking up with Brett.

"It was on the plane . . . Joyce was asleep. I was beyond paralyzed, beyond depressed, but I wasn't suicidal. Just numb."

Mitch tried to imagine the devastation of Valerie's decimated anticipation. She had been *so incredibly high* – she had met the man of her dreams, she was going go back to his hotel room after the show – then she was plunged, so abruptly, so completely, so irretrievably low, like an egg dropped out of an airplane. She must've felt the very terminal velocity of disappointment. The penny hadn't split her skull, but the opportunity forever lost had definitely affected her.

Mitch wasn't sure he wanted to discover just exactly how much it had affected her . . .

"I couldn't sleep. My mind was full of Eddie, of what might've been . . . But there was no use thinking about that, was there? Eddie was dead. It might've been his native weather that had taken him, or maybe it was a mugger."

Mitch remembered seeing the article on Variety.com, quite by chance. *Canada Mourns Favorite Son.* Eddie had been a nice guy, and Mitch had been shocked and saddened by his one-time co-star's sudden, perhaps malicious death. He and Ronny Prince had sent a wreath.

"I scrolled through the movies available on the flight. The main feature was *The Notebook*. The last thing I needed was a bittersweet tale of love and quiet, peaceful endings, starring two Canadians. I took out my phone and looked at Eddie's pictures.

"My favorites have always been the two stills of you guys from *Two's a Crowd.*" When Mitch looked uncertain, Valerie showed them to him on her phone. The ghost of Eddie's curious smile made Valerie smile, as it always did.

"I was looking at this very picture . . . And I heard Eddie's voice. He said, 'Hi, Valley,' just as plainly as if he was sitting right next to me. I was startled. I looked around, to see if it was all some kind of twisted joke. I expected to look up and see him leaning over the seat. That's how clear his voice was."

In your head. Realization harshly jarred Mitch. He saw Norman Bates, wrapped in a blanket at the police station. Stark colorless shadows: the blank gray wall, Anthony Perkins's black hair and black eyes, his maniacal grin. And Mother's voice over: *I'll just sit here and be quiet, just in case they do . . . suspect me . . . They'll see and they'll know. And they'll say, 'Why she wouldn't even harm a fly . . .'*

"Of course, he wasn't there. I looked back at the picture. Eddie said, 'I'm sorry about how things turned out, Val. I was really looking forward to getting to know you better.'"

These were Mitch's own words, the very phrase he had thought of concerning Valerie. He had just gone right on ahead and *gotten to know her better*, without bothering to find out ahead of time that she was a stark, raving lunatic. Brilliant programmer Valerie Whitly, creator of the world's hottest infotainment service, was not afflicted with Janna's self-loathing, self-destructive delusions, but Mitch now knew that she was still just as nutty as the oft-mentioned fruitcake.

"I opened my mouth to answer him," Valerie continued. "But there was no one there to be talking to. The whole situation was just *unbelievable* . . . But I could hear Eddie. Somehow, from the other side . . ."

Mitch thought of Jackie from Torrance and her fortune-telling grandma.

"I got up and went to the restroom. I asked Eddie all kinds of things. How could this be? Where was he? Had he just slipped on the ice, or had someone murdered him? I figured that no one could hear me talking in there, over the drone of the engines.

"He said he didn't know where he was, didn't remember what had happened. He said, 'What difference does it make? I'm talking to you, am I not?'"

334

Valerie studied Mitch's expression. He tried to keep it blank, interested, as if it was an everyday occurrence that the woman he'd been sleeping with for a week suddenly confessed that she talked to a dead man, and that he talked back.

Mitch wasn't entirely successful at keeping his face neutral.

Valerie squinted suspiciously at him. "Remember, when we were chatting on the system, and I told you that I talk to Eddie all the time?"

Mitch nodded, not daring to speak.

"Why did you cut me off?"

That had been the first kernel, the first inkling of her madness. Greg had heard it, and not wanting to hear anymore, had ended the session. Mitch thought that he should've realized right then, just like Greg had . . .

But Greg had still hoped that Valerie would log on and talk to him again, that she would ask him about his poor, possibly murdered Canadian co-star. Valerie would finally get to hear the answer to the one question that could never be answered IRL, and Greg could later benefit from her gratitude.

But Mitch knew now that Valerie never would've asked him that question. Greg had seen a flash of crazy and had killed their session, but he didn't know how far it went. Valerie wouldn't bother to ask Mitch about Eddie, because she already knew. They were buddies. *They talked all the time.*

Valerie was waiting for him to reply. "I didn't . . . it wasn't me . . ."

"That's what I thought. Just another bug. So I freaked out over nothing. I know how this all must sound to you, Mitch. And that's why I went looking for you that night. I ran a trace – found you in the Prep Center. I was shocked to see you in there, let me tell you."

Not half as shocked as I am right now.

"Nobody knows that I talk to Eddie, except for Joyce. It's all just so . . ."

Insane? Bonkers? Nuts? Cray-cray?

". . . Unusual. Everything that I hold to be true tells me that Eddie can't be talking to me. Yet I hear him. Maybe there is an afterlife."

All dogs go to heaven, Mitch thought, feeling a little nuts himself. *And Canadian actors, too. You're a film buff, aren't ya, Val? Ever seen Psycho, have ya? Or Friday the Thirteenth? Or how about Fight Club? Primal Fear? Dressed to Kill? The Three Faces of Eve? Christ, you've seen enough movies! Hearing voices in one's head is a Hollywood staple! How can you possibly not know that it's you that's talking for Eddie?*

Mitch could tell from the look on her face that the idea had never occurred to her. The *unusual* phenomenon of conversing with her

335

favorite dead actor was just a wondrous miracle to Valerie Whitly. The possibility that it defined madness had not crossed her mind.

Mitch heard a voice himself, that of David Mills, the doomed cop from *Se7en*: *I've been trying to figure something in my head, and maybe you can help me out, yeah? When a person is insane, as you clearly are, do you know that you're insane? Do you just stop and go, "Wow! It is amazing how fucking crazy I really am?" Yeah. Do you guys do that?*

"So when I opened my big mouth and told you about it," Valerie was saying, "and then we got cut off – I panicked. I thought that you were just an operator – I thought that you'd somehow figured out who I was, that you would tell the whole floor that I was talking about my family to a simulation on TTAMS, talking about Eddie. I couldn't be havin' that."

Mitch blinked to hear her use Greg's expression; then he remembered that they had gone to college together.

"But now that I know you, I know you won't tell anyone. I trust you, Mitch." She snuggled against him.

"Of course not, Valerie."

I'll never tell a living soul. My daddy always said, never sleep with anyone crazier than you are, and this is twice now that I have inadvertently ignored his advice. Apparently I'm attracted to nuts. No, Valley, I won't tell. It'd make me look as insane as you. Can't be havin' that.

Valerie smiled. "I haven't told you the best part."

How could it get any better than this? Mitch asked himself hysterically.

"Riding back from the airport, Joyce and I were quiet, but she could tell that my mood had changed. She knows me, Mitch. She's my best friend. She asked me if I was okay, and I told her I was. I asked her to give me a few hours, and then I had something to tell her.

"I knew that it was weird. It's still weird, even though I'm used to it. I always tell myself, when I get a spare minute, I'm going to read up on the afterlife."

Mitch suddenly believed for a moment that he should turn screenwriter. He had the pitch: brilliant programmer hears voices, but it's not because she's as mad as a hatter, as balmy as a March hare. Oh, no. How commonplace would that be? It's because the souls of the departed have figured out a way to communicate with the living via the miracles of modern electronic technology . . .

He heard Ronny Prince's voice. *It's been done.*

Valerie continued, grinning. The big reveal was coming. "I went to my room, flopped down on my bed. I would unpack later. It wasn't like I was ever gonna need all those coats and gloves and warm clothes."

Not ever again.

"I opened my laptop. The pictures are bigger." Valerie giggled, and Mitch thought of Ophelia, her mind completely gone. "I said to Eddie's picture, 'This is so great. Now I can talk to you whenever I want!'

"He said, 'Now we can finally get to know each other.'"

And that's the crux of it all, right there, Mitch thought. *The seed, the root of her insanity.* Getting to know Edison Forbes had been presented to her, and on a silver platter. He had been friendly . . . Who knew what incredibly wonderful things could've been in store? Then all the *what might have beens and happily ever afters* were cruelly yanked away by an uncaring universe. Valerie had been so close, on the very doorstep of finding out: *What was Edison Forbes really like?* The door was ajar, the light of curiosity-at-long-last-satisfied beckoned . . .

Then the door was slammed in her face, locked, the key thrown into the abyss. Valerie's mind, as the cliché goes, had quite simply snapped in response. Fate had decreed that she would never know Eddie, the one thing she had wondered so much about, for *so long* . . .

But we couldn't be havin' a disappointment like that. Death had rendered Eddie incommunicado on this plane of existence, but Valerie would still get to know him, because now he was talking to her from the other side.

"Then he said, 'What if it could be like that with anybody, Valley?' I didn't understand – I was confused for a minute."

You're confused, all right, and it's been for more than just a minute.

"I thought about mediums and séances, Mitch. I thought maybe Elise was there with him, that he was gonna bring her around to talk to me, too."

This had to be what Valerie meant by *the best part.* She didn't just have a split-personality, like Norman Bates with his mother, like the narrator from *Fight Club* with Tyler Durden. Oh, no. Valerie had developed *multiple personalities. That was the best part! Not only Eddie Forbes, but her aunt, too, and Christ only knows who else* . . . Mitch discovered that he was holding his breath.

"But that wasn't it."

Thank God for small favors . . . Mitch exhaled, relieved, amazed that he could find only a split-personality a relief.

"Eddie said, 'I mean other actors, Val. What if you could talk to any other actor, living or dead? What if they would be friendly to you, say anything you wanted?'

"I asked him how that could be, and he said, 'You know all about motion-capture, right?' He did the voiceover from *The Six Million Dollar Man: Gentlemen, we can rebuild him. We have the technology. We have the*

337

capability to make the world's first bionic man. Steve Austin will be that man. Better than he was before. Better . . . stronger . . . faster.' "

Where does she get this stuff? Mitch wondered. *The Six Million Dollar Man?* That was from before *he* was born. *It's the internet, and a parent's fond memories. Her mother had probably once said, 'There was this show when I was a kid, Valley . . .' A child's curiosity plus YouTube equals dead Canadian actors telling her about Steve Austin.*

"Eddie laughed. 'I know you can do it, Valley. Not a bionic man, but a computer-generated simulation. A Max Headroom kind of thing." Another one from before she was born. "A face on a screen. Just like the monkeys you did for *Dawn of the Planet of the Apes.* But they'll be Hollywood monkeys, Val! People in facial motion capture devices, pretending to be celebrities, talking to their fans, just like you're talking to me now.' "

Mitch was speechless. *Though this be madness, yet there is method in't.*

" 'You'll make a whole lot more than six million bucks,' Eddie added."

Valerie smiled dollar signs, an expression Mitch had often seen on Ronny Prince's fat face. *Let's make lots of money.*

"I've made much more than that, Mitch, *my brother and only friend.* And I owe it all to Edison Forbes, dead though he may be."

****

Mitch Barlo liked the owner of TTAMS. He liked her a lot. Maybe all geniuses were insane, dependent on dead muses for their inspiration. But still, he was rather glad to drop Valerie off at the office the next day. He had to meet with Ronny, discuss doing the three-sisters deal. That was crazy enough – the script wasn't really his cup of tea, as the saying goes – but it was Hollywood crazy. He was familiar with that.

When the limo idled up to the curb, Valerie said, "Could you sneak back here tonight, Mitch? Maybe just for a minute? Hide in the Prep Center like you always do? I want to surprise Joyce. She's a big fan, although she'd never admit it. I'd like her to meet you." When he hesitated, she added, "I'm not gonna tell her about . . . us."

Mitch considered. He knew that he couldn't just drop Valerie Whitly like a bad habit, no matter how crazy she was. She was too prominent in this town. Such a thing was just not done to women like her. It was . . . impolite. He heard Ronny's voice: *She'll talk, and she won't say anything nice.*

Besides, Mitch was fond of Valerie, just not romance-relationship fond. Unlike Janna, she'd revealed her insanity too soon. But still, he liked her. They would always be friends – how could they not be friends, after all they'd shared?

So it was with an infinite sense of relief that Mitch realized, now, as they were parting, that Valerie wasn't asking him to continue what they'd had for a week. It had been delightful, but anything more, well . . .

She wanted to introduce him to her buddy, the CEO of TTAMS, the hot executive that his agent had so wanted to meet, but Valerie wasn't going to divulge their brief *us* to her friend.

Why not meet her? Mitch decided that he had a few choice words for Joyce Vinson, anyway, formerly the sole keeper of Valerie's secret. For all intents and purposes, really, *her sister's keeper.*

"Sure, Val. Say this evening, like seven?"

"It'll be fun. She'll be so surprised!" Valerie giggled. Mitch still found her adorable, even if she was a lunatic.

She gave him a quick, fun kiss and alit from the limo.

****

Joyce wasn't onsite. It was the weekend, after all, but when Valerie called her, she said she'd be right in.

"That's okay, Jo. Enjoy the rest of your day. I've got stuff to do. Maybe this evening?"

"Of course, Val. I miss you! Just text me."

Valerie hung up and began slogging through a week's worth of emails – production stats, hardware and software performance reports, happy descriptions of TTAMS's staggering bottom line – *Christ, how it does pile up!* She was barely into the first day's communiques, when she looked up to see Greg Castro standing in her doorway.

"How was your vacation?" he asked evenly.

Was there a tiny, gritty edge to his tone? Was it resentment? Had he really just glanced at the clock, as if to say, *Gee, ya finally came back, but ya couldn't make it in 'til one o'clock in the afternoon?*

Valerie was unmoved by Greg's annoyance. He had more than sufficient time accumulated: he was here nearly as much as she was. He could also take a vacation, if he so desired, so Valerie ignored his undertone of bitchiness. Her work ethic was above reproach.

"It was too short," she replied shortly, and returned his level stare.

Greg held it, then looked away. He entered the office and threw himself down into the chair in front of her desk. He smiled. The umbrage of a hard-working employee for an uncharacteristically irresponsible boss evaporated. They were friends again.

"I've got a surprise for you, Val. I've been meaning to tell you, but I just haven't had a spare minute." Greg offered his best *you know how that is,* apologetic grin. "But I'm pretty sure you're gonna like it."

As her Number 3 employee spun his tale of some fortunate operator and his friends in high places, of the curious actor and his hidden workstation in the Prep Center, of his enjoyment of talking to his fans, of the revenue he was bringing in, Valerie endeavored to look surprised, then interested, then pleased. At last she smiled. Relief flowed through Greg. He loved it when Valerie smiled like that.

When his saga was concluded, she said, "I can't begin to tell you how much I love it, Greg." *You have absolutely no idea.* "Tell Mr. Barlo he can stay on as long as he likes. Give his operator buddy a raise for bringing him onboard. Just keep it all on the down low, will ya? If everybody knows . . . it'll be a distraction. Let's just keep it our little secret – you, me. The actor and his friend."

We all have secrets – the ones we keep, and the ones that are kept from us. Where have you been for a week, Val?

"Of course," Greg said. Then he eyed her cautiously. "Would you . . . Would you like to meet him?" He hoped that his longing ambition for her grateful friendship didn't show.

Valerie smirked; her eyes flickered to the screen in front of her so the Ops Director wouldn't see their mirth. Apparently Greg was unaware that she had already met with Mitch Barlo, here in her office – he certainly didn't know anything else they'd done. *Maybe you should keep better tabs on the activities of your secret employees, Greg, my brother and only friend.*

"I'm a little swamped right now, Greg. Just back from vacation and all." She gave him back his *you know how it is* expression. "Maybe some other time."

Her desk phone buzzed. It could be no one else but Joyce. The number to Valerie Whitly's direct line was as closely guarded as a Vatican secret.

She smiled at Greg – *What're ya gonna do?* Here was yet another workaday interruption; they couldn't even have a meeting on a Saturday afternoon without the phone ringing off the hook. Valerie pushed the speaker phone button, said brightly, "Shello?"

"For Christ's sake, Val, would you please, I beg you, I *entreat you* – would you please talk to Brett? We're in the lobby. He followed me here. He said you won't answer his calls, so he's begging me to bring him up there right now. I told him you don't want to see him, but will you please just talk to him?"

"Hold on a sec, Jo." Valerie noticed that Greg was frowning again. "I'm sorry, Greg. I have to take this. Tell Mr. Barlo I said, *Welcome to TTAMS*. Tell him that I'll talk to him . . . sometime."

Greg's frown remained. "Okay, Val. I'll see you later." He stood, turned, and stalked stiffly down the steel steps.

Valerie discovered that she was pleased with Brett's persistence. She wasn't thinking about Mitch now, nor the put-on meeting they'd have to enact for Greg's benefit.

She took a deep breath. "All right, Jo. Put him on."

"Hi, Val," Brett said softly. It was not a sexy whisper, but Valerie found that she was put in mind of the many times that he *had* whispered her name, mornings and evenings and afternoons spent in bed with him . . . *Ah, Brett, honey* . . .

Although Valerie had been thinking about him, reconsidering, maybe . . . he would not win that easily. "What do you want?" she asked coldly.

"Let me come up there and talk to you, Val."

"This is a place of business, Mr. Cooke. I have a ton of work to do today. Perhaps Ms Vinson can make you an appointment."

Brett was stunned by her icy, boss's demeanor. There was silence for a heartbeat. Then . . . "So you will see me? If I . . . make an appointment?"

Valerie tried to keep her voice stern. "Apparently, it's either that or I'm gonna have to call security to get rid of you."

Brett was hesitant, but Valerie still caught a hint of his old, familiar, lady-killer's confidence when he said, "How 'bout dinner then? Maybe six?"

"I've gotta get some work done, Brett. I've been out of the office for a—"

Brett didn't want to hear about her *vacation*. "All right. How about eight?"

"Okay, Brett," Valerie said quietly. It wasn't really like she was giving in. She was just facing her problems head-on, sooner rather than later.

"And I'm a Chinese jet pilot," Eddie's voice said in her mind.

Valerie smiled. He was right. Not only was she giving in by agreeing to see Brett, she was looking forward to seeing him. The conversations that she'd had with Mitch, the gloriously fun week that she had spent with him – Valerie felt that she was a stronger person for making the actor's acquaintance. She was no longer the confused, frightened idiot that she'd been when Brett had just shown up in the garage. Mitch had freed her from all that. Valerie was *not that chained up little person still in love with you.*

Eddie started to take exception to this, too, but Valerie cut him off, saying to Brett, "I'll see you then."

"I can't wait, Val." It still wasn't his sexy voice, but all of his confidence had returned with those four little words. Valerie told herself (and Eddie) that she may or may not still be in love with Brett, but she did *so* enjoy his confidence. She felt her own swell – she could handle Brett.

"Put Joyce back on, will you?"

"He's smiling, so it must be all good." Valerie could hear her friend's own smile.

"It used to be," Valerie said, and grinned at Joyce's surprised bark of laughter. "I've still got a dogpile of work to do, Jo–"

"Yeah, me, too. Brett just skipped out of here, Val. He literally *skipped.* I'm so glad that you decided to talk to him. So he'll leave me alone, and because . . . he's different now. He's grown up. I think he's serious about making a go of it this time."

"You always know best, Jo. I'll listen to what he has to say." *Especially if he's whispering it in my ear* . . . Valerie shivered, and chided herself for behaving like a tramp. *A week with one pretty, confident man's not good enough for me. I'm already thinking impure thoughts about another one. Ah, Brett, honey* . . .

"I'm pulling for you guys, Val," Joyce said.

"I appreciate it. Do me a big favor, will ya, Jo? Come up here, like sevenish tonight? I've gotta get through this email. But there's something I want to show you before I leave."

****

Joyce climbed the steel steps promptly at seven o'clock. The best friends hugged, as if it had been far longer than a week since they'd last seen each other.

Joyce held Valerie's hands out at arms' length. "I see you got a little sun. Where did you go?"

The programmer shook her head. "Like *Agatha,* Jo. I'm sure I'll tell you someday, but not right now."

Valerie sat down behind her desk, and Joyce took the chair in front of it. She let the subject of Val's mysterious week-long disappearance drop. Maybe she had been off somewhere, plotting revenge against Brett, as had the character in the movie she'd described. Joyce smiled to herself: apparently those plans had changed.

And Joyce knew that trying to get Valerie Whitly to talk about something she didn't want to talk about was fruitless, like arguing that there was a better-looking actor in the world than Edison Forbes, like attempting to teach a pig to sing. It would just make Joyce look foolish, and she had no desire to annoy her friend, after missing her for a week. Valerie looked great; her smile was bubbly and infectious. Wherever she'd been, it had restored the roses to her cheeks.

"What did you want to show me?

****

Greg was calling him, and Mitch considered that in the busy world of modern life, why, he could just go right on ahead and not answer the phone. If Valerie had mentioned their *vacation* together, then Greg could rant, he could threaten, he could express his betrayal, to voicemail. Mitch had absolutely no words with which to answer his friend. He had no real excuse for his behavior. *She didn't pick you,* wasn't good enough.

But Greg was his friend, or at least he had been. And sending your friend to voicemail because taking his call might be uncomfortable was just chickenshit.

"What's up, Boss Man?"

"I've got some really good news, and some pretty shitty, definitely annoying news."

"Good news is good news," Mitch said lamely.

At least he's not calling me a son of a bitch. Not yet. Mitch relaxed a little. If Valerie wasn't planning on telling her best friend about their week-long bacchanal, then she surely wasn't going to describe it to her Ops Director. Her employee.

"Enlighten me," Mitch said.

"Valerie finally decided to come back to work this afternoon. I still don't know where she was." Greg sighed. "What I told her – it was actually Baker's idea. I just went up there and said that I had a surprise for her."

It's good for me that she didn't have a surprise for you.

"I told her everything, after a fashion. That you were friends with Baker, that you'd expressed an interest, so we brought you onboard. She didn't say that she already knew. I didn't say that I knew she already knew. She said she loved the idea."

Mitch smiled to himself. *She loved it for a week, anyway.*

When Greg didn't go on, the actor asked, "What's the shitty part?"

"Ah . . . It doesn't have anything to do with you, Mitch." He fell silent again.

"What, Greg?"

The tech sighed once more. "I was there in Valerie's office, and Joyce called on the land line. She was in the lobby. Valerie put her on speaker, then Joyce gave the phone to Brett Cooke."

Mitch was a good actor, an Oscar-contender. Though Greg hadn't intended it as such, Mitch knew a cue when he heard one. "Who?"

"He was Valerie's boyfriend in college." Greg laughed humorlessly, bitterly. "Another dark-haired, blue-eyed pretty boy, like you and Eddie Forbes."

"And she hadn't seen him since college? Did he move away or something?"

Mitch was fishing. Greg knew about Valerie's obsession with Edison Forbes, although Mitch would've bet that the tech couldn't even begin to imagine the startlingly insane depth of *that* well. How much did he know about other-woman-texting Brett Cooke and Valerie's relationship with him?

"I dunno, Mitch. All I know – when Valerie started working with me at Fox, she was single. She never mentioned Brett Cooke again. I was glad. I'd always found him to be a smug asshole. Full of himself. He got more girls than he deserved. He didn't need to have Valerie, too."

Mitch pressed. "But was it a bad breakup, Greg? Maybe she won't want to see him again."

"I don't know anything about it. All I know is that Valerie hasn't had a boyfriend since, except for some wormy Canadian Foley guy."

Greg lowered his voice. "While we were working at Fox, Valerie took off for the weekend with this sound guy. It hit me when she was talking to you, Mitch. If anything she was saying about meeting Eddie Forbes was even remotely true, the only time it could've possibly happened was when she was gone with that snowback Foley twerp. Maybe he knew Eddie. Maybe they'd worked together . . .

"But then I thought, maybe *it's just my imagination, runnin' away with me*. Just because some four-eyed sound guy is Canadian, doesn't mean that he introduced Valerie to her idol.

"But when she was talking to you, I remembered the timing.

"I used to have a Google notification set up – if Eddie's name appeared on the internet, I'd know about it. I figured, maybe then I'd have an excuse to talk to Valerie about whatever he was doing. But I never got the chance, Mitch. The only notifications I ever got were a bunch of articles, all at once, from Variety.com and *The Toronto Star, The*

Toronto Sun. All bearing the bad news that Edison Forbes was dead. He'd been mugged, or he'd slipped. Hit his head. Bled to death.

"If it could possibly be true, if somehow, the Foley guy did know him, then the only time Valerie could've met Eddie Forbes was the weekend that he died. That's when they were gone.

"Then, when she started telling you that she *talks to him* . . . It was just too nuts, Mitch. Nobody wants to believe that somebody they love is crazy . . ."

Can I get an amen?

"But she's still got all those pictures of him on her computer, she's still obsessed with him . . . So I crashed your session. I didn't want to hear any more about how she *talks to him*. It wasn't until later that I realized that she was probably making it all up. It was all just part of the fantasy of TTAMS, of talking to Eddie's co-star. She probably just figured that a simulation wouldn't know that he was dead. I shouldn't have cut her off, but I panicked. She sounded so sincere, like she really believed what she was saying, like she believed that she talks to a dead Canadian nobody. It was just too crazy to think about.

"But now, I'm sure. Valerie's never been to Canada, with that sound guy or anyone else. She never met Edison Forbes."

Mitch could tell that Greg wasn't sure about anything. He pictured the Ops Director chewing his fingernail, talking himself out of the idea that his lady-love was a lunatic.

"The timing's just a coincidence. Valerie knows Eddie's dead."

She does indeed, my friend, but that doesn't stop her from talking to him, nor he to her.

Greg sighed. "Anyway, like I say, Valerie's never had another boyfriend since college, except for that Canuck sound guy, and that didn't last. But now asshole Cooke's back, and she's gonna see him again. That's the shitty part about today's news."

Mitch felt a stab of jealousy. He'd thought that his weeklong romp with Ms Whitly had caused her to forget this cheating pretty boy from her past; apparently he was mistaken. But then a silky relief whispered to Mitch. Not only did he not have to worry about cute-but-crazy Valerie deciding that she wanted to continue their little thing, she wasn't going to tell anybody about it, either. Not her girlfriend, not Greg. Not if she was getting back with Brett. Valerie and Mitch would continue to be friends, but that was all. Greg would never find out about the actor's ill-advised, week-long consolation of his beloved. Mitch wouldn't lose the tech's friendship.

"I'm sorry to hear about all this, Boss Man. Is there anything I can do?"

"If she ever talks to you again, execute the original plan." Greg laughed and it was lighter now. "It's like I've said all along. Eddie's dead. No one Valerie knows can ever tell her what he was like except you. You tell her, she comes around and thanks me for bringing you onboard . . . It could still bring us closer, make us better friends, even if she is seeing that jerk Brett Cooke."

"I will try my damnedest, Greg, if she ever talks to me again," Mitch told the Ops Director with an utterly heartfelt sincerity. *I'd like to thank the Academy . . .*

Mitch knew that he'd never talk to Valerie on TTAMS again. If she wanted to cry on his shoulder, if things didn't work out with her college sweetheart this time, she'd just call him. Maybe drop by the house for a little swim.

And if for some reason she did contact him through the service again, if Greg's keeper alerted him, and he became an unseen auditor once again, it would all come to nothing. Valerie was never going to ask Mitch about Edison Forbes; all the prompting in the world would never *lead her to it*. She knew everything about Eddie that she wanted to know, because she'd made it all up herself.

"Are you coming in tonight?" Greg asked.

"Yeah. About seven."

"I'll be off the clock by then. I'm thinking about drinking myself into a stupor and sticking pins in a Brett Cooke doll."

Mitch laughed. *I'll help you.* He wondered for a minute what it was that Valerie liked so much about some guy that she thought had cheated on her in college . . . But then he let it go. No sense in analyzing the bullet he had dodged. Getting involved with the owner of TTAMS would not have been a good idea. On so many levels.

"I'll make it a short shift," he told Greg. "Those of us that work for free can do that. I'll come by and see you. Tell you all about this dog of a script my agent sent over."

"That sounds great, Mitch. I know a little bit about movies. I'll give you my best Roger Ebert opinion."

****

"You've never experienced a TTAMS session, have you, Jo? My service is making you rich, and you've never even tried it. Not one single time."

"You know I'm not into movies like you are, Val."

"I'm a lawyer, Jim, not a fan. Unless it's Mitch Barlo, maybe?"

Joyce wagged her head slightly in agreement. "He's a good actor."

346

"I believe the word you used was *fine*, Counsellor." Valerie turned her laptop to face Joyce, then came around the desk and pulled another chair away from the wall. She sat in it and smiled. "I want you to talk to Mitch Barlo on TTAMS, Jo. As a personal favor to me."

Joyce opened her mouth to object. It was ridiculous. She didn't have the imagination that Val did, didn't possess her bottomless capacity for delusion. She couldn't pretend that a simulation of an actor was anything more than that, nothing more than an operator on the floor below, reading prompts off a screen. He would only look like Mitch Barlo – the whole thing was only making them rich – because of Valerie's brilliant programming.

But Joyce didn't decline. She had missed Valerie, had worried about her. She was glad to see her smiling, happy face again. Joyce figured the least she could do for her friend was this. She wouldn't have to talk to the fake Mitch Barlo for too long, anyway: Valerie was due to go out to dinner with Brett soon.

"Okay, Valley. I'll play your silly game."

"Great!"

The laptop's desktop background was a shot of Edison Forbes wearing a black fedora, from *Desperate Caper*. He smiled seductively at Joyce until Valerie hit a couple of keys and he blinked off, leaving a black screen. At the system prompt, she typed, *Locate MB426312*.

Y:\system> OpsPrepCent10T

Satisfied that Mitch was onsite, Valerie backed out to Windows, then called up the TTAMS home screen. She waited while Joyce entered the username and password to her never-before-accessed TTAMS profile. The system welcomed her, asked which star she would like to contact.

"Type his name and hit return, Jo. But don't do anything else."

Joyce complied. She got the landing screen, a cartoon-like mock-up of Mitch Barlo. These landing screens had been Greg Castro's idea, Joyce remembered. He'd said something about mimicking the graphics from some famous old music video, but Joyce thought that in reality, Greg just liked to make good-looking people look foolish, even if it was only for a moment.

Valerie turned on the mike and the webcam, then said, "Now, normally, you'd click here, and it would bring up a list of his movies and characters. Then you would choose which Mitch you wanted to talk to. But I have a little surprise for you tonight, *my brother and only friend.*"

Valerie again hit a few keys, causing a small black window to appear. Joyce noted that it had the same *Y:\system>* prompt as when

347

Valerie had blacked out the entire screen a moment before. But that was the extent of Joyce's observation. She didn't wonder what the programmer was doing, what was going to happen next, why Valerie was guiding the system instead of letting it guide them. Joyce didn't know anything about how computers worked, and had no interest in learning.

Valerie typed *MB426312, session override* and hit *Enter.*

A window opened and showed them the simulation of Mitch Barlo's face. Valerie made it full screen, and he blinked in surprise. Joyce also blinked. The simulation seemed utterly real.

"Dammit, Val," Mitch said good-naturedly. "I was talking to Andrea from San Diego. She was explaining how Billy's quick end in *Stutter and Scream* represents modern youth's loss of innocence in our fast-paced technological world. Or something like that. She forgets how old that movie is. Now you've sent her to the blue screen and killed her own technological innocence." The simulation grinned. "Or something like that."

"She'll be back. Like I told you once, your numbers are amazing. Could you hold on for one second?"

The simulation nodded, and Valerie clicked off the mike and webcam. "He can't see us or hear us right now."

"But we can still see him," Joyce said. She watched the fake Mitch Barlo look to the upper left hand corner of his screen. He smiled at whatever he read there.

"So, what do you think, Jo?" Valerie demanded excitedly.

Joyce was unsure what reaction was expected from her. It was true that the motion-capture simulation of good-looking Mitch Barlo was stunningly lifelike. Even Joyce's stunted, lawyer's imagination wouldn't have to reach too far to convince her that this was really him. But he hadn't done anything yet.

"What do you want me to say, Val?"

"Oh, my God, Jo!" Valerie gestured at the screen. "That's Mitch Barlo!"

"Obviously."

"No, Joyce. Honey. It's actually Mitch Barlo. He's downstairs in the Prep Center."

"Really." Joyce treated Valerie to her most withering *How dumb do you think I am?* glance. "Since when have we started hiring real actors? That might take a chunk out of the budget."

"This isn't costing us a dime, Jo."

"You've got to be kidding, Val. I know that I've never logged onto the system, but why do you think that you can make me believe that this guy is really–"

"Do you think that an operator would talk to me like that? *Dammit Val, why did you send my subscriber to the blue screen?* Seriously? I don't think even Greg would dare to address me like that."

"So you're telling me that you met with Mitch Barlo and talked him into working here?"

Joyce had spoken to the actor's agent – his name escaped her at the moment – and had requested the meeting for Val; then she had forgotten all about it. It wasn't her meeting after all, and she knew that in Hollywood, TTAMS embodied Teddy Roosevelt's advice: *Speak softly and carry a big stick; you will go far.* Joyce knew that a request for a meeting from her firm would not be ignored.

Joyce knew that Valerie had to have met with Mitch Barlo, but since she'd never mentioned it, the fact that it had no doubt occurred had slipped Joyce's mind. TTAMS was in early negotiations for expansion into the Japanese market; right now, the greater percentage of Joyce's attention was centered on that.

"No, you've got it backwards." Valerie fluttered her hands, annoyed that she had to waste time with the explanation.

She wanted Joyce to talk to Mitch. She wanted her to experience what it was like to be a fan, getting to interact with her favorite star. TTAMS was making a fortune by providing the illusion of just that, but this time, for Joyce, Valerie was making it real. And all Joyce wanted to do was dissect it. She was worse than the Cara training simulation.

"I wanted a meeting with him, because . . . I uncovered him working in the Prep Center one night. Hiding out."

"The real Mitch Barlo."

"Yes, Jo! Look at him! Our simulations are good, but not that good." Mitch was looking at his phone. "Besides, if he was a real operator, he'd get fired for what he's doing right now. If he was a real operator, he'd be smiling at the screen, waiting for us to come back." Valerie sighed in exasperation. "You can't *just go* with anything, can you? You have to see the contract, the signatures . . . But there's none of that this time, Jo. *Pay no attention to that man behind the curtain.*

"This is an anomaly. Mitch is friends with one of the operators. He expressed an interest in how the system works, so Greg let him in on the down low. He's everything but on the payroll. He enjoys pretending to be someone pretending to be him, talking to his fans. I found out he was here quite by accident. But now we . . . We talk all the time. We're friends."

Like you talk to Eddie? Like you're friends with Eddie? These thoughts paraded through Joyce's head like bikini girls holding up round cards at a boxing match. For a split second, Joyce feared that Valerie had snapped completely, that she had convinced herself that the operators on the system she created were real stars after all.

Valerie grinned and clicked on the mike and webcam icons. "We're buddies, aren't we, Mitch?"

"Indeed we are, Val." The simulation didn't even look up from his phone, and that fact alone convinced Joyce that it was indeed the real Mitch Barlo on the other side of the connection. The owner of the company was talking to him. No employee would be so cavalier with the boss.

Now Joyce clicked off the sight and sound icons. She felt an unaccustomed thrill race through her. "Oh, my God, Valley! It's really him?"

Valerie nodded, grinned, eagerly sharing Joyce's fan's enthusiasm. "I asked him to come in tonight, especially to talk to you."

Suddenly Joyce was running with the rush of being a fan, of letting that singular excitement course through her mind, her body. Mitch Barlo was fine, he was single, he was Valerie's buddy, she was going to talk to him . . . "What should I say?"

"Say whatever you want. But no talking dirty right away. He might think you're a reporter."

Valerie clicked the icons. "Sorry to keep you waiting, Mitch. It took a minute to convince – let me introduce you. Mitch, this is Joyce Vinson, my right hand man and my best friend in the whole world. Joyce, this is Mitch Barlo, someone that needs no further introduction." Valerie winked at him and Joyce was nonplussed to see the famous face grin back at her.

"Nice to meet you, Joyce."

Joyce opened her mouth to speak. "That remains to be seen," Valerie interjected, then smiled innocently at the shocked expression of *I can't believe you just said that about me to Mitch Barlo* stamped on Joyce's features. "One more second, Mitch." Valerie clicked the icons again. She giggled and shook her head. "The look on your face."

"It's really him?"

"I wouldn't lie to you." *Not entirely, anyway.* "Here's a quick rundown. Like I said, I've talked to him a few times online, on the phone. We've become friends, because . . . we talked about our problems, Jo.

"It was just like Marianne Jackson said. It was like therapy. He told me about Janna, and I told him about Elise. We shared our pain about their deaths. We helped to heal each other. If you'd like, I can call up the transcripts of our heart-to-hearts."

"I thought we didn't keep—"

"Who wrote this program, Jo? I can keep whatever I want." Valerie grinned. "He's a great guy. I trust him. I told him all about Eddie—"

Joyce grabbed her friend's arm in astonished surprise. "You didn't!"

"I did. Like I say, I trust him. He's not gonna tell anybody. We're friends." Valerie smiled fondly at the screen. "I like him a lot. In another world, maybe . . ." She let the thought die. "Talk to him, Jo. He's a great listener. He's gorgeous and he's single . . ."

"Oh, my Christ, Val! He's a movie star! He wouldn't be interested in—"

"He's just a man, Jo. And you're gorgeous and single, too. If you don't give it a whirl, if you don't show Mitch Barlo the same bon vivant, girl-about-town that you showed to Mortie Fellows, I'll never let you live it down."

Joyce grinned. "I'll try, Val." She looked at the screen. "Damn, he's cute."

It just takes one actor to make a girl a fan, Valerie thought smugly.

"This is my only request, Jo. If he winds up asking you to meet him IRL, asking you out—"

Joyce squeaked at the impossibility, the *possibility* of that. The unimpressed lawyer was gone – Joyce knew not where. She'd been replaced by someone who had a little bit of a warm for Mitch Barlo, star of stage and screen – someone who was just as thrilled as she could be, because she was going to get to talk to him. *Joyce Vinson, TTAMS subscriber.* Well, almost . . .

"If he asks you out, you'd better go." Valerie smiled. "But if he does, I want you to tell him that Valerie said that that bullshit would get him fired if he was a real operator. No fraternizing with subscribers IRL." She clicked the buttons. "I've gotta go, Mitch. I have a . . . late meeting. But I leave you in Joyce's capable hands." She waved. Mitch told her goodbye. He saw her leave the office, over Joyce's shoulder.

For a second, Joyce Vinson just blinked vacuously, as if she was a simulation herself. Finally she said, "Valerie says you guys are friends?"

"Yes." A neutral smile. Mitch didn't know what level of friendship Valerie had reported to her business partner.

Joyce studied him curiously. She licked her lips, paused. But the suspense was killing her. She had lived with it for years, had never been able to discuss it with another human being, and now Valerie said she'd just gone right ahead and told this famous stranger, because she trusted him.

"She says that she told you about . . . Eddie?"

Mitch's killer smile dimmed a few watts. Several, in fact. "It's funny you should mention that, Ms Vinson. When Val said she wanted to introduce us, I thought that that was just the subject that I'd like to discuss with you." His smile faded entirely. His attractive mouth was now set in a grim line.

Joyce had once aspired to be a trial lawyer, had anticipated handing out her share of scathing cross-examinations. This dream had not come to fruition, but she hadn't had time to miss it. She was a negotiator now, a broker of deals, wherein everybody pretended to love everybody else. Just how much that love was going to cost all the parties involved – it was Joyce's job to mediate that.

But still she recognized the tone of an interrogation when she heard it, even if it was in Mitch Barlo's low, rich voice, even if it was coming out of his world-famous, good-looking face.

Her smile faltered. "Is that a fact? Well . . . Please proceed. Ask me anything you'd like."

The simulation sighed. *No,* Joyce reminded herself. *It's not a simulation. This isn't a TTAMS session; it's a teleconference. That's really Mitch Barlo, and he's abandoned being a cute, smiling star, because his good friend Valerie told him all about her conversations with Edison Forbes, who just happens to be dead.*

"I really only have one question. Why haven't you gotten her some help?"

Joyce's mouth dropped open in shock. Only her professionalism stopped her from saying, *Who the fuck do you think you are?*

Mitch continued. "She *hears voices,* Ms Vinson. You're her friend. Haven't you ever considered that perhaps that calls for a little psychological intervention?"

Joyce smiled thinly to cover her outrage. "You say you're her friend, too, Mr. Barlo, but you don't seem to know her very well. Valerie doesn't need any *intervention.* She's the happiest person I know. Sure, she's had a little rough patch here lately. If she told you about Eddie, I'm sure she told you about Brett."

The actor gave a barely perceptible nod. He knew about Brett. *Mr. Wonderful. God's gift to women, according to Greg. And apparently Valerie.*

"But even that hasn't fazed her. She went away for a week – I don't know where she was, or what she was doing–"

352

It was me, Consigliere.

"But whatever it was, it helped her to make up her mind about Brett. She's gonna give him another chance, I think. She never gave him half a chance in the first place. The whole thing hurt her very much–"

"I know. She told me."

Joyce narrowed her eyes at the actor's interruption. "But they've both grown up a lot. It's like this, Mr. Barlo. If Brett's quit texting the world, if he acts like Valerie thinks a boyfriend should, then she'll be the happiest person in the world. In college, Brett was perfect to her. We all knew he was a ladies' man, but he was always faultless to Val. Until he wasn't. Then, she saw his one fault as insurmountable, and even though it nearly killed her to do it, she dropped him like the well-documented bad habit.

"But if Brett talks her into taking him back – and I'm pretty sure that he will – then Val will again be happy, safe in her mild delusion of his perfection. Brett can handle it. He thinks he's pretty perfect his own self. He's another man, not conceited but convinced, just like her rock star father.

"I figure that's part of the motivation for his return – Brett'll never have another a fan like Val. No one'll ever love him as completely as she does."

"Funny you should mention how much of *a fan* Valerie can be, Ms Vinson."

Joyce sighed. "Ah, yes. You don't care about Brett – you're concerned with Valerie's conversations with Edison Forbes." The CEO's expression softened. Here was a man that Valerie trusted; she had confided her secret to him and he was genuinely worried. Joyce sought to reassure him.

"I want you to know that I appreciate your concern, Mr. Barlo. It shows that you care about her, just like I do." Joyce paused, sighed again.

"The first time Valerie ever beheld his Canadian Majesty was on Netflix. It was the day we graduated from college, the day she broke up with Brett. The day she bought two bottles of pills from a drug dealer-slash-bartender name Brad, because she'd considered offing herself, because, oh, my God, Brett still had dating apps on his phone, just like the college kid he was at the time.

"I picked *Sonny's Diner* out for her, at random. I'm sure you know how much Val likes movies – I thought watching something would take her mind off of stupid Brett. I just eeny-meeny-miney-moed a television series, because it would last longer than a movie.

"I went out to get a pizza, and when I got back, Valerie was hooked. Here was the best-looking man she'd ever set eyes on, playing in some lame Canadian sitcom that nobody had ever heard of. Valerie was happy again. Deliriously so, like turning on a light switch. Brett who?"

Joyce smiled fondly. "Val actually used to make up conversations with Eddie, before we even met him. Ask her sometime about what he – and you – are supposed to be saying in those stills from *Two's Company*."

"*Two's a Crowd.*"

Joyce's smile was beautiful and kind, and Mitch couldn't help but smile back a little. This woman obviously knew Valerie, loved her.

"My point is this. Crushing on Edison Forbes helped Valerie get over Brett. Even though she was obsessed, like a Beatles' fan, like one of her dad's groupies, it wasn't like she thought she was ever going to meet him. She wasn't delusional then, didn't think she could fly up to Canada and commence happily ever after with him. She just thought he was *really* attractive. She wondered what he was like.

"Then all of a sudden Liam Cote arrived, told Val that he knew Eddie Forbes, that he could introduce them. The possibility of happily ever after must've occurred to her then."

Joyce giggled. It wasn't as adorable as when Valerie giggled, but Mitch still found it charming. "Valerie was grateful to Liam . . . Well, I guess you could say that she liked Liam well enough, even though he wasn't really her type. It wasn't really him she liked. It was his connections."

Ah, yes, the inestimable value of connections in showbiz. You're her best friend and all, Ms Vinson, but I bet you don't have a clue how well Greg Castro also knows her. He aimed to score a little of Valerie's gratitude his own self, like you say, based on my connections to Eddie.

"I was just glad to see her with a boyfriend again, even though it was obvious to me that it was really just a convenience thing. They were both using each other, but neither of them minded." Joyce grinned slyly. "Except for Brett, Valerie had never had any trouble with getting overly attached to men in college. Until she met him, all the pretty boys had always been just a pleasing diversion to her. *Catch and release*, she used to say."

Mitch pictured a hook and a big shiny lure hanging out of the corner of own mouth. He was glad that Joyce Vinson didn't know it was there.

Joyce's grin faded. "Valerie finally got to meet Eddie. He was nice. But then he died, and I was *so worried*. She'd finally got to meet the man

354

of her dreams, and then just like that, he was gone. When she told me that he was talking to her, I was just as freaked out as you are, Mr. Barlo."

"Please. Call me Mitch." He flashed that Oscar-nominated smile.

"If you insist." Joyce lowered her eyelashes shyly. She picked a non-existent bit of dust off the desk, thinking, *Goddamn, he's cute*. Joyce felt that she might be blushing, so she cleared her throat and continued quickly. "I thought that maybe it was just grief; Val had suffered a terrible shock. But she wasn't grieving. She recognized that Eddie was dead, that she would never see him again, that he'd never make any more movies. But she wasn't sad, because he still talked to her. I waited for it to go away – even Val herself admitted that it was–"

"Unusual."

Joyce smiled again. "Yes. Even she thought it was *unusual*. To this day, she says, *You don't tell anyone that I talk to Eddie, do you?* You must be special to her, Mitch, if she told you. Somewhere in the back of her mind, I think she *knows* it's nuts. Maybe, all this time, she's been waiting for it to go away, too.

"A few days after we got back from Canada, she starts telling me about Eddie's idea for this service, where fans could talk to fake movies stars. She called one of her techie buddies from school – snatched him right away from Fox. Before you knew it, the three of us were launching TTAMS. The acclaim – *the money* – has been rolling in ever since.

"Valerie Whitly is successful, beyond her wildest dreams. She's powerful, in the town that makes the movies that she's always loved. That power has allowed her to meet Hollywood's elite, to . . ." Joyce blushed again. "To become friends with people like you."

Talk to a Movie Star, befriend him, sleep with him . . . then throw him over for your ex-boyfriend . . .

"Brett was gone and Edison Forbes was dead, but despite all that, Valerie was happy again, Mitch. Happy, busy. She had TTAMS to occupy her. My mother had a little magnet on our refrigerator. I looked at it my whole life. It was a quote from Aristotle: *Happiness is the meaning and the purpose of life, the whole aim and end of human existence.* My dad stuck up another one next to it that said: *If you think money doesn't buy happiness, you don't know where to shop.*" Joyce smiled again.

"So I say, so what if Valerie's a little crazy, Mitch? She's also happy, happier than most of us. She's always been odd, for as long as I've known her, with the whole always-quoting-movies thing. I think a little crazy runs in her family, from the maternal line at least. Family history says her grandmother died from missing her grandfather. Like

Val, her mother's wa-ay too much into movies. She used them to demonstrate every talking point in Val's life. Her aunt was a suicidal obsessive with her own delusions.

"But Valerie's delusion – talking to Eddie – it's harmless, Mitch. She's happy, and Eddie's advice, his suggestions – Val's conversations with her imaginary friend have made her a millionaire. It's not like she doesn't know he's dead – he's just a little less dead to her than he is to us. I figure – she used to make up little tête-à-têtes with him when he was alive, before she ever met him, when she was just an anonymous computer geek from Riverside. Now, she's invented the hottest service in the world, she's rich – who cares if she still talks to him?"

"Imperfection is beauty, madness is genius and it's better to be absolutely ridiculous than absolutely boring."

"Who said that?"

Valerie would know. "Marilyn Monroe."

Joyce clapped her hands in delight. "See? Valerie's okay, Mitch. She's certainly saner than most of the people in this town."

Mitch smiled. "I would have to agree with you on that."

He saw then that Joyce Vinson was right – Valerie's *unusual* conversations with dead Canadian actors had not been detrimental to her. She had achieved what she'd always wished – she had longed to know what Edison Forbes was really like – in her mind, he'd become exactly what she thought he should be. Plus there was the added dimension that every Number One Fan dreamt of: having her favorite actor available for a few words whenever she wanted to talk to him. Just like on TTAMS.

An awkward silence descended. As when he had spoken to Denise from Riverside, Mitch realized that he and this very special subscriber had been discussing topics entirely too heavy for what should've been a light-hearted TTAMS session.

But Mitch was a good actor. If the change-of-subject cue wasn't forthcoming, he'd just ad-lib it himself. "So tell me, Ms Vinson—"

"Please, call me Joyce . . . Mitch." *Oh, my God, I just called Mitch Barlo by his first name!*

But Joyce was so cool that ice cubes wouldn't melt in her pockets. Not unlike Valerie, she knew how to talk to pretty men. She said, "I feel like we're friends already." *Oh, my God! Friends with Mitch Barlo!* Joyce smiled at him and allowed the potential awesomeness of *that* to bounce around in her mind.

"I feel the same way." Mitch offered her a shy smile; she recognized it immediately from *Shamus Alive. Damn, but he's cute!*

Mitch's smile again took on mega-star wattage. "So tell me, Joyce. Which one of my movies is your favorite?"

****

The Oscar-nominee and the CEO talked for hours. Once each was content that the other had Valerie Whitly's best interests at heart, the topics soon ranged all over the spectrum, from current events to historical ones, from politics and the law to the latest memes rocketing across the internet. Mitch talked about show business without quoting movies. Joyce told him about the business side of TTAMS without boring him with administrative details.

Mitch ignored texts from Greg Castro, from Ronny Prince. Joyce had to return one of hers, but she did it quickly: she told Marvin to go ahead and handle the teleconference with Japan. *I give you carte blanche,* she texted him, feeling entirely like the Grinch after his transformation. Marvin was a good lawyer, a slick, competent negotiator. He could handle one meeting.

Joyce found the actor to be intelligent and clever, and at times, uproariously funny. Mitch discovered that the CEO possessed her own species of droll wit, and a dead-on ability to gently skewer the minds and motivations of the agents and Hollywood lawyers and studio wheels with whom she did business every day.

Just like Ronny had said, Joyce Vinson was hot, and even better than that, there didn't seem to be even the slightest whiff of craziness to her. Mitch had decided to attempt to attune himself to the possibility of this aspect in beautiful women from now on. He had hit the round-the-bend jackpot twice already, and vowed to be a little bit more observant before he dropped another marble onto the roulette wheel the next time.

To his relief, Mitch found not a hint of mental health *unusualness* about Joyce Vinson. It was always possible that she was hiding it, that it might come out later – but for the moment, she came off as a sassy, confident, intuitive, supremely well-adjusted lawyer. After a while, he forgot about looking for any possible instabilities and concentrated only on her dark-eyed beauty.

The TTAMS interface was almost better than real life for Joyce and Mitch. They were talking face to face, but there was no noise, no waitresses or old friends (*or fans,* Joyce thought with a grin) that could interrupt them, as there would've been had they had been chatting in a bar or restaurant. The privacy of the interface lent an extra level of intimacy; they were close enough to catch each other's smiles and giggles, but there were no real world distractions.

Other common first-meeting concerns were also eliminated. Mitch didn't have to worry if it was too soon to touch her hand or her shoulder; Joyce didn't have to be on the alert for such gestures, to wonder if they meant that he genuinely liked her, or if he was just seeing how familiar he could be, and how soon.

The absence of the ability to touch made both keenly aware that just such a phenomenon existed, however. Mitch contemplated how soft her shiny, dark hair might be; he pictured loosing in from the confines of its business-like bun. Joyce considered Mitch's stubble, black interspersed with a little gray, as it had been in *A Random House Is Not a Home*. She almost felt the roughness of it on her palm, as she imagined gently caressing his beautiful face . . .

The fact of their attraction began to manifest itself in short pauses in the conversation. They were *thinking about* each other instead of *talking to* each other. The time was nigh to part and consider the prospects solo.

Just like Valerie had predicted, Mitch asked Joyce if she'd like to have dinner with him. "Tomorrow . . ." He looked at the blue bar on the side of the screen. All his prompts had gone red, hours ago. The session had eventually timed itself out, stopped offering new prompts. It was long after midnight. "I guess that would be today. If you're not too busy."

"I can move some things around." Joyce reckoned it was Marvin's time to shine. Japan was important, but having dinner with Mitch Barlo was just too incredible of an impossibility to pass up.

"Where would you like to go?"

Joyce was suddenly painfully aware that she was *talking to a movie star*. "You pick, Mitch. I don't know where you famous people like to eat."

That killer smile. "Anywhere you'd like, Joyce." He winked. "If you don't mind a few photographers." When she blanched at that, he said, "Why don't you just come up to my house? Alex Behrn is my personal chef."

"All right," Joyce replied, remembering Valerie's admonition to be a bon vivant, girl-about-town.

"Say sixish?"

"Sixish sounds great."

There was another pause. They smiled silently, appreciatively, at each other.

"Let me walk you to your car," Mitch suggested. "I'll meet you in the lobby."

Joyce had forgotten that he was onsite. She couldn't quite say where she had placed him – in some distant aerie of *Oh, my God, I'm actually talking to Mitch Barlo*, perhaps. The fact that he was just downstairs had totally slipped her mind.

He winked and logged out.

Joyce sat there, spellbound, for a good ten seconds, reading but not comprehending TTAMS's farewell message: *Have a great day, Joyce, and come back soon!* At last she snapped out of it, and closed Valerie's laptop, this wonderful electronic contrivance that had allowed her to talk to *Mitch Barlo*, who was now waiting for her in the lobby. She found a compact in her purse, checked her face. Her face was fine, but her heart was skipping along at an alarming rate.

He was just as devastating in person as he had been on the TTAMS link, but Joyce was cool. She remembered that Valerie had been in control of herself when she had met Eddie Forbes, and Joyce surely didn't have even remotely the same kind of obsessive *thing* for Mitch Barlo, but *Sweet Jesus, he's fine!*

When Joyce found out that he intended to wait in the alley behind the building for a limo – he'd already called it – she insisted on giving him a ride home. When they arrived at his house, Mitch insisted that she come in. The living room was still a startling white, but Janna's portrait was gone.

They sat at the butcher-block table in the kitchen and ate gourmet left-overs and talked until dawn. Reluctantly, Joyce told him that she had to be back to the office in a few hours. Mitch walked her out to her Porsche and they shared a friendly hug. They lingered in each other's arms, however, thinking about the possibilities.

****

Brett chose a quiet booth, conducive to conversation. *To apologizing*, Valerie thought. They each ordered a cheeseburger and fries, like the old days. Valerie added a Gin Rickey, because she thought she might need it. Brett ordered a bottled water. He was driving.

Valerie narrowed her eyes. *"Welly, welly, welly, welly, welly, welly, well. To what do I owe the extreme pleasure of this surprising visit?"*

All the good memories came back again to Valerie with Brett's smile. "I've missed you so much, Val. Nobody in the world's like you. You've got a line for every situation. You're so funny."

Valerie's lip curled wryly. *"Funny like I'm a clown, I amuse you? I make you laugh, I'm here to fuckin' amuse you? What do you mean funny, funny how? How am I funny?"*

Brett's voice took on an automated tone. *"Shall . . . we . . . play . . . a . . . game?"*

"Warriors, come out to play-ee-ay!"

"Behind every great man is a woman, rolling her eyes."

"Check out the big brain on Brett."

"I have come here to chew bubblegum and kick ass, and I'm all out of bubblegum."

Valerie smiled craftily. "Who did you text today? Let me see your phone."

Brett handed it to her immediately. *"Machete don't text.* Not anymore. I don't want anybody but you, Val." Brett smiled brilliantly. *"The last time I was inside a woman was when I visited the Statue of Liberty."*

"And you want to be my latex salesman?" She handed the phone back to him without looking at it. The waitress brought their cheeseburgers deluxe, and Valerie murmured, *"Feed me, Seymour."*

They ate in silence, smiling, watching each other. There was only one word in Valerie's mind: *Ssssssssssssmokin!* Sure, Mitch Barlo was funny and witty and a good listener; he was a talented actor, and he was talented in other arenas. He was definitely attractive, had made millions off of his pretty face. But he was no Brett Cooke.

And Eddie . . . Eddie remained, and would always remain, the prettiest man Valerie had ever seen. His expression alone just did it for her. But Eddie was dead, in another world, available only for advice and clandestine chats that she couldn't tell anyone about. Valerie would always love Eddie, but Brett was here, smiling at her, *wanting her,* and he was just as hot as the Fourth of July.

Valerie reckoned that Joyce was right – when had Joyce ever steered her wrong? Brett had grown up. He'd made this grand gesture, moving back to LA because he wanted to try again, and even though she had freaked out and ran away the first time she'd seen him, he'd been patient, waiting while she disappeared for a week to think about it. Valerie thought that Brett had probably believed all along that she'd come back to him. When you looked like he did, you were confident about such things, and Valerie *so liked* his confidence.

She decided that he had waited long enough. Maybe it *would* work this time. She knew it would work for tonight.

The waitress cleared away their dishes and brought Valerie another drink, and when she departed, Brett impulsively reached across the table and took Valerie's hand. *"Miss Elizabeth, I have struggled in vain and I can bear it no longer. These past months have been a torment. I came to* LA *with the single object of seeing you . . . I had to see you. I have fought against my better judgment, my family's expectations, the inferiority of your birth by rank and circumstance. All these things I am willing to put aside and ask you to end my agony."*

Valerie supplied the next line. *"I don't understand."*

"I love you."

Now Valerie grinned. *"Listen, I appreciate this whole seduction scene you've got going, but let me give you a tip: I'm a sure thing. Okay? Wanna make 14 dollars the hard way?"*

"I'm your huckleberry." Brett's smile was glorious. *"Hey everybody, we're all gonna get laid!* Check, please!"

****

A strategy meeting regarding the Japanese market expansion was scheduled for the following morning, and all the department heads were gathered around the polished conference room table. They didn't care if it was Sunday, and they could all be at home with wives and husbands and kids. Not when there was this kind of money to be made. They were all bright-eyed and bushy-tailed, ready to talk dollars and cents, with lots of zeros.

All except for the CEO, Valerie noted with surprise. Joyce looked a little frayed around her normally razor-sharp edges. Valerie watched her unsuccessfully attempt to stifle a yawn. Her employees were still babbling quietly amongst themselves, so Valerie did what only the boss could do. RHIP and all that. She took out her phone and sent her friend a text.

So did u enjoy talking to a movie star?

Joyce didn't look up; she didn't dare. It didn't pay to be grinning mindlessly in staff meetings. She replied, *He's awesome, Val, just like u said. We talked all night.*

There'll b a dip in his stats.

I didn't get any sleep at all. After this meeting, I'm taking the rest of the day off. To recover. We're having dinner 2night. He has a chef. ☺

Valerie wondered what Alex would think of the cavalcade of TTAMS executives dining with his famous boss.

Then let's light this candle.

Valerie was a little worn out herself, seeing as how Brett had ever-so-slowly and deliciously showed her exactly how much he'd missed her, how much he loved her, how much he sincerely wanted to make it work this time. And Valerie had responded in kind, *all night long,* as the song said.

We were all feeling a bit shagged and fagged and fashed, it being a night of no small expenditure . . .

Valerie nodded at Greg, and he called the meeting to order. "Sorry that you all had to come in on a Sunday, but it couldn't be helped. This Japan thing is requiring a little extra effort from all of us."

****

The meeting concluded, and again the department heads gathered in groups of twos and threes and murmured amongst themselves. The mood was like a congratulatory party; there was no need for haste in leaving the conference room, as few of them were returning to their offices today. They'd just come in for this important meeting.

Loudly, Joyce said, "Excuse me, Val. I'd like to clarify legal's position with you on . . ." But then she could no longer keep a straight face. She took Valerie's elbow and steered her out of the conference room, then down the hall into the lobby, where no one could overhear them.

"Well? What did Brett say?"

"Brett said he wants us to live happily ever after." Joyce was surprised to see a happy flare of insanity flash in Valerie's eyes, like the bright blue of a gas jet turned up to a higher intensity. "Do you think that's possible, Jo?"

Joyce considered her warily. "Sure, Val."

Joyce reflected that she'd always seen the crazy dancing there behind Valerie's eyes, from the moment she'd met her, but she'd only seen this extra flare of derangement every now and then, such as when Valerie had first discovered Edison Forbes's awesomeness on Netflix.

She had been in control of herself when they visited Canada – her fantasy of meeting and at last getting to know Eddie seemed to be actually coming true, was it not? So there was nothing to be delusional about then.

The next time Joyce had seen this bright blue incandescent glow of instability was after they had returned to LA, and Valerie had told her that Edison Forbes, cold in a morgue in Canada, not yet in his grave, had started talking to her. It was there once more when she'd told Joyce about his idea for TTAMS.

Val's always been a little bit nuts, Joyce said to herself, *from the day we met.* Like she'd told Mitch, she thought that maybe in ran in the Carlin side of her family.

But as she again read the madness in her friend's beautiful eyes, Joyce realized that Edison Forbes was not the original trigger to it. Neither Valerie's obsession with him, nor his tragic death – it hadn't been Eddie at all that had brought Val's crazy out of the shadows and into the spotlight. She might hear his voice in her head – but he'd led her to be a millionaire. Val's fantasy of Eddie Forbes, dead or alive, had been absolutely harmless to her.

It had been Brett Cooke, not Eddie, that had caused the lunacy to take up more or less permanent residence with Val. In college, she'd convinced herself that they were going to share a fairytale life together, just like in the movies, and when that didn't happen, Val had coped by making up her own fairytale life. She saw the black-haired, blue-eyed Canadian actor, and since Brett had been fired from the set, Valerie cast Eddie as the romantic lead in the movie that was to be her life. The Canuck performed flawlessly. He was always perfect to Valerie because he wasn't real, because he could never let her down. After he died, Val just expanded her delusion from a movie to a mini-series, from *I Was Eddie's Biggest Fan* to *My Life With Eddie*.

But Eddie had come along A.B. (after Brett); he had been second choice for Val, really, seeing as how she had been forced to abandon her first choice. It had been Brett all along, but Valerie had made do without him, since she believed he had betrayed her. Eddie had just been Brett's understudy.

Now that Brett was back, making happily-ever-after promises – Joyce had no doubt that he had used exactly that expression – Valerie's original delusion had returned. Not a never-ending, every day fairytale romance with Eddie, in her head, in her imagination, but a never-ending, every day fairytale romance with Brett, in real life.

Joyce decided to go with the hope she saw in her friend's eyes. "I always thought you guys were meant for each other."

"You really think so, Jo? I'd like to think so . . ."

"Just like in the movies." Joyce hugged her and Valerie smiled. The jet of crazy receded.

EPILOGUE

A little less than thirty days later, TTAMS's second in command climbed the diamond-stamped steel steps for a quick meeting with her boss. When Joyce entered the office, Valerie's eyes flickered up to meet her friend's for just a second, then returned to the screen before her.

"Mitch Barlo hits the red carpet with gal pal Joyce Vinson for the premiere of his new movie, The Erskine Dilemma. Vinson is the CEO of Talk To a Movie Star. Which needs no explanation." Valerie grinned in delight.

Joyce was astonished. "No way."

Valerie turned the laptop around and displayed the picture from People.com. "You didn't notice the cameras? The flashes?"

"He said there'd be . . . He said to just smile."

"You look great, Jo. Where'd you get the dress?"

"I'm not a hermit like you are, Val. I've got a few dresses. I've been to a few parties."

"Not to mention The Conga Room. And now movie premieres."

Valerie paused and waited for Joyce to tell her all the details. She hadn't seen very much of her friend over the past month, because the talks with Japan were heating up. There had been a few tours for their upper echelon players, many more meetings. From founder to CEO, right down to the operators, TTAMS was jumping: busy, busy, busy!

Valerie had been forced to call Marvin in order to schedule just these few minutes with Joyce this morning, because like the famed cat, her curiosity was positively killing her. There was Joyce's picture on People.com with Mitch: she was stunning, radiant, and the movie star looked positively smug in his happiness.

Valerie had to hear about it. There hadn't been time until now, and she just couldn't wait for another second to find out, so she went ahead and asked. "How is it, Joyce?"

"Oh, it's all right. It reminded me a lot of that *Bourne* movie, with fewer stunts and more mysterious clues. I think you'll like the ending, though. It's kind of a surprise."

Joyce was kidding. She had to be.

"I don't mean *the movie*, Jo, for crying out loud. I mean, how is it with you and Mitch? What exactly is required of a *gal pal*? Is Mitch . . . Does he . . .?"

****

While she and Joyce were in college, B.B. (before Brett), Valerie had once upon a time gone home to Riverside for a weekend, and when she'd returned to Mr. Vinson's guest house on Sunday evening, she'd discovered that Joyce had taken a rare plunge into the dating pool. Valerie found a devastatingly attractive young man sitting on the couch beside her in the living room.

"Valerie?" he said in surprise. "How have you been? I didn't know that you and Joyce—"

"Yep. We're roomies." Valerie looked curiously at her friend, and Joyce grinned brightly. "How've you been, Jonathan?"

"Oh, I'm the same. You know. School."

The intercom buzzed, and Jonathan went outside to pay the pizza man. When the door closed behind him, Valerie said proudly, "Look at you!"

"Quit acting like I'm a virgin, Val."

"Not hardly. But you're usually so picky . . . Jon is a cutie, though. I suppose you found him at Q's?" Joyce nodded. "Yeah, that's where I met him, too. It was right before the end of last term. You were busy studying for exams." Valerie made a face. Exams had always come almost embarrassingly easy to her.

"After Q's, he insisted on taking me to Long John Silver's because I had mentioned that I loved their hushpuppies. After that, we came back here . . ."

Valerie then proceeded to describe to Joyce the marathon and athletic romp she'd enjoyed with Jonathan, right here in this very house, whilst Joyce herself was shut up in her room, enmeshed in learning to be a lawyer. Valerie was specific, detailed; she made gestures, practically drew diagrams. It was just how she was. Valerie enjoyed her adventures with the opposite sex to the very fullest.

She finally concluded, "And those five little freckles on the corner of his butt? Aren't they adorable? I wanted to take a Sharpie and connect them, call it *The Constellation of Jon* or something. *Second star to the right and straight on 'til morning."*

Valerie giggled, paused. It was only then that she registered Joyce's open-mouthed look of appalled disbelief. "What?"

Joyce cleared her throat. "It the future, will you do me a favor? If you notice me sitting here with some guy that you went out with, don't tell me about it, would ya? There is just something off-putting about the idea that you–"

"I've said it before and I'll say it again. You're a prude, Jo. He doesn't mean anything to me, and I know he doesn't mean anything to you. He's too pretty to be your type."

Joyce objected. "I like pretty men, too."

"Only if you think that he might have a mind or at least a personality, too."

"Whereas such considerations have never concerned you."

Valerie grinned slyly. "If you've spent the whole weekend with Jonathan, then I know you know that no *such considerations* lurk behind those gorgeous eyes. He sure is cute, though. So what difference does it make if I've already–"

"Just don't tell me, okay?"

Valerie already knew the answers to the questions that she'd just asked Joyce about Mitch. She knew quite thoroughly that he *was* and that he *did*, that the one-time *People Magazine's Sexiest Man Alive* lived up to the name behind closed doors, and in spades.

But it wasn't like Valerie could reveal to Joyce that she knew.
She didn't want to make her friend uncomfortable by letting on that she'd been to the Mitch Barlo well first, that she was already aware that it was deep and warm and satisfying. Valerie couldn't tell Joyce that she'd drunk her fill, that it had taken her a week to fully chart all the waters . . .

Still, Valerie wanted to hear Joyce's opinion of the sexy actor and his many and varied charms. She'd eventually heard all about Jonathan, and every other one of Joyce's conquests since, right up to and including Mortie Fellows. (Final analysis: *Meh.)* So when her friend hesitated to talk about Mitch, Valerie was surprised.

"Come on, Joyce, you can tell me. I promise not to give TMZ an exclusive."

"To tell you the truth, Val . . ." Joyce blushed as if she was going to make some huge confession. But it was just the opposite. "To tell you the truth, I don't know yet. We haven't . . ."

Valerie blinked speechlessly. She gestured at her computer screen; then the words finally arrived. "But you . . . You're still seeing him, right? It says right here, *gal pal Joyce Vinson.*"

"I see him every spare moment I can, Val, but we haven't . . . I've got Japan hanging over my head every second of the day–"

"Domo Arigato, Mr. Roboto." Valerie heard the gloriously familiar sound of cash registers.

"What?"

"It's an old song, Jo. *And thank you very much, Mr. Roboto, for helping me escape, just when I needed to . . .*"

"Right." *The things she comes up with.* "Anyway . . . Mitch has started pre-production for *Taming the Trio*–"

"He's gonna do the sisters' movie?" Again Valerie was surprised. Mitch had been reluctant about the part when they'd done the read through . . .

"Yeah. But I guess Ronny requested a rewrite before Mitch'll sign–"

"Who?"

"Ronny Prince. His agent."

Valerie remembered listening to Mitch talk to his agent on the phone. But Mitch had never bothered to introduce them . . . "When did you meet his agent?"

When did you hear about Taming the Trio? But Valerie and Mitch were friends, after all. Maybe they talked on the phone.

"We've had dinner with him a few times."

"You've had dinner with his agent, but you haven't . . ."

"There hasn't really been time, Val."

"That's the most ridiculous thing I've ever heard come out of your mouth, Jo. You can't make time to nail Mitch Barlo? Seriously?"

"It's . . . There's more to it than that, Val . . . He's . . . Look. Before I forget. He wants me to invite you and Brett to dinner on Friday night. He says this whole pre-production thing with *Trio* should be wrapped up by then, and he wants to celebrate a little bit before shooting starts, because he'll be even busier then."

Suddenly, Joyce giggled. She put her hand over her mouth like a schoolgirl, lowered her voice. "Actually, Val, I think that after this party, we might finally get the chance to . . ."

"To hell with the party then."

"No, Val! He says he misses you. He says he wants to meet Brett."
I'll bet he does.

"He says he wants to . . . show me off."

"I'm already impressed, Jo. I've been impressed since the day we met."

"You know what I mean. To other people. To show people that we're . . . together."

"If you're sure it won't cut into your first–"

"It won't."

"We'll be there."

****

Morris Baker answered his phone. "Haven't seen you in a while, Movie Star."

"I've been busy, my friend."

"The roar of the greasepaint, the smell of the crowd?"

Mitch laughed. "Something like that. I want you to come to my house on Friday, Morris. I'm having a little party."

The operator grinned. "Will there be starlets?"

"No starlets. Starlets are a pain in the ass. Trust me. Just a couple of single girls . . ."

"I will be there. What does one bring to a Hollywood party? I'm fresh out of coke."

Again Mitch laughed. He wasn't sure if Baker was kidding or not. "Just bring your charming self, Morris. Do you like Italian?"

"Women or cuisine?"

Mitch pictured the girl he had invited for Baker. Sloe-eyed Minnie Alverson, a costume designer he'd met while filming *Two of Swords* at Paramount. Dark-haired, cute and bubbly, she might be Italian. "Perhaps both," he told his operator. His good friend.

"I will be there," Baker repeated.

****

Mitch called Greg Castro next.

"This Friday? I dunno, Mitch. Joyce has got me up to my eyeballs in reconfigurations. Gotta impress the Japs."

"Joyce is gonna be there, Greg." Mitch paused, then said slowly, "I've got a little confession for you, Boss. I've kinda been dating *your* boss."

The Ops Director barked astonished laughter. Mitch was only kidding, but Greg most assuredly didn't like the direction of the jest. It wasn't funny to even suggest such a thing – that he, Mitch Barlo, famous, world-renowned pretty boy, was suddenly, cavalierly, dating

368

Valerie, right under Greg's nose. Like it was *no thang*. He didn't like the actor talking about Valerie like he knew her, like he liked her, like she would be amenable to *dating him*. Greg didn't like that at all.

Where the hell was this coming from all of a sudden? Valerie hadn't talked to Mitch lately, at least not on the system. Greg's keeper had been silent. She'd been too busy with this Japanese bullshit, and Mitch hadn't even been in to work for weeks.

Greg suddenly felt very worried. What if they'd been talking on the phone, outside of his ability to moderate? What if they'd been speaking *in person?*

But that was just ridiculous. Valerie would never go for Mitch – there was only one movie star that had ever impressed Valerie, and he was cold in his snowy Canadian grave. Besides, that asshole Brett Cooke had been hanging around, taking her out to lunch, waiting for her after work. Valerie was not dating Mitch Barlo.

"You had me going there for a minute, my friend," the tech said at last. "The idea of you and Valerie . . ."

Oh, shit! Of course he'd think of his lady-love. "Not Valerie, Greg. I'd never do that to you." *Not again.*

"Even though you could."

Mitch was a little bit taken aback by the bitter tone of this statement. But on the other hand, everything was fair in love and war, especially in this town, and Greg was feeling threatened.

Mitch hurried to clarify. "Not Valerie, Greg. Joyce."

"You're dating Joyce."

"Call up People.com."

Greg did as he was bid. "Well, I'll be damned." He whistled in admiration. "Who knew? All it took was one Hollywood pretty boy to melt the Ice Princess. Good for you, Mitch."

"So you'll come to the party? I want you to set down your torch for Ms Whitly for a minute, Greg. There's a girl that I want you to meet."

Greg echoed Baker, and just as hopefully. "A starlet?"

"Script supervisor. From Paramount."

"She sounds . . . plain."

"She's not, Greg. Trust me. Would I introduce you to a plain woman?"

****

369

The Director of Technical Operations for Talk To a Movie Star arrived early to his famous good friend's Hollywood Hills manse. Greg hadn't seen Mitch in a month, except on People.com. He hadn't talked to him, either, except for the call for the party invite, when he'd dropped the astonishing bomb that he was *dating Joyce Vinson.*

Jesus Christ and Mother Mary, how in the hell had *that* happened?

Greg had arrived early so that he might ascertain the answer to this most curious of questions, right from the horse's mouth.

The two of them answered the door together, and it was cute to Greg, in a happy, impossibly-rich-and-powerful-couple kind of way. The Oscar-nominee and the CEO. The executive and the movie star. His friend and his boss.

But Joyce and Greg had been sort-of buddies in college. They'd had a drink together a couple of times, if they ran into each other at Q's. She'd never been overly bossy to him at work, was always polite and friendly, in fact, which was more than he could say about the way she treated Marvin and the rest of her personal staff, or TTAMS staff in general. And at Mitch's house, with his arm around her, Joyce seemed to have left all vestige of that bitchy executive behind.

She was dressed in a white, expensively-simple Mexican peasant dress. She looked almost girlish to Greg; he was surprised by her glowing beauty. He was positively nonplussed when she gave him a quick hug of welcome, kissed him on the cheek, told him it was great to see him.

They exchanged a few words, then Joyce flounced gracefully back to the kitchen. Greg was amazed to see that she was barefoot. He knew that she was not cooking for a Hollywood Hills dinner party all by her lonesome, but still she seemed definitely comfortable in the role of the lady of the house.

Curiouser and curiouser.

"You want the tour?" Mitch asked.

Greg shook his head, glanced in the direction of the setting sun. "Step into my office."

They went out onto the patio. Mitch left the door ajar, so he could hear the bell. Greg said quietly, "You gotta tell me, yea and verily, how all this came to pass, Movie Star. How you got Joyce Vinson up to here your house, dolled up *como un campesino, como Carmen Miranda.* I believe I might be witness to some kind of miracle here. How *did* all this come about?"

"It's a long story."

"I'm all ears." When Mitch hesitated, Greg pressed. "Come on, Mitch. You're dating someone I've known since college. You gotta tell me about how that is."

The doorbell rang and Mitch told him to hold that thought. He went to the door and admitted Minnie Alverson and Julie MacElrey, colleagues from Paramount, from *Two of Swords*. He took them out to the kitchen to introduce them to Joyce and Alex. Minnie was intrigued with the preparations, while Julie could not possibly have cared less. This was good for Mitch's plan, because he wanted to introduce Julie to Greg Castro, had invited her specifically for that purpose.

When they'd worked together at Paramount, the script supervisor had been dating a stuntman. That hadn't lasted, but Mitch thought she might be interested to meet another man with the same kind of rugged, outdoorsy looks. Greg was in reality about as outdoorsy as a plastic plant, but he *looked* like the type Julie liked.

And she certainly was Greg's type: blonde and beautiful, with laughing blue eyes that could turn serious in a heartbeat. She was not as whimsical as Valerie, but she was just as brilliant: she was the youngest script supervisor at Paramount. Hitchcock said, *To make a great film you need three things – the script, the script and the script,* and Julie had a knack for making the good ones flow with a seamless continuity, and she had an instinctive talent for keeping the bad ones from turning out to be complete stinkers.

Mitch took her out to the patio and introduced her to Greg. He asked what they were drinking, and when he went back inside to mix their requests, the doorbell rang again.

Morris Baker walked in and flopped carelessly onto the white couch. "Nice little place ya got here, Movie Star," he said with a grin, not impressed in the slightest. He pretended to be Mitch Barlo for a living, and a lot younger one than the one that stood before him. The one that stood before him was his friend.

He held out a bottle in a paper bag. "It's called a *Carignane*. I Googled it. It's supposed to go with Italian."

"Women or cuisine?"

Baker wiggled his ginger eyebrows. "Perhaps both."

"I'm making drinks, Morris. You want this or something else?"

Baker smiled. "I'll have a Presbyterian. You know how to mix a Presbyterian, Movie Star?"

"I'll have Alex do it."

"Who?"

"My . . . the chef. I think he was once a bartender."

"Weren't all chefs once bartenders? Or is it the other way around?"

Mitch grinned. "Make yourself at home, Morris–"

"You got a mirror? Maybe a razor blade?" Again he grinned. "All right. Enough with the *Coke Ennyday* jokes."

"Silent screen fan are you, Morris?"

"Nah. I used to be Douglas Fairbanks for a little bit, before I was you. But he was incredibly not popular."

"Owing to his lack of appearance in talkies, maybe?"

"No doubt. Plus the fact that he's been dead for a million years."

"Like the dinosaurs."

Mitch went out to the kitchen to deliver the wine to the chef and to press-gang him into making drinks. The actor wondered idly if fans would still be talking to him on some future incarnation of TTAMS after he'd gone to the great green room in the sky. This train of thought led him to Edison Forbes; the next stop on the line was Valerie. As if on cue, the doorbell rang again.

Morris Baker didn't stand on ceremony: he got up and answered the door on his host's behalf.

"Good evening, Ms Whitly," he said and offered his hand. When he saw no recognition in her eyes, he added, "I'm Morris Baker. I work for you."

Valerie smiled, and Baker was charmed to the roots of his hair, as were all of her employees, especially if she smiled at them. "You must be Mitch's friend."

"That I am. Welcome to his home."

The man himself arrived at the door, slightly out of breath, thinking, *Hasn't anyone ever heard of fashionably late?* He was not used to all his guests showing up at once, on time. Mitch smiled at Valerie and said, *"What took you so long?"*

Brett recognized the last lines from *The Player*. *"Traffic was a bitch."*

Valerie introduced Brett to Mitch and Morris as *her friend.*

Mitch shook his hand, noting Brett's resemblance to Edison Forbes, but not to his own, black-haired, blue-eyed self. Mitch wanted to hate the good-looking kid – Valerie's choice of her ex over him had been a brief, sharp, whip-sting to the A-lister's ego. Mitch knew that such a feeling was monumentally unfair – he wasn't even interested in Valerie. And besides, Brett Cooke already had enough enemies here because of Valerie's choice.

Greg had never referred to him without saying *that asshole* in preamble, and from the look on Baker's face, the boss's boyfriend wasn't making any points with him, either. *Everybody loves Valerie,* Mitch thought. *Greg, Morris. Me, at least for a week. But only fortunate Mr. Cooke has been able to get her to love him back.*

Alex appeared with a tray of drinks, like some face-saving maître d', and Mitch smiled gratefully at him. Baker retrieved his Presbyterian, and Alex went to serve Greg and Julie on the patio.

Mitch was feeling a little flustered. He was not used to parties where he genuinely looked forward to talking to everyone, where they all arrived at the same time, smiling and friendly, with no hidden agendas. A random line from Shakespeare occurred to him: *Why the devil should we keep knives to cut one another's throats?*

But these people weren't like that. These people were his friends. Even Alex, who was an employee – Alex winked at him as he went back out to the kitchen. It was about time the boss had a dinner party again, so he could show off his skills.

All of Mitch's guests tonight liked him, not because he could be beneficial to them in some way, business-wise. His actor's mind couldn't help but remember Sally Field's famous Oscar acceptance thanks: *I can't deny the fact that you like me, right now, you like me!*

He wanted to entertain all of his friends, to talk to each of them, but there was just not enough Mitch Barlo to go around. He took stock – Greg and Julie were still on the patio, entertaining each other, according to plan. Minnie had returned to the living room; Baker toddled back and introduced himself. *This is all good.* Mitch congratulated himself on his matchmaking skills.

Now to amuse Valerie and her beloved. He took them out to the kitchen to greet Joyce, thinking he would be glad when dinner was served and they would all be in the same room.

Brett and Joyce shared an exuberant, almost triumphant hug, and Mitch felt a thin, white-hot wire of jealousy knife through him, accompanied by another flash of dislike – no, it was hatred, again – for Brett. But then a multi-pronged logic soothed the A-lister: Joyce had told him all about Brett, that although they'd been great pals in school, she'd never trusted him, had never been involved with him romantically.

Added to this was the idea that had slowly began to fill Mitch over the last month, like a smooth, sweet, warm molasses: it was the definite possibility that Joyce was falling in love with him, and he with her. He intended to explore all the possibilities of this concept, slowly and thoroughly, after his friends went home this evening. He had just this weekend before work again reared its not unwelcome, money-making head. Principal photography for *Taming the Trio* was to begin on Monday, and Mitch wanted to establish the groundwork for a possible future with Joyce before that. He thought she was great; he had immense hopes that they would be together for a long time.

Mitch also dismissed her hug with Brett because of the smile Valerie gave him. It said, *Don't worry, Mitch, they're just friends. Not as good of friends as we are, but then neither of them are ever gonna know about that, now are they?*

Leaving the old friends in Alex's capable hands, Mitch went back to the living room to check on his other guests. He was amazed at his desire to make sure that everyone was having a good time. There was the matchmaking aspect – he wanted to assure himself that Julie and Greg and Minnie and Morris were getting to know each other. But he also wanted to make sure that everybody's drink was full and that all conversations were flowing smoothly. This was never a problem at biz parties: cliques formed and gossip was transmitted within their circles, totally without need of input from the host, seeing as how he was often the subject of the gossip.

Mitch discovered Baker and Minnie staring conversationlessly at anything but each other. Baker looked at him with a kind of blank embarrassment, then smiled faintly and rattled the ice in his empty glass. Mitch took it from him and watched in horror as Baker retrieved his phone and began scrolling through it. Short of an Amish shunning, there was no ruder gesture to demonstrate your boredom with someone you'd just met.

Minnie's feelings were mutual. Her expression said to Mitch, *No love connection here, Chuck.*

We'll be back in two and two.

Before the actor could jumpstart the conversation, the door to the patio opened and Julie stalked in, the picture of annoyance. "You've got to be kidding, Mitch. Like my granddaddy used to say, *I've seen better heads on a nickel beer.*" She shook her head in disbelief. "I need another drink."

"In the kitchen," Mitch said helplessly. Julie stomped away. Baker watched her appreciatively.

Greg stepped inside and grinned at Baker and his host. *"That gal's got entirely too many brains to have an ass like that."*

"Can I get an amen?" Baker agreed and winked at Mitch.

Greg opened his mouth to guffaw, then noticed Minnie sitting on the couch. He blushed at the misogynistic, unkind-though-not-inaccurate line he'd just quoted from *Roadhouse*. In speechless chagrin, he retreated back out onto the patio to hide.

Her drink refreshed, Julie reappeared. She said to Minnie, "You should go out and talk to that guy, Min. Maybe he can get Suri to stop calling you *Triple A.*"

Baker looked up from his phone in surprise. He smiled at the blonde, then looked at Mitch: *Are you sure she's not a starlet?*

Baker looked back at Julie and was pleasantly surprised to find her smiling at him. She explained, "Minnie's car broke down and she needed a tow. She said, *Suri, call me Triple A,* and Suri said, *From now on, I'll call you Triple A.*"

"I fixed that myself, Julie," Minnie said.

"That's what you get for having an iPhone," Baker opined.

Julie sat next to him on the couch and smiled at him again. His pleasant surprise expanded. She shared a significant glance with her friend across the glass coffee table. "You should go out there and talk to him anyway, Min. Enjoy the view." She winked at Baker. "If nothing else."

Minnie understood. "All right." She smiled at Mitch. "Will you join us?"

Mitch was amazed. Perhaps his matchmaking skills weren't so good after all. "I'll be right there, Min."

The costume designer arose.

"He's a great guy," Morris said, in a further effort to hasten her departure. He said to her back, as she stepped outside, "He's my boss."

"What is it that you do, Mr. –?" Julie offered her hand.

Morris Baker shook it and introduced himself. Julie said her name and allowed her hand to linger in his for an enticing extra second. She liked the chubby redhead already. She found his relaxed manner adorable; he was intriguing in a big teddy-bear kind of way.

The smiling ginger was certainly more attractive than the know-it-all lumberjack on the patio. He'd mentioned that Frank Sinatra had once owned Mitch's house, told her that Marilyn had no doubt slept here. He'd obviously been consulting his *Maps To the Stars' Homes* app, as if she was a tourist and would be impressed by his encyclopedic knowledge of the area's history. *As if.*

Morris answered her question. "I'm not Mitch Barlo, but I play him on Talk To a Movie Star."

"Christ, Morris, that's from before you were born!" the real Mitch Barlo exclaimed. It was from an ancient Vicks commercial: *I'm not a doctor, but I play one on TV, and if your child had a cough . . .*

"Those who ignore history are doomed to repeat it, *my brother and only friend.*" Baker smiled winningly, charmingly at Julie.

Apparently he's familiar with Santayana, too, Mitch thought, *even if he did misquote him. And of course he's seen A Clockwork Orange, just like Valerie.*

"What do you do, Julie?"

"I'm a script supervisor at Paramount."

"Then you get enough of the movies at work," Baker replied wisely and winked at Mitch.

Can I get an amen? Mitch's expression replied.

Valerie stepped into the living room and announced in her best Magenta-from-*The Rocky Horror Picture Show*-southern-twang, *"Dinner is prepared."*

Mitch automatically supplied the audience response. *"And I helped."*

****

Once everybody was seated at the table, the party's host felt less like the legendary chicken with its head cut off. Alex presided, joined them – he was a five-star chef after all, and none of Mitch's guests tonight viewed him with anything less than the respect that he was due for that. He was not an employee to them.

Joyce sat beside Mitch; she clasped his hand, smiled into his eyes. The anticipation of what was to finally occur tonight, after their guests had departed, was like a living thing between them.

She considered Brett and Valerie across the table, giggling, happy, in love again. Valerie had returned to the one pretty boy that she couldn't live without, and like Joyce had told Mitch, Brett loved having a fan. He had matured enough to realize that he needed only one.

Ah, Brett, you are so cute . . . Joyce thought, without a trace of wistfulness. She had always been able to deny Brett's undeniable attractiveness, but for a moment, her also-gorgeous high school sweetheart Jeremy returned to her mind . . . Joyce squeezed Mitch's hand again. *I've got to admit that Val's right and has been right all along,* she thought. *Nothing beats a pretty boy . . .*

Mitch returned Joyce's smile and thought for a hot second that if they proved as compatible in the bedroom as they did outside of it – and he had little doubt that they would – he might just ask her to marry him. Not tonight or tomorrow, of course. But maybe in a few months, when he was done shooting *Trio.* Ronny would applaud. Announcement of nuptials for sadly-widowed Mitch Barlo would be added publicity for what they both regarded as a lukewarm comedy at best. *Let's make lots of money . . .*

He looked across the table at Valerie. She gave him a quick smile, then went back to talking to Minnie about costume design. Mitch reflected that people rarely escaped the real-life phenomenon of making the same mistake, over and over again. He had almost done it, had almost become involved with another nutball . . . *There must be something about crazy that I like.* But he had broken the cycle – he liked Joyce just fine, and there was not one thing crazy about her.

Valerie turned to ask Alex something about the *Acqua Pazza*, and Mitch watched Minnie gaze adoringly at Greg Castro, seated to her left. Greg leaned in close, put his arm lightly around her shoulder, whispered in her ear. Apparently the Ops Director wasn't so shy after all, at least not when he had a woman that was obviously attentive. They giggled; then Mitch observed a brief, kind of astonished look on their faces. Then they smiled, as if they were alone in the room.

That's it, right there, Mitch thought in wonderment. *They've just clicked.* Greg consulted a non-existent watch on his wrist – *no one under forty wears a watch anymore,* Mitch thought, *unless it's to demonstrate his wealth. Ronny's got about five, but if you ask him what time it is, he looks at his phone.*

Greg whispered in Minnie's ear again and she nodded. *Maybe I'm not the only one that's gonna get lucky tonight,* Mitch thought. *Valerie who?*

Since his Minnie and Morris match-up had failed so spectacularly, Mitch glanced down to the other end of the table. Baker was telling Julie, "So we went to see Meteor Crater in Arizona when I was about eight. I don't remember much – a long, long road, with some cows alongside it. My mom and sister made Dad stop the car. They got out and tried to pet the cows, but the cows ran away."

Who pets cows? Mitch thought.

But Julie was completely attentive, as if Baker was discussing some great philosophical truth in which she was interested. *She's interested in him,* Mitch said to himself. *Who'da thought that?*

"Anyway," Baker continued, "we get up there, and there's a parking lot and some buildings. Dad says to the guy, 'Where's the crater?'

"The guy says something about admission, and my dad says, 'We gotta pay to see the crater? You people didn't make it. So why do we have to pay to see it?'

"The guy says something about how they had to pay to make the parking lot, and the Visitors center. The buildings. Dad says, 'We got buildings in LA. They're free.'" Baker grinned. "He told us to get back in the car. So I never did see Meteor Crater."

377

Julie laughed genuinely, and Baker lifted his chin in techie pride and shot Mitch a smile. *What did I tell ya, Movie Star? I do all right.*

****

Mitch's very first dinner party for the not-famous was an unqualified success.

The after-dinner conversation revolved around TTAMS. Alex again raved to Valerie about how much he enjoyed her revolutionary service, although he didn't go into as much detail about his conversations as he had when they had spoken alone.

Minnie told them that she had chatted extensively with Edith Head, the famous costume designer. "You guys got the glasses and that weird bowl haircut just right," she told Valerie in admiration.

"You didn't talk to any movie stars?" Julie asked with a shade of derision. As Morris Baker had so shrewdly deduced, Julie got enough of movie stars at work. She had never used TTAMS.

"We also have directors," Valerie said with a little indulgent grin. She recognized a non-fan when she saw one, and pitied Julie a little bit for what she believed must be a complete lack of imagination. "And a few other famous behind-the-scenes types, like Ms Head. Gossip columnists from the Golden Age – Hedda Hopper and Louella Parsons."

"For people who are into more than just stars," Greg said. "For the ones that are into the history of cinema, who want to talk to Hollywood pioneers."

You are as boring as a pioneer, Julie thought. She made a face and Morris grinned at her.

"It was all Joyce's idea," Valerie said. "She wanted to give us some respectability, some film school cred, like Greg says. So we come off as something more than just Rent a Famous Boyfriend."

"Renting a famous boyfriend is enough for me," Alex admitted.

The chef's preferences aside, Mitch thought that none of his female guests would need to be renting a famous boyfriend for a while. Nor would Greg be staying up late with software manuals, nor would Baker be eating stale M&M's all by himself, late at night in TTAMS's deserted cafeteria.

The actor recalled what Baker had once said to him about TTAMS and its subscribers. "It's not real, Mitch. They know it. You know it. It's just a way for them to pass the time until life picks up. They love you excruciatingly – it hurts so good – for $9.95 a month. But then an

IRL man comes along and they forget all about talking to a movie star. Most of them don't even bother saying goodbye."

Life had picked up for Mitch. And Valerie. And things were definitely looking good for Minnie and Greg and Julie and Baker. The actor remembered Audrey, his fan, the subscriber who had told him goodbye. She wasn't renewing her subscription because she was getting married. Her life had picked up, too.

"If things don't work out, they're back, talking about movies again," Baker had said. Mitch reckoned that he was right about that, too, that there were still millions of lonely single ladies (and men) that would continue to talk to a movie star until their lives picked up. The service certainly did in a pinch when there were no real partners around. Mitch had discovered that for himself. TTAMS would continue to make millions.

****

The dinner had been excellent, the company and conversation enjoyable, but Mitch's guests did not linger over their digestifs. Each was eager to learn more about the treasures they had uncovered at the actor's house, and the host himself was not sorry to see them go. His own treasure awaited.

Alex was the first to leave. He said to Valerie, *"I watched myself in Red River and I knew I was going to be famous, so I decided I would get drunk anonymously one last time."* When she didn't get the reference, he winked and said, "I'm going to have a few more words with Monty before I retire for the evening." Alex wiggled his eyebrows.

"Tell him I said hi," she said.

After he was gone, Morris Baker remarked, "He'll be talking to Dougie. He sits two booths down from me." He smiled at Mitch, shook his hand. "It's been real, Movie Star." Julie also said goodbye, and arm-in-arm, they walked out to his Civic.

Greg embodied more than a little of Ronny Prince's philosophy. Thinking that he would no doubt partake in some of his famous good friend's expensive liquor, he'd taken an Uber to Mitch's house, and he was glad of it this time, gladder than he'd been about too many things in his life. Minnie had volunteered to give him a ride home.

Valerie sighed. "You know what they say, Mitch. *Crowd control's the thing. If you're not careful, two's a crowd.*"

Mitch grinned from ear to ear. Valerie's quote memory was eidetic. She'd only seen it once, but she remembered his line from –

"What's that from?" Brett asked.

"An old Edison Forbes movie," Mitch told him. "Straight to video."

"Who?"

Mitch blinked in utter astonishment. *The other man, Brett, my boy, that's who.*

"It's not important, Brett," Valerie said.

She again thought of *The Odyssey*. Odysseus is told that in order to placate Poseidon, he must take a pair of oars and walk inland until someone asks him what they are. Only then would he know that he'd reached a place where the people knew nothing of seafaring ways. There he was to raise a temple and educate them about the sea god.

But Brett knew enough about the great shining temple of Hollywood, about the movies; more than anyone else Valerie knew. What he knew was more than enough. She didn't need to educate him about Eddie Forbes.

On the way home, Valerie received a text from Greg. *Forgot 2 tell u. Stevenson wants 2 sit in on meeting w/ Nippon 2morrow. I say no. Y so serious?*

Valerie grinned. Mark Stevenson was indeed rather serious. *Ur the boss.*

C u then, Val.

Valerie swiped the text box away. Eddie smiled at her from the familiar photo. He said, *I guess we won't be talking too much anymore, eh, Valley?*

She opened her mouth to answer, but then just spoke to him in her mind, where he always spoke to her. *I'll always love you, Eddie.*

I'll always be here if you need me.

I know you will, Eddie.

****

Also by LM Foster

A Passing Resemblance
Contrariwise – A Tale of Twins
Corvino
Crypsis
Duck Feet
Peter's Sisters

Two Green Keys:
Two Green Keys
Adapted for the Screen

One Wilde Ride Trilogy:
Part One: It Might Have Been
Part Two: An Exceptional Boy
Part Three: What Should Never Be

Stars and Guitars:
Talk To a Movie Star
Where The Guitars Play

Tom and Wiley:
This Carnival of Strange
Wiley Royce
Generally Recognized as Safe
Wiley Royce Versus The Martians

www.ingramcontent.com/pod-product-compliance
Lightning Source LLC
Chambersburg PA
CBHW061305170626
46817CB00001B/67